VALLEY GIRLS

From the author of
DONE DIRT CHEAP

Sarah
Nicole
Lemon

AMULET BOOKS
NEW YORK

VALLEY GIRLS

Three
Brothers

Yosemite
Falls

The Nose

Middle
Earth

Yosemi
Village

El Capitan

Rilla's
House

Camp 4

Cathed
Rocks

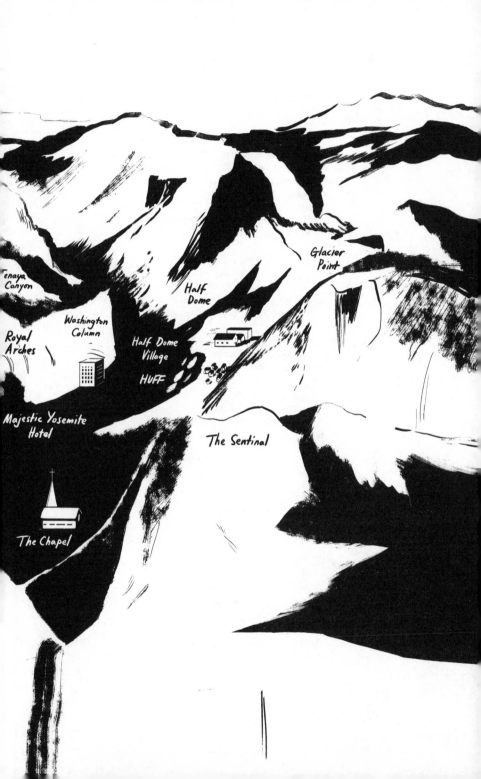

Cataloging-in-Publication Data has been
applied for and may be obtained from the Library of Congress.

ISBN 978-1-4197-2964-5

Text copyright © 2018 Sarah Nicole Lemon
Jacket and map illustrations copyright © 2018 Na Kim
Book design by Alyssa Nassner

Published in 2018 by Amulet Books, an imprint of ABRAMS.

Printed and bound in U.S.A.
10 9 8 7 6 5 4 3 2 1

Amulet Books are available at special discounts when purchased
in quantity for premiums and promotions as well as fundraising or
educational use. Special editions can also be created to specification.
For details, contact specialsales@abramsbooks.com or the address below.

ABRAMS The Art of Books
195 Broadway, New York, NY 10007
abramsbooks.com

To L, J & M
and the muchness
of your minds

"ON BELAY?"

Real adventure is defined best as a journey from which you may not come back alive, and certainly not as the same person.

—Yvon Chouinard, Yosemite climber, founder of Patagonia and Black Diamond Equipment companies, in *Let My People Go Surfing: The Education of a Reluctant Businessman*

one

SHADOWY PALMS WAVERED IN THE STREETLIGHT, AND A MOON ROSE
blue and waned over the San Joaquin Valley. Seventeen-year-old Priscilla
"Rilla" Skidmore leaned against the metal pole of the empty bus stop in
Merced, California. All around her, the air seemed cavernous and wide.
You're alone. All alone, it breathed.

She pulled her denim jacket tight over her sweatshirt. This was the
best thing for everyone. Mom said it. Dad said it. Thea said she would
do whatever *they* thought was best. The only one who thought leaving
home in West Virginia to live with her older sister in Yosemite National
Park *wasn't* a good idea was Rilla.

Rilla's phone had been taken away in exchange for a burner meant to
last only for the bus ride, her friends left in confusion, and her Lab mutt
left wandering the house looking for her. Rilla, who had to fit anything
she loved in a duffel bag and board a bus in West Virginia, spent three
days cramped and quiet, seeing America from the curbs of interstate gas
and bus stations and trying to remember Curtis's number to apologize.
Best thing. She tucked her chin, trying to ignore the new bite to the western wind. For everyone else, sure. For Rilla, this loneliness didn't feel like
it could be good.

Her heartbeat thumped a roller-coaster rhythm. Up and down. Resigned
and expectant. She pulled her last smoke from her pocket and bent against
the wind to light it. With her bag between her boots on the sidewalk, she
waited for the last person who might want her: her half sister.

3

A boy dropped his bag by her feet with a heavy clink of metal, startling her out of her thoughts. "Got another one of those?" he asked, gesturing toward her cigarette.

Rilla shook her head. "Sorry. I'm out." The last place had carded her, and she was down to this cigarette and one emergency joint in the bottom of her bag. She was supposed to be done smoking anyway. It was part of the plan. She'd had three days to hash out new rules for a new life—to turn everyone else's *best thing* into her own. She took a deep pull and held the cigarette out to him as an offering.

The boy reached for it. "Do you have much further to go?" he asked through a rush of a smoke.

"No idea. I think I'm close? It feels like I've been on a bus longer than I've been alive." She pulled her hands into the sleeves of her jacket and hugged herself in the chilly May wind, glancing quickly at him and away, trying to get a look without him noticing.

He was a tall cowboy stuffed into a thin, black puffer jacket and old corduroy pants. Tangled earbuds dangled from around his neck, swinging as he curled forward to relight the smoke. His straight mouth and strong jaw landed him just this side of clean-cut and boring, but something she couldn't pin down gave him a lurking edge of intensity. His gaze cut to the road, and in the amber light, as he took a deep pull on the cigarette, his eyes gleamed.

Her heartbeat surged, as if racing to match that ephemeral intensity. He caught her staring and offered the smoke back.

She waved it off, trying not to blush. "I'm quitting."

"Where're you from?" he asked.

"What?"

"Your accent."

Rilla frowned and pulled a strand of her long brown hair back from the wind as it swept across her face. "I don't really have an accent."

"Is it Kentucky?"

Kentucky? She made a face. "I do *not* sound like I'm from Kentucky."

"I hate to break it to you, but you have an accent."

She drew back. *Did she?* "But like . . . not like Kentucky. I'm from West Virginia."

"Same thing." He put the cigarette back to his mouth and looked in the opposite direction. "At least, west of the Mississippi. I get it. I'm from southern Ohio. I know people who have been to Antarctica more times than they've been to southern Ohio."

Rilla opened her mouth to respond, but a lone truck swung into the parking lot, headlights blinding. Her stomach dropped, and she held her breath as the engine cut and door opened.

Thea.

Thea had left West Virginia with short black hair and multiple piercings, as the lead singer in a band who poured fake blood on herself during shows. Even then, Thea was the most responsible person Rilla knew.

Goth Thea did not climb out of the truck, but it was Thea nonetheless. Her face emerged out of the night, split with the warm, natural smile she'd always kept hidden. Her natural, dark brown hair was pulled over the shoulder of her purple windbreaker, her face tanned and makeup-free. At seventeen and twenty-five, they looked more like sisters than Rilla remembered. Without Thea's goth persona painted on, they both looked like Mom.

"Rilla!" Thea stepped onto the sidewalk and folded Rilla into an iron hug.

A surge of relief flared through Rilla's whole body. Thea was still taller. Thinner. Stronger. She smelled, impossibly, like she always had—orange and thyme. All things Rilla remembered from having an older sister. She buried herself in Thea's arms, stomach in a knot. Thea might have *said* she would do whatever they thought best for Rilla—but what else was a decent human being supposed to say? It was hard to believe Thea wanted her when everyone else had sent her packing.

Thea pulled back. "How was the bus? Terrible, right? You ready to get back in the car?" Her smile flickered away from Rilla and deepened as she looked to the boy. "Look at you, Walker. Ah. Congratulations." Thea lifted her arms, and Rilla stepped out of the way.

The boy—Walker—dropped the cigarette, a wide grin spreading across his face that made him look younger. He bent and gave Thea a friendly hug. "Hey, boss."

Thea groaned. "Not so far. I'm up to my eyes in administration. And parking duties."

Walker looked horrified. "Parking? I finally get on the team, and you've abandoned me?"

"It's the price I pay for living the dream," Thea said, reaching for his bag. "I haven't even been climbing this season."

"What?" Walker asked, swatting Thea's hand away and picking up the bag himself. It clinked with that same metallic sound as he threw it, bulging and awkward, over his shoulder and stepped off the curb, into the shadows toward the truck. "What are you even doing with your life?"

Thea grabbed Rilla's duffel. "Listen, whippersnapper, I got real tactical shit going on these days. Those minivans don't park themselves."

"Oh. Well. My apologies, *Ranger Martínez*," Walker called dryly.

Rilla swallowed, shouldering her backpack. The wind snapped at her neck, biting open the loneliness she'd thought a warm welcome would resolve. Rilla rushed to catch up with Thea.

"You feeling okay? Relieved to be out here?" Thea asked. "Ready to buckle down and pull it together?"

Rilla knew what she was supposed to say to the long-gone sister who'd doubled back to disaster. "Yep. All good. I'm fine." She did two thumbs-up to prove she was whatever normal was. Thea knew all the sordid details via Mom, but Rilla didn't want to rehash any of it. "That bus ride was eternal, though. We broke down in Salina, Kansas. I probably smell. Someone was cooking liver and onions on a hot plate the last few hours. I—"

"Sorry to make you ride crammed in the middle after that bus," Thea interrupted. "But it's all I've got."

Just then, Walker hollered, "Are you tying me to the hood or something?"

Rilla gulped back the rest of her chatter.

"Rilla'll get in the middle," Thea answered. She took Rilla's bag and threw it alongside Walker's.

The door hinges squeaked. "Come on then, West Virginia," Walker called in Rilla's direction. "I want to get there."

Rilla ducked underneath Walker's outstretched arm, sliding into the middle of the blue vinyl bench seat. He followed, putting his arm on the back of the seat to make room for his shoulders.

Rilla was aware of every part of his body filling the cab—from his fingers draped on the vinyl seat behind her neck to his ratty sneakers pushed up onto the floorboard. But it was hard to tell if he noticed—folded up and turned in on herself as she was.

Rilla smoothed back her hair and tried to avoid making eye contact with herself in the rearview mirror. She'd put makeup on in the bathroom in L.A. that morning—dark eyeliner and coats of mascara to make her narrow blue eyes as cutting as she could manage. But it looked all smudged and terrible by now, she was certain.

Thea shut her door and the dome light clicked off, bathing them in darkness.

Folding her hands in her lap, Rilla looked out the front window, at the amber-lit street and more lines on pavement.

Mom had reminded her before she boarded the bus—girls like her didn't get chances like these. They didn't leave Rainelle. They didn't see the country. They didn't get to start over, in a place where they could be anyone. They didn't see their feet past a pregnant belly at the end of age seventeen. Rilla's shoulders had sagged listening. Those were all truths her mom knew by experience, and none of Rilla's protests convinced her this wasn't the same. Rilla had never envisioned leaving like this. She'd never really envisioned leaving at all. Come hell or high water—and both surely came—West Virginia was home.

On the bus, she'd decided California was a chance to prove to everyone at home that they were wrong about her. Wrong about it all. Thea probably wouldn't want her for long, but in that time she'd make everyone back home sorry. She'd show them.

Suck it, everyone back in Rainelle.

two

"DON'T GET INTO TROUBLE," THEA'S NOTE SAID AT THE END. INSTEAD OF something sisterly, or *love you*, or even a smiley face, there was a scratched admonition on the back of the map of Yosemite Valley.

"Get your schoolbooks from the office. You can eat in Half Dome Village—just sign my name on the sheet at the register. Call Mom and tell her you're okay. And don't get into trouble."

Rilla folded the map into a tiny square and tried not to let it sting. All her eagerness to prove herself had drained away.

Last night, Yosemite Valley had been nothing but a blurry blob of darkness before Rilla had dropped straight into a squeaky cot in the attic. Fourteen hours later, she'd crawled down the attic ladder to find the Valley drenched in sunshine, and Thea at work.

Alone, the silent house echoed in her chest. No one to call. No one to kiss. No one to even talk to.

Rilla stared at the brown painted porch steps of the bare-bones crafts-man bungalow Thea shared with three other rangers. The small house was plunked in a meadow in the heart of the Valley, in a neighborhood without fences, driveways, or different paint colors, and Rilla sat, unable even to lift her chin to the massive cliffs bordering all directions and the oaks shaking their silvery leaves in the crisp wind. This was supposed to be her new home, these mountains her new keepers. But she and Thea had done this before, just the two of them in Rainelle. Rilla remembered—when Thea got a chance, she left Rilla behind. Rilla couldn't help but assume that it would happen again.

The sun touched the back of her neck—warming away the spring chill. All the wonder and awe she should have felt were missing. All she could see was *don't get into trouble*. All she felt was alone.

Standing, Rilla tucked the map into her pocket and set off to complete Thea's other instructions.

She picked up her books from the tiny school a short walk down the road, and found her way to the viewing platform of the massive waterfall she heard all night in her dreams. The rush of thick, white water pounded car-sized boulders and surged down toward the bridge she stood on. The mist washed over her, cold, even in the sun. The waterfall was the most beautiful thing she'd ever seen, but watching it from the bridge where tourists all clumped to take photos and smile made her feel very small and forgotten.

She kept walking. Dazed. Lost. Exhausted. A boy who she thought was Walker passed across the parking lot, but when she called out, he didn't respond. Her face burned and she picked up her pace, ignoring the tourists whose heads had turned.

Even with all the people, she felt out of place. It was clear from the winter paleness of her soft limbs, she was not here for anything Yosemite had to offer. It felt like everyone could see she was one of those *rebellious* teenagers dragged into the wilderness against her will, in hopes the awe of things bigger than herself would unlock the stubborn set to her jaw and the daggers she tried to shoot from her eyes. She kept walking, letting the asphalt path lead her through the Valley in hopes of finding the food Thea had mentioned.

The cliffs looked the same. The meadows blurred together. The map made no sense. The crested wave of Half Dome stood as her only landmark. Her phone died while sending a fourth text to a friend from home who hadn't yet responded.

By the time Rilla wandered into a warm cafeteria filled with people eating at gleaming wood tables arranged around stone fireplaces, she had forgotten the shape and sting of Thea's note, and thought only that she was tired, hungry, and overwhelmed.

A guy who looked like he *definitely* had a weed hookup stood behind the counter, serving mashed potatoes—friendly and non-threatening, with soft brown eyes and messy blond hair that touched his shoulders, even in the hairnet. Rilla had promised herself on the bus ride, she'd stop smoking in California, but with everything changing all at once, it felt like too much to ask that she also change.

Rilla smiled and tried to make her eyes friendly. "I'm new."

"To what?" he asked, holding up a spoonful of mashed potatoes over her plate, his eyes questioning.

"Here."

His forehead creased.

"I'll take some," she said to the mashed potatoes. "I thought weed was legal in California, but I couldn't find it in the store over there."

He chuckled. "I'm sure the tourists would be a lot more chill. Did Amber send you?"

"Yes? Sure!" She said it with a wink in her voice. If she had to be sent by someone, consider her sent. Let him and whoever Amber was figure their shit out later.

He rolled his eyes, but his smile was as friendly as the rest of him. "I get off in an hour. I'll meet you outside. My name's Jonah."

"Rilla. See ya," Rilla said, sailing away with her tray.

The mashed potatoes were disgusting, but a hefty dose of hot sauce resurrected them into something edible. She took her time eating and nursing a cup of hot tea. Inside, she was shielded from the massive cliffs, surrounded by the murmur of people and the smell of warm food. The prospect of a friendly face cheered her almost as much as the food. It was true—going off with a strange boy for some smoke was probably under the umbrella of what Thea considered *trouble*. But Rilla could handle herself. Thea had forgotten what it was like at home.

"Where are you working?" Jonah asked as they walked out of the busy hub of Half Dome Village, into the fading afternoon light.

"Oh, I don't work here. I just live here."

He swung a look over his shoulder. "How did you get so lucky?"

"My sister lives here. I moved in with her. She's a park ranger."

"They just let you move in with her?"

"Special perks for wayward baby sisters." She arched an eyebrow and put on her best villain face, in what she hoped was a charming take on the truth.

He laughed. "You'll fit right in."

Jonah was from Arizona, and ran ultramarathons—a hell Rilla had previously not known about where a person ran thirty-four or more miles *for fun*. He seemed to understand she didn't know anyone and had just been looking for a friend, chatting easily about some *Mont Blanc* trail run and how running that far was an incredible experience, as he led her off the wide asphalt path, between two drab canvas tents built on wooden platforms.

"I'll have to take your word for it," Rilla said. "If you see me running, I'm being chased."

He laughed.

She followed him down a dirt path with tents on either side.

"Well this is what you're missing over there in your luxe meadow housing," Jonah said. "Welcome to HUFF."

The tents were made of dirty canvas, built on raised platforms, with steps and screen doors. On her way across the Valley earlier, she'd seen similar ones by the Merced, filled with tourists. But these looked different. Some of the canvas was patched and doors were ripped. Steps were draped with clothes and rusty bikes were propped against the sides.

"This is summer employee housing," Jonah said. "Not like the fancy ranger houses."

She thought of her cot in the attic, shoved in between the storage boxes, and nodded. "Why is it called HUFF?"

"They used to throw hot coals off the top of Glacier Point right there." He pointed to the trees and Rilla lifted her chin. Unease rippled through her chest to see the massive wall looming over them, smoky gray and shadowed in the late afternoon light. It was bigger than anything she'd ever seen.

"They called it the Firefall." He snorted. "They stopped doing that in sixty-eight, but this is still called housing under Firefall. Or HUFF for short. Rilla, say hello to everyone. Everyone, say hello to Rilla."

Rilla tore her eyes away from the cliff, to a circle of people in camp chairs all staring at her. An open bag of chips and hummus sat in the middle of a piece of beige carpet laid in the dirt.

Rilla swallowed and lifted her balled sweatshirt fist in a wave. They were all older than her—college age. She tried to look mature and experienced. When they asked her where she was working, she shook her head. "I live here."

"Like permanently?" A girl leaned forward. "Really?"

Rilla shrugged. "For now." She didn't know what would happen. How long Thea would tolerate her. The breeze stirred her ponytail, and she shrugged, throat tight because she had no real answer.

"Where are you from?" someone asked.

"West Virginia," she said quickly, thankful for a question she *could* answer.

Another snorted. "Wow, I didn't know they had pretty girls in West Virginia."

Should she react to that as a compliment or an insult? It felt like both. Rilla's smile stayed frozen in place, as she pretended she hadn't heard it.

"Do all y'all work here?" she asked, sitting in the chair Jonah pulled up for her.

Everyone nodded, staring back at her with the unmistakable look of standing in the warm house and looking out at the person left in the chill.

Alone. A shiver ran up her spine. It was a feeling of emptiness in the air where she kept clutching to find something that she'd always thought would be there. A sudden expansion of a room, where she expected to find a wall, a door, something to hold on to, but the dark kept going.

"So, what's West Virginia like?" a boy with an Australian accent asked. "Is it like the *Beverly Hillbillies*?"

Jonah rolled his eyes and reached for the chips. "This is how Brock is seeing the country, by getting drunk and asking people the most offensive things about their state."

But Rilla didn't care. Everyone's eyes were on her for a moment, and she wanted to make the most of it.

"West Virginia is not like the *Beverly Hillbillies*," she answered. "It's like the *Beverly Hillbillies* meets the *Fast and the Furious*. With trucks."

A flicker of laughter ran through her audience. But she was only getting started. "I know this guy, right. His name is Depraved. No, that's his actual name. Yeah, that's a different story—how Depraved got his name. He buys wrecked trucks, like wrecked titles, and fixes them. Three years ago, he bought this wrecked duck boat from World War II. The kind that can go in water and land . . . *you know.*" She took a deep breath. "Anyway, that's not the story. The story is he had this snake."

Out loud in California, she made it funny and real as she told the story of Depraved and his big python, Samwise, that often sunned itself in the window of his souped-up Duck Truck, eventually surprising some boys from her high school who tried to steal the truck-boat as a prank. Rilla's eyes danced, her hands leapt, and she pulled the story up and down in a bright rhythm that melted the chill of being an outsider and brought her into the center. It gave her a sense of power, and the warmth of an audience chased away the chill of being alone.

Their laughter made Rilla laugh, and once she started laughing, she laughed so hard she slid down in her chair and wiped tears from her cheeks. She'd paid her way with a story—for the night at least—but deep inside, the feeling of shit and shame grew, as if their laughter was another insult and compliment. Everyone had made fun of Depraved's Duck Truck for years, but when Rainelle flooded last spring, Depraved drove down and spent an entire night ferrying people to safety. Rilla closed her eyes and wiped her tears, remembering the sound of water in the streets and the scared faces of the Monroes as they sat, wet and dejected, clutching the only belongings they could hold in their hands in the back of Depraved's Duck Truck.

And suddenly, Rilla wasn't sure whether she was laughing or crying.

A cute boy with dark curls, dimples, and an honest-to-god French accent passed a joint in her direction, and she shoved down her feelings and reached for the familiar unlacing of all that had been cinched tight the last few hours of sobriety. "California has the best weed," she said through her grin, knees pulled up in the chair. Someone handed her a beer and she opened it and held it between her knees.

Jonah laughed and took the joint. "That's the altitude. Careful with it. It'll wear off in a few weeks."

Now that her stomach was full, spine unlaced, and the sound of something like friends rang in her ears, Rilla noticed how it didn't smell like West Virginia, but like something newer and less complicated. The wind sang a song of dry dust and pine. It pushed into her bones and blood, and urged her onward—into something *also* newer and less complicated. As soon as she found her way back to Thea's house, she was going to start again. Tomorrow would be better. Less terrifying. Rilla would start over, for real this time.

She abandoned her broken chair to wind herself along with the music in the cute French boy's lap. His green polo shirt wrinkled in her grip. His curls smelled like girl's shampoo. His hands braced her thighs. It felt so good to be touched. To be wanted.

Night fell and the little canvas neighborhood moved along at its own pace—people were dancing, laughing, ,moving in and out of the circle as they finished the hummus, did laundry, and went for showers. The screen doors to the canvas tents swung back and forth in perfect cadence with the mountain wind.

After Jonah left to shower, Rilla bummed a smoke and wandered away, spilling out of the line of tents to stand under the trees and away from the crowd. A few tourists passed on the path, carrying shower caddies and toothbrushes for the bathroom. They didn't notice Rilla or the slivers of light coming from the row of tents just beyond them. She lit the smoke and the cold wind caught in her chest, wrenching her out of the warm haze.

The dark felt enormous. The granite wall behind her even more so. The trees moved in the wind, as if they would shift and crush her without ever hearing her cries. At home, she was a villain. Here, she was nothing. This was a mistake. A horrible, wretched mistake.

Thea. She'd be home by now, wondering where Rilla was. Digging for the map in her pocket, Rilla unfolded it and squinted, trying to simply find her place.

Rilla flicked her cigarette away and stepped back toward the crowd, clutching the paper in the wind to ask someone.

"Hey, you," an authoritative voice yelled.

Rilla didn't realize he was talking to her, until he grabbed her elbow. "Stop."

She turned and blinked at the face of a park ranger.

"Did you just drop that cigarette?" he demanded.

"Uh. No." The lie was out like breathing. *Always deny, everything.* It was one of her mom's most repeated rules. She swallowed and tried not to look guilty. She was a Skidmore—they never did well in front of law enforcement.

His features hardened. "I watched you. Don't you know how dangerous that is? Go back and pick it out of the grass, before you burn down the whole Valley from your carelessness." He let go of her elbow, and she wobbled unsteadily for a second.

"Have you been drinking?" He looked past her, into the alley between the tents and the crowd beyond. "How old are you? What's your name? Do you work here?"

"Twenty-one," she said, struggling with the rapid-fire questions. "Priscilla Skidmore. I haven't been drinking, though. I didn't know about the cigarette. I don't want to burn anything."

But he was already moving on. "I'm going to do a series of tests. Touch your nose with your pointer finger."

Rilla touched her nose. Heart pounding in her ears.

"Now with the other hand."

She swung her other hand up and poked herself in the eye. *Shit.*

"How much have you had to drink tonight?"

Did it look like she just fell off the turnip truck? "Nothing. Ossifer." She licked her lips and tried again. "Officer." That time she nailed it. How much had she had to drink? Her nervousness lit a fire to the two beers she remembered.

"You're slurring."

She was not. She was nervous. "Stop making fun of my *ass-sent.*"

A white light blinded her eyes. "Place your hands on top of your head."

No. No. No. This couldn't be happening. It felt like her wrists lifted of their own accord.

Don't get into trouble. But she hadn't meant to. She didn't want to be here. She didn't want to be alone.

He took one hand off her head and wrapped it behind her back with the cuffs.

Rilla was definitely in trouble.

three

EVEN IN RAINELLE IT FELT LIKE EVERYBODY REACTED TO A VERSION OF Rilla that she herself couldn't see. In Yosemite, she thought she'd be set free from that—able to get out from the shadow of her own caricature and find the real Priscilla Skidmore. But if this night was any indication, her shadow had followed her here. It was the only thing that explained why she was in jail for drinking and a little bit of pot. In *California*. Of all states.

Rilla wrapped her fingers over the edge of the old pew bench, shivering uncontrollably under the gaze of the two park rangers who had busted the party and were now processing all the arrests. Shame watered in her mouth, stronger every time the rangers glanced in her direction. They had to call Thea. They knew who she was. They probably knew what had happened in West Virginia, and it's why they looked at her with so much derision as compared to everyone else.

Rilla tried not to let them see she noticed.

Thea walked in a little after 5 A.M. With her straight shoulders and a thrown-back head, she marched to the empty desk beside one of the rangers.

"Martinez?" he asked without looking up.

"Miller," Thea said, opening a drawer and looking through it. "I'm going to take Rilla home."

Rilla slumped. Just when her life couldn't get more shameful.

"Oh, are you?" Ranger Miller asked dryly.

"She's been through enough. She wasn't driving or making a scene—"

"You need to talk to the judge first," he interrupted.

Rilla froze, feeling Thea's eyes on her.

"What?" Thea retorted. "She looks sober. She's sitting there completely calm and alert."

"Well, she *is* drunk." Ranger Miller's facial expression didn't change throughout the entire conversation. Did it ever change? He had the face of a hot guy who wasn't actually that hot and didn't look anything but a not-that-hot dick. Rilla narrowed her eyes: *Dick Face. Ranger Dick Face.*

"She blew a .07." He began clicking his pen, studying Thea.

"She's terrified and exhausted and a *child*," Thea said sharply. "These kids are all way older than her. Right now, she just needs a safe place. I'm taking her home. If the judge has anything to say about it, you tell him to come talk to me."

"Go ahead," Ranger Dick Face said, waving his pen. "It'll just make the decision this fall that much easier for everyone."

"You'll be as liable as me, Miller," Thea said over her shoulder. She held her hand out for Rilla to take.

Rilla stared at Thea's open hand and didn't move. Never had she felt this shitty. Not even when she sat in a Rainelle jail with her bloody nose and swollen eye.

"Oh, trust me. I'll make sure everyone knows what happened," Ranger Dick Face said.

"That you were harassing vulnerable children?" Thea asked.

"That you were insubordinate," he barked.

Rilla burst up. "*Stop* being an asshole to my sister. She didn't do anything."

"Rilla." Thea pulled on her arm. "No. It's fine . . ."

Rilla shook her off and took a step toward Ranger Dick Face. "I was just an easy target."

He frowned and looked straight past her to Thea. "Maybe work on getting her to take responsibility for her actions."

"Rilla," Thea snapped. "Let's go."

"Thea didn't ask for this," Rilla said as Thea tugged her out of the room. "Leave her alone."

"Come on," Thea said softly, squeezing Rilla's hand.

Rilla's skin crawled with the horror of her sister being so kind. It made her hate herself and everyone around her.

"Go to hell, Martinez," Ranger Dick Face said as they went out the door.

"Meet you there," Thea said before letting the door slam shut behind them.

Thea kept a firm grip on Rilla's hand until they were outside, in the glimmering blue-gray of coming sunrise. The moon hung low, nearly resting on the top of cliffs that walled in the narrow valley, and winking as if it hadn't lost sight of her since the bus stop in Merced by the Japanese maples.

"How dare you?" Thea finally asked. "I had you one day. I got home and you were gone. I was worried you went back to West Virginia, or had fallen off a cliff somewhere and would die before I found you. *Why the hell did you do that?*"

"It was an accident. I just got . . ." Rilla ducked her chin. "Lost," she said in a near whisper.

"Didn't you stop and think that after everything that had happened I might be worried when you fucking *disappear*? You didn't answer your phone or text me back. What if that guy—what was his name, Curtis?— had followed you out here?"

"*Oh my god!*" Rilla snapped. "Stop. That's ridiculous and not how it was at all." She cringed just to think about how Thea had probably talked about her. "Anyway, my phone is dead and I'm out of minutes."

"Mom didn't . . . ?" Thea stopped. Frustration clamped her features into lines, and her words were clipped and tight. "Ugh, of course she didn't send you out here with anything but a burner. Forget the phone. You didn't think, even once, that maybe you should come home? You were gone all night!"

"Just send me home," Rilla said quickly. The end of Thea's rope was much shorter than she'd even expected, but there was relief in not having to wait all summer for this moment.

Thea threw her hands up in exasperation. "Why would you even want to go back?" Without waiting for Rilla's reply, she stormed ahead.

Rilla glared at Thea's back. Well, *there* was the sister she once knew. The one who got angry and left. Rilla needed to go back to West Virginia, before she did any damage to her sister's pristine new life. Before Thea started regressing to smashing fake blood bags over her head while screaming about futility.

They walked in silence between the shadowed cliffs, and Rilla forced herself to look up.

She'd seen pictures of Yosemite, of course. After Mom had bought her bus ticket and California turned out to be real and not just a threat, she'd sobbed under her pillow and then googled *Yosemite National Park*. A mile wide and roughly eight miles long, the Merced River wound through a grassy meadow and woodland floor. The Internet was full of photos of tall waterfalls lit in sunlight, the Valley spread through wide-angle lenses, with the famous cliffs keeping watch on each end: El Capitan and Half Dome.

What she hadn't seen—hadn't understood—in all those pictures was the *scale*.

How it kept going, on and on. Beyond the limits she didn't even know her mind had placed on trees and rocks and sky. It was as if she'd walked into what she thought was the world, and suddenly it grew up around her, lurching from the depths of the earth to push tall and proud toward the stars. The whole world was bigger than she had imagined it could be, and she much smaller in it.

"Drugs?" Thea asked, falling back in step beside her. "Weed? Something else?"

It took a second to realize Thea was asking if she'd done them. Rilla's throat tightened and she kept her face even. "No." No more. Not after last night.

"Have you talked to someone about what happened? At home?"

Rilla didn't respond. She was sure if she opened her mouth, she'd cry. Her face flushed hot and horrified. A flash of tightness crossed her collarbone, a blur of heat and anger pressing into her skin, and she had to look down. "I don't want to talk about it. It's over. No one listened in the first place."

"I'll listen," Thea said.

Rilla rolled her eyes. "Yeah, *okay*. It wasn't like you think. It wasn't this huge thing Mom is making it into."

"You're saying Mom . . . *our mom* . . . overreacted?"

Rilla tightened her jaw and glared at her. This was exactly what she feared from Thea. From anyone. "I don't want to talk about it."

Thea sighed as they crossed into the open meadow. "Fine. But what good does it do anyone if you come all the way out here and just keep doing the same things?"

Rilla swallowed. Her throat ached. "I'm trying."

Thea snorted. "If this is trying . . ." She shook her head. "Girl, I can't keep you if I don't have a *job*. This is a seasonal position. I just got here two months ago. There's one opening for a permanent park ranger. At the end of the season they're going to decide between me and Miller."

Rilla blanched. "Ranger Dick Face?"

Thea made a face. "Gross." She shook her head, and the porch steps creaked under her boots. "Why do you think he did all that with you and seeing the judge? He knows it's good for his career for me to seem unstable. If he can get me in trouble, he can keep me out of a job. If he can get *you* in trouble, he can keep me out of a job."

"Is that what y'all do all summer? Just bust people having a good time?" Rilla asked.

Thea shook her head. "They do these once or twice in the early summer, to weed out the employees who are going to be a problem all summer."

"What's going to happen to them?" Rilla asked.

"The ones who were arrested? They're going home."

"I want to go home," Rilla said. She didn't really, but she did at the same time. It was both things at once. She didn't want to feel this small. She didn't want to wait for her sister to get fed up and send her home. She wanted time to belong in this vast landscape. But she only said, "I don't like it here."

"You don't even know where here is," Thea said, rolling her eyes. "Baby girl, you're so West Virginia it's ridiculous. Look at you." Thea swept her hand up and down.

Rilla frowned and looked down at her boots and cut-offs, the gauze top, thin and drab from a long night. "What?"

Thea snorted. "Nothing. Just . . . and your accent. God, sometimes it's hard to believe I ever talked like that. Ever looked like that."

"You didn't look like this. I'm prettier," Rilla shot back. What did everyone see that Rilla couldn't? What was she supposed to be ashamed of?

Thea laughed.

"Not all of us hate where we come from, Thea," Rilla said.

"I don't hate West Virginia. I just never want to go back."

"Well, I do want to go back. I have friends there. I have a *family* there." Family who hadn't left her.

Thea's eyes widened and she nodded slowly like Rilla was too young and dumb to understand. "Okay, sure. That's a word you can use. But hey, guess what, girl? You're not going home." Thea whipped the door open, before continuing. "Don't party. Don't get into trouble. Don't do stupid-ass things that are going to get me fired. The Valley is a small world. You can't get away with anything."

Rilla's stomach sank.

Thea sighed. "If anything, do it for yourself. You're in Yosemite for the summer. This is a chance not many people get." She'd already opened the door. "Come on before I let a squirrel in."

The falls above continued to crash and roar in Rilla's ears, as she followed Thea inside.

Thea stepped into the galley kitchen just inside the door, and Rilla ignored the sleepy looks from the other rangers sitting in the living room, eating breakfast, and working on a laptop in a recliner. Rilla's body tightened with exhaustion and unshed tears. She kicked off her boots, adding them to the pile by the door.

The house was small—only one bathroom, two bedrooms with bunks where Thea and the other rangers slept, a little galley kitchen, and the living room filled with shoes, coats, laundry, piles of books, and outdoor gear. The lopsided squares of commercial carpet askew in the center of the main space looked suspiciously like leftovers from the carpet in the dining hall at Half Dome Village.

"How's it going?" one of the rangers asked.

Rilla straightened and swallowed. "Fine," she choked over her swollen throat, chin high as she stepped over a saddle someone had dumped right in the entrance to the hallway.

"You'll feel better if you eat," Thea called from the kitchen.

But Rilla couldn't be around anyone. She made it to the end of the hall, up the ladder leading to the attic Thea had shoved her into, before the tears came.

Throwing herself belly down on the cot, Rilla sobbed into the wool blanket until her eyes were exhausted of tears and her face itched from the wet wool. Turning her chin to the side, she stared at the light through the cracks in the floor and listened as, one by one, the women below left. Until all that remained was her puffy, itchy face and the dull roar of the waterfall outside.

•

Rilla woke a few hours later, from dreams bright and sickening, her sweaty cheek smashed into the edge of the cot mattress. She blinked at the slatted underbelly of the roof, straining her neck to look out the only window. Still in California. Thea hadn't kicked her out.

Sleep hadn't calmed the pitch of her feelings, and she hated that she didn't understand what she wanted. One second she found herself consumed with homesickness, and the next all she wanted was to *belong* here. Like Thea did.

A clammy feeling crawled over her, but she dragged herself out of the cot and slid to the floor. She needed water. Her dreams—hazy and unformed—still lingered on her skin, and her stomach churned with the lingering sensation of a narrow escape.

Shuddering, she eased downstairs to the shower.

The house was silent and cold. She rushed in the shower and crawled back up the ladder to her warm attic. Sitting on the floor, she steadily combed out the snarls in her hair until she felt like she might be able to stand up. She pulled on a sweatshirt, sunglasses, and hat, and shoved a cold Gatorade under her arm on her way out the door.

She didn't know what to do next. It was the day before all over again. Except, somehow, she had to do something different.

Unscrewing the Gatorade cap, she carefully took a sip, and sank into a chair on the porch. The same Valley sat awash in sun. The same loneliness aching all around her.

The cool dry wind gusted, lifting the heavy ends of her wet hair and stirring the oaks overhead. She closed her eyes, feeling it over every inch of her skin. The white lines of all the roads that had led her there, on that porch, ran through her mind and left her stomach churning again. She wanted to go home. She wanted to see Curtis. It was all she truly had. She had nothing here.

"Thea around?" A voice shattered the stillness.

Her eyes struggled to open.

Walker stood below. One leg up on the steps. He wore sunglasses, with a leather cord tucked behind his ears and around the back of his neck, and dust-smudged red track pants with blue stripes running down the sides. No shirt.

She shook her head. It hurt. The sweat from her bottle dripped over her fingers, onto her thighs. The wind flattened her hair against the rusty metal of the chair.

"Know where she is?"

Rilla unscrewed the cap and took another sip before answering. "I sure don't."

"You all right?"

"I'm fine," Rilla said. "Do you want to leave a message?"

"I guess she's working a lot these days?"

"I don't know. I mean, I just got here," Rilla said, eyebrow raised until she remembered she was wearing a hat and glasses and it was a wasted effort. "What do you need?"

"Just tell her I was looking for someone to climb with." He hooked his thumbs under the straps of his pack and looked away. There was a long pause.

Rilla squeezed the bottle between her fingers and frowned.

He pulled off the step. "Later." The grass swished as he walked past the house.

Squinting against the sun, she watched him go, long muscled arms swinging at his sides.

Homesickness washed over her with a lurch of her stomach, and the Valley all around seemed to reverberate with emptiness. All she wanted was to not be alone.

"Hey," she croaked.

Walker kept going.

Rilla pushed out of the chair and called over the railing. Louder. With certainty. "Walker."

He turned.

She gripped the edge. "Can I come? Climbing?"

four

HOME—*RAINELLE*—WAS NESTLED IN THE MOUNTAINS ALONG SAM Black Church Road, surrounded by woods and wild. But despite her surroundings growing up, Rilla had never hiked anything farther than a trail to a party or a tree-stand, and she'd only ever climbed to get something she couldn't reach otherwise. Sitting on a rock, where Walker had told her to *stay* while he disappeared up a steep gully, a sudden wave of anger washed over her.

This was stupid. What did she think she could do . . . move to California and suddenly become one of these tourists with hiking poles and SPF clothing? Like, *let's go die in the wilderness, Bob. Yuk, yuk, yuk. Pointless and avoidable death for the win!*

Rilla stared at the gray granite wall in front of her, her jaw clenched tight. The gentle asphalt path that circled the Valley and promised a quick return to Thea's place sat just out of the corner of her eye. But if she went back, it would only be to an empty house. She didn't know what she was doing. Here, with climbing. Or in life. Her eyes stung, but she took another careful drink of her warm Gatorade. She wouldn't cry. *No more crying.*

"West Virginia," Walker said from behind her.

Rilla jumped. "How did you?" she sputtered. "Where—"

Walker adjusted the sunglasses atop his short, dark-blond hair. "I rapped down."

She blinked a long, slow beat.

"Um. Right," he said. "Rappelled. I set up a top-rope, a rope at the top, and rappelled down the rope. You haven't ever been climbing before?"

She shook her head.

"Okay, no biggie. We got this." He tilted his head. "Come on."

Forcing herself up, Rilla followed him farther along the base where two stretches of a bright green rope ran down the cliff and coiled at the bottom like a thin, vivid serpent.

"What do you do here? Are you a ranger?" Rilla asked. She was pretty sure he lived in the park, and now she understood there was a reason.

"I'm on the Yosemite Search and Rescue Team. We get to stay in the park for free, in exchange for our search and rescue skills."

Rilla's spine straightened. *Well, hello.* "Oh. How old are you?"

"Twenty."

"Hi, Walker!" a bright voice called.

He turned and lifted his hand in reply to a girl with long red hair, walking with her friends.

"Climbers?" Rilla asked.

"Hikers," Walker said, digging through his pack. "Hang on. I swear I had one . . ." He dug through the top. After another moment, he started pulling things out and setting them in the dirt. A balled-up sweatshirt. Some clinking metal bits that looked totally foreign. A big black notebook. Another book with a photo of a climber, mid-pose on the cover.

"Shit," he muttered to himself. He shook the bag.

The wind stirred, sending dust spinning into the books. Without thinking, Rilla bent to retrieve them. One was a guide book full of photos. But it was the black notebook, which had fallen open to a detailed ink illustration of a mountain, that caught her eye.

The sketch included notes and lines showing a path to the top. It was beautifully drawn, and also made no sense. Rilla flipped to the next page.

A half-finished charcoal of some people—mid-laugh around a fire—was on the next page, and the opposite page dated entries. "The weather fucking sucks," began one. Too late, she realized Walker had drawn them. This was his notebook. His journal.

"Hey," Walker snapped. "What are—"

She slammed the book shut, trying not to look guilty. "I didn't realize . . ."

"That's mine." He snatched the book back. Two spots of red rising on his cheeks. Anger? Embarrassment? She couldn't tell.

"I didn't realize it was personal," she said, handing back the guide book as well. "They fell out of the bag, and I didn't want them to get dusty."

He glowered, taking the guide book and dumping both back into the pack. "Let's just stick to climbing." He pulled a long stretch of rope out of the coil, the muscles in his side flickering lightly under little folds of skin as he bent. "A figure-eight knot is the basic knot in rock climbing. It is essential to learn, as this is the main point of contact between you and anything that keeps you alive."

The lack of a shirt hadn't seemed unnerving when Walker had showed up at Thea's doorstep—it hadn't read as nakedness. But now that Rilla stood within touching distance and felt less like death, it was hard to ignore the grace of his movements and the substance to his body. That intensity seemed to simmer under his skin, and it was hard not to watch for it like the sun behind clouds, wanting to feel it directed *at* her.

"Got it?" Walker asked, shaking a finished, intricate knot in front of her.

Shit. She'd been staring at him, not the rope. "Can I see it again?"

He started over.

At first, it was a relief to focus on the knot and the way his body was a welcome distraction from the rest of her feelings. But as he started through a second time, for no reason, the charm turned sour.

He shifted his weight in her direction to show the double overhand knot he said was her backup, and her heart raced at his closeness. But it felt like she had bitten into something sweet, and made her head throb. She tried to focus on his hands, but kept chasing after the origins of the sickening feeling.

Suddenly it hit her. He was humoring her. He was trying to be nice because he felt bad for her.

Her cheeks burned and mouth watered. Stepping back, she focused on his hands, on the slide of the rope—flexing her fingers as he went. She'd show him. She'd show them all. Starting with this dumb fucking knot.

After another moment, he held out the rope for her to try.

She took it—her brain suddenly unable to recall what he'd done, let alone connect it to her hands. The limp green coils twined in her fingers. She moved her hands, but the rope went the wrong way. The seconds ticked past. The wind waved the tops of the pines. All she wanted to do was one thing right. One thing. He'd *just* shown her. Her throat swelled with the threat of tears.

Walker pointed to the rope. "Around this way." Taking her whole fist into the palm of his hand, he pulled her through the motions.

It didn't help—his hands were warm and rough and utterly distracting. She wanted to do this on her own. She wanted to show herself she could. It was silly, but it mattered.

Walker let go, pointing out the places for her to push the rope back through. "Great job!" He congratulated her in the same overly cheery, supportive tone as she finished. Like a dog who'd finally shit outside.

Ripping the knot apart, she flexed her fingers and began again.

The third time, Rilla did it perfectly. Neat and elegant. Sweat beaded on her back and her head spun, but she pulled it apart and did it again. And again. And again. And—

"Okay." Walker took the finished knot away. "I think you got it." His tone had softened.

Which only made it worse. He could see her cracks.

She cleared her throat and put her hands on her hips. "What's next?"

He pulled out a snarl of thick nylon webbing and hard plastic loops. "This is a harness. Waist. Leg loops. Gear clips to these, but you won't need to worry about that." He pointed out the pieces, but they didn't look like anything but a snarl. "You tie in through these front parts and clip in to belay from this big front loop." He hooked a big finger through the sturdy nylon loop in the front of the harness and swung it to her. "Put it on. Like pants."

She fumbled, managing to catch it and step through the leg loops after he pointed where to step. How did she keep this on? Clutching the waist belt to her, she glanced at Walker.

He gripped the webbing on either side and pulled it up farther. "Your waist. Not your hips."

Her breath caught. That intensity—right under his skin—close to her. It was a one-sided charge. Reacting. It didn't make sense—he wasn't *that* attractive. But her heart thumped in the back of her throat, and it felt like he could lift her off the ground if he tugged too hard. She leaned back, trying to get distance. This wasn't how she wanted to feel.

"Pull the leg loops up as high as they'll go," he said, backing away.

"It's supposed to assault you?" she asked, yanking the leg loops into her inner thighs as instructed.

His mouth twitched, like he might have a real smile somewhere instead of that tacked-on, handsome shit he put out. "Yes." Offering her the end of the rope with the figure-eight follow-through half started, he tucked the tail into the top of her waistband. "Double back, then follow- through."

Rilla hated how he kept using words that made no sense. She hated how her head felt light from the push and pull of blood reacting to him. She hated everything. "You don't take new people climbing much, do you?"

He frowned.

She did as he said, rope cinching the top and bottom webbing together as she finished the knot with only a little hesitation.

Walker pulled the other end of the rope to his harness, opening a metal contraption he took off one of his gear loops. "This is called a Grigri."

"Gree-gree?"

He nodded. It was about the size of his palm, and he stuffed a bend of the rope into it before replacing the cover and clipping the whole thing to the belay loop.

"This goes to your climber." He yanked on the rope running up the wall.

The tug pulled up on her harness, cinching it tighter between her legs and around her hips.

God, why was he so compelling? It was like her hormones were the only thing not completely trashed.

"And this is your brake," he said, pulling on the rope that spit out the other end. "This stops the climber from falling. A Grigri has assisted braking, but it's just an aid. Don't ever take your hand off this part of the rope. Ever. Never."

Yeah. Okay. When were they going to start climbing? "Can I try?" Rilla asked.

Walker unclipped the Grigri from his harness and re-clipped it to her belay loop—his hands close to the space between her hipbones.

She bit her lip and then hastily pushed it back out in case he caught her looking like a moony-eyed middle-schooler.

Walker backed away, pulling the rope with him. "If your climber says *slack*, it means they need more rope. When the climber says *take*, you want to bring the rope back in."

Carefully, she practiced feeding the rope back and forth through the Grigri, and locking it off in case of a fall.

Before she felt comfortable with it, he switched the Grigri back to his harness and handed her a helmet that looked sort of gross. "Okay, let's go."

It felt like he was in a hurry. He tied the knot on her harness in a matter of seconds, not giving her a chance to do it.

She buckled the helmet under her chin and looked at the wall out of the corner of her eye. All this other stuff was easy. Distracting from the real thing. Now she had to climb. She'd asked him to take her, after all. There was no tapping out now.

She turned to the wall. Her stomach rolled. The helmet shifted over her eyes. This was fucking stupid. She was stupid. She pushed the helmet back and reached.

The stone was cool on her sweating hands and she grabbed hold of whatever protruded and looked up. Shit.

"Don't look up. Look at your feet."

"Yeah, yeah," she muttered, getting her feet on the wall and moving up. Sweat rolled down her back, but the faster she did it, the faster she'd get it over with.

"Go on, I've got you. You're fine." He said it smoothly, in the same lying tone he'd used when telling her he didn't mind, that he could take her.

"You're full of shit," she said, still moving.

He sighed, the rope pulling tighter. "Okay, West Virginia."

The wind had died and she seemed to be sweating everywhere. She'd gone far enough. Tied the knot. Did the belaying thing—sort of. Climbed. She could be done now. "Let me down."

"You're barely off the ground." His impatience was obvious now.

"I want down."

"You can do this." His tone grasped for enthusiasm. "You wanted to do this."

She pulled herself closer to the wall and looked awkwardly through her legs. "Yeah, I did it. Now I'm done."

"You can go farther. Come on." His sigh pulled on the rope. "I don't want to come back out and do this again because you didn't finish."

Her face flooded with heat. "If I want to do it again, I'll find someone else," she snapped.

That shut him up. "What's wrong with me?"

Only that he was an asshole. "I don't want to do this." She was shouting now, but she was still high above him and her fingers felt slippery on the granite. "I'm done. Let me down."

"So, come down," he yelled back.

Oh. She took her foot off and tried to find where last she stepped from.

"No, not like that. Sit back in the harness and hold the rope."

She swallowed and tried. Closing her eyes, she saw herself go back and let go of the wall. *And fall into nothing.* "Nope." She screeched, eyes flying open. "Nope. Nope. Nope."

"I have you," he said.

"You are not as helpful as you think."

"Come on, just relax, take a deep breath, and trust me. I got you." The rope cinched even tighter. A cord strung between them. But it wasn't enough. She took a deep breath, squared her shoulders. "I'm going to try to climb down."

"Don't do that. Just trust me. Feel me?" He tugged the rope and it yanked her harness tighter around her, digging into the tendons of her inner thighs.

She fixed her gaze to her hands. *Let go. Let go. Let go.* They didn't let go. "*I can't,*" she wailed.

"You can," he bellowed.

"You're wrong."

"I am not fucking wrong."

Ugh. He was no help. She had to get down. And pretend he wasn't even there.

Looking around at her feet, Rilla spotted the last little cleft she'd stood on and reached her foot down. The whole thing felt precarious, like if she tried to crouch or move down she might fall. This had been the worst idea. People who did this clearly had no other problems in life and needed to experience human misery. Rilla's toe couldn't find the cleft and she couldn't risk pulling away any farther to look for it. She was going to die or be stuck there forever.

Yanking herself back up to where she was safe, she dropped her forehead to the granite and started to cry, fingers cramping from holding so tight to the wall.

When someone touched her, she screamed.

"Calm down," Walker said soothingly. "I got you." He showed her the Grigri, locked off and holding them both.

"Don't tell me to calm down when I'm stuck twenty feet off the ground," she snarled.

"That's definitely the time you *should* be calm." He looked down. "You ready to come down now?"

"Shut up."

"All right, West Virginia." He put his arm around her waist and cinched her tight against him. "Let go."

She didn't want to, but with his arm there and the pull of his body away from the wall—the assurance of that weight—she could force her fingers to uncurl. Even so, a little scream escaped her throat as the rope stretched with their weight, pulling away from the rock.

Walker lowered them to the ground.

As soon as her feet hit the dirt, she yanked away, angrier with each second at everyone and everything. Mostly herself. Her tears were drying stiff and salty on her cheeks. Rounding on Walker, she opened her mouth to unleash her ire.

Before Rilla could even get a word out, a female voice interrupted. "Walker Jennings, stop torturing that poor girl."

five

THE WAY WALKER'S FACE TIGHTENED, RILLA EXPECTED AN EVIL STEP-
mother draped in the skin of his favorite dog. Instead, the girl who bounded
on top of a rock was only a little older than Rilla, with long, straight blond
hair and pale blue eyes—not beautiful, but compelling in that wide-open,
California girl way. "Don't you know anything by now?" The girl wagged her
finger in Walker's face. She wasn't wearing any makeup, and her hoodie and
leggings were streaked with dirt. Somehow, the effect was one of instant
coolness. Like she was one who *actually* just woke up like that.

Rilla hunched, wiping her cheeks—thankful her angry tears had been
surprised away like a case of the hiccups.

The girl patted Walker's shoulder and shook her head. "We've *got* to
get you some manners."

Walker's jaw clenched. "Petra, this isn't . . ."

The girl leaned on his shoulder and started talking over him. "I keep
telling him this is terrible foreplay, but does he listen?" She held out a
hand. "Petra Moore. Nice to meet you."

Rilla swallowed and offered her sweaty, damp hand. "Rilla."

"How's your vacation going, Rilla? Apart from this creep?" Petra
jerked her thumb over her shoulder.

"No, I . . . um." Rilla choked on her spit, swallowing quickly to answer.
"I live here."

"Oh, you work here." Petra's eyes flickered with interest. "What do
you do?"

"No. I just live here. With my sister."

Petra straightened off Walker's shoulder. "Wait. *Live* live here? Are you serious? And this your first time climbing?" She glanced over her shoulder to Walker's bare chest and rolled her eyes. "Oh, *honey.*"

Rilla's cheeks burned. "Turns out, this one's not a great teacher," she said, knowing it was petty, but trying to salvage a scrap of her dignity.

Walker yanked the rope down with a glare her direction. The rope whizzed and sizzled, dropping to the dirt with a thump.

"Rope," he said, in a deadpan.

Petra laughed. "If only all his liaisons could say such darling things, I'd like them more." She said *liaison* with the same thick, buttery accent the French boy had the night before. It rolled off, casually. Effortlessly. And then was gone.

Rilla swallowed, her tongue thick in her mouth.

"Everyone's at Angels' Bowl," Petra said. "Which, incidentally, is how you should try seducing girls from now on, Jennings."

Walker's face was all thunderstorms. "I was doing. A favor. For a friend."

"Yeah," Rilla jumped in hastily. "We're not . . ." But she trailed off, embarrassed.

Petra laughed and hitched the rope higher on her shoulder. "Have you been up there? No, if you're new to the Valley. Well, you're coming. You have to. I won't let him annoy you."

"Yeah, okay." It was out of Rilla's mouth way too fast to be cool. Of course she was going to go. The two of them together—Walker and Petra—looked like a movie she'd never be in. They looked like they had always been and would always be in Yosemite. And anything with Walker—someone Thea clearly seemed to trust—was probably okay, or would at least make a good excuse.

Despite Walker's bluster and Petra's needling, Petra set aside her rope, and she and Walker worked together to repack the gear, before all three of them headed off across the Valley.

Walker and Petra kept talking—arguing—as they circled up toward the base of the massive cliffs, with an exchange, that for all Walker's crankiness and Petra's antagonizing, made small curls of jealousy form in the bottom of Rilla's stomach. She couldn't tell if her jealousy was over the easy way they fought, or because it was clear she'd never be that cool.

Her freak-out while climbing seemed more and more illogical. He probably thought she was afraid of heights. It wasn't the height. It was the insecurity. If she'd just taken a second and *thought about it*, she could have pulled herself together.

Rilla dodged the swing-back of a branch, her calves aching as she struggled to keep up. They weren't even breathing hard. How much longer was this goddamn hike? She opened her mouth to ask, but Petra yelled, "Only a little farther."

Soon, the narrow, unused path leveled off, and they emerged out of the manzanita bushes, onto an open shelf in the cliff side. Granite rimmed a shimmering blue pool, and a thin waterfall cascaded down the cliff that continued to rise above them. The wind puffed in a cold and unfettered updraft. Rilla dragged in deep breaths, sweaty, her head buzzing faster than normal.

"There you are." A girl with a shiny brunette bob and an oversized sweatshirt shaded her eyes in their direction as she lounged on the rock. "I stopped by, but you weren't there." It seemed like she spoke to Walker, but her eyes flickered to Rilla, looking her over coolly before turning away.

"I found him tormenting this poor girl on her first time climbing," Petra said, plopping onto the rock. "Rilla, this is Caroline, Walker's sister. Caroline, this is Rilla."

Oh. *His sister.*

Caroline didn't look at her. "You're on call, right?" she asked Walker.

"Rilla is Thea's younger sister," he said to Caroline, dropping beside her.

"Oh, the one with the poly parents?" Caroline asked.

The what? Rilla put her hands on her knees and suddenly felt like she was going throw up. They knew about her parents? What else did they know about her?

Petra was still introducing her. "Rilla, this is Hico. Hico, this is Rilla."

Rilla waggled her fingers at a short, strong-looking Mexican boy with shaved dark hair. She *had* to get it together. She wasn't pretty enough to not have a good personality. "Hico?" she repeated.

"It's a nickname," he said. "It's a long story."

"Rilla was going to be Walker's next victim," Petra said to Hico.

"Not like that," Walker snapped over his shoulder. "She's Thea's sister."

"Martinez's sister?" Hico glanced at her, confused.

Rilla was used to it. "Half," she said in a flat tone. "We have the same mom."

"Oh, right. Nice to meet you, Thea's sister."

"It's Rilla, man. Come on." Petra snapped her fingers. "I just said it a minute ago."

"Did Adeena and Gage and them make it back yet?" Caroline asked.

Petra answered, "I looked over the edge and they were maybe two pitches away. I told Eammon to send them up here when they get back."

"How was Pink Panther?" Caroline asked.

"Done. I mean, it was fine. I kept expecting to have a hard time with it, but it went pretty smoothly. You said the crux was right below the anchors?"

Caroline looked annoyed.

Rilla wanted to put her head between her knees and raise a white flag. They were all going along on a rhythm Rilla just couldn't find. Instead, she kicked off her sandals, edging her feet into the water. The ice-cold clarity sent a shock through her spine and she took a deep breath, feeling more alert. Back home, this would be a puddle in a ledge—but here the scale transformed it.

More people emerged out of the brush, coated in dust, ropes slung over their chests. Petra introduced them as Gage, a Korean engineering major from San Francisco whose given name was Jospeh, but "no one called him that"; and Adeena, a Pakistani mountain climber.

It took a beat too long for Rilla to realize Pahkistahn was Packistan, and to cover her stupidity, she blurted out the first thing that came into her head. "Ha! Like a mountaineer." At home, a mountaineer—the West Virginia football team mascot—was a white-bearded man in buckskin with a rifle. Here, she'd met one in the flesh who turned out to be a girl only a little older than her.

Adeena's eyes narrowed. "Nice to meet you," she said with a slight trace of an accent.

Rilla got the sense she'd said something wrong.

Two more people were introduced, but Rilla didn't even bother to try and remember. She didn't care. She didn't care they were all older. Fit and tanned. Educated. Nice. *Fuck them.*

Everyone peeled off their shoes and socks, and waded out into the pool.

"So, you moved here with Thea?" Hico asked when Petra seemed satisfied with intros and Rilla had joined them in the pool. "And you're a climber?"

"Yeah. No. I . . ." She licked her lips. "That was my first time."

"Oh, was it, Walker?" Hico smirked and nudged Walker without looking. "Her first time."

Walker turned, a smile half-cocked, but when he saw it was about her again, he narrowed his eyes before looking away.

"No. I'm uh—" *What should she say? Shit.* She hadn't thought this through at all. Rilla looked at her feet in the water and thought for something that would keep her safe from revealing desire and failure and the edge of desperation she tasted in her mouth. "When juvie is too full in West Virginia the judge just asks where you want to go." She shrugged. "So, I picked Yosemite." She studied the cliff as if it was the most interesting thing she'd ever seen.

"When juvie is too full?" Hico laughed, then abruptly stopped. "Wait, *juvenile*? You're under eighteen?"

A flush of heat washed up her neck. Oops. "I'll be eighteen in a month."

"Oh, you're a baby. What have you been doing that got you into trouble, baby Rilla?" He patted her shoulder.

Rilla wanted to bite his hand like an agitated dog. The last thing she wanted to do was even hint at what had happened to get her kicked out of West Virginia. She fixed her eye to him over her shoulder and coolly replied, "I murdered someone."

He froze, confused.

She winked and stood. "Nah, I'm kidding." She lunged for the closest string of words that would obviously be a ridiculous lie. "I smuggled cocaine over the border in carrots. Code Name: Cocaine Carrots. Canadian, obviously."

Walker's gaze flickered to her, expression impassive.

Hico laughed. "People," he addressed everyone. "The next route you put up, please name it Code Name Cocaine Canadian Carrots."

Rilla's skin itched and tightened as everyone looked at Hico, then her. She couldn't read their expressions. She inched toward Petra, who stood with Gage on the far edge of the shin-deep lip that surrounded the water. They were studying a section of the cliff that rose out of the water, half-heartedly pulling themselves out before dropping back onto the shelf.

The problem, it seemed to Rilla, was obvious—the air was cool and the water was *ice*. Like, it had melted sometime in the last week. Her feet were already numb, and the wind raised chicken skin on her arms. If you started climbing, you'd have to go for a swim. There was no other way to get down off the thirty-foot block of rock.

Rilla didn't know *rock climbing*, but she sure as hell knew friends around a swimming hole. At home, they'd head out with coolers and inner tubes on Summersville Lake—spending their afternoons float-ing around, scampering up to ledges of sandstone, or tops of massive boulders, and diving back into the crystal-cold water. To Rilla, the space between *rock climbing* and climbing up a rock was enormous. She was terrified and intimidated of this formal thing with ropes and rules and packs of gear Walker had shown her, but she wasn't afraid of cold water.

"What's at the bottom?" Rilla asked, eyeing the deep blue water just beyond her toes.

Petra swung around. "A cold swim. I don't know. It's deep enough to dive off the top."

"Well, then there's nothing to worry about, I guess," Rilla said, stretch-ing for the rock. Her limbs were unsettled and uncomfortable; and if she didn't move *right then*, she was going to self-destruct. If she fell, she'd just fall into the water, and if she made it to the top, she could just jump off. All things she knew.

Petra backed away in sloshing steps, and the hum of conversation went quiet behind her.

Adrenaline hit. With it, peace.

Rilla exhaled and pulled herself out of the water, bare feet scrambling for purchase on the granite. It was slick. Slicker than the sandstone at home. But with the adrenaline and the knowledge that she was paying her way again, except this time with an action, she gritted her teeth and scrambled—nearly springing to holds in an effort to just get it all over with. Her breath came hard. Her heart pounded in her ears. She pulled herself over the next ledge, clutching fistfuls of soft grass. *Suck it, Walker.* But triumph didn't hit. Her legs shook and her arms felt like they'd been poured into concrete. This was a terrible idea to climb hungover. She was going to throw up.

Crawling on all fours, she managed to get away from the edge before heaving her Gatorade into a patch of wildflowers.

Take me home, country roads.

That stupid John Denver song rang in her ears, tauntingly, and she remembered she should have been at school right now. If she hadn't messed everything up, she'd still have her friends, her mom would still be there with hangover cures and mild annoyance, and Roosevelt, her chocolate Lab, would still be licking her face while she slept on the couch. Suddenly, she was crying. Big, wrenching sobs like she was still throwing up. The breeze caught her hair and she opened her eyes on the view. She jerked upright and gasped.

She was so fucking high. *In the air.*

Between the hike and the little scramble, she'd risen so incrementally, Rilla hadn't realized how far she'd come. The tops of the pines were far below, and over the edge, the wall swept sheer and warm to sudden death. The edge itself seemed to shimmer with its own forces of fate. She pulled away and her back slapped on the granite that continued to rise overhead.

Holy shit.

She closed her eyes on the height—on the feeling of her body untethered and adrift. Her heart raced against her ribs. It was quiet all around and inside. Blessed quiet. The ache in her chest eased. She tipped her head against the rock and closed her eyes to the sunshine. And in the quiet, her thoughts formed clearly enough for her to hold on to them.

She would come down off this cliff, and find a way to keep moving.

She didn't want to go home and see the pity in everyone's eyes. Pity that she'd been sent away. Pity that she'd come back the same. She had to prove everyone wrong—Thea, her mom, all her friends back home, even these climbers below. She had to prove she wasn't what everyone thought, and could be what they didn't expect. If she didn't, she'd lose everything—any home, any family. She couldn't change the past, but she could change herself. And by changing herself, her future would have to follow.

Rilla opened her eyes, setting her shoulders and standing to her feet. *Details later. Big picture now.*

All she had to do was keep going.

Pressing firmly against the wall, away from the edge, Rilla made her way back to the edge she'd ascended.

The pool shimmered in the breeze thirty feet below, sparkling like a sapphire inlaid into silver granite. The people—strangers in every way, no matter how nice they'd all seemed—sat talking with their feet in the water. Occasionally studying the cliff with their eyes shaded. They'd forgotten her already.

Rilla's stomach turned, and the exhaustion and fear left her empty. But she had to get down, she had to keep going, and there was only one way. She backed up, lifted her chin at the empty space, ran, and . . .

Jumped.

Straight and sure. Her body snapped tight, hurtling with a snarl toward the bottom of the hole. The water swallowed her, filling her ears and nose, and pausing her heart with its chill. But there was relief in its cold baptism. She arched her body up for the sun, as her clothes swirled around her limbs. Her stomach rolled and unknown fear shook out in every inch of her body as she thrashed.

Her head broke.

Petra hollered encouragingly.

47

Instantly, Rilla felt the panic on her face and how visible it all was. The fall and the force of the water had sheared back pieces of herself she had never intended to remove. With one deep gasp of the wind, she locked the cold and the fear into her chest, teeth clenched tight to keep it from escaping.

Petra hollered something, her smile becoming clear as she stood on the shelf and held out a hand.

Rilla's ears buzzed. She couldn't quite hear, but she swam over and took Petra's hand, letting herself be hauled to stand on the lip. Her shirt was plastered to her bra, and her hair hung in strings. The breeze so cold she wanted to jump back into the water.

"I thought you didn't climb?" Walker said accusatorily.

Rilla swallowed and unhinged her clamped jaw. "I don't," she managed to say, hiding the trembling by bending to wring the water out of the bottom of her shirt.

"That water looks cold." Petra laughed. "I don't mind the jump, but I don't want to swim." She shivered.

Rilla tried to chuckle, but it came out more like a hiccup. She flashed Petra a casual smile and shrugged it off. "On the plus side, I think I'm finally sober."

Petra looked confused, but she didn't ask. "You're making me reconsider why I haven't made it to West Virginia yet. I've heard the New River Gorge is amazing."

"It's one of my favorite places," Caroline said. "You should totally go, Petra."

"Oh, that's right, is that the closest climbing to you?"

Caroline shook her head. "We're closer to the Red."

All Rilla wanted to do was to listen to someone talk and not feel totally lost. She sat down and clutched her knees, trying to keep the trembling under control.

"You have to do it *now*, Hico. She's never climbed," Petra said, sloshing toward the base of the cliff.

"The climbing isn't the problem," Hico replied. "It's the swim."

The wind died and the sun hit her back, easing the shudders wrenching at her spine.

Rilla closed her eyes. She could do this. She could do this. What *this* was, she was still uncertain. But she kept telling herself she could, over and over.

"What was that shit?" Walker asked, his tone low and clipped.

No one answered. Her eyes flew open and found him watching. "What?" she asked stupidly, dropping her gaze. Unfortunately, staring at the hard lines of his forearms draped over his knees just turned her mouth cotton dry like she hadn't *just* crawled out of the water.

"You don't climb?" he asked.

"I've never been climbing," she said.

"What did you just do?"

"Cliff-jumping." Just like at home. Minus all the warmth, friends, and inner tubes.

He was silent.

Rilla tugged her eyes away from his arms.

His jaw worked, eyes on Hico and Petra on the cliff. "Did I do something?" he asked tightly. "To upset you? Earlier?"

Oh. She hadn't expected him to ask. She'd cried and frozen on the wall ten feet off the ground less than two hours ago. But now her mind was blank, staring again at the sun on his skin. He was tanner than he'd been at the roadside in Merced. It was only a few days and he'd managed to change. Meanwhile, she had traveled the span of the country and stayed the exact same person she'd been at home. "The rope upset me," she finally said. "I've never climbed with a rope."

"You don't like safety?" He asked it as if it was a joke, but as he said the words, her spine straightened and she couldn't look at him again. Before she could come up with a retort, he nodded and repeated in a serious tone, "You don't like safety." As if that said much more about her than she'd ever intended to tell him.

"You're full of shit." she retorted. "If you didn't want to take me climbing, why didn't you just say so? If I can't trust you to tell the truth about how you feel, why should I trust you to tell the truth when you say I'm not going to fall? Why should I trust you at all?"

A muscle in his cheek twitched, and he looked at her. But this time, for real. The intensity under his skin gathered and fixed directly on her.

She forced herself against the urge to shy away, staring right back into his cornflower-blue eyes. They looked like the pool from above—the same fathomless blue water dropping into unseen currents and holes she might get sucked into and never escape. Her body hummed. Something passed between them—but what it was, she had no idea.

She wasn't sure how long that moment lasted. Petra called for her, and Rilla ran off to climb, feeling all the while as if she and Walker were still sitting on the granite. The moment they'd accused each other of fear and deceit had left something massive and new, uncovered.

•

Rilla made it back to the house in mostly dried clothes and what she felt was a reasonable hour around dinnertime, half expecting Thea not to be home. But Thea was on the phone on the steps—still in her ranger uniform, with her shirt untucked, hair loosened from her braid, and bare feet. She lifted her head as Rilla walked up, eyes sunken with dark circles.

Rilla ducked her head, ashamed to think Thea looked haggard from her late-night rescue efforts.

"Mom wants to talk to you," Thea said over the phone.

Oh. Rilla bit her lip and nodded.

"Mom." Thea paused. "Mom," she said again. She rolled her eyes. "Mom. Rilla's here. I'll let her hang up." She handed over the phone.

Rilla's stomach tightened, but she pressed the phone to her ear and looked at her feet in the dry grass. The rock had left scrapes on her legs, and she focused on the sting to keep from feeling the one in her chest.

"Hey baby," her mom said. "How is California?"

"Good," Rilla answered.

"Get all settled in with Thea?"

"Yeah."

There was an awkward pause. "Daddy said to tell you he loves you. I'm doing all right," Mom went on. "The house is lonely though. I went over to Ashlyn's the other day just because I couldn't handle the quiet . . ." Mom kept talking.

Rilla looked up and found her sister watching her, chin in her hand, eyes dark and sad.

Rilla turned her back to Thea. "That's great, Mom. I'm doing great. Thea has to wear a cowboy hat."

"Oh really?" Mom was distracted. "Oh, that's right, they wear Stetsons, don't they? I'm not surprised, Dad . . ." Mom meant Marco, Thea's dad. *Daddy* always meant Tom. Dad was Marco. Rilla had thought every family was like that, until somewhere in third grade when Alison Andrews said Rilla couldn't be invited to anything because Rilla had three parents. ". . . always looked good in a Stetson. He had this black one . . ." Mom launched into a story about a man that left her eight years ago, her tone bright and energetic as if it hadn't meant anything at all.

Rilla listened to the story, laughing in all the right spots. It made her feel less homesick. "Your mother is many things, but first and foremost, she's a survivor," that's what Granny had said before she died, and it'd stuck as the best way to summarize her mother even to herself. Rilla didn't understand all her mother's life, but she knew this was how she coped with loss, even though it made Rilla's chest ache to feel the hole of a man she'd once called Dad. She could understand the sadness in Thea's eyes—Mom probably talked to Thea the same way.

"You've been keeping out of trouble?" Mom asked, but with a conspiratorial tone. "I don't know why I ask though. Your sister is such a hard-ass—*everything* is probably trouble."

Rilla looked down. "Yeah, we're both . . . uh . . . adjusting."

Mom laughed. "You'll manage. I know you will. It'll be good for you to be on your own a little. I was on my own at your age. Grandma kicked me out. I was pregnant."

Not with Thea, but with a baby Rilla only knew of as having not made it.

"At least we know Thea gets it honestly." She laughed again. Mom always had a great laugh. And hearing her made Rilla feel reassured this was all part of the process.

"You're going to be okay, baby. I know it. Don't miss me too much."

"Love you," Rilla said.

"Love you too."

Mom hung up. Rilla handed the phone back to Thea.

"What did she say?"

Rilla shrugged.

Thea's eyes narrowed. "You okay? Where were you at?"

"Not in trouble," Rilla snapped.

"Did I say you were? I asked where you were."

"I don't know. In the woods. With Walker and some climbers."

Surprise flickered on Thea's face. "Rock climbers? Walker?"

Rilla nodded.

Thea pushed back her hair, eyes narrowing. "Hmm . . . well, you have all that schoolwork to catch up on."

"I know."

"Don't forget about it. If you do a little every day it won't be bad."

Rilla nodded. "I know."

Thea still didn't move. "You feel okay about Mom?" she asked like she was expecting something else.

Rilla stepped over her sister. "Not everyone has mommy issues like you," she said, heading inside and shutting the door on whatever Thea planned to say next.

six

THE NEXT MORNING, RILLA OPENED HER EYES TO THE GOD-AWFUL
sight of Thea hunched under the eaves, kitchen tongs brandished in one
hand and a new cell phone in the other. "I'm cooking bacon. Get it while
it lasts," she said, tossing the phone onto the blankets.

Rilla rolled over, an involuntary moan escaping as her muscles protested every movement. The sides of her back felt as if someone had
wound the length of her muscles into snarls overnight; and her hamstrings were definitely two inches shorter than they'd been when she
went to bed. The cold morning air wasn't helping. She turned on the
phone and texted a friend from home, Layla.

Hey got a new phone, finally. Call me! It was mid-morning back
home; Layla was sure to reply soon.

Rilla pulled on a pair of socks and climbed down the ladder to the
hallway. It was a little easier today—to walk past the strangers in a strange
house.

Thea was in the kitchen, cooking bacon under a wall of oppressively
dark walnut cabinets. Rilla leaned on her elbows just inside the kitchen
door, on the edge of the pea-green counter, logging back into social
media and inhaling the smoky-salt scent of bacon. "This weather is giving me whiplash," she said to Thea's back, switching over to the camera
to see what manner of death she looked like today.

Rilla frowned and held the phone farther away. Sorcery. Her hair
looked frizz-free and tousled in a way she'd never ever be able to replicate

54

on purpose, and her cheeks were flushed pink, making her look alive. She took a selfie and flicked over to Instagram, trying to ignore that Layla still hadn't replied.

"It's the desert. Cold at night, warm in the day." Thea set a plate in front of Rilla and licked her thumb. "Did you get any schoolwork done last night?" Thea opened a cupboard next to an honest-to-god rotary phone and took out a glass.

Rilla put the #hangoverselfie on Instagram and picked up her bacon. "I looked at it." She passed the pile of books on her way to bed.

"I can't believe your grades were *all* failing. Don't you remember how much you loved school?"

Rilla remembered. She remembered when Mom, Dad, and Daddy were in jail for check fraud, and Thea hid it from everyone so they wouldn't get separated. Rilla would spend hours in the library after school, until Thea came to get her from work. Funny how Thea was doing the same things Mom always did when it came to remembering the reality of someone else's life. Rilla decided not to answer.

"They wanted to make you redo junior year," Thea continued. "But I told the principal about your situation, and they agreed to let you make up the work over the summer. I told her it'd be different. You'd be different here. With some stability." Thea filled the glass and handed it over. "Right?"

Rilla took a sip of the water and nodded. "Right." Her throat felt dry. She took another drink, and her phone lit with a notification. A friend from home had commented on her photo.

You can take the girl away from the Skidmores, but you can't take the Skidmore away from the girl.

Rilla made a face. *The hashtag was supposed to be funny, Bobby Jo. A joke.* West Virginia got involved and suddenly Rilla felt tragic. Rilla put the phone down.

Thea's neatly wrapped chignon bobbed briskly as she lectured, flipped pancakes, and made three other plates.

"Aw, shit," one of the women said, coming out in a hooded sweatshirt that hit her knees. "Bacon!" She grabbed pancakes off the pile.

"Rilla, this is Jessica. Jessica, this is—"

"The baby sister," Jessica said, eyebrows high on her forehead like she had finally hit on something interesting while channel surfing. She seemed around the same age as Thea. "Hey, *Rilla.*"

Rilla forced a smile.

Another woman came into the kitchen, smiling at Rilla like she already knew her.

Rilla pressed her lips tight and glared at Thea's back. When had Thea turned into a person who told *everyone* her business?

"I'm Lauren," the smiling woman said. She had shoulder-length black hair and tattoos covering one arm.

"Hi," Rilla said curtly.

Thea turned, giving Lauren a look Rilla didn't understand.

"Still settling in. Got it," Lauren said, taking her plate. She gave Rilla the universal look of *oh shit, you're in trouble*, and disappeared.

Thea resumed her lecture as she finished cooking the pancakes. "It's stupid that you waste your brain like this . . . this is manageable. If you *work hard* . . . I know you can do this. You just have to *want* to do it."

As if Rilla didn't try and still, somehow, didn't get it right. As if she wanted to fail. It almost made her not hungry for the fluffy pancakes Thea piled on her plate. Almost. Rilla dumped syrup over the pools of melting butter.

"My schedule is on the calendar on the fridge," Thea said, wiping off the griddle. "When I'm not here, you need to be doing your schoolwork. I'll leave my computer on the counter. Don't leave the Valley. Be smart. Be safe. And be home by nine thirty."

Home was in West Virginia. Rilla couldn't feel like California was home—there was nothing here to make it hers, and it would be ripped away whenever Thea decided. Rilla stuffed a bite into her mouth and tried to shift the conversation. "Do all rangers have to work this much?"

It was the wrong question. Thea's forehead creased. "I don't work that much. They're just long shifts."

"How did you get into this job, anyway?" Rilla asked, cutting her pancakes. "Do you have a boyfriend, or is this basically your life?"

Thea shrugged. "I like this. I don't know what you mean by *is this my life?* You can have a life without a boyfriend."

Rilla poked at her pancakes. *This wasn't going well. New direction.* "Walker says you climb? I went with them up to this hole in the cliff. The water was so cold it gave me a headache jumping in, but . . ." She paused to shove a mouthful of pancake into her mouth, and continued talking over it. "I mean, I didn't hate it. Walker tried to show me—"

Thea looked up from where she flipped through mail. "Walker is great as a person, but he's not a guy to get involved with. You know that, right?"

Rilla blinked, fork midair. Was she that obvious?

"I worked with him all last year. I mean, I'd say this to his face and he knows it—he goes through girls quickly. Plus, you definitely don't need to be involved with anyone right now." Thea raised her eyebrow. "Don't you think?"

Rilla's pancakes now tasted like shame. "Sure. Yeah, totally," she said, and finished eating in silence.

Layla hadn't replied yet.

After breakfast, Thea left for work and Rilla went back to bed. She woke covered in sweat. This weather made no sense. Stripping off her pajamas, she sat on the floor in her underwear, staring at the *seen* receipt on Layla's unanswered text. There were more comments on her Instagram.

OMG, girl, you're going to kill yourself.

When the going gets weird, the weird turn pro, huh?

Who you been fucking already ho?

Skidmore never dies.

Lolololol you look so high.

Rilla swallowed and turned the phone dark, putting it facedown on the floor. A sweaty, sick feeling clamored on the edges of her ribs and into her throat. The people she knew were still commenting on her social media, but wouldn't return a text, like they were all relieved distance would do something they hadn't known how to do themselves.

Deep down, she hated that they weren't wrong—that she had been partying, that it *was* everything they'd thought. But *she* wasn't.

Right?

The waterfall whispered outside, and she closed her eyes, rolling her shoulders to try and loosen the aching muscles. The pool from yesterday shimmered in her memory. The way everyone had gathered—dirty, weird, and oh-so-stupidly cool and older. If she were someone like that, it would prove everyone at home wrong about her. It would show she was meant to be something bigger all along. No one back home knew what she was capable of.

Doubts pinged somewhere in the back of her brain. But Rilla ignored them, pulling on leggings, a football T-shirt from home, and her sandals. She somehow had to find Petra and become a climber. Rilla quickly shook out her hair, did her eyeliner and mascara, and left the phone facedown on the bed. *Fuck you people.* At the last minute, she doubled back to pick it up—just in case Thea called.

Out in the Valley, it was almost as if Rilla imagined yesterday. No one looked familiar. The Valley, while small in square miles compared to the surrounding wilderness, was still huge and full of strangers. If Petra and the others couldn't stay there, where did they stay?

Rilla walked the same path she'd followed Petra and Walker along the day before, scanning each passing face for someone she recognized.

Along the road, a ranger SUV passed and hit its brake. Rilla slowed, thinking it was Thea. In the rearview, she locked eyes with Ranger Dick Face. *Not Thea.* The SUV began to reverse.

Hurriedly, she turned off the path into the woods. Let him get out and chase her. He'd have to burn calories. Her heart raced, and she kept glancing over her shoulder. But he didn't follow.

Walking all the way across the Valley to the cafeteria in Half Dome Village, she found Jonah serving corn instead of mashed potatoes. They shared a cigarette outside on his break, but he still had most of his shift to go, so when he went back inside, she aimlessly set off the way she'd come. After crisscrossing the meadows, she found her way back to the path, on the far edge of the parking lot of something labeled "Camp 4."

A long line of people waited in front of the ranger shack, snaking its way through the rows of cars. Most were young. Everyone was fit, thin, light on their feet, older, cooler, and unlike her. Beyond them, a whole little village of tents and cold campfires spread under the trees.

Rilla crossed her arms over her chest and pretended she did not feel like a heavy-pawed bear, with her un-toned arms and normal-as-fuck body, bumbling past a flock of birds aching to take flight. A sick feeling unspooled in the bottom of her stomach. Maybe she should just go back to Thea's and try to find her schoolwork. She had been a disaster at *real* climbing anyway.

The late afternoon sun was high, and dust and chatter billowed up under the whispering cedars. Her skin tightened with each step. She told herself she was looking for Petra, but she kept catching herself scanning for a six-three, muscled cowboy in weird track pants with good forearms.

Her phone buzzed and in her hurry to get it out of her pocket, she flung it onto the dirt. Oh shit. If she broke it the first day she had it—

She picked it up, relieved to see it was fine. The text was from Layla, finally.

Who is this?

Rilla, she replied.

(typing)

Rilla's stomach tightened.

Oh. Hey.

Hi. How is everyone? I made it to Cali.

Cool.

Rilla's chest seemed to be cinching tighter.

Hey that stuff with Curtis was totally blown out of proportion, Rilla typed. It was hard not to regret ever hooking up with Curtis in the first place—with the amount of grief it had caused them both. But he'd been a football player, hot, and he had made her less of a joke. Until now.

K.

I mean . . . it was just an argument.

No response.

Rilla bit her lips tight.

Nothing.

Do you have his new number? Rilla texted, stomach hurting.

(typing)

Rilla bit her thumbnail and stared.

The response was one word. *No.*

Rilla stuffed the phone in her pocket, not feeling any better for finally having made contact with someone. The path circled around toward the road, and her steps slowed. All she wanted was to call Curtis, drive out to the river, and make out in his truck. The past forgotten. Everything erased. Maybe it wasn't good, but it was something she'd actually had.

A passing car slowed, the window rolling down. Rilla turned and blinked away the moisture in her eyes, pretending not to see it. The last thing she should be doing is giving directions to a clueless tourist. But the car stopped and Petra's white-blond hair peeked out from the driver's seat. "There you are," she called, as if Rilla had made a date and stood her up.

Rilla swiped at her eyes. *There she was.* Like magic.

"You coming?" Petra asked, patting the seat. "You can sit up front. Backseat's full." She jerked her thumb toward Hico and Gage crammed into the backseat with huge packs on their laps and a plastic storage container set between them. Hico sat with a spaced-out expression in a cut-off hoodie. On the other side, Gage, with messy hair and a buttoned-up plaid shirt, looked half-asleep. Both boys' limbs splayed in exhaustion.

"I can't be out too late," Rilla said, ignoring that Thea had also told her not to leave the Valley.

"We'll bring you back." A car behind them honked. "Come on," Petra hollered.

Hoping she wasn't about to do something Thea would disapprove of, Rilla jumped in—catching the door as they sped away under the pines.

seven

THIS WAS WHAT SHE'D ENVISIONED WHEN SHE THOUGHT OF A NEW LIFE
in California.

Rilla draped her arms and head out the open window, hair whipping in the wind. A massive tower looked over them—a sun-drenched mono-lith of peachy granite that stayed firm in the sky as the trees moved past in a blur.

"What is that?" Rilla breathed, jaw unhinged.

"*El Capitan,*" Petra said, with reverence in her voice.

The overstuffed hybrid doggedly huffed up Big Oak Flat Road, driving out of the Valley, into the late afternoon shadows as it fractured thick beams of dazzling gold over the ridgeline. Beside them, the massive walls fell away toward the bottom, where deepening purple shadows gathered over the Merced, as if night crept up from the ground.

Rilla leaned farther out, trying to see around the car to catch a glimpse of the foaming water at the bottom. Instead, she noticed the sheer face of Half Dome reflecting the sun, the streaks of snow still at the top, and how narrow and deep the Valley was—like a tight scar cut into the wide mountains behind her. The prow of El Capitan sat as a guard over the entrance. Things she hadn't seen, at the bottom. Things that could only been seen moving up.

And then it all went dark.

Rilla pulled away, tasting the stone and earth of the tunnel wall. It hit her—she had just gotten into a car with virtual strangers who were all older than she was. She didn't even know where they were going. She should have been more cautious.

"This is my new gumby," Petra said to the boys, patting Rilla's shoulder. "After yesterday, I have to try and make a climber out of her."

Rilla smiled and slid back into her seat, heart in her throat. "What's a gumby?" she asked, hoping it wasn't bad.

"Someone who is new," Petra said.

"Someone who is new, doesn't know what they're doing, has no common sense, is not super coordinated, and is liable to fuck everything up," Gage said from the back.

Rilla shot him a look over her shoulder. "What did I do to you?"

He laughed. "Don't let Petra bullshit you."

"I meant it the way I said it," Petra said. "She's new, like we all were once."

It was one thing for Rilla to think she could become a climber like them, sitting in the attic with quiet fury gathering in her blood. It was another thing to sit here feeling very young and lumpy and *new*.

"Well, you couldn't have picked a better place to start climbing," Gage said, sun lighting his face as he leaned against the door. The sunglasses, coconut-scented tree air freshener, and ChapStick hanging on the rearview mirror tilted as Petra followed the mountain road. "It's like going to heaven to become a believer."

Rilla looked back to the road ahead, hand open to clutch at the wind. Outside the window, the trees and brush were changing. The air was sweeter and cooler.

Petra turned off the smooth asphalt to a dirt road. The car hopped and wiggled and squeaked; and the manzanita bushes flattened and puffed as they flew through the shallow valley, passing the few standing charred pines and cedars. The trees were so big and old, they'd managed to absorb the fire and remain alive, unscathed at their core. Great clouds of golden dust boiled up and rolled into the open window. No one moved to prevent it, they just accepted the gentle layer of dust settling on their skin. Maybe that's why they all looked so tanned.

Led Zeppelin blared, familiar and eternal.

The sun deepened.

Hico and Gage rattled in the backseat, expressions immovable.

Rilla sank into her seat, feeling at ease for the first time since she'd arrived. Though they were surrounded by a ring of snow-capped mountains in the distance, the wide-open feeling stood in stark contrast to the immensity deep inside the Valley. For a place so huge, the Valley felt as if it could fold in on her at any minute. Here she was closer to the sky. Let loose and un-cinched. For one brief moment, she didn't have to convince herself she was okay here—she simply *was*.

They turned down smaller and narrower dirt roads to a dead end at a big house with nothing but trees and far mountains in sight.

"Welcome to the Grove," Petra said, turning off the car.

"Wow," was all Rilla could think to reply, not taking her eyes off the house as she unfolded her legs and crawled out of the dusty hybrid.

The redwood-trimmed structure stood below the edge of the hill, in the midst of a clean forest of pines. In some ways, it felt like West Virginia; but when Rilla took a deep breath—expecting the pungent scent of pine and earth—there was nothing to smell. The scent of home was just a thread for her to follow, not a world to sink into.

"My grandparents are traveling through Europe this summer, so they let me use it," Petra explained, leading them onto a catwalk to the uppermost deck of the house.

Rilla blinked. She knew rich people, but not people *that* rich. And their granddaughters didn't look like this. Petra's twin braids were sloppy and falling out, and she wore a pizza-printed tank top that looked so hideous the thrift store probably had given it away. Money did not look like that in West Virginia. But then, maybe there was a point where you had so much money you could afford to look poor.

"It's not Camp 4," Hico said. "But it's as close as we're gonna get."

"Who even wants to be in Camp 4 anymore?" Petra said. "Bea stayed there at the end of her trip and said she was kept up half the night by a kid crying. And, oh my god, all the rules."

"I meant what Camp 4 was, not as it is now," Hico said.

"It's still Camp 4," Gage said. "Just . . ."

Everyone seemed to silently nod in agreement to whatever Gage didn't say.

"What did it used to be?" Rilla asked, thinking of the birdlike line watching her huff past the ranger shack.

"It used to be this," Petra said with a spin to raise her hands to the roof. "Except, a short walk to climbing, instead of the drive."

"It used to be the climber's campground," Gage said. "Where people lived for months. Climbing, as we know it, was basically born there. There's so much history there."

Petra stopped and turned back. "Get the other side, will you, Rilla? God, can you imagine the golden years of Camp 4?" Petra took one side of the container Gage and Hico were trying to carry along with their packs.

Hico handed over his side to Rilla with a relieved-sounding "thanks."

The container yanked on her arm, much heavier than she expected, but Rilla gritted her teeth and kept her gait smooth, hoping no one could see her struggle.

"I can smell the food from here. I'm starved," Hico said, opening a sliding glass door.

Fragrant spice, fried meat, and warm bread all mixed with the smell of a stranger's home, enveloping Rilla like a cozy blanket. Though unfamiliar, it was the kind of smell that made Rilla feel at home. And hungry. Her stomach growled.

"Rilla?" Adeena shouted from the kitchen. "Damn it!" She pounded her spoon on the edge of the pot and glared at Petra.

Rilla remembered being introduced to Adeena the day before, but she was surprised she hadn't noticed how short Adeena was. Somehow, she assumed all climbers were tall—with Petra and Thea, who were five-ten and change, and Walker, who was easily six-three. Both Gage and Hico were tall enough she just added them to the tall category. But Adeena was tiny—no taller than five feet and narrow framed, with thick, wavy black hair falling out of a ponytail, light brown skin, and wide green eyes. Not what Rilla expected either Pakistanis or mountaineers looked like.

Adeena lowered her chin to Rilla. "Did she abduct you? This jackass stuffed you into the trunk to get you here, didn't she?"

"Ha! I told you I'd find her first," Petra smirked.

Rilla's heart raced, trying to think fast enough to be clever and funny in reply. "Um . . ." She readjusted her grip on the container.

"Dude. Tell me where this goes, or I'm dropping it here," Petra said to Gage.

Thankfully, everyone's attention shifted from Rilla's grasping for words.

"Just dump it," Gage said to them, pointing to the floor beside the door. "We didn't sort anything out."

Rilla followed Petra, shuffling the container back toward the door.

"He's not fucking anything up in there, right?" Petra asked Adeena, sitting on a stool on the edge of the kitchen island.

Rilla quietly joined her, careful not to knock any of the food or draw attention to herself.

A white boy with shattered blond hair, a British accent, and long, lanky limbs frowned over the boiling pot he stirred. "Hey, my sister-in-law is Pakistani. That's why we signed up for the same meal."

"Don't worry, I'm keeping an eye on him." Adeena raised an eyebrow in his direction.

He rolled his eyes.

"We're lucky I found her tonight," Petra said. "Otherwise, we'd have to seduce her with Gage and Hico's food and we all know how that would go." Petra glanced to Rilla. "It's not good," she said in a low whisper.

"I heard that." Gage bellowed from the hall.

Petra rolled her eyes.

"This is really the only thing I can cook," Adeena said. "And like, macaroni mix-ins. If my mother was here, she'd tell you I don't actually cook this very well and I need more practice."

"It seems like you should be looking for a girl who can be seduced by granola," Hico said from the couch in the living room beyond them.

"If we can't give her Walker, we have to give her something. Granola isn't going to cut it," Adeena said, shoving the wisps of her hair back over her forehead and studying the contents of her skillet.

A snort of exasperation escaped the British boy.

Rilla's cheeks warmed. "Listen. I don't . . ." she protested.

Adeena and Petra looked at her, bemused, like *go ahead and deny it.*

"Yeah, *okay,*" Hico said.

"We all have our weaknesses, all right?" Rilla muttered.

Both girls cracked up.

"Don't we all when it comes to Walker," the British boy said.

"Walker will sleep with anything thin and blond," Petra said.

Rilla tried to look like she didn't care, even as her stomach sank. She searched the memory of Walker's face, that intensity directed at her, but the memory was foggy—all she was certain of was how she felt under his gaze. "Are you guys search and rescue climbers too?" she asked.

"Oh god, no," Petra said. "We're just dirtbags. Out of school for the summer, or trying to string together enough money to climb. Eammon usually lives in a van, but he's upgraded this summer."

"I don't know what to do with all this space. I'm going to be spoiled," the British boy said.

"But you," Adeena said to Rilla. "You live in the Valley? And you don't work there?"

Rilla nodded.

"How did you manage that?" Adeena asked.

"By being the actual worst," Rilla said with a laugh. She tossed her hair and put a little wickedness into her grin. She didn't say anything more. Whatever they assumed would be safer than what was true.

"It would be a waste if she didn't climb," Adeena said to Petra. "I have to take her."

"Agreed." Petra nodded. "But I'll take her. Since this is my home crag."

Adeena rolled her eyes.

It had been a great idea—back in her attic and staring at her miserable Instagram—to become this epically cool climber and tell everyone to shove it. But to actually climb . . . Rilla gulped. It was within her ability to make herself seem cooler than she was, but climbing, she'd learned, stripped all that away.

"Why doesn't your sister take you?" Hico asked.

"Does she climb?" Petra glanced at Rilla. "Sorry, I don't know your sister."

"Yeah. She was a climbing ranger last year," Hico said. "Not the SAR site."

"Thea's trying to get a permanent position," Rilla said.

"She's a law enforcement ranger this summer," Hico explained. "When I saw her last, she was directing traffic."

There was an awkward pause. Rilla studied her nails.

"Rilla, let me show you around before we eat," Petra said, pulling up off the counter.

Relieved, Rilla followed as Petra gave her a grand tour.

The Grove, as Petra jokingly called the house, though Rilla wasn't sure she got the joke, was a luxury home at odds with its contents—like Thea's house in the Valley, there was a proliferation of outdoor gear, clothes, mangled shoes, and dust; and underneath the smell of food, an undercurrent of something sour and mildewed. *Unlike* Thea's bare-bones, pine bungalow in the Valley, the Grove was all redwood and granite, tall windows, and a two-story stone fireplace under an exposed beam ceiling.

It was the most gorgeous and lived-in house Rilla had ever seen. Even the screened-in porches flanking the sides of the house had sleeping bags stretched out and packs leaned up against the wall. Her mom wouldn't have been able to spend more than ten minutes without needing a smoke to calm down from the mess. For all her flirting with disaster, her mother's house-cleaning was something she took seriously.

"I'm just going to get a massive cleaning done at the end of the summer and not worry about it now," Petra said at one point, leading her over a pile of dirty clothes in a hallway. "If I can't pay someone to fix it, it deserves to stay broken."

"Does everyone just live here?" Rilla asked. "How do y'all afford to do this?"

"Well, we don't have to pay for the house. There's a few of us who saved to be here all summer—we can eat pretty cheaply, and we rotate through these big meals where everyone chips in a few dollars. Everyone else comes and goes," Petra said, shutting a door. "You aren't allowed to stay for more than two weeks in the Valley, total. Non-consecutive. So these are climbers who need a place to stay near the climbing, but can't stay in the Valley. Not everyone can live out of a cool van like Alex Honnold."

Rilla didn't know who Alex Honnold was, but at least that explained why it was such a big deal Rilla lived in the Valley. No one else got to do that.

"You can try to evade the rangers." Petra shrugged. "Or you can stay here and catch a ride with whoever is going to the Valley that day. We use it for a base camp. Everyone pays a little bit to use the laundry, but other than that, it's free. We're still in Yosemite, and there's always someone to climb with." She cracked open a door. "You decent?"

"Sort of," Gage yelled.

Petra shrugged. "Good enough." She opened the door and showed Rilla the bathroom. Complete with a half-dressed, still damp Gage. He didn't seem bothered by Petra's tour, but it was hard not to notice the flex and roll of muscle rippling under his skin as he toweled off. Rilla glanced to the floor, trying not to look embarrassed, but embarrassed that she felt like she needed to avert her eyes. The bathroom was luxurious —a copper tub and separate river rock shower—but also a horrendous mess with piles of clothes in corners, the countertop splashed with muddy water, and the trash overflowing. "Does Walker's sister live here too?" Rilla asked as they went back into the hall.

"Caroline? Yeah. There's a handful of us here for the entire summer. She keeps to herself a lot though. I mean, she's a great climber, but . . ." Petra trailed off.

"She seems a little detached?"

"She's trying to turn this into a career. Caroline really only climbs with climbers she thinks are on her level. She spends a lot of time on her social media. Like, her Instagram probably tells you a lot." Petra pressed her lips together and frowned. "I don't mean to sound catty. I can't imagine handling all that bullshit commercial stuff that goes into monetizing a passion, so what do I know?" Petra led her to the top of a twisting metal spiral staircase. "Let's eat."

Rilla followed Petra back to the kitchen. Being here was nothing she could have imagined herself doing even a week prior. Like she'd been dropped into a dream of her life and any minute the alarm was going to go off and she'd be late for school in Rainelle.

Back in the main area, more people she didn't know and hadn't been introduced to gathered in the border between the kitchen and living room, eyeing but not touching the trays and platters of food arranged on the counter. Looking around, Rilla was certain she was the youngest. And the least in shape.

A winning combination.

"Ajeet?" Adeena asked.

Everyone straightened and bowed their heads, and a lean, dark-haired climber began saying something in a language she didn't understand.

A half second too late, Rilla realized it was a prayer, and ducked her head.

After the blessing, everyone lined up, buffet style.

Rilla fell in line behind Petra, plate to her chest as she surveyed the food—most of which she'd never seen.

"This is Chapshoro," Petra said with a confident accent on the word. She peeled back a portion of the folded flat bread, showing her the inside. "It's chopped lamb and beef, onions, chili peppers, tomato and coriander. I don't know if you like any of that."

"Oh, it's so good though," Hico said, reaching around them to grab one. "I want to go climbing in Pakistan with Adeena again, just to be fucking *fed*."

"That was only time I've seen a climber come home fatter . . ." Caroline said, coming up to the back of the line.

"*But the food! Don't judge me!*" Hico roared over a mouthful, in mock anger.

"Guys, my mom would have ten pounds on all of you in a week," Adeena said.

"Hey, you made it back," Petra said to Caroline, who had just joined the rear of the line.

"Barely," Caroline said, picking a plate off the stack. "That was an ugly day."

Rilla took some and moved to the next dish. Everyone in line, aside from Hico, waited patiently or offered up opinions on how to tell if she'd like the food. Rilla took it all, including chili sauce for the Mamtu—a type of dumpling—and followed Petra out onto the big deck. Everyone perched on steps or chairs or sat, legs folded and their plates on the redwood, diving in with fingers and forks.

For a moment, it was silent. The last of the pink sunshine slid into purple. Someone began a story about getting turned around during a climb and ending up in Italy when they were supposed to be in France, and trying to get a sheep herder to give them a ride back to the border. And as Rilla ate—swiping her dumplings through the chili sauce and savoring every bit of the spice and meat and dough—the dust turned into a purple haze, and the shadows gathered into something reminiscent of home.

If asked outright, Rilla wasn't positive she'd have been able to tell anyone those countries bordered each other. When she got back to Thea's, she was going to find her schoolbooks. If they were going to take her to magical houses in the woods, feed her, and tell her great stories, she would do anything to meet their expectations—even study.

In the lull between stories, Petra announced to everyone that in the near future, she and Rilla were going to climb something called Snake Dike, and Rilla was going to come back to the house as a real climber; while Adeena argued that Rilla should climb something shorter and more manageable for a first time.

Forgetting that climbing was probably the *worst* way to convince everyone she was cool, Rilla stuffed another dumpling in her mouth and nodded an emphatic agreement.

eight

AFTER BEING DROPPED OFF IN THE CAMP 4 PARKING LOT AFTER DINNER
at the Grove, barely in time for curfew, Rilla hustled through the meadow
grass, trying to make it home before Thea discovered she'd been out of
the Valley. Her phone was quiet—but she couldn't trust the spotty service.
Across the meadow, dim amber light glowed from the kitchen window of
Thea's house, and muffled music drifted out into the dark. Rilla trudged
through the grass and tiptoed up the porch, opening the door quietly to
slide inside.

"Speak of the devil, and she appears," Walker bellowed over the country music.

Rilla's spine snapped straight.

"We were just talking about you," Thea said. She and Walker were
playing cards—empty dinner plates pushed to the side on the cluttered
table.

Rilla stayed frozen in the doorway. "Um. What about?"

"I was telling him about the time you raced Frank down the Meadow
River during that ice storm."

"Oh." Rilla narrowed her eyes, uncertain how Thea was swinging the
story. It'd started out as a stupid bet with her cousin. They'd gone sliding
down the frozen river until Frank hit a bad patch of ice and dropped
through. The hole kept tearing at the edges and Rilla had raced back, without thinking. She'd kept sliding on her stomach around the ever-widen-
ing hole until they both were able to crawl to the bank. Thankfully.

"She said she couldn't tell whether you were stupid or smart," Walker said.

"And it's still that way today." Thea laughed, reaching to turn down the radio.

The food in Rilla's stomach turned into stone. It was hard not to wonder how many other stories Thea told about Rilla's life, without her ever knowing. Rilla's face heated, but she kicked off her sandals and slid a finger under her eyes in case her makeup had run. "I'm obviously smarter than you," she said, eyeing Thea's hand meaningfully. She didn't really know her cards, but Thea hadn't ever been good at poker.

Walker laughed.

Thea slapped her cards facedown and frowned.

"What's with the card game? I thought you two would be climbing?" Rilla said, trying not to sound nasty. This friendship between Walker and her sister bothered her—a jealousy, but the sibling kind, where it seemed her older sister left and found someone to replace her.

Thea groaned. "I'm too exhausted."

"And it's dark now anyway." Walker laid down his cards.

Thea laughed and shoved away from the table. "More tea?"

"Sure," he said.

"Want any, Rilla?" Thea asked.

"Yeah," she said.

Walker's eyes met hers; and for a moment she was back at the pool, sitting beside him.

He looked away, gathering up the cards.

Rilla shifted awkwardly and tried to look like she was doing something with her phone.

"What were you up to?" Thea called from the kitchen.

"Oh. I ate with some friends," Rilla said.

"Want to play?" Walker asked, shuffling the cards. "I'll deal you in."

"Sure." Rilla sat at the bench.

"You in this hand?" he yelled to Thea in the kitchen.

"I'll skip," Thea called.

Rilla leaned forward and put her chin in her hands, watching the cards fly across the table as he dealt. His fingers were smudged and she wondered if it was from dirt or from drawing. He didn't seem like the artist type—which made it all the more interesting to Rilla.

"When you going climbing again?" Walker asked.

"I don't know," Rilla answered, pulling her cards off the table. She kept her face still, feeling his eyes on her as she arranged her cards.

"I'll take you again," he said.

"No, thank you."

"I promise it'll be better."

She snorted and stared at her cards. "You had your chance."

He didn't respond.

She glanced up. He wore a fluorescent-green T-shirt and his sunglasses were on the table, but his hair still stood like the glasses were pushed up on his head. His lower lip pursed as he moved his cards. He was too attractive for his own good, she could just tell. Those blue eyes flicked to her. "How many?" he asked.

She held up two fingers.

Without dropping his gaze, he gave her two cards.

"Rilla, do you want honey?" Thea asked.

Something beeped. But it didn't sound right.

Rilla frowned. "Is that the microwave? That's a weird microwave."

Walker put down his cards and leaned back, the beeping continuing, as he took something out of his pocket.

"Is that a pager?" she asked, stunned. At the same time, Thea called from the kitchen doorway. "Is that yours, Walker?"

He laughed and looked at it briefly, before shoving it back into his pocket. "Gotta go save some lives," he said.

"Ugh. I hate you. Get out of here, with your gloating." Thea hit him on the head with the tea box still in her hand.

"This isn't over." He pointed to Rilla, with a glint of teasing in his eyes. "Hopefully, I'll make it back alive to finish."

"Get out of here, drama queen. Stop flirting with my sister." Thea opened the door. "Don't fuck anything up."

He saluted, picking up speed down the steps and disappearing into the night at a jog.

"Was he flirting with me?" Rilla asked, totally unable to help herself and trying very hard to keep her voice nonchalant.

"He flirts with everyone," Thea said. She disappeared into the kitchen and reappeared a second later with two mugs. "I'll finish his hand."

"Thanks," Rilla said, taking the mug and picking up her cards. She was almost afraid to breathe—sitting here, drinking tea with her sister. It was everything she'd wanted California to be, deep down. Maybe the tide was turning. She looked at the cards and tried to come up with something to say. "Why do they use pagers?"

"The cliffs do weird things to digital signals."

"Pagers aren't like cell phones?" Rilla asked.

"No." Thea frowned at the cards and picked one out. "They use radio signals."

"Oh. So, how come you can't go?"

"It's not my job."

"How come? If it's something you love . . ." Rilla eyed her sister. Thea looked annoyed. Which could be her questions, or could be her hand.

"It's really hard to get a position like that." Thea tossed her cards with a sigh. "I don't have anything."

Rilla dropped her cards. "Do you want to play again?"

Thea yawned. "Mmm . . . I need to sleep. Maybe tomorrow?"

Rilla nodded and started gathering the cards. All she kept trying to do was engage her sister. To talk like they used to. But she kept doing the wrong thing, somehow. It felt like Thea would rather be anywhere other than with her. She'd sat here and ate with Walker, played poker with Walker, laughed, and been herself. This curt person who needed to go to bed wasn't Thea. Rilla was doing something wrong still. Maybe it was just that she was a walking reminder of everything Thea didn't want to remember.

"Do you ever want to go back to West Virginia?" Rilla asked, turning on the bench. "Seriously?"

Thea paused at the beginning of the hall. "No." She yawned again. "Good night."

Never.

Rilla stared at the cards in her hands.

"You two make me feel like I need to call my sister," someone said.

Rilla jerked up.

Lauren—the ranger with the dark hair and tattoos—sat in a corner on her laptop. Rilla hadn't noticed her.

"Yay," Rilla muttered.

Lauren just smiled and shook her head, still focused on the screen. She wore a big T-shirt, the thick glasses she'd been wearing before, and her hair in a messy ponytail, like she was ready for bed—except she was still wearing her uniform pants. "She loves you."

Rilla shrugged. It wasn't that she doubted her sister's love. But right now, it just felt like a love stretched thin, without much substance for the everyday.

"My little sister is the good one." Lauren clicked and peered at the screen. "She's a nurse with two adorable kids. Mom never wants to visit me." She rolled her eyes to the messy cabin. "Can't imagine why," she said dryly.

"Yeah. I'll just be out . . ." Rilla said quietly, putting the cards on the table. She dug out her phone and headed to the porch.

The Valley seemed the same—despite Walker's jog into the night. No moon, but bright stars peeked out beyond the trees and rocks. Easing her breath out, she dialed Curtis's old number.

The phone rang. Her breath held tight.

It rang. And rang. And rang.

And Rilla stared into the night.

Three days later, Rilla felt like a toy everyone had fought over and then forgotten about. No matter where she walked in the Valley, or how long she waited on the porch, trying to do homework while she watched the edges of the meadow for someone she recognized to cross through, the magic of the Valley did not conjure her anyone. Not this time.

Rilla kept texting anyone she remembered from home, hoping she didn't sound like the desperate, insecure person that she was. But even if they did reply, no one talked for long. And no one would give her Curtis's new number, no matter that she just wanted to apologize.

Worse, while stalking everyone on Instagram, she'd found Caroline's account. Despite Petra creating expectations, Rilla was *still* surprised at how beautiful and professional the feed looked. Like, a more-gorgeous-than-you'll-ever-be girl sitting cross-legged on a cot, tied to a giant rock wall, laughing like a dork, as she ate from a tin can. There were pictures of Caroline climbing in tight pants without panty-lines or weird bulges or anything awkward. The comments on those numbered into the thousands and included a lot of not nice things, but Rilla didn't pay much attention to those. The most recent ones were Valley sunsets, and climbing gear laid out. Rilla clicked one and saw the meal Adeena had made. Everything looked like a goddamn advertisement. Rilla kept scrolling. Before Yosemite there was Argentina. Arizona. Spain. Mountains bigger and higher than anything Rilla could imagine, even with Yosemite's reset to her sense of scale. Food she'd never seen. Beaches she could only imagine. The one picture Caroline had posted of her and Walker for #nationalsiblingsday had a ton of comments about her hot brother. Those comments were made by girls prettier than anyone in Rainelle, let alone Rilla.

Rilla made a gagging noise and closed the app. How on earth had she thought she could be friends with Caroline? Or have a chance with Walker?

It was like all the embarrassment she should have felt, caught up in one rush of red-hot agony. Oh god, they probably hated her. They probably thought she was the dumbest person. They were probably talking right now about that awkward girl who had no idea. The *nerve* she had . . .

Rilla looked at the phone, and found herself clicking it back on.

Caroline was from southern Ohio, which was a similar place to central West Virginia. Caroline was on her own, with her sibling, like Rilla. It was impossible to look at those pictures and not feel that all Rilla needed to do to fix herself was be like Caroline.

Irritated at herself for even remotely believing in magic and her ability to be that cool in the first place, Rilla resolved to never think of climbing again. She was definitely afraid of heights. It was a ridiculous sport. She already had a problem with recklessness. She didn't have a death wish, no matter what anyone thought. It was stupid.

She closed Instagram. There. *Done.*

Determined to forget climbing, she spent her days at HUFF, hanging out with Jonah. He fed her leftovers from the kitchen, and she tagged along as they went through the routine of every day—work, food, and laundry. She took a spot in the makeshift living room formed of a rug and camp chairs in the dirt, rushing to make it back to Thea's at a reasonable hour. When she wasn't with Jonah, she unpacked her clothes, hung

Christmas lights in the rafters of her attic, and tried to do homework.

In the middle of the week, Thea had her weekend. She had a serious-slash-awkward conversation with Rilla about how Ranger Lauren was actually her girlfriend, while Lauren leaned on the counter and tried to look supportive, but kept grinning at them like she found the whole thing hilarious, except she was wearing her glasses and they made her eyes bigger in a way that almost cartoonish, so Rilla kept trying not to laugh when she looked at her.

Finally, Thea finished her speech.

"You had to wait to tell me this?" Rilla asked as soon as Thea stopped talking. Maybe that was why Thea was on edge about everything. But, like, how terrible did Thea think Rilla was that she'd be upset about this?

"I just didn't want to overwhelm you," Thea said.

"Okay. Well. Good to know. Anything else?"

Thea frowned and glanced to Lauren.

Lauren shrugged.

"No?" Thea said, with no confidence.

"Thanks for updating me on your relationship status," Rilla said, hopping off the kitchen stool and grabbing an apple before heading back to the attic. It was disconcerting though. To find out something this big about a person she'd known her whole life. Had she missed it? She didn't want Thea to know how she felt—it might make Thea feel like she had to send her home.

It took forty-five minutes of getting distracted remembering things from their childhood, given this new information, before Thea was the same old Thea, and Rilla was restless again.

She finished one unit of trigonometry out of sheer and total boredom; but after she discovered Thea's laptop had movies, schoolwork didn't stand a chance.

•

"Your sister probably doesn't want to go back to West Virginia because she's got a girlfriend. Not because of you," Jonah said, handing her a coffee a tourist hadn't liked the look of. He usually worked in the cafeteria, but was covering the shift of a friend.

"West Virginia has lesbians," Rilla snapped, exhausted by the constant comments about things West Virginia was or was not, as told by people who had never lived there.

He raised an eyebrow. "Yeah, but do they get married and have babies and put those babies in Montessori preschools?"

"Monta what?"

"Exactly." He poured the milk.

She made a face and took the latte outside.

By the fifth day, she'd given up—on homework, magic, and hope.

Guilt and loneliness mired her in misery—where the only cure was more misery and Pop-Tarts from the store in Yosemite Village. She sat in a dark attic on her phone, stalking people at home on slow-ass Internet. Hating herself. Hating everyone else. Making herself sick on Pop-Tarts because no one was around to tell her to stop. Until suddenly, Adeena knocked on the door.

"We're going climbing!" Adeena announced as Rilla hid behind the door, blinking and shielding herself from the intense sunshine like a vampire fresh from death. "Don't worry, I'll ease you into it. Bring water and wear comfortable shoes. I'll come back before sunrise tomorrow morning. I need to catch my ride." Adeena waved goodbye.

Rilla was so excited she'd been invited to climb with Adeena, she almost forgot it was an activity she'd just spent five days convincing herself she wanted no part of. A pit of nervousness grew in her stomach, but she wasn't about to chicken out. Before going to bed, she laid out layers of clothes and stuffed her backpack with water and an extra sweatshirt. It took her three hours to fall asleep. She managed to wake up, dress, and slip outside with peanut butter toast before Adeena arrived in the early hours before dawn, Petra in tow.

"Long story," Adeena snarled over a granola bar as she glared at Petra's headlamp light. "Don't worry, I'll make sure she doesn't kill you."

"I am a fantastic climbing instructor," Petra said as she stabbed a plastic spoon into an open packet of instant oatmeal. "I worked at a gym in Burbank."

"No. No, we shall *not* do this." Adeena stalked off. "Call me when you lead a team up the Trango Towers."

"You didn't *lead* it." Petra's eye roll was visible even in the headlamp glow. "Come on," she said to Rilla over a mouthful of oatmeal. "You're going to like this."

Rilla slung her backpack onto her shoulders and followed, afraid to say anything in case it would be wrong. It was hard to tell what she could say to either girl that would endear her, especially when she didn't understand why they argued or what they were even arguing over. It was like waiting for the beat to start dancing, but always somehow missing it.

They started across the Valley toward the sheer, shadowed face of Half Dome looking off into the distance—a dark wave, frozen at its steep crest. Her breath hung as a silver cloud and she shivered in the purple dark as she followed the gentle bobbing of Petra's headlamp. This was it.

Her stomach flipped in sudden nervousness. She was going climbing.

"BELAY ON."

*Between every two pines
is a doorway to a new world.*

—John Muir

nine

RILLA SPENT THE FIRST TWO AND A HALF HOURS STARING AT THE BACKS
of Adeena's and Petra's contrasting ponytails as the sun crept high along
the mountain ridges. Adeena only came to Petra's shoulder, but their pace
was the same. Fast. *Up.* So much hiking that Rilla forgot to be worried
about climbing, and got pissed she'd been tricked into exercise.

A huge group of college-age hiking boys clustered on the stone steps
carved out of the gorge around Vernal Falls, taking photos of the roaring falls and white water surging down the narrow ravine. Rilla would
have wandered off the path and died somewhere in the land of well-
defined biceps, ugly-ass wraparound sunglasses, and "*brah*" if it weren't
for Petra yanking on the shoulder strap of her backpack and pulling
her along.

"Down, girl," Petra said.

"It's just . . . it's so pretty," she sputtered, and looked back at the boys.
"Sniff."

Adeena laughed.

Rilla tried not to look back.

Unfortunately, that meant she was focused on how much her legs
hurt, how thin the air seemed, and the weird flashes behind her eyes like
she was crawling her way into goddamn Mordor.

The trail wound up a deep gully, and the wind caught great tufts of
mist from the falls, dusting the rocks with mist-heavy emerald moss and
Rilla in a layer of sparkling, bone-chilling wet. At the top, Rilla slowed, her

hand clutching the railing for support, thinking they'd surely pause to catch their breath.

Nope.

The two girls dropped back and matched Rilla's pace, but they didn't stop.

By the time Rilla staggered to the top of a second waterfall, she was somehow pouring sweat and still freezing from the first waterfall. "I'm out of shape," she wheezed, figuring it was better to admit it than pretend her death wasn't happening, as if she could hide it. Out of shape and wet. Both Adeena and Petra were dry, she noticed. The bright, technical fabric of their shirts had released the waterfall, while Rilla's cotton layers clung to it.

"Yeah. You are," Petra said, biting into an apple.

Adeena made a choking sound.

"*She* said it. I just agreed," Petra said to Adeena, then looked to Rilla. "Eat something."

Rilla blinked at their arguing, a terrible sinking feeling in her stomach. She hadn't packed food. Adeena hadn't said to pack food. Why hadn't she thought to pack any food?

"Get something now, before we start hiking again," Petra said.

Rilla looked down. "Oh, I'm not hungry."

Silence.

She couldn't bring herself to look up, pretending she was suddenly super interested in the rocky soil underfoot.

"Look sharp," Petra said.

Rilla lifted her chin and caught the granola bar Petra tossed her. "Thanks." Food seemed counterintuitive to getting in shape, but Rilla ripped the bar open and demolished half in one hungry bite.

"I always pack way more food than I need."

"Another reason you're not an alpinist," Adeena said, peeling an orange as she sat cross-legged on a rock.

"You just never know, Dee. Don't come crying to me when you need snacks."

Adeena closed her eyes and shook her head as if to say Petra was absurd.

The dull roar of the foaming Merced filled the silence as they finished eating. Even though it was mid-morning, the sun hadn't climbed high enough to light the depths of the canyon walls, leaving the bottom still dark and blue in shadow, and the mist of the river like smoke. It should have warmed up by now, but the air was still cold and thin. Rilla subtly stretched her hamstrings against the rock so she wouldn't maim herself standing up too fast.

"Holding up?" Adeena asked.

Rilla's mouth was too full of granola bar to answer. "Imph mphinnn," she managed.

"It's going to be a long day, but the climbing is easy," Petra said, screwing the lid back on her Nalgene. "Good conditioning. Want some water?"

Rilla swallowed. "I have a bottle. Thanks."

Petra nodded, with an approving smile. "Let's get this hiking shit over with."

"I like the hiking. It's so relaxing," Adeena said.

"You would, *alpinist*."

Adeena threw an orange peel at her. "You're lucky to have me, otherwise you might get lost on the way up without a string of bolts to guide you."

Petra just laughed and turned off the path, into the rocks and trees.

Adeena stood off the rock. "It won't always be this hard. I promise. And even though I would have taken you on something shorter for your first time, this is something you can do."

"What was your first climb?" Rilla asked. "Was it like this?"

Adeena smiled, looking carefully where she stepped. "A mountain near my home in Gilgit, in Pakistan. My brother was a guide. I had been begging to go, so he took me for my twelfth birthday. It was a three-day trip. Our mother was so angry." She laughed softly.

Well then. Rilla pressed her lips together. No more complaining to Adeena. "When did you come here?"

"For school, last year. I have family here, too."

"Your brother?"

There was a long beat. "No."

Rilla frowned, but felt like she'd just stepped off the path and she didn't press. "This is kind of my first time. I never climbed at home."

"This is your home now, isn't it?" Adeena asked.

Rilla didn't know how to answer.

They hiked deeper into the backcountry, around Liberty Cap and Mt. Broderick, both of which Rilla spent a good fifteen minutes thinking were Half Dome until she realized they weren't. They walked a near invisible course that Petra and Adeena seemed to know—through a boggy meadow Petra called a lake, into more open, rocky land spotted with massive sequoias, firs, and patches of grass scattered with lavender-colored lupine. When Rilla asked how they knew the way, Adeena pointed out the little cairns Rilla hadn't noticed because she'd been so busy hunting for signs of her impending doom.

The white-peach granite of Half Dome's massive shoulder became visible—a looming thing through the trees that seemed to create its own force. They paused for water and Adeena pulled out a scarf.

"You going to pray?" Petra asked.

"I'll keep our asses covered," she said with a laugh, turning off the trail.

Rilla wanted to ask—about the stop, the cloth, the way Petra understood. She didn't know how to ask and Petra didn't explain. Instead she studied the dome and waited.

Dread settled into Rilla's bones like beads of mercury, and though they walked ever toward it, the dome never moved. "How high is it?" she asked when Adeena returned, almost not wanting an answer.

"From here?" Petra asked.

"Yeah, sure."

"The climb itself is eight hundred feet," Petra said.

"But that only gets us a quarter way to the top," Adeena added. "From Valley to the summit, we'll go a total of almost five thousand feet today. The summit is eight thousand eight hundred feet above sea level."

"You're such a nerd," Petra said.

"I forgot sport climbers' brains were underdeveloped." Adeena flounced ahead.

Petra walked faster and passed her.

Rilla wanted to ask what the difference was between alpine and sport, but she didn't want to draw attention to her lack of knowledge, so she just tried to keep up, staring at the dome as she trudged behind. The magnitude of what she was about to do hit her in the chest. Even with Adeena and Petra, it felt way too big. Too impossible. Just yesterday, she had held her pee for three hours, because it meant another trip on that damn attic ladder. And she had spent that whole time clicking through all of her ex-boyfriend's photos and eating a box of Pop-Tarts. This—Half Dome—wasn't something she could do. Sweating more than she had been five minutes ago, Rilla rushed to catch up with Adeena and Petra, who were—*shocker*—arguing. This time, about which direction they should be taking.

"Okay, but I really *can't* climb," Rilla interrupted. "I cried when I did it with Walker."

"Girls usually do," Petra said without missing a beat.

Adeena cackled.

Rilla swallowed, her stomach tight. She could *literally* die doing this—inexperienced, out of shape, and in way over her head.

As if hearing her thoughts, Adeena turned, shading her eyes. The sun slanted dark shadows on her face. "It looks intimidating, I know. Even if you know what you're doing, you should always be a little scared."

That wasn't helping.

"Don't listen to her," Petra interjected. "You don't need to be scared. It looks more intimidating than it is. We'll haul you if you need it."

"Just focus on the trail ahead of you," Adeena coached. "If you can hike, you can do this climb."

Rilla shaded her eyes to look up the wall. "I feel like I'm in one of those rescue-your-teenager programs or something."

"You'd be having to walk a lot farther, trust me," Petra said dryly "Want some gummy bears?"

"You went to one of those outdoor rehab programs?" Adeena asked Petra. "Those are real?"

"My parents caught me smoking weed when I was fifteen and ..." Petra jerked her thumb over her shoulder. "The whole summer. I think they just wanted to go to Corsica alone."

What the fuck was Corsica? But Rilla didn't ask, taking the gummy bears Petra offered and biting their heads off as the group resumed hiking.

Rilla frowned and tried not to look at the dome anymore. She *could* turn around, hike back to the cot in the attic, pull the covers over her head with the Pop-Tarts, and never come out. Maybe even, she should.

But if she did that, that's what she'd have to do for the rest of the summer. She certainly couldn't show her face to Petra or Adeena or Walker, or any of the other climbers ever again. And somewhere inside, she couldn't live with herself if she didn't grit her teeth and take the chance she'd been given to try.

ten

THE WIND WHIPPED AT RILLA'S T-SHIRT. SHE ROLLED HER SLEEVES UP
to keep from getting a farmer's tan, and focused on Petra, who stood
with her pack on, sunglasses down, and hands raised to the wall. Petra's
white-blond ponytail fanned out in the breeze and metal bits hung,
clinking, off green webbing slung across her chest.

"Belay on?" Petra asked, as if that should mean something.

The rope threaded through the Grigri Rilla had used with Walker,
clipped to the big loop on the front of her harness between her
hips. She grabbed it, but couldn't remember what to do. "Walker
didn't . . ."

"That's because Walker is an asshat and didn't take you seriously."
Adeena said. "He's a fantastic climber, but not the greatest teacher. Don't
tell him I said that."

Petra stayed quiet, poised to leave the ground while Adeena talked.
"She says, *Belay on?* Now, if you're ready, you say *On belay.* You're the belay.
Are you on? Can she trust you? Are you ready?"

Rilla swallowed and looked at the rope. She couldn't be trusted. She
wasn't on. She didn't remember how to do this. But she didn't want
to expose herself. "On belay," she said faintly. The wind snapped at her
braid.

"Louder," Adeena ordered. "You're a team. You have to communicate."

"*On belay*," Rilla said, louder.

Petra immediately rocked forward on her toes. "Climbing," she said.

"She's telling you she's about to climb," Adeena said. "Now, you have to tell her to *climb on*. That means from that moment on, you're the person to keep her alive."

"Wait." Rilla gripped the rope tighter, heart thumping in her ears. "What's supposed to hold her?" The rope hung slack between the two of them, nothing in between Rilla's Grigri and the knot Petra had tied to her harness. If Petra began to climb and fell, she'd just *fall*. There was nothing Rilla could see to do to stop her.

Adeena pointed to the metal bits hanging at Petra's side. "She'll set one of those pieces of protection—*pro*—every so often along the way. Either in a crack or on a bolt. Then, it'll be just like when you did it with Walker."

Rilla squinted up the wall. This was such a bad idea. *A Bad Idea: The Priscilla Skidmore Story.* Caroline's Instagram feed popped into her head, and she clenched her jaw. She wanted to be that, so badly. But she stood frozen, unable to start. And *she* wasn't even climbing.

"I'm not going anywhere," Adeena said. "I'm your backup. And Petra's done this climb a thousand times. She doesn't even need you."

"I could do this with no hands," Petra said, balancing on her toes and waving her hands in the air to demonstrate. "Now. Climbing."

Rilla took a deep breath. It was this or Netflix and staring at her undone homework all summer. "Climb on," she said.

"All right!" Adeena fist-bumped the air.

Petra began moving up the wall, rope trailing behind her.

Rilla's stomach turned and turned, and her palms were sweaty, but she carefully fed out rope as Petra moved.

In less than a minute, Petra paused and reached for a piece of *pro* at her side. A few seconds later she called, "slack" and began pulling up on the rope that trailed down to Rilla.

Adeena lifted up the rope from the pile. "*Slack* means give her more rope. Keep your hands on the brake and feed it through the Grigri."

Rilla's hands got all crossed, and her fingers trembled as she tried to feed the rope out without letting go, like she'd practiced with Walker. She couldn't even seem to recall Walker's face at that moment, let alone what he'd taught her.

"She's not going to fall," Adeena said. "You don't have to rush. Think about what you're doing and do it. Don't make a mistake because you're nervous." She clamped a hand over Rilla's right fist, pushing it to Rilla's thigh.

Oh. Her brake hand. She remembered now. Rilla's cheeks warmed. She'd unthinkingly lifted the brake and let go. The thing Walker had told her never to let go of.

"Calm down," Adeena said. "Then feed it without lifting your hand."

Rilla stopped. Petra wasn't going to fall. They were okay. She was safe. She took a deep breath in through her nose and looked at her hands, carefully managing the rope through the Grigri. Her hands felt like they would shake if she let go, but she wasn't in a giant knot anymore.

Petra pulled up all the rope Rilla had let out. "Clipping." Then a second later. "Clipped."

Rilla glanced at Adeena for an explanation.

"She's got the rope clipped into the pro now," Adeena said. "*You* tighten up that slack. The reverse of what you just did."

Following Adeena's instructions and trying to move as smoothly as possible, Rilla pulled the rope taut without getting crossed or letting go. Allowing herself one relieved sigh, Rilla anchored the rope at her hip and tipped her chin to Petra. "Got you," she yelled.

Adeena smiled. "See? You're doing great. Just go smooth and steady and *think*. I promise, you've got this."

Rilla nodded, a whisper of a smile crossing her tensed jaw as she stayed focused on Petra's upward movement.

The sun blistered Rilla's shoulders and the wind kissed away the burn. And somehow, in the wind and the sun and the intensity of watching Petra and listening to Adeena's instructions, Rilla forgot everything else. All that was real was her focus on keeping Petra secure. It made her feel useful. Like she was needed—because for this one second, even with Adeena there as backup, that was true.

They continued on until Petra called down that she was off belay and Rilla could pull the rope out of the Grigri and tie in.

Tie in?

Rilla stared stupidly at her waist and tried to remember how to tie the knot.

"Let me know if you need a refresher," Adeena said.

Rilla pushed air out of her cheeks and undid the rope from the Grigri. "Let's see." Clipping the Grigri to her harness, she double backed the rope, and knotted it with a figure-eight follow-through. Walker's blue eyes flashed in her memory. "I forget how to tie the backup knot."

"Don't worry about it," Adeena said. "It's not really a backup. It's just to keep the tail from whipping in your face if you fall. People just call it that." She shrugged.

"Oh."

"That tail is pretty short. You're fine."

Rilla hated it when the rules changed. It left her unsettled and on edge—a terrible feeling anytime, but definitely when she was about to ascend a cliff. Swallowing her feelings, she dropped the rope and tried to move on.

"You ready?" Petra called. "I'm going to belay you from up here." The rope went taut, pulling upward on Rilla's harness. "When you're climbing, use your legs more than your arms. Push up, don't pull. Take your time."

"Okay." Rilla nodded. Her heart raced. It was too late. Too late to turn around. Was this peer pressure? She was going to die from peer pressure.

"Okay?" Adeena asked. "Don't forget to have fun."

Rilla nodded, her heart firmly fastened into the back of her throat.

Adeena stepped back. "Tell your partner you're climbing."

Oh.

Shit.

Rilla stepped to the edge of the granite, fingers trembling as she skittered over its surface, looking for anything where her hands could rest. "Belay on?" she croaked into the fathomless sky.

"On belay," a thin voice replied.

"Climbing," Rilla said.

"Climb on."

This was just like playing. *Playing.* Rilla told herself as she pushed off the ground. Her body weight seemed to double. Her limbs too long or too short or too something. Her fingers slipped and she scrambled to move up. *Playing.* She reached and pulled, remembering halfway Adeena's admonition to *push.* As she went, the rope stayed taut, and after a few heart-pounding moments, Rilla relaxed.

Petra hadn't been lying. The climbing was easy. For a moment even, it was fun.

A thick stretch of granite had cooled millions of years ago as a fold—creating a perfect space for her to grip the blunt edge and step along its curving line up toward Petra.

The rock itself was smooth but finely textured, rough and sharp against her bare fingertips like a heavy grit sandpaper, and her shoes—the ones Petra had handed her—stuck firmly.

Rilla pulled level with the one metal bit Petra had shoved into a crack and stopped. Her stomach turned. This was what she'd put her trust in. A little piece shoved into the wall and attached to the rope with some carabiner and webbing. *This.* Somehow, knowing that was scarier than if she'd simply climbed up here without anything keeping her secure.

She kept moving to the overhanging lip, where instead of a piece, the rope was dropped into a carabiner and webbing hanging off a bolt.

"Look at you, dude. No sweat," Petra said when Rilla had almost reached the ledge Petra belayed from. Two separate stretches of webbing with carabiners attached Petra's harness to a pair of silver bolts drilled into the clean rock. It looked tidy, but complicated. How did anyone know how to do this enough not to mess it up? Rilla stepped carefully on the narrow ledge, and the rope between them shortened to only a horizontal foot.

A lot of sweat. And terror. But she'd done it. She'd *fucking done this shit.*

Rilla laughed and shakily leaned against the wall.

The world spread out in front of her. Far in the blue-gray distance to her left, the falls outside her attic window formed a streak of faintly moving white. The wind gusted in her face, cold and dry, and the kind of breeze you only get high above the ground in wild, empty space. All around, the peaks of the high Sierras were thick with snow.

She felt free. Alive. Focused. Like she was capable of anything.

"First pitch down," Petra said. "Seven more to go."

What? Rilla jerked to Petra. "*Seven* more? We have to do that seven more times?"

"You're in training now," Petra said in a chipper tone. "Let's get you anchored so you can belay Adeena up here."

Rilla tipped her chin up—surprised and somehow not surprised to see that the dome looked very much the same as it had at the bottom. The eighty feet she'd just climbed seemed to make no difference in the distance left to go.

eleven

RILLA CRAWLED ON THE RAISED SPINE OF GRANITE LIFTING OUT OF THE
dome like some prehistoric snake frozen in the act of diving for the depths
of the earth. Nearly forty feet of rope blew in the wind ahead of her, shorten-
ing as she climbed to Adeena.

They were only halfway up the curve of the dome—but the angle was
leveling off and when Rilla finally reached Adeena and Petra at the anchors
of the eighth pitch, she could stand and walk.

"You did it," Adeena shouted.

Petra pumped her arms in victory. "See?"

"I did it!" Rilla yelled to the wind, dropping onto her back on the granite. She smiled so wide it hurt, cheeks aching, and raw from the wind and
sun. She couldn't even imagine herself doing this, and yet, it was done. She
had done it. Whatever happened, no one could take this moment. With the
granite against her backside and the sunshine on her face. She grinned to
the sky.

"You've officially completed your first multi-pitch," Petra said. "Peanut
butter crackers?"

"Ooh. Yes, please." Rilla sat up so quickly her head spun.

"Here, take some of these." Adeena scooped a handful of almonds out
of her bag. They were coated with flakey salt that smelled faintly of wood
smoke. "They're better fuel than crackers."

"You did not just come at my crackers," Petra said.

"Oh, I definitely did. What are you, ten? Peanut butter crackers?"

"Peanut butter, Dee," Petra said. "It has protein."

"That's not even real peanut butter."

"It's . . ." Petra frowned and looked at the package. "Canola oil, soybean oil, sugar, wheat . . ." It was quiet a second. "*Peanuts!*" Petra shouted triumphantly. "In your face!"

Adeena rolled her eyes. "Oh, the pinnacle of western nutrition."

"Whatever, you lost, I win. All that counts."

Petra's competiveness didn't seem to bother Adeena, who just flopped back on her pack and threw an almond at her, laughing.

Rilla still didn't know how to act—whether this was all a joke, or whether there was something real at the root of their arguing. Inside, it made her want to stay very still, like a rabbit in the grass, waiting to see if the way was clear.

Rilla hooked her arms over her knees and stared down the climb they'd just come up, crackers in one hand and almonds in the other. Below them, another group of climbers was nearly halfway up the last dike. She'd been so focused on getting up here, she hadn't paid attention to anything behind.

"Is it always this busy?" she asked Petra, interrupting their arguing to point down the dike.

"I was surprised we didn't have to wait when we got here. It's usually busier," Petra said.

"It's been cold this spring," Adeena said, standing and brushing off her pants. "And the cables on the back for hikers aren't up. I think that cuts down on traffic."

"You did good today," Petra said to Rilla. "Did we get you hooked?"

"Yes," Rilla said confidently. She could see why people did this. The taste of the wind and the edge of fear. The feeling of pride and accomplishment that she had just done something not many people could or would ever do. That she'd done something she herself was afraid of. She didn't know how she would ever do it again, but she wanted to.

"You're going to become the next Lynn Hill now, right?" Petra teased.

"Who?" Rilla asked.

"The patron saint of women climbers."

"In Yosemite, at least," Adeena added.

Rilla laughed. She laughed—not because she thought Petra was absurd, though she did—but because her entire body felt lighter and stronger and sharper, and she could hardly believe she sat here, laughing.

"You have a chance hardly any other climber in the world has," Petra said. "You live inside *Yosemite Valley*. In a house. With a bed. And a kitchen?" Petra squinted at her.

Rilla nodded.

"A kitchen! And this is your backyard." She flung her arms wide. "This is your fucking backyard."

"Well, yeah . . . I guess." Rilla's heart beat faster—whether from fear or exhilaration, she wasn't sure. She didn't want the privilege of living in Yosemite to be wasted on her. She looked around, at the mountains surrounding her. Maybe there was a home here.

"We're going to turn you into a climber," Adeena said.

Rilla clutched the plastic wrapper in her fist. She understood the words, but didn't believe them. The wind whipped her hair into tangled wisps about her face. In silence, they watched the climbers below them struggle slowly upward on the dike, before standing, hoisting their packs, and heading up the steep slab toward the summit.

After another forty minutes, Rilla took back all the good things she felt—certain death was imminent. Her calves burned, and the cold wind scraped her lungs. Snow fell into her shoes no matter how carefully she stepped. Somewhere near the top, she paused to catch her breath, and a sudden wave of head-spinning nausea slapped her in the face, making her gag. "I'm going to be sick," she gasped. "I need a minute." She sank onto a rock and closed her eyes.

"Altitude sickness," Adeena said. "Be careful. It slows your head. It'll get better once we start going down. We can stop again if you need it."

Rilla waited until she caught her breath and stood—following on, silent and nauseated. Her eyelids drooped, heavy and weirdly swollen. They crossed the barren moon landscape of the top of the dome in a thin line, one after another, with Petra leading.

She was *on top* of Half Dome. She should be running around, high kicking and Instagramming all over the place—but all she wanted to do was get off.

They wound past impossibly balanced cairns—rocks stacked one on top of the other to stand taller than Rilla's head. She slipped in the snow as she tried to stay in Adeena's and Petra's footsteps.

Adeena grabbed her wrist. "Hold up."

Rilla slid to a stop, lifting her head and realizing they'd crossed the top and now stood overlooking the back side of the dome. Even the altitude sickness didn't dull the thrill of seeing what lay beyond the dome she'd gotten so used to seeing every time she looked east. They stood on a gentle edge before the plummet. As far as she could see, there was nothing but white and gray jagged peaks, charcoal valleys, blunt domes, and the scrubby dark sage of evergreens. Oblivion spread before her. Oblivion, with no way down.

"How do we get off?" Her heart was already racing, thumping in her stomach and throat. It didn't feel like it could go any faster. The edge of panic rippled against her.

"We'll go down the cables route," Petra said. "As soon as the people ahead clear out."

"I thought you said the cables were down."

"They are. But they just drop them down on the rock. The boards are left," Petra said. "It's not suitable for most hikers, really. But it works."

"Why don't you sit," Adeena said. "Drink something."

Rilla sank onto a rock, shivering in the icy wind.

"See if this will fit." Adeena handed her a ball of quilted nylon. "It will be warmer."

Rilla stupidly held it up, before realizing she needed to put it on. Slowly, she pulled it over her sweatshirt. It was too tight to zip and her arms and shoulders strained in Adeena's tiny jacket, but she clutched it across her chest with numb fingertips.

This was totally how people died. Even with Petra's and Adeena's experience she could see how the altitude numbed you and slowed you enough to make mistakes you wouldn't normally make.

Another group was ahead of them. Not climbers, but hikers who had made the climb to the top of dome using the thick wire cables lying flat on the rock. Petra stood at the edge, watching their progress as they disappeared over the swell.

"Hey," someone hollered across the wind.

In unison, the girls looked up and behind them. A man came toward them from the summit, waving and running over the snow and rocks.

"He's going to slip," Adeena said, before yelling back to him. "Slow down."

He didn't slow. The strings on his hat bounced off his shoulders as he ran up to them. "My partner is . . ." He looked at the three of them wildly. The panic in his eyes made Rilla's chest tighten. "Something's wrong," he said.

Adeena and Petra bolted off after him, snow flying into the wind. Rilla pushed up to follow, holding the jacket tight across her chest. Her pulse pounded hard even though she'd just been resting. She ran as fast she dared up the slope, back to the summit, where a man leaned against a rock.

"It's like altitude sickness, but this altitude should be fine. He's diabetic, but he's got a pump. I don't know . . ." the guy said, looking down at his buddy. "Rob. How're you feeling? You awake?"

He looked pale and sweaty. He shrugged.

"He has a pump?" Petra asked. "So, it shouldn't be his insulin, right?"

"Sometimes altitude fucks you up when it didn't before. Can he get down?" Adeena asked.

"No. I mean, yes he has a pump. No, it shouldn't. I don't think I can get him down though. Maybe with your help. You guys were the climbers ahead of us, right?" He didn't look up from his partner.

"But we can't hike him out," Petra said. "Can he walk?"

"Barely."

Rilla sank down to a rock, her stomach tight and the nausea heavy. It felt like she could see the curve of the earth on the horizon and it made her almost feel the sensation of spinning through the cosmos. The sick man sat across from her, looking like she felt. The voices of the more experienced climbers blurred together, muffled by the wind. "Shit, if we can't get him to walk . . . could we contact someone?"

He must be terrified. She'd be terrified. His mouth was open a little. Brown eyes glazed. As if he too felt the world spinning in space and couldn't stand upright against those forces. Rilla's granny had been a diabetic. No pumps—just shots, so many shots. One day, when Rilla was nine and helping in the garden, Granny had sat down, unable to move anywhere else. Looking pale and sick, just like this man. She'd swatted at Rilla's hand. "I'm fine, girl. Just this heat." She'd fanned herself and the air had smelled like the warm, sharp scent of tomatoes. It hadn't been the heat.

"It's his diabetes," Rilla heard herself say. She crawled forward, feeling like she might puke. Her head throbbed, but she wasn't sick like he was.

"He has a pump, but that's to keep his blood sugar from going too high. But it's probably too low, because he's working hard. Does he have one those of blood sugar stick things?"

Adeena looked to the other man. Petra looked to Adeena.

"I don't know . . ." The guy who'd ran to get them whirled around and started digging through what Rilla assumed was his partner's bag.

"It's okay. We're going to figure this out," she said, surprised how calm and relaxed she sounded. Her heart raced.

The other man looked up from the shambles of a backpack. "This?" He held up a little thing that looked like a step meter.

"That's it." Rilla grabbed it and stuck it into Rob's limp finger. In seconds the readout showed it was too low.

"Does he have glucose tabs? Petra, do you have those gummy bears? We have to give him a little at a time."

The guy looked confused. "I can get it." His words came out raspy and dry. He tried to reach out for it.

Rilla stopped him. "I'll bring the bag to you," she said.

Someone shoved the bag to her. Opening it wide, she looked at the sick climber—Rob. He nodded. In a few seconds, she'd found the little packet of glucose tablets in an interior pocket. She kneeled on the rock and took a deep breath, breaking one out of the package and closing it into his mouth.

He shut his eyes in relief.

Petra handed him a bag of gummy bears.

He took the bag, but didn't eat any.

"How long have you guys been climbing together?" Petra asked.

"We just met the other day. I didn't even know he was diabetic until we started. I didn't think it was a big deal."

"Usually it wouldn't be. He was prepared for it," Rilla said. His partner wasn't. If something had happened to Petra or Adeena, she'd have been the one unprepared. Rilla didn't want that to happen again.

In fifteen minutes, she checked again, before giving him another dose of glucose and repeating until he was on his feet, color returned to his face. He gave each girl a warm hug in thanks—along with his partner—and they all headed toward the descent.

Rilla walked backward down to the sub-dome, slowly feeding the cable through her gloved grip as she lowered from board to board, like Adeena instructed. Trying to keep from puking.

Halfway down the back side, it was as if someone snapped their fingers and Rilla woke. The nausea lifted. Her heartbeat calmed. Her fingers were cold but not buzzing with numbness, and the heaviness left her body. The cold wind kissed her cheeks, and she carefully walked down the face, staring blissfully at the fathoms of open space. Adrenaline flooding the places the sickness had left vacant in her blood, sweeping her spirit back up into heady ecstasy.

She was alive.

•

Rilla continued to die and come back. Her feet were freezing in the sub-dome snow. But swelled once they warmed. Her legs and arms and back stiffened and gnarled. It was just hiking down; but down had its own woes. After the first four miles, her toes pushed against the front of her shoes so much they were numb and aching, and her thighs trembled from supporting each step.

"How did you two meet?" she asked Petra as they descended the never-ending turns of the forested trail.

"Um . . . what was it, that comp?" Petra asked, looking to Adeena.

"Yeah," Adeena said. "At a climbing gym in L.A. I did this competition, and Petra came up and started talking. She was putting together this group for the summer, and offered a spot in the house. So . . . we kept in touch. I wasn't sure what I was going to do this summer, but figured Yosemite was a chance I couldn't pass up."

"We climbed together after the comp too . . ." Petra said.

"Oh yeah, that's right."

"Adeena is new to sport climbing," Petra said.

"Well, not new. But yeah," Adeena said.

"What's the difference?" Rilla asked, hobbling around a boulder.

"Alpine uses a variety of climbing tools and techniques to climb a mountain. Ice, snow, just plain hiking . . ." Adeena said. "Or climbing like we did today."

"Sport climbing," Petra said. "Or traditional climbing is more like a blank sheer wall. In sport climbing you always clip into bolts. In traditional climbing, you place the protection along the way. It's shorter and more intense than alpine."

"It's not more intense," Adeena said. "It's just a different kind of intensity. It's more like a sprint and alpine is a marathon."

"We used a bit of gear today," Petra said. "But mostly just quickdraws for the bolts."

Rilla nodded, still not sure she understood. "How did you get into climbing?" she asked Petra.

"I didn't actually climb until the end of high school. I was a soccer player," Petra said. "Until I busted both my knees."

"Oh, I'm so sorry."

Petra shrugged. "I started climbing during rehab. It's hard and required my brain to engage in a way that let me forget I couldn't play anymore."

"Is that why you're so competitive?" Adeena asked. "Your American sports complex?"

"I'm not competitive," Petra said.

Adeena snorted. "Okay. That's why you told Caroline you got the Pink Panther redpoint?"

Petra narrowed her eyes. "I did."

Adeena stepped ahead and didn't say anything else.

"Anyway," Petra said to Rilla. "Climbing pretends it's not competitive. But it is." She stepped over a fallen tree. "How did you end up here with your sister?"

Whether it was the way they'd all climbed together, Rilla trusting them as much as they trusted Rilla, or the exhaustion starting to dull her defenses, Rilla opened her mouth, and wearily confessed the truth.

"I got in a fight."

"With your mom?" Petra asked.

Rilla stepped over a fallen log and shook her head. "Not my mom. It was with my boyfriend, but it wasn't like you're thinking."

"Oh, Rilla," Adeena said, stopping abruptly, mid-trail. Her look was so concerned, it made Rilla cringe.

Petra frowned. "What?"

"No. No." Rilla took a deep breath, trying to slow her heart. "That's what I mean. It wasn't like that." She closed her eyes, willing her heart to calm, but behind her eyes it was red and violent and she heard herself scream and Curtis's arms grapple after her. Her eyes burst open. "No," she repeated. "It wasn't like that. I started the fight and it was all mutual. Yes, we got out of hand. Both of us. And in the school parking lot . . ." She sighed and resumed walking. The two other girls had no choice but to follow as Rilla explained. "So, it blew up into this whole thing. They took us both to jail, and then wanted me to press charges. I didn't though, because it wasn't like that. No one would listen."

Adeena shook her head, eyes down.

Petra's face was smooth—her eyes free of that private judgment so many people had when they looked at Rilla. "So, you came out here? After that?"

Rilla nodded, following the twisting trail. "My mom called Thea, I guess. First time in my life my mother's overreacted to anything. I mean, it would have been fine. It was over. But . . ." Rilla shrugged. "That's what happened."

"Well, it's good you're here now," Petra said, linking arms with both her and Adeena and pulling them close. "Both of you."

"Tragedy can birth new beginnings. I lose sight of that sometimes," Adeena said softly.

"I'm not *tragic* tragic. Just tragically dumb," Rilla said.

"No. You are neither," Petra said, so confidently Rilla felt it must be true.

"You helped that man today," Adeena said.

Rilla shrugged. "It just happened that I knew a little about it, is all."

Adeena shook her head. "It doesn't always work like that. You did great today. You should feel proud."

And Rilla did, a little. Somewhere deep inside. It was a spark that was highly likely to be snuffed out, but it warmed her for the moment.

The afternoon shifted into evening, flooding the cedars and the snow with beams of light so thick she could taste it. A coyote ran across their path, looking at them over its shoulder like it was rubbernecking at an accident. It shook its shoulders, mangy gray fur shivering, and slipped soundlessly into the trees. In those moments, she forgot about her agony and only remembered what a privilege it was to exist in this wild, cruel world.

Then Petra grabbed the back of her pack and pulled her along.

She ran out of water in Little Yosemite Valley, and Adeena showed her how to fill her water from the Merced and make it drinkable with tablets.

The sun sank behind the mountains. Darkness unspooled in the trees. They passed the place they'd turned off the trail in the morning, and even Adeena and Petra seemed tired. The same canyon walls bore different shadows and their steps wound eternally down. Rilla stumbled through the mist, soaked again in the heavy clouds of silver.

In the purple alpenglow, they finally hit the paved trail. And in twilight, Rilla's numb body staggered back into the Valley.

It had been amazing. But she was *never* going to do that again. *Never ever. Ever.*

twelve

THE PULSE OF HOT SHOWER WATER ON HER SHIVERING, TIGHT BODY
was as pure and raw an ecstasy as Rilla could ever imagine. The sound
of her cot sighing as she crawled in and lay, stomach down, in the soft
flannel sheets and fleece blanket, another.

The white Christmas lights she'd strung in the rafters glowed softly,
making the dark attic warm and pleasant and dreamy as the waterfall
roared outside her window. She closed her eyes and her body felt as if it
still stood on that little ledge on Half Dome, viewing the waterfall from
across the Valley. She was grateful. Deeply grateful. For every bit of pain
that had brought her to this moment of knowing how grateful a person
could be for the simplest of things. This raw aching that looped back
into delight that was the most pleasure she had ever experienced. And . . .

She fell asleep.

thirteen

SIXTEEN MILES. EIGHT PITCHES OF CLIMBING. RILLA TURNED THE
numbers over on soundless lips, listening to the ceiling fans hum above
her as she stared at her phone's desperate attempts to snag Internet.
Sixteen. Eight. Sixteen. Eight. A blank screen with a winding wheel stared
back. Never mind yesterday, *this* was looking into the abyss.

She sighed, sinking deeper into the corner of a worn leather sofa in
the Half Dome Village lounge—a sparse rectangular building filled with
couches and comfortable chairs arranged around a stone fireplace. Most
everyone sat, staring at their own slow-moving phones. A few people read
books, or whispered over a guidebook. One or two napped. The air was
warm and drowsy, and clear sunlight streamed through the windows.

It'd taken Rilla a half hour of gentle, slow walking on tender feet to
cross the Valley, and she didn't plan on moving—it was the only place she
could sit, all day, and be steps away from food, coffee, and a bathroom.
She'd even brought a schoolbook.

She was the only high school student in the little Valley school, and
when she'd met with the principal to pick up her books, she'd also been
given a ten-page, single-spaced letter detailing what she needed to complete in order to be reinstated into her senior year in the fall—whether
it was here or in West Virginia. Everything was due by a date in August.
So far, all Rilla had done was put the pile of books on the floor by her cot
and let it gather dust. But today, she'd brought a book.

Her swollen and bandaged feet were propped up on a battered coffee table, in her softest pair of wool socks, and the only shoes able to adjust for the swelling—sandals. She didn't even care that the blue wool socks came to her mid-shin, her shorts were men's boxers patterned with lobsters, and her only clean hoodie was from middle school and basically three-quarter sleeves. She was never repeating yesterday again. Sixteen miles. Eight pitches. Not a single picture. Did it even happen?

Not that Instagram was loading anyway. Switching over to her messages, she stared again at the few and brief text conversations she'd had with friends from home. *People*, she amended, with an empty feeling in her stomach. Not friends. No one had told her people could break your heart like this. Cutting you out and discarding you. If they could just see Rilla as a climber, they'd want to be friends again.

"Looking like a climber already," Hico said as her cushion suddenly tilted the wrong way and he smashed into her tender side.

She winced and shifted upright. "Uh, hey guys."

"Stop manspreading," Gage said, kicking Hico's knee with a battered flip-flop.

Hico moved and Gage sat beside him, crunching the three of them onto the two-seater.

Both boys put their feet up on the table. Hico wore rainbow socks, black basketball shorts, a long-sleeve T-shirt, and dug into his strawberry yogurt with a fork. Gage, in a plaid button-down and pants, unwrapped a sandwich on his lap and pulled packets of hot sauce out of his pockets, before painstakingly cutting a packet open with a little pocketknife from his keychain. She remembered him out of the shower and again found herself looking away and blushing.

People snuck glances at their little group, as if her friends' presences were disrupting the quiet. Rilla shifted and tugged her shorts down.

"Nice lobsters," Hico said, over another fork of yogurt. It dripped on his chin and he licked it off. "Heard you did Snake Dike yesterday."

"How'd it go?" Gage asked, dousing his sandwich in hot sauce.

A man to the left in a cloth chair cleared his throat loudly and lifted his eyebrows at his tablet screen.

"How'd it go?" Gage repeated in a whisper almost louder than his original question. He took a big bite of sandwich and waited, chewing.

"I can't walk," Rilla whispered back. "I might be dead. I'm not positive."

Hico snorted. "Well, you made it back on your own two feet, so that's a win."

"Is that how you decide a win?"

"More or less," Gage said. "Sometimes just alive is good enough. Feet are incidental."

"Incidentally, my feet are busted," she said.

Hico muffled a laughing at the sight of her wool socks. "We can see, girl. We know. But your cat-eye is looking . . ." He winked and clicked his tongue in approval, and Rilla felt her spine involuntary straighten. He was cute. They were all cute, in individual ways. And she was goddamn susceptible.

"What?" Gage asked.

Hico pointed at her eyes. "Her makeup. I got three older sisters. Do you know how hard that shit is?"

Gage narrowed his eyes and studied her face. His eyes were dark and deep.

Rilla's pulse fluttered. "Why is Hico eating yogurt with a fork?" she asked Gage, feeling strange at the scrutiny of her makeup.

"I'm catching a judgmental undercurrent in your whispers," Gage said. "Hico, why don't you enlighten her as to your fork."

"I could only steal a fork," he said sulkily. "The spoons were out of reach."

Rilla snorted.

"This is how you do me after my compliments? At least I'm not wearing my underwear in public," Hico said.

"These aren't underwear," Rilla whispered furiously.

"Dude, you can pee through the hole there." He waved circles at the general area of between her legs, yogurt going along for the ride.

"Watch that," she said, grabbing his wrist and moving his yogurt fork back to where it would drip somewhere else. "If I had a dick, *dick*. I don't. Therefore, not underwear."

"Excuse me, can y'all keep the language down," a woman said in a friendly tone Rilla recognized as being cutthroat church lady.

"I'm sorry, ma'am. I can imagine that is quite disconcerting to hear. We'll be more careful," Hico said with a tone so earnest, the woman looked suspicious.

"It's almost ten thirty," Gage said, crumpling the wrapper from his sandwich and standing. "You ready, man?"

"Where you guys going?" Rilla asked, wishing they would ask her along. Even if she could barely hobble.

"Getting wilderness permits to head into the backcountry for a climb called Pharaoh." Gage looked at his phone. "It's far enough out we'll have to camp overnight. Heard it's rad, though. A buddy did it last summer and I can't get it out of my head." He held out the phone to show her.

The picture was gorgeous. Purple light, silver granite, endless mountains, and wide smiles of everyone in the photo. The kind of thing that made you want to be that cool. That ecstatic. Her body ached and her feet wept, and still she handed the phone back, half wishing they would invite her along. She'd say *no*, obviously. But to be asked . . .

"Looks really cool," Rilla said, trying not to sound wistful. "Does everything involve hiking?"

Hico laughed. "You could spend your whole life in the Valley and never run out of things to climb. I hate hiking, but I'll do just about anything for something beautiful." Hico stood. "The office opens at eleven, so we better go get in line. See ya."

Gage waved.

The boys left, Hico's rainbow socks turning brilliant in the sun before the door closed behind him.

The couch slowly expanded to adopt its original shape. The fan hummed above her. Someone near the unlit fireplace snored.

Rilla picked up her phone and stared at the still-blank screen, at the loneliness facing her.

She found Curtis's Instagram again. He had posted a picture of a Solo cup on his truck two days ago. *Hey, how are you?* she messaged him, feeling reckless and desperate. In the quiet, her heart thumped hard as she watched the message send and sit there.

Rilla picked up *The Scarlett Letter* and tried to read.

Fifty pages later, there still had been no reply, and Rilla hobbled over to the grill to order lunch, a sick feeling stirring in the pit of her stomach every time she thought of the unanswered message. She huddled in a corner of the deck, under the eaves to keep out of the crisp wind, waiting for her order number to be called, when Ranger Dick Face came up the steps.

She took a step sideways to escape. Dick Face was the *last* person she wanted to see right now.

But he was already in front of her, smiling. "Hey Rilla. How is everything going?" he asked, with only a wisp of tightness in his jaw.

She pasted a smile on her face. "Great."

"Yeah? You been staying out of trouble? Catching up on your schoolwork? Can't have Thea's baby sister being a dropout." He laughed and scratched the bridge of his nose, gaze scanning the mostly empty deck around her.

God, did Thea tell *everyone* her business? Even the guy she was competing with? Rilla inwardly groaned. "Um. I'm not—"

"You know. Most of your friends from the other night aren't here anymore."

A few people from HUFF had been fired after that first night, including the French boy she'd made out with. "I didn't really—"

"When I have a problem with people in the Valley, it's usually solved one of two ways."

Titus called her order from behind the screen.

Rilla lifted her receipt. "My—"

"Either they're leaving in a few days, on their best behavior," Dick Face continued. "Or they're leaving in cuffs and banned from the park."

Rilla's neck and face burned.

"The question I want you to ponder is, which way would *you* like to leave? I don't like people here who take unnecessary risks with the park, like your stupid move with the cigarette. I also don't like people who break the law. It's my job to protect the park from those kinds of people."

"Obviously." She bit her lips tight and clenched her fists, trying to keep everything locked inside.

"It's a good thing you and Thea will be leaving after the summer season anyway."

He said it with such confidence, Rilla almost lit on fire. How dare he assume he would beat Thea. "You have no idea," she seethed.

He shrugged. "Well, we'll see, won't we? And uh . . ." He grabbed her burger from Titus's surprised hands, and handed it to her. "Here you go. I recommend the veggie burger next time. Meat isn't great for your arteries, or for our environment." Turning, he walked away.

"What a dick," Titus said from behind the screen.

"Yeah." Rilla clutched the paper-wrapped burger and glowered. He really was a dick. It hadn't just been his face. Rilla needed to be extra careful not to get into trouble, or else he'd make her *and* Thea pay for it.

The wind died and a shiver ran up her body in the sudden quiet.

She should just go home now and save Thea the trouble. Except no one wanted her there either. Unwrapping the burger and taking a bite, she shuffled inside the outdoor store to get out of the chill.

Rilla scanned the racks of brightly colored jackets and technical shirts, slowly chewing. All she could taste was Ranger Dick Face's words. The bit of pride warming her chest—from sore feet, sore back, and the hazy memory of helping someone—turned cold.

On her way out the door, she caught sight of a blown-up and framed photo hanging on the wall above the racks—it pictured a woman rock climbing.

The woman's blond hair blew in the wind, and her limbs were tanned and toned, but she wasn't pictured in the way Rilla was used to seeing women do things in pictures. She crouched and stretched low, angled toward something beyond the camera. Her body was coiled not in a pose, but with purpose. Toward something above her that made her forehead crinkle and her eyes narrow against the California sun. Behind her swept dramatic peach-and-gray granite reaching dotted trees, thick and lush like moss at granite's base.

With a sudden thrill, Rilla forgot about Ranger Dick Face and Curtis. She didn't know who this woman was, but she knew that yesterday, this woman had been *her*.

Rilla's raw fingertips tightened on the half-eaten burger, remembering the feel of unyielding granite. Remembering the feel of the wind and the sun. If someone had taken a photo, it would have shown her body coiled and intense, her eyes squinting against the sun, into the future, and her long brown hair snapping in the wind. A hunger hit her mouth that had nothing to do with food. It was like lust, but instead of for another, it was for herself. For her future. She wanted be that woman in the photo. In every way. Never mind she'd really only tasted it. Never mind the agony she still felt in her body. Never mind it was ridiculous to think Rilla Skidmore, seventeen, high school dropout, from Rainelle, West Virginia, could be anything like that. Or even if she could, Thea might at any minute send her home. That woman, immortalized in that moment, was someone Rilla wanted to be, in every line of her forehead and every stretch of a limb.

With a thrill of purpose that made her feet hurt less, she went to the counter.

The man, to his credit, didn't blink at her socks, lobster boxers, and too-small hoodie. "Can I help you?"

"Yes, sir. I'm just curious. What climb is that picture?" She pointed to the wall.

He didn't answer right away. A smile twitched on his mouth and he studied the photo. "That's Lynn Hill on the Nose of El Capitan." He pointed to the map under the plastic counter. "It's the first big thing you see when you come down into the Valley. You can't miss it."

She remembered staring out the window of Petra's car, mouth open in awe. At the way Petra had reverently said its name. *El Capitan.* She hadn't even realized people could climb something that huge. Half Dome was already in the mountains—it's base already high. It felt different—somehow more attainable. But El Capitan started in the Valley and rose clean and unhidden. It felt untouchable.

Petra's wide arms and excited shouting, *"This is your backyard"* rang in her ears.

Staring at the place the man pointed on the map, a surge of longing ran through her. She could do this. Or at least, she could try. And if she could stay busy climbing and doing schoolwork all summer, she'd be less likely to cross paths with Ranger Dick Face. She'd become a person Thea would be proud of, and make everyone at home regret the way they'd treated her. She'd become a person she wanted to be. She'd find a home . . . in California.

Rilla smiled. "Thank you kindly." Her mind whirred dizzily around a plan.

First, she'd need her own gear. She made a beeline for the back corner where the climbing gear hung on the wall, ticking off a mental list of what she'd seen in Petra's and Adeena's packs. *Harnesses. Ropes. The pieces of pro that had anchored them to the wall. Carabiners. Quickdraws. Webbing. Shoes.* She should start with a harness. Picking one a random, she looked at the price.

$156.99

Her fingers froze, and her throat tightened.

Slowly she let it drop, scanning the rest of the gear on the wall. A harness was incredibly important and probably cost more. One of the little doo-dads couldn't cost more than that.

She picked a piece of pro like she'd cleaned out of the wall the day before and looked at the tag, praying it wasn't as bad.

$64.95

Instantly, her brain tried to add up Petra's sling full of pieces, clinking together like the ring of a cash register. Plus the pile still in her pack.

Dropping the cam, Rilla turned and rushed for the door without looking at anything but her feet. Her burger was clutched, smashed, and cold in her hand. She'd forgotten about it. This had been a silly mistake. She should have known better. She threw it in the trash and walked as fast as she could. *Away.*

Trying to get to the woods before she burst into tears in front of someone, she reeled off the path toward the river. It was impossible not to notice Walker, in a fluorescent shirt, and a beautiful girl with long blond hair tucked under his arm. Like they were there just to drive the point home—there was an uncharted valley between her and the things she wanted. It wasn't really about climbing. Or about something as stupid as a boy she barely knew. It was that she'd, for one second, let go of what she'd left and reached for something ahead—and had her hand slapped in consequence.

With tears streaming down her face, she crossed into the dark shelter of the pines, feeling stupider the more she cried, and crying harder the stupider she felt.

fourteen

RILLA FOUND JONAH DRINKING WATER IN THE SHADE OUTSIDE THE SER-
vice entrance to the big cafeteria. His gaze swept over her—a bemused
smile flickering across his face as he leaned against the brown slats of the
building and looked at her. "You're looking more like Yosemite today."

"Lobsters are so California, I know." She tugged at her shorts, pretending to curtsey.

He smirked.

"You working right now?" she asked.

"I need to finish putting the trash in the dumpster." He gestured
with his middle finger to the pile of slick black trash bags. Flies circled
overhead.

The sound of clinking metal echoed in her head and she blurted out,
"Give me five bucks and I'll do it for you."

He laughed. "Five dollars? That's a little steep."

"A dollar a bag? That's five."

He took another drink of his water and seemed to think. "You're just
going to give it back to me for weed."

"I mean . . . I keep trying to stop." She crossed her arms. "Can I go running with you sometime? Is there, like, a secret formula for being good at
sports? I just want to get like . . . not as much as a lazy toad. I don't want to
run ultramarathons or even a marathon. Or even a half. Or quarter. Or—"

"All right. Fine. Take my money. Just stop talking." He rolled his eyes.
"You have a deal."

Rilla grinned. "Deal." Trying to avoid stepping in the puddles leaking from the garbage, she grabbed one off the top and lugged it over to the Dumpster. A trail oozed behind.

"What do you need five dollars for?" Jonah asked.

Rilla hauled a bag over her head, sore muscles screaming and her stomach rolling from the curdled smell. It fell over the edge of the Dumpster and dropped inside. She made a face at her sticky hands. "I don't know. I don't have a job."

"You could get a job here."

"Don't you have to be eighteen?" she asked, grabbing two bags this time.

"Oh. Right. Yeah. You're right."

"Are you here just to run?" she asked, before realizing it sounded sort of harsh. "I mean, what made you want to work in Yosemite?"

He shrugged, smoking. "I wanted to travel, but didn't have money just to travel. So, I'll work here. See what I can do next. I can run anywhere, but not everywhere is this beautiful."

The last bag didn't quite make it over and Rilla squealed and jumped out of the way. It plopped on the asphalt. Thankfully, intact.

"I think I made out on this deal," Jonah said.

She heaved the bag over in a second effort. This time it made it in. "I need to go wash my hands," she said.

"I'm going to go clock out. I'll meet you outside the bathroom." He kicked up and went inside.

Holding her hands far from her body, she trudged up the hill to the bathrooms and washed her hands, face, and arms until she couldn't smell trash on herself anymore.

Jonah waited outside with a fountain soda in his hand. "My treat." He handed it over and then dug in his pocket. "And your five dollars."

She smiled and stuffed it into the top of her sock. "Thanks."

"Want to see something?" he asked.

"Sure. As long as it doesn't involve a lot of hiking."

"Oh, were you hiking?" He snorted.

"Don't make fun of me," she said, sipping the icy root beer and following him toward the woods. "I was actually climbing and hiking. Sixteen miles."

He looked back, a mixture of impressed and genuine surprise on his face. "Priscilla Skidmore!"

Rilla couldn't help but glow. "See?" She grinned over the straw. "I'm not always a stoner."

"You did Half Dome?"

"Sure fucking did." She skipped ahead, gleefully forgetting all about her aching feet. Her blood sang sharp and bright and if only—*if only*—everyone in her life could look at her the way Jonah had in that split second.

"Wow. That's really incredible. You don't need my help to run. If you can walk sixteen miles, you can go for a jog."

"Well, it hurt a lot," Rilla admitted. "I kinda swore I would never do it again."

He laughed, leading her up a thin footpath. They wound through house-sized boulders that had sloughed off the cliff and crushed part of the camp, reclaiming tents and cabins to the crawl of the forest. It was quiet and cool. The sounds of the busy Valley fell away as if they were an hour into the wilderness. Her feet were sore, but the walking wasn't nearly as painful as when she first started that morning, even when they reached the bottom of the wall under Glacier Point, and Jonah started up the scree at the base.

Still, her breath was heavy by the time Jonah stopped on a wide ledge.

"Oh," she said with a smile, looking around her. They were level with the tops of the trees, and the deep blue sky was perfect and boundless.

All the tourists, cars, and signs of life had been swallowed by the trees. She couldn't even see the roads from this angle. There was nothing but the proud cliffs standing watch over the sweep of the Valley in each direction.

"Like the couch?" Jonah pulled a Baggies out of his shorts and began stuffing a bit of weed into the pipe on his lap, curled over to protect it from the wind.

"It's a nice spot." She sat beside him, pulling her legs up in the wallow of granite curved out of the wall. Resting her shoulders back, she stared at the stretch of the magnificent view.

At least Ranger Dick Face wouldn't catch her up here.

She took the pipe and lighter from Jonah, and held the smoke so long in her lungs Jonah made a joke about whether she was still alive. But when she exhaled, everything loosened and unwound in her spine, and she wiggled her toes as the wretched feelings of failure and frustration slipped off her skin like oil on water.

A solitary cloud sailed across the sky—it's shadow slowly sliding over the wall across the Valley. The granite swirled and arched, and her gaze lazily followed their lines in the sunshine. Thin shouts echoed from somewhere, whipped and distorted by the wind, and it was hard not to wonder where Adeena and Petra were today. Maybe they were climbing again, feeling relieved they didn't have to haul her around.

Hey-o. Give me some slack, the wind cried.

She checked her Instagram, heart dropping when she saw Curtis had replied to her DM. *Thanks for apologizing. I forgive you. How's California?*

"What's wrong with your face?" Jonah asked.

"Huh?" Then she felt the glower etched into her expression and shook her head, tucking the phone away. Her face burned with shame to think if Thea or Mom or anyone knew she'd messaged him in the first place. She didn't even love Curtis or anything, it was just—it was that *he* loved *her.*

Got it, the wind said.

She blinked. "Did you hear something?"

"No? You seem distracted. I mean. Even more than usual."

She frowned, scanning the cliff around them, beside them, below them. "I'm just . . . I thought I heard a friend. A climber friend."

"Climbers are all assholes."

"Really? All of them?" She raised an eyebrow.

He shrugged.

"Screw you. I want to be a climber," she admitted, hoping he wouldn't laugh.

"Well, you won't get a better chance than this," he said matter-of-factly, leaning against the rock.

"It's expensive," she argued.

"You seem like an enterprising young woman." He raised a meaningful eyebrow. "Who recently relieved me of five dollars."

She laughed, leaning forward on her hands. "It's dangerous."

"Would you like it if it wasn't?"

She snorted. "It's not something I'm good at."

"I guess that's why they call it learning to do something." He folded his arms against his chest. "It seems like you're trying to talk yourself out of even trying. Why do that? This is your chance to try something you seem interested in. You can't expect to wake up a good climber, when you haven't put in the work and effort toward becoming one."

She winced. He was talking about climbing, but somehow, she felt the truth of it in the deepest parts of herself. It was true. That was what she'd been expecting—to change the minute she determined she should. Terrified when she was not immediately the things she envisioned. Panicked she never would be. Maybe . . . *maybe,* it wasn't that she couldn't change, but that she was afraid to try all the things required to change. Maybe it was like he said, she kept expecting to change without putting any of the work and effort into changing.

He shook his head. "Your five fell out," he said, reaching down and putting the money back into her hand.

She looked at the crumpled bill and her buzzing thoughts narrowed down to something clear and sure. She could find a way to make money in the Valley. She could do her schoolwork and figure out how to climb. She could pack her own snacks and learn fast. She could prove to everyone, she was something. For the first time, the thought of the impossible was more excitement than dread. Fear, but with longing. The future unknown, but with potential that had not been there before.

It wasn't a question of if she could succeed. It wasn't a question at all. She could *try*.

Stuffing the five back into her sock, she took the lighter, relit the weed, and put her elbows on her knees. And as another cloud slid its shadow over the Valley, she let her thoughts do the same—let the sorrow and fear and hope skim the surface of her mind so that in five minutes when she was done, she could stand and go down into the Valley and begin.

"CLIMBING."

When people say, "It can't be done," or "You don't have what it takes," it makes the task all the more interesting.

—Lynn Hill, first person to free-climb
The Nose (5.13+) on El Capitan

fifteen

RILLA PUMPED HER LEGS AS FAST AS SHE COULD.

Heavy boots thumped behind her. "I know where you live," Ranger Miller—*Dick Face*—yelled.

Rilla risked a quick glance over her shoulder.

He was gone. The only things behind her were ogling tourists, clutching bags and children closer.

Shit. He'd caught up faster than she expected.

Rilla's side hurt and her lungs drew sharp, but she turned and doubled her speed. Her sneakers flapped on the asphalt, sending shocks up her bones as she hurtled through Half Dome Village. She hopped curbs. Pitched right. Left. Right again. Around tourists. Past Andrew, the pool boy, who paid her three dollars to clean out the filters of all the disgusting shit that accumulated from heavy use of the heated pool. He was laughing.

"Shut up, Andrew," she spared a precious breath to holler as she glanced at the road and made sure she wasn't going to get run over by a bus, a clueless European driving an RV through America, or any of the tourists rubbernecking out the windows. All clear.

Run. Run. Run.

She had to beat him.

The road behind her, she kicked up gravel and bounded into the meadow. The wooden planks of the meadow path beat a new rhythm against her feet. Ahead, a tall stand of dark pines clustered along the Merced. The gray granite Royal Arches rose high above them as a backdrop. The way it looked right here was almost as if she could hold out both hands and touch either side of the Valley. An illusion. All she needed was to get to Thea's before Ranger Miller got there. If she beat him, even by a hair, it would be fine.

Quick as a flash, she entered the trees, hopped off the planks, and kicked up pine needles and dirt behind her in tufts. The sharp cedar air seared into her lungs. Golden light filtered through the trees, enticing anyone who wandered through to slow down and breathe deep. But Rilla sped past.

She slowed for the rocks at the river's edge, and waded through a shallow part of the Merced, straining her thighs against the current of the water. Her foot slipped and she slowed nearly to a walk. She couldn't afford to fall—not in this frigid water, with deeper, darker currents farther down. God, it was hard to run through a river. This was a first in an escape route. She pressed on, and it became shallower, licking at her ankles, until she was just soggy sneakers on the bank. Up the other side, she redoubled her speed and crossed the road.

Someone honked.

Rilla kept running, her shoes squelching in the dirt.

Now running on the opposite side of the Valley, she turned and ran west, with Half Dome at her back. She knew the long impenetrable wall bordering her side of the Valley for all its names now. She knew them from paging through the guidebooks with Adeena and Petra, looking for easy climbs they could top-rope before the sun slid into night. Maybe one day, though, she might know the walls by touch.

Rilla wove around the Benzes and Caddys waiting for the valet at the four-star hotel sequestered behind a grove of oaks in a meadow under the cliffs. Almost home. Almost.

She drew sharp breaths through her nose. The sweat stung her eyes. Was that a siren? Her ears strained over her heartbeat.

Shit. It was.

She hurdled the bushes into Yosemite Village—past the little store, the firehouse, the jail she'd spent the night in—and flew through the mulch of the cultivated beds around the visitor center and administrative offices. There were more tourists here, near the waterfalls and most food options. She dodged a clustered Japanese family with a baby in a buckled carrier and construction workers pushing wheelbarrows, slipping back into the woods. Almost. Almost. She was going to throw up. No. She was going to make it. Tightening her fists, she pushed the last bit of energy she had into her feet.

Finally, the edge of her meadow.

Ranger Stafford stood outside, grilling in the front of the house with his twins in a kiddie pool. He shook his head as she passed, turning his back as if he didn't want to see. Leena and Lamont, his twins, stilled in the pool, waved and laughed.

Rilla would have laughed if she didn't have a stitch in her side and her heart about to explode out of her chest.

That was definitely a siren following her home.

Shiiiiit!

With all that she had left in her legs and lungs, she sprinted through the dry grass for the back of Thea's house and lunged for the rusted fire escape.

Her sweaty hands slipped on the rungs, but she made it to the back roof, and jumped for the window. She clutched the edge and let her legs do the work—sneakers pawing at the siding and pushing her up. Three weeks ago, when she first moved here, she couldn't have done this. Maybe escaped, but never have gotten back inside. She grunted and groaned, pulling herself over the edge and into the narrow window opening. She couldn't fade now.

The siren sounded like it turned into the meadow.

Shit.

She fell onto the floor in a greasy, sweaty, gasping heap.

Home. But she hadn't beaten him yet. Still on the floor, Rilla kicked her sneakers off. Ripped her shirt up. She crawled onto all fours. Closed her eyes. Her heart slammed against her ribs—*calm down, calm down, calm down.*

Her clothes rested where she'd laid them out and she leaned against the bed as she wrestled into them. Tanktop. Gym shorts slipped over sweating skin. New socks. The same things she'd worn to lunch with Thea and Lauren. Rilla yanked out her ponytail, and her face felt like it was on fire.

The siren stopped. He was here.

Come on. Come on. Her fingers trembled as she scooped ice out of the cooler under her cot. Rubbed it over her face. Neck. The bright red splotching on her thighs. Oh god, she had to stop breathing so fast. Her side cramped. She fought nausea. Grabbing perfume, she sprayed a cloud and wiggled-slashed-rolled through it as she plopped on the floor, opened her books, and tucked her hair behind her ears.

Made it.

Her heart beat so loud, she couldn't tell if it was in her ears making her head swim, or if it was the sound of Ranger Dick Face's knocking. She waited, ears straining.

"Rilla?" Thea shouted from below.

Rilla took a deep breath, willing her heart to steady. Calm. Calm. She'd been studying the last hour. These ridiculous problems in trigonometry. She rubbed the pencil across her fingers, the lead smudging her calluses. "Just a second." *Shit.* Her voice sounded ragged and just the reply had used all her air.

Slowly, she stood. Fighting the dizziness. Her face was hot, but not actively sweating like under her hair, thanks to the ice and her clean, cool tank top. She had this. Escaping in a small town was a thing she knew as well as she knew anything.

Carefully, she descended the ladder. Walked down the hall. A confused, slightly annoyed expression arranged on her face. "Yeah?" she asked Thea.

Ranger Dick Face stood sweating and red in the door.

She couldn't resist. "Why are you so sweaty?"

His face contorted with rage. "Come with me, you little monster."

sixteen

THEA LEANED BACK, GLARING IN THAT WAY RILLA FOUND ESPECIALLY
chilling when it was directed at her. "Excuse me?"

Dick Face blinked, a flash of panic crossing his eyes.

"What has she done?" Thea demanded.

Lauren sat up and leaned her elbows on the back of the couch, to
watch.

"She was selling . . ." He had to stop for air. "Water bottles. At the
bottom of." He put his hand up and braced himself against the door.
"Vernal." *Gasp.* "Falls."

"Do you need to sit down, Reid?" Lauren asked. "Or would you like
some water?"

He glared at them each in sequence, taking off his Stetson and waving it over his red face before gesturing to Rilla. "I got you. I saw you. I
know it was you. There's no way out of this one, Thea."

Rilla widened her eyes, then made them normal. She didn't do inno-
cence nearly as well as irritated injustice. She folded her arms. "What are
you talking about?"

"Don't lie to me," he seethed.

"Oh god, you're like a bad parody of yourself," Thea said, coming back
with a glass of water.

He took it. "I saw her. It's done. Over."

"I don't know who you saw, but I've been upstairs since lunch doing
trig."

"Bullshit," he said over the water glass.

Thea turned to Rilla, dead-eyed and irritated. "You been selling water bottles at the bottom of Nevada Falls?"

Rilla kept her face still. "Nope."

Thea's eyes got narrower. She knew.

Lauren snorted and turned back around. Rilla resisted glaring at her.

"I came home with her from lunch," Thea said. "And she went upstairs to do schoolwork. Reid, I haven't . . . seen her come through here at all."

"She obviously went out a window."

Rilla groaned. "Are you kidding me? What do I have to do here? Even if I'm studying, you're somehow figuring out a way to get me into trouble. *You're* why people hate cops."

Thea held up her hand. "Rilla, you're not helping."

Ranger Dick Face's face was red as a rooster. "You. Can't. Escape."

A shiver ran up Rilla's spine, like she had, for a moment, looked into the red, sweaty face of all her worst fears, but she tightened her arms around herself to hide it.

"Reid. Come on. You can't do it this way," Lauren said from the couch. "The fact is, you've got two rangers who say she's been in her room the last three hours. A girl who isn't sweating and breathing hard. A girl who says she wasn't there. And you."

Rilla wanted to hug her. But she just tried to look innocent.

Thea leaned against the door. "Yeah, are you saying she ran back here faster than you?"

"I drove partly," Dick Face said defensively.

"You're only proving the point."

"Well, there was traffic."

Lauren groaned. "Come on, man. We have one day off together, and you're killing it."

Ranger Dick Face shook his head, stubborn and snarling and disgusted.

Rilla knew she'd won. "Can I get back to my homework?" she asked. "I'm almost done with this stupid unit."

"Aha!" he exclaimed, pointing his finger at her. "Mistake. You never want to get back to schoolwork."

Rilla glared at her sister. Could Thea just stop talking about Rilla at work?

"Yeah, get upstairs," Thea said before swatting at Dick Face's finger. "Reid, knock it off."

Rilla turned for the hall and her face split with glee.

Nailed it.

She climbed the ladder and crawled across the floor, over the incomplete trigonometry and dirty clothes. Lying on her back on the cool wood planks, she breathed deep of relief. Her left hand brushed the edges of Thea's, June's, Lauren 's, and Jessica's storage boxes. Her right hand was under her cot. But she was exultant. She'd done it.

Pulling the wad of money out of her sweaty sports bra, she peeled apart the damp fives and ones. Fifty-two dollars.

It had been warmer the last week, almost hot at midday, and Rilla had carted a big bag of ice-cold water and soda bottles a mile up the trail toward Half Dome. The vending machine in the outhouses had broken, and based on the crowds in the Valley, she had hoped the water fountain wouldn't be much of a competition. It wasn't. She'd sold out within forty minutes. It helped that it was a Saturday and there were crowds everywhere, even for the water fountain. Two bucks a pop to sweaty, tired tourists and she was looking at a gross pile of sweaty money. A perfectly acceptable amount to go toward another piece of gear.

The ladder creaked.

Quickly, Rilla stuffed the money under her cot, inside the sheet. She'd go to the outdoor store as soon as Thea was finished with her and Ranger Dick Face ended his shift at 4 P.M.

"Well, you're grounded," Thea announced, ducking under the eaves.

Like Thea could enforce a grounding. "Can you even stand up in here?" Rilla asked.

Thea had the decency to look embarrassed. "So, that's why you needed those drinks at Walmart last week."

"I have no idea what Dick Face—"

"Don't call him that," Thea snapped.

Rilla rolled her eyes. "I don't know what *Ranger Miller* is talking about. I've been doing math." Rilla gestured at the open homework. One of her notebooks was folded back weird from when she'd crawled over it.

"And all that thumping five seconds before Reid knocked?"

"One of my legs had fallen asleep."

Thea sighed and pinched the bridge of her nose. "What on earth do you need money for?"

Rilla frowned, her throat automatically tightening. She was currently, technically a high school dropout . . . rock climbing would be the last thing Thea would think she'd care about. If Thea knew Rilla was taking these risks to earn money for gear, she'd probably forbid the whole thing. And always, the fear that Thea would send her home to West Virginia shimmered behind their words. If Thea didn't want her and Mom didn't want her in West Virginia . . .

"I outgrew my clothes," Rilla said. It was true. "I don't have anything for summer that fits." She'd been climbing every afternoon for two weeks with Adeena and Petra in the short slabs near the Valley floor, running with Jonah in the evening, and eating her fill for all three meals. She felt stronger, lighter, but nothing she brought out west fit—it was all too small.

Thea's face contorted. "Why didn't you just ask?"

Rilla blinked, not expecting the emotion on her sister's face. "I, um . . ."

"Honey, we can get you some clothes." Thea sank onto the cot, tucking her hands in between her legs.

Rilla shifted nervously. "But, I'm already eating . . . and living here."

"Rilla! It's . . ." Thea took a deep breath. "It's not a big deal. Next time we go into town. Can you make it until then?"

She nodded, feeling guilty. It was hard to ask for more when Thea had already given her so much.

"How's homework going?"

The guilt deepened. "Good."

"You don't want to be held back."

"No shit," Rilla muttered to her knees.

"You're smart." Thea smoothed the covers of Rilla's bed and shook her head. "Stay outta Ranger Miller's way. He *is* a dick. And he will eventually get you."

"I hear you."

"Mm-hm." Thea eyed her. "I'm worried about you."

"Don't be," Rilla said. "I'm doing good."

"You look better than when I got you, that's for sure. I know it sucks to not fit your clothes, but you have more color and you look less exhausted."

Rilla shrugged. A tan and some sleep *not on a bus* would do that.

Thea looked at her like she was waiting for Rilla to say something. Again.

But Rilla didn't have anything to say. "Sure."

"All right . . ." Thea sighed, and went back downstairs.

Rilla heaved a relieved sigh, before rolling over to her elbows and trying to do trigonometry. Her phone sat on the floor, just under the bed. Dark and quiet. No one knew her number, but no one from West Virginia had asked. The stab when she remembered wasn't the same sharp desperation she felt at first. Now, it was more a deep, raw ache. Like something healed over on the surface, but festering somehow below.

She copied one problem into her notebook, before getting irritated at the soft, blunt, unsharpened pencil. If she was going downstairs, she might as well sharpen all her pencils, so she wouldn't be interrupted next time she started her schoolwork.

It took twenty minutes to find all the pencils she'd brought. She'd forgotten she put them in with her toiletries. It had made sense when she packed, she was sure.

Downstairs, there was an old-fashioned pencil sharpener screwed to the side of the kitchen cupboards. Rilla dropped her handful of pencils onto the counter, and shoved the first one into the machine.

Whirr. Whirr. It sang a rusty song that reverberated in her teeth.

She pulled it out. It had barely sharpened.

Shoving it back in harder, Rilla sighed and resigned herself to the task. Only a little bit more and she could maybe squeeze in a climb before she had to babysit for Ranger Stafford and his wife's twins, across the meadow, that night. The fifty-two dollars burned a hole in her pocket. From experience, she needed to spend it quick, or she'd end up spending it wrong; but fifty-two wasn't quite enough for the shoes she needed. Everything else, she could borrow a little longer. With shoes, she could climb the many massive boulders, for practice, without needing other gear.

The pencil suddenly snapped.

She pulled it out. It'd over sharpened and snapped off inside the pencil sharpener. Shit. She eyed the hole. Now she had to fix the sharpener before she could finish sharpening anything. "Thea, where's a screwdriver?"

Thea answered from where she was cuddled on the couch with Lauren watching a movie. "The drawer at the end."

Rilla went all the way down at the end of the counter and wrenched the old drawer on its sticky tracks. It was stuffed full of papers, scissors, knives, mail, paper clips, nail clippers, magazines, and candy wrappers.

How was anyone supposed to find anything in this drawer? She pawed at the top and then yanked the drawer all the way out. Clearing a space on the counter with her arm, she dumped it over with a crash.

"What are you doing?" Thea asked from the couch.

"Finding the screwdriver," Rilla said. She pulled the garbage can over to dump the used wrappers and weird trash. Carefully, she stacked all the papers to the one side, stopping only to read the most interesting. *Ah! The screwdriver.* She set it to the side carefully, where she would find it again, and went back to sorting out the trash. The garbage can was so full, the last bit of wrappers fell off the top. She had to take it out. Rilla shifted to the can, tied the bag in a knot, and yanked it toward the door. Outside, she hauled it around the house to dump it in one of the locked bear cans for trash collection.

"Hey there," Walker said, in a tone so bright and friendly, she nearly jumped out of her skin.

seventeen

OH, GLORY BE. WALKER WAS SHIRTLESS. AGAIN.

Call it Yosemite magic, call it her own mind-clouding hormones, but it didn't even feel douchey—and it should have. A soaking wet, navy bandana was tied around his head, grimy hair curling off his neck. The clothing he did wear—dirty canvas pants and pack with rope, empty water bottles, and a bouncing helmet—made him look sort of homeless. Rilla kept her chin lifted, so she wouldn't accidentally start counting his muscles and begin to drool. "Uh . . . Hello," she said. Honestly, she'd expected him to ignore her. "You heading out?" she asked, thinking he might be heading to a climb.

"Coming home. I am supposed to be on a wall, but we had to bail. There's a big storm coming and we were going slower than I thought."

"Really?" She eyed the expansive blue sky and frowned. It'd been sunny nearly every day she'd been here. She'd almost forgotten about rain.

"I gotta drop this off, and then I'm going to get some hot food. I'm starved."

"Cool." She turned around and threw the garbage bag into the bin. He was still standing there when she dropped the lid. He looked at her expectantly. The silence an awkward beat.

Was he inviting her along?

She took a tentative step that let her follow or bail, depending on his face.

"You hungry?" he asked.

"Starving. What were you guys climbing?" She fell into step beside him, blood singing so hard it made her fingertips tingle.

"We were on Tangerine Trip. It's usually pretty easy. A little wet. With a storm coming . . ." He shook his head. "We bailed."

"Pretty easy, and a little wet?" She snorted. "I mean, that's what *they all* say about me."

Walker busted out in a laugh so booming, her face instantly flushed. Her comment had been more nervous tic than funny. The old Rilla coming out. But if he was laughing, she was going with it. Especially with the way his skin tightened over his stomach muscles.

"Oh is *that* what they call you?" he asked.

"Tangerine Trip is a little long for a nickname when my given is so short. They call me TT for short."

He laughed.

Her brain wasn't even working. "You're laughing too much," she said, hitting his arm. Because *oh my god*. If she couldn't lick his arm from elbow to shoulder, she might as well take her chance to touch it. "I didn't know you had a sense of humor."

He gave her this look like *of course* he had a sense of humor.

She rolled her eyes. *Okay.* She swallowed and steadied herself. Pulled it together. She felt weirdly drunk.

"You climbing today?" he asked.

"Yep. I'm meeting Petra and Adeena later." She flexed her fingers, feeling the ache in the tendons. "We've been working our way through the slabs."

"They got you leading yet?"

Rilla shook her head. "Not really. Petra's shown me how to place gear, but I haven't led anything."

"I'll teach you to lead," he said, just shyly enough to make her pulse skyrocket. "If you'll ever go climbing with me again."

"That's a hard *no*," she said quickly—though it wasn't because it was a *no*, but because somehow the *no* gave her power, and she couldn't resist holding on to it for as long as possible.

"Are you going to make me grovel?"

She shrugged. "Why do you care?"

"I need to redeem myself! The last thing I wanted to do was make you hate climbing."

She rolled her eyes. "Don't give yourself too much credit there."

"So, you'll go climbing with me again?"

She gave him a smile out of the corner of her mouth.

"I didn't hear an answer," he said, eyes falling to her mouth.

"No," she said casually, looking away as if it didn't really matter. They crossed through the parking lot, and into Camp 4.

It was mid-afternoon and as quiet as Rilla had ever seen it. It was still full somehow—people clumped around their picnic tables and unlit fires. Eating or reading. Talking.

Rilla walked side by side with Walker through the camp. As they passed, people glanced up from what they were doing. Some looked at Walker with recognition. Some watched them like they were trying to figure out what was happening. A surge of warmth hit Rilla's chest—a thrill—walking beside him like she was part of this. Like they were the gods of this sunshine and granite world. She might be faking it just then, but she was determined to become part of this. This was how she wanted to be looked at, always.

"So, you're enjoying climbing with Petra?" he asked, loping up the gentle, rocky slope to the cluster of canvas tents, pulled away from Camp 4, under the shade of incense cedars.

"Yeah, she's been great. I know you don't like her, but . . ."

"I like her," he said defensively. "Clearly she's better than me at teaching."

He dumped off his pack into the canvas tent. The breeze shifted and a heavy wall of the smell of his sweat hit her full in the face.

He must have smelled it too, because he touched his chest. "Sorry."

"You're fine." She swallowed and tried not to breathe deeply.

"I need a shower."

"I assume it's in your plans."

"Do you think a clean shirt would help?" He frowned and looked away thoughtfully. "On second thought, I'm not sure I have a clean shirt . . ."

Was he asking just for her? She couldn't tell. It made her nervous. He made her nervous. Even when he smelled disgusting. "If you meet anyone you want to smell nice for, tell them you just came back from your assault on El Cap. It's an aphrodisiac."

"Well, duh. I crushed it *and* rescued a kitten. While baring my biceps." He flexed, and she wasn't sure if she was going to die from the smell, or the aesthetic.

"Well, you've been warned. Don't get downwind."

She shifted and pretended to inhale, clutching her throat and tipping back as if she'd died.

"Very funny. I'm getting a shirt."

He disappeared into the canvas tent, leaving her awkwardly standing by herself at the picnic table outside. The wind felt cool on her arms, as the sun disappeared behind clouds. She shivered and looked around.

Standing in the middle of the SAR site tents pulled away from Camp 4, where only the search and rescue climbers lived, felt like standing in the middle of someone's house. Everything was lived out in the open. Like HUFF. But the tents here, like the one Walker had disappeared into, were lived in and ragged on the edges in a way the ones at HUFF were not. Faded tarps were strung up over the roofs—leading one to presume they leaked—and tied to the cedars or tall wooden stakes to make overhanging porches. Under the tarps were all manner of earthly possessions, similar to Thea's overstuffed cabin and closet and the house in the Grove. Bikes leaned against the trees. Milk crates were stacked as shelves. Worn chairs waited for missing occupants. A fire smoked between two of the canvas tents, its coals all banked. A box of cereal sat out on the picnic table under one of the tarp porches. It looked like someone's leg hung off a cot through a ripped screen door, but she couldn't be sure.

Walker came back out in a wrinkled white undershirt smudged with dirt at the hem. He winced, running his hand down his flat stomach. "Okay, let's go."

He pulled a bike from the side of the tent and got on. "Lady's choice." He grinned and looked back and forth between the back axle and the handlebars in front.

Laughing, she hopped lightly onto the back of the bike and gripped his shoulders.

He kicked off and her teeth chattered as they rode down the rocky hill and back onto the footpath of Camp 4. Thank god he couldn't see her face. All that white T-shirt against tanned skin and dark blond hair curling on his neck . . . ugh, how could he be this disgusting *and* disgustingly hot? They were going to eat. Were they on a date? Her stomach flipped and she couldn't help the grin that threatened to split her face in half.

He abruptly turned.

She yelped and clutched at his neck.

"You're choking me." His hand pulled at her fingers and she loosened them, cheeks hot and heart all aflutter.

They rolled into Yosemite Village, parked the bike, and headed into the grill.

"I'm starved," he declared, tipping his head to the menu and lacing his fingers behind his head, arms up, before he caught sight of Rilla's face and lowered his arms with a sheepish face. "Sorry."

"Seriously, man. You could kill everyone in here."

His cheeks flushed; but before she could decide if he was actually blushing, he stepped to the counter to order.

Trent lazily leaned on the counter. "How's it hanging, Skidmore?" He asked while Walker signed the clipboard.

"Good." Rilla muttered, avoiding eye contact. Trent was in his mid-forties and one of the long-time employees that seemed like he was there because his main passions in life included collecting dolls and being a serial killer, and this was how he funded his needs for tarp, rope, and mint condition dolls.

She ordered, signed the clipboard with Thea's initials, and joined Walker at the table, where he leaned on folded arms, watching passersby.

Rilla pulled her leg up on the chair and leaned back. "How's the rescue business?"

He smiled. "Good. Not too busy yet. How's Ranger Miller?"

She groaned. "Oh no."

"Oh yes. I thought that was you streaking past. I knew for sure when I saw him running after you."

Rilla wanted to put her face in her hands and hide from embarrassment, but she just poked at the salt shaker. "Well, it's an unorthodox exercise program for him, I must admit. But it seems to be working."

Walker laughed, lacing his fingers over his stomach.

"Are you originally from Colorado?" That's where he'd gotten on her bus. Her fingers had smelled like beef jerky and her hair a little bit like the joint she'd smoked outside a gas station in Salina, Kansas.

Then, he was just a boy. Who came down the center aisle with the slanted evening light casting long streams across his chest and face. His eyes had roved over the bus, looking for an empty seat—their true color distorted into an intense purple in the deep gold sunlight tipping over the edges of the still snow-covered Rockies.

He shook his head, *no*. Then said, "Yes."

She gave him a confused look.

He stretched his fingers, still looking at people around them. "I'm from southern Ohio, but I've been living in Colorado since I left home at seventeen. With summers here."

She tried to control the eagerness in her voice. "Did you move out at the same time as Caroline?"

He nodded. "She's only a year older than me. We moved to Colorado together." He paused a moment, then glanced at her. "You're seventeen?"

She nodded, dropping her gaze. "I'll be eighteen at the end of June." It felt weird to say it so specifically. As if he knew she was thinking about them together. That thought only made her brain immediately conjure up a question about what he looked like naked, and then she was blushing. "What brought you to Yosemite?" she asked quickly to cover her embarrassment, even though it was an overly stiff and formal question.

He laughed. "Are you kidding? Other than the climbing, perfect weather, and great people?"

"Yeah." She nodded, still trying to control her blush.

"I bet your friends back home are jealous," he said.

She shrugged. "Sure."

He narrowed his eyes. "You and Thea have the same mom, right?"

She nodded, hesitant at this new vein of conversation.

"You two are pretty different."

She shrugged. "Thea's dad is Mexican."

"Oh. That's not what I meant," he said hastily. "Thea's talked about your dads."

"What do you like to draw?" she blurted out before she could think how to say it better.

It was his turn to flush, and he shrugged. "Copying route maps helps me remember them better. That's all."

It wasn't all—that drawing of people that she'd stumbled across wasn't a route map. She frowned and raised her eyebrow. "Bullshit."

He snorted. "Like you're not. Full of bullshit, I mean."

"I've been very forthcoming."

He rolled his eyes. "I think it's safe to say we both have things we don't like talking about."

She stuck her tongue at him.

He leaned forward and laughed.

The silence was awkward. She rubbed her ear.

Walker stayed maddeningly quiet as he stared at her with this grin half-cocked.

"What?"

"You don't like safety," he said, that shit-eating grin still plastered on his face.

She primly picked up her burger. "And you're full of crap if you're trying to convince me you're safe."

"I'm not safe?"

Her gaze flicked to his. That pulse of intensity in his blue eyes.

His eyes, which tightened at the corners.

She wanted him. Badly. It'd been easy in West Virginia—to avoid this. This real thing she couldn't help but feel when looking at him. No one had been the things Walker was. A boy from places she knew the shape of, who'd made his mark in a world still foreign to her. Maybe that's why he had that shell around himself always. Maybe it's what made him full of it. She bit her lip and tried to come up with words to talk to the boy from Ohio. But she didn't want to talk about who she'd been in West Virginia either; and instinctively she knew that to get intimacy, she'd have to exchange it.

That wasn't what she wanted. Not right now. He was right.

She was afraid.

eighteen

IT WAS OBVIOUS THAT THEY'D ALREADY BEEN CLIMBING. PETRA AND
Adeena stood by the ranger station of Camp 4, where they'd told Rilla
they'd meet her. Their pants were smudged with chalk and dust, and
their hair windswept. It wasn't that Rilla expected to be invited on the
long routes that far surpassed her skill level—but she hated that she
wasn't. It made her feel every inch of her space on the fringe of the group.
If they were the gods of Yosemite, she was yet mortal, craning her neck
up to look high into the golden sunshine, at places she couldn't touch.

Literally.

Walker stopped the bike, and Rilla lightly hopped down. Maybe it
was the way Adeena's and Petra's eyes went wide, watching her hand
slide down Walker's arm. Maybe it was just that she had enough experience climbing to be able to want something more than just tagging
along. Whatever it was, a sudden determination flooded her veins—she
could *do* something worthy of the gods. She was ready. She wanted it.
This evening's climb was the perfect chance to show them.

"Where you guys heading?" Walker asked.

"To the Camp 4 walls for some Yosemite educating," Adeena said.
"Our girl here is doing pretty good."

"Doggie Diversions?" Walker asked.

Rilla assumed it was the name of the climb Dee and Petra had selected.

Petra nodded, shaking out her braid. "You want to come? This teaching a gumby thing is good for my technique. It's giving me an edge."

Gumby. Rilla didn't want to be a gumby anymore. She wanted to belong.

"You can keep your edge," Walker said, with an eye roll. "I've got a meeting. The weather report is in and we're gonna get nailed. If you see anyone heading out, tell them to stay put. I don't want anyone stuck on the wall."

"Hopefully everyone looked it up," Adeena said. "But we'll tell anyone we see."

"Thanks." Walker kicked off the bike. "See ya," he called over his shoulder as he pedaled away.

Both girls immediately snapped to Rilla.

Adeena raised her eyebrows. "Um, do you have things to tell us?"

Rilla grinned the cheesy grin she'd been trying to keep inside since she'd taken out the trash. "*I know!*" she squealed. "It wasn't like that, though. Just friendly. Nothing remotely illicit. God, I want to be very illicit with Walker."

Petra adjusted her backpack and laughed.

"He's too average-white-boy for my taste. I like that Lahore business-man look," Adeena said with guttural vowels and her walk shifted into something like a mockery of masculinity.

Rilla laughed at the obvious joke without having a clear picture of what the joke even meant. It made her realize, somewhere deep down, that Adeena had a life before this no one knew the rhythm of and jokes no one understood.

"Blasphemy. He's *classic* white boy," Petra said. "And what are you even talking about, Dee? You love the All Nighters. *James.*"

Rilla snorted. James? The so-pretty-it-hurt one from the famous British boyband the All Nighters?

"Stop weaponizing my love for James," Adeena said. "He's perfect. I shall not hear anything to the contrary."

"I mean yes. You could say Walker's a little boring," Rilla conceded.

"Walker or James?" Petra asked.

Adeena glared.

"Walker," Rilla said. "Except he's not. So…" She trailed off dreamy-eyed.

"You just can't see anyone other than Hico," Rilla said, elbowing Adeena. "And James."

Adeena laughed. "We're friends. Me and Hico. Obviously, me and James are soon to be married."

"Mm-hm. Hico asked me out like a year ago," Petra said. "But I don't date climbers."

There was an awkward beat in the conversation and Rilla didn't dare look at Adeena. Petra was competitive on every level—even in silly conversation, she often threw those kinds of things out. It was just how she was. It never seemed like she was trying to be mean, just that she always needed a game to win, a race to beat, or a war to fight. Everyone seemed to ignore it, so Rilla followed suit.

Adeena shrugged. "Well, *no one* is dating Hico. And anyway, how can you eliminate a whole group of boys like that? No climbers?"

Petra mimicked the sound Gollum made in *The Lord of the Rings*.

Adeena busted out laughing. "Okay. Okay. Some of them are kind of Gollum-y," Adeena said. "You don't know this, Rilla, because all you're thinking of is Walker. Who is not that. Neither is Hico," she said. "Imagine this short—they're always short—"

"Always," Petra laughed.

"With long arms, and a bit bent . . . kinda . . ." Adeena stooped a little, widening her shoulders in an imitation.

They laughed.

"Yep, so sexy." Petra laughed and Adeena straightened and caught up.

"There's that, and then there's the guys who do better at organizing their gear than doing . . . anything . . . else."

"And the bros," Petra added.

Rilla made a face.

"I still contend you're painting with a very broad, United States–specific brush," Adeena said.

"The point is. I'm attracted to independently wealthy men who like the idea of adventure more than the execution," Petra said. "And consider funding my worldwide climbing trips part of that adventure. I need to be the star."

Adeena rolled her eyes. "Okay, while we watch for independently wealthy fantasy men, I want to hear every detail of this Walker thing."

The three girls fell in step together, and Rilla divulged the details of her *not-date, definitely friends, but like maybe-date* with Walker as they hiked the short path past Camp 4, past the SAR site under the stirring cedars, to the rocky base at the bottom of the cliff. No clouds encroached on the sky, but the late afternoon sun carried an increasingly angry tinge of red.

Adeena clambered up the climb quickly, placing cams and nuts along the way for protection, while Rilla watched carefully from the bottom. This was her chance. She was rested. Strong. She was ready to show them she could go higher and longer. That she could be trusted as a team member. She cracked her knuckles nervously and watched Adeena.

"You nervous?" Petra asked.

"No. I'm excited," Rilla said, ignoring the quivers deep in her stomach.

"Good. You've come a long way since that first climb with Walker."

"Thanks to you and Dee," Rilla said.

"It's part of the fun." Petra fed out rope. "Bringing new people climbing. You're doing great."

"Can I clean the route?" She would climb as if she was leading—instead of putting the protection, she'd take it out. If she did it without making a mistake, it would show them she was ready to lead.

"You sure?" Petra asked.

Rilla nodded.

"Sounds good," Petra said. "Leave it!" she shouted to Adeena, who had just reached the top. "Rilla is gonna clean it."

Rilla grabbed the guidebook, worried about the description of *tricky*. They were only doing the first pitch, because Petra had been worried about the time. The description of the climb made it sound like a thing she would encounter over and over again all over Yosemite. Rilla frowned and looked up at the wall. "Who's Joe Faint and Yuu-von Chow   . . . I don't know how you pronounce this name."

"Who?" Petra looked up.

Rilla held up the book. "Here."

"Oh. Yvon Chouinard." She pronounced it with a buttery accent and it sounded like *Ee-bon Shwee-nahh.* Stretching a length of rope, Petra looked back to Adeena. "A Valley dirtbag, like me and you." She looped another stretch. "And the founder of Black Diamond and Patagonia. Like, the fleece pullovers all the preppy girls like? His company." Petra pointed to Rilla's side and nodded. "Your carabiners. Look."

Rilla looked down at the sleek carabiner she'd borrowed from Petra. Her thumb moved over the inscription. *Black Diamond.*

"Joe Faint?" Rilla asked.

"His partner on this route. Their names are in there because they put up the route, and climbed it first—that's called a first ascent. In climbing, the belayer for a first ascent is just as important as a climber. Anyway, Joe did an amazing rescue of some injured climbers before there was any search and rescue in the park, actually." Petra picked at some tape on her fingers and looked up. "Pretty awesome to think we get to have the same experiences as the greats."

Rilla looked at the climb again—the polished opening between granite blocks that dropped back into darkness and tunneled toward the sky.

In the same places the gods first ascended, so could she. Her stomach fluttered with nervousness.

The bushes rustled, and Hico and Caroline pushed out of the scrubby trees.

Rilla's stomach dropped. Now she *was* nervous.

"I'm dead," Caroline declared, looking exactly like her Instagram, but in two sloppy braids, a pair of army surplus pants, and a big hoodie. "Carry me to the car."

Hico dropped to the ground, using his pack as a pillow and crossing his feet—cheeks flushed dark with the sun. His socks today had Chewbacca up to his knees. His eyes drifted to Adeena.

"What'd you guys end up doing?" Petra asked.

"Supernatural?" Caroline glanced to Hico. "Right?"

"Yeah."

"What's the grade?" Petra asked, eyes still up on Adeena.

Rilla glanced at the book. The Yosemite Decimal System—grade or rating—was a system for rating the difficulty of climbs. The climb Rilla was about to get on was rated 5.7. The hardest climbs in the world were 5.15. But in between, after 5.10, it got broken down in a, b, c, d to rate the increasing degree of difficulty in between number grades. She had made a list, in her math notebook, of all the climbs under 5.10 in the Valley that appeared in the guidebook.

"I don't remember," Caroline said. "It's got a tricky arête I sucked at. Ugh."

"5.11d," Hico mumbled. "I think."

"You didn't know, huh?" Petra said, skeptical eyebrow raised at Caroline. There was an undercurrent Rilla could feel. Over the last two weeks, she got a sense that Caroline and Petra were in some kind of rivalry—a different one from the friendly competition Adeena and Petra had running.

Caroline laughed. "I honestly didn't. But that's fun. Oh well . . . we all have to suck some days." She sighed and looked up at Adeena, coming down the wall. "Oh, I love this one. Can I go next?"

For Caroline, a 5.11d was sucking? Rilla inwardly groaned.

"We were setting it up for Rilla. We're running out of light soon."

"You can jump in," Rilla said quickly. "I'm sure we'll have enough time." And if she was lucky, they'd run out of time and she wouldn't have to climb in front of Caroline.

"Pull the rope at the bottom, Dee," Caroline said, slapping her hands together. "Mama's ending the day on a good note."

Hico moved his pillow over by Rilla's legs. "Have you seen Caroline climb yet?" he asked Rilla as Caroline put her harness on.

Rilla shook her head.

"We're all good, but Caroline is great. She's trying to free-climb The Nose."

"Don't jinx me, man," Caroline said. "I hear you telling people." She glanced up. "Wait, are you anchored at the top of the first pitch?"

"Yeah. It's getting dark. We were just out to do this real quick for Rilla," Petra said.

"Wait, free-climb The Nose? Like without ropes?" Rilla was surprised, Caroline didn't seem like the kind of person to climb without anything to protect her from falling. Not *at all.*

"No," Hico said as Caroline started climbing. "Climbing without any protection is called free soloing. Free-climbing is when you use gear and protection, but climb it all straightforward, with hands and feet, not falling, or grabbing gear, or using aid climbing. Only five people have free-climbed The Nose. It would be a big deal."

"I'm going to do it this summer too," Petra said. "Well, in the fall when it cools off a little."

Hico looked toward Petra with a dubious frown. "You're going to free-climb The Nose?"

"Yeah," Petra said, looking up as Caroline climbed.

Hico snorted softly. "Go for it."

"I'll belay for you," Rilla said.

No one acknowledged she'd said anything. A red flush of embarrassment crawled up her neck, and Rilla felt like she must have sounded desperate.

"Look sharp, you're missing Caroline," Hico said.

Rilla turned and rested her chin on her shoulder, looking up at the wall. Caroline was already mostly finished with the first part and pulling through the upper crack. After a few minutes, it was clear what Hico had been worried she'd miss. Seeing her in all those places on her Instagram was one thing. Seeing why she'd been sent all over the world to climb, was another. Caroline moved like nothing Rilla had really seen. Fluid and effortless. Like a ballerina. Grace and raw power on sharp granite in a heady wind. Suddenly, Rilla realized Caroline was a better climber than Petra. A better climber than all of them.

For a second, Rilla had felt like being this person was attainable. Now, she saw it was farther away than she thought. She'd only needed to get this far to see how much distance there truly was between herself and all she wanted to become. The more she got of what she wanted, the more she knew to want.

Rilla picked up the book and reread the description. Chimney. Then another crack. She squeezed her hands into fists, remembering how she was to put her hand inside the crack, make a fist, and move it around until her hand was locked—stuck—into the crack in the same kind of way the gear they placed worked. Her fist—or fingers, arms, whatever fit— kept her body on the wall, while her feet moved her up. She shook out her hand and looked at the sky—at the Valley bathed in crimson and the creep of darkness. She had this. But a nervousness grew in her stomach like the cloud cover. Damn Caroline.

"Time for some old fashioned shimmying," Hico said when Petra called her over. "Good luck."

"Thanks for letting me jump in," Caroline said, handing over the rope. Rilla gave a nervous smile and tied in.

"Did Caleb and them head out today?" Adeena asked Caroline.

"Yeah. Why?"

"Did they check the weather?" Adeena asked.

"I think they're planning to bunker down. It didn't look that bad when they checked last night."

"I just saw Walker, and he . . ."

Rilla turned her back, tuning out the conversation and tying her knot with trembling fingers. She couldn't care about anything else right now. Nothing except proving herself in front of everyone.

The first pitch of the climb was only about fifty feet, but the wall kept going up beyond the anchors. She stepped inside the start of the chimney, her body gently hugged by the cool granite. She closed her eyes to steady herself, and she was back in Rainelle, gripping the edge of her desk, high, and bored, but not high enough to not feel the itch to move deep down in her bones and buzzing in her head and the clock ticking above the door. Savannah Hayworth smelled sickeningly of vanilla and when she turned to talk to Laurie, sitting behind Rilla, the curled ends of her hair swept across Rilla's desk, making her fingers crawl and itch.

The man who was responsible for the fleece pullovers Savannah wore every day climbed this for the first time. He stood in this exact spot.

She opened her eyes and exhaled, putting her palms to the granite. The ghosts here weren't like West Virginia; but there was something aware and alive all the same. She just didn't know yet if she'd fit into it.

Adeena and Petra talked about the weather. The coming rain. And if certain people in the house were going to make it back in time. Caroline was silent and watching. Rilla looked down, suddenly uncertain quite how to begin. Terrified to try and fail while they all watched.

"Running out of daylight," Hico said.

Rilla shoved her feet onto one side of the wall and pressed her back against the other. It got her off the ground. Awkwardly. She cleared her throat and began inching up the chimney. Keeping her back pressed tight. Her hands bracing herself to move her feet up, just as she'd been taught.

"All right, you're doing it," Petra said, keeping the rope taut as Rilla moved up.

Rilla paused in between movements, self-conscious as she looked down between her arms and legs. "Am I though? This does not feel pretty."

Adeena laughed—she'd stretched out on the ground beside Hico, head propped up on her bag. It made Rilla's heart squeeze in envy—envy for what? It made her feel sick to realize she wanted the relationship—the shared bond—with Walker, just as much as she wanted to hook up with him.

"Take your time and figure out a rhythm," Petra said.

"Bump and grind," Hico yelled. "Bump and grind."

"Let her just figure it out herself," Caroline said to them.

Petra probably rolled her eyes, but Rilla didn't look. She took a deep breath and went back to wiggling her way up the chimney. It got worse and worse. She was still wearing shorts and a tank top, and having to smash herself into the rock any way she could, meant wide swaths of her skin were getting shredded by the granite. Despite the cool temperature, there was no breeze in the chimney, and she was soon dripping sweat. Adeena had done this from the ground up, without the rope secured at the top, and with all the risk and responsibility of going first. Caroline had done it in a similar way—dropping the rope into the gear Adeena had placed. Rilla was the follower. No risk. No responsibility. This was easy. Especially for someone who wanted to show them she could climb like them. That she could learn to lead.

Wincing, Rilla stretched her arms and dug her fingers into a seam at the back of the chimney. In her head, it played out crystal clear—the slip of her foot and the sickening wrench of her fingers, still locked into the seam. Ugh. She pushed and tightened and every muscle snarled with tension. Slippery. Tenuous. The worst.

She was going to lose it.

She was going to fail.

Somehow, she pushed upward. Her cheek scraped the granite. Her feet felt uncertain. But she was doing it. A guttural wrench of air burst from her lungs and she managed to work her fingers out, give them a shake, and stick them back into the crack.

"Take a second. Try something different, if what you're doing isn't working. Look outside the crack, or whatever. There's no rule that says you have to get deep up in there," Petra called.

"Focus on a rhythm," Adeena said. "It just has to work for you."

Caroline was silent.

Probably standing there, watching with pity. Or maybe she'd left. Why would she stay to watch the *gumby* climb anyway?

Rilla swallowed against the sick feeling, gritted her teeth, and kept going. All she could think was that this was horrific, and horrible, and she was bleeding, and Caroline was still there—or she'd left—and Rilla didn't want to do it. *She didn't want to do it.*

But somehow, it got done. She managed to get the gear out of the wall and hooked on her harness, cleaning the route without dropping anything or falling. And in no time at all—but what felt like a century—she pulled even with the anchors.

"Got you," Petra yelled. "Tell me when you're off belay."

"K," Rilla yelled. She leaned back in the harness, feeling raked over and brutalized. Her body trembled. Bled. She'd done the best she could. It might be enough. She wiped at the sweat around her eyes and looked at the anchors.

Adeena and Petra had drilled the process of cleaning anchors into her head, and she'd done it a few times while climbing. It wasn't brand-new. But the consequences of messing up were so extreme, it was impossible to not feel a bit of nervousness tight in the back of her throat.

"Can you do the anchors now? We need to go find some people," Petra yelled. "Sorry."

Caroline said something Rilla couldn't hear.

"Yeah," Rilla yelled down. Swallowing, she shifted her hips closer to the anchors. Took a carabiner from her harness and clipped herself to the anchors. Took another carabiner and clipped it the opposite way. "Off belay," she yelled down.

Okay. She closed her eyes, trying to remember the steps. The blood pounded red in her eyes, and when she opened them the wall was bathed in the same red haze from the sunset. Every second that passed ticked loudly in her head, reminding her she needed to get down.

She started untying the rope from her harness. Deep breaths. People were waiting. She couldn't fuck up, or she'd fall and there'd be nothing to catch her. She'd untie, pull it through a bail biner—a cheap sturdy biner they could leave behind—and then retie and lower out. It was awkward though—the rope was slippery and heavy, and had it felt this awkward before? She gripped the end, trying to thread it through the biner. This didn't feel right. Shit. This didn't feel right. What . . .

And then the rope slipped.

Thwissssss, it sang. Straight from between her legs. To the ground.

Rilla froze. Hands open. Eyes wide.

That did not just happen.

Oh shit. Oh shit. Oh shit.

She'd dropped the fucking rope!

"Rilla?" Petra yelled.

"I dropped the rope!" Rilla screeched. "Oh my god. I dropped the rope."

Oh my god, I dropped the rope.

She closed her eyes. It was getting truly dark now. And here she was stuck on the wall. How could she screw that up? *What had—?* Her mind raced through the steps of cleaning the anchor.

Fuck.

She'd forgotten to pull up a long stretch of rope and tie it to her harness. That way, if she'd dropped the end, the rope would still be tied to her. Rilla swallowed, her throat so tight it ached. After all that effort, she'd gone and done the dumbest thing *ever.* Gumby indeed. All she wanted to do was get down and go home. But she was stuck.

"Hang tight, Rilla. We're sending someone up."

Rilla buried her face in her bleeding hands and groaned. This couldn't be more embarrassing if she'd sat down and tried to come up with a way to epically embarrass herself. She'd dropped the rope.

The wind blew and clouds gathered on the darkening sky. Chills ran up her arms. The sweat dried while she waited, trying not to think about what they were talking about below. Suddenly she remembered she was supposed to babysit. She was going to be late if she didn't get down quickly.

It couldn't get worse until it did.

Caroline appeared below. Climbing smoothly and quickly.

Of course they sent Caroline.

Rilla scooted over, giving Caroline space at the anchors. A second rope was tied to her harness. "Hey," Caroline said with a smile. "Lose something?"

Rilla blushed and looked at her feet. "Stupid, I know."

"It's fine. Shit happens." Caroline clipped herself into the anchors, threaded the second rope through the anchors, and tied Rilla in.

Rilla let her, feeling mortified and like a child who needed her mom to tie her shoes.

"She's on belay, Hico," Caroline yelled. "Double-check everything. You're tied in. Your rope is fed through the anchors." Caroline's finger ran from the knot to the anchors.

Rilla nodded, following.

"Now, unclip and he'll lower you. One at a time, just in case," Caroline shifted away.

Rilla pulled herself toward the wall, unclipping the draws she'd been using, so her weight sank into the rope.

"Tell him when you're ready to lower," Caroline said, tying a knot and clipping the rope to her harness in preparation to thread herself through the anchors and be lowered. The very action Rilla had missed.

"Lower, Hico," Rilla yelled.

In the twilight, she dropped. Hanging her head in shame.

nineteen

RILLA BURST INTO RANGER STAFFORD'S HOUSE TWENTY-FIVE MINUTES late, still bleeding from a hundred scrapes, and breathing hard. "Sorry I'm late." She gasped.

They were waiting on the couch. Ranger Stafford in his nice jeans and polo shirt. Mrs. Stafford, with her arms and legs crossed, side-eyeing her husband.

"Thea'll be right there if she needs her," he said.

"I promise. I'm responsible. I just got stuck on a climb..." She trailed off, realizing dropping a rope was not going to help reassure them she was responsible. "Long story." She leaned on the counter and gulped back her breath. "Where are the twins?"

"They're asleep. And hopefully, they'll stay that way." Mrs. Stafford unfolded her legs and stood. "Okay. I guess..." She looked over Rilla and frowned a little. "Thea's off tonight?"

Rilla didn't know.

"Yes," Ranger Stafford said. "Rilla will call right away if she needs anything."

Mrs. Stafford nodded. "Okay. We'll be back in a few hours. We were going to run to town, but I don't know if that's a good idea with this weather coming."

Ranger Stafford grabbed his ball cap. "I'm sure we'll be fine."

Mrs. Stafford sighed through her nose.

"We'll just head over to the Lodge for a drink tonight. Shouldn't be long."

"All right. Have fun!" Rilla held the door. "We'll be great." The wind gusted as Rilla shut the door, and she nearly lost her grip before getting it closed.

The sudden silence seemed deafening. She turned and looked around the house—it was exactly like Thea's, and also totally different. The same layout, carpet, and furniture. But interspersed with baby toys, half-folded laundry, and family photos. All that waited for her in this house with silent sleeping twins was the brutal, fresh memory of her shame.

Groaning, Rilla sank into the couch and covered her face with her arm. What had she done? She'd ruined everything. Walker probably knew by now, and he'd never want to talk to her again. How was she supposed to show her face in the Valley after tonight?

Her phone was in her pocket and she shifted, digging it out to text Thea she'd made it to the Staffords'. Trying to avoid replaying the whole evening over in her head, she flipped to Instagram and found herself scrolling through her feed.

It was a mistake. Salt in an open wound.

Prom.

She'd forgotten all about dropping the rope as she stared at photo after photo of her former friends—the only people she'd ever known, her whole life—spinning in tulle and sparkles, laughing and dancing together. She was supposed to be there. They were supposed to miss her. No one missed her.

Rilla laid her head on the arm of the couch and pulled her knees to her chest. She was cold and everything hurt and mostly it hurt in places she knew couldn't be cleaned and bandaged. She missed home. She missed being Rilla Skidmore, requisite bad girl. She even missed the stupid jokes about her *moves*, the kind of thing that came with your mom being an ex-stripper. At least in West Virginia she knew her place and everyone expected her to be a fuck-up. Unlike now, where she kept trying not to mess things up but did anyway. She dropped the rope, which was bad enough, but then *in front of everyone.* She was lucky someone had been there, like Caroline, who could climb up to get her. Otherwise, she'd have been stranded.

The wind howled at the roof and her tears overflowed. She pulled up her calls and dialed her mom, putting her phone to her ear.

The phone rang. Clicked.

"Hey Rilla," her mom said.

"Hi."

"What's going on?" her mom asked. "How is California?"

"Sunny." Rilla stared at the ceiling. "I want to come home."

"Is Thea giving you a hard time?"

"No. She's fine. I miss everyone." If she came back she couldn't help but feel like she could force them all to love her—even knowing that's not how it worked. "Everyone makes fun of West Virginia. I'm tired. I just want to come home and have everything be normal again."

"I know. I know it's hard to leave," Mom said.

"I didn't do anything. It was just a mistake. I'm done with Curtis," Rilla said. "I'll pay for the ticket home."

"Rilla." Mom sighed, long and heavy. "You can't come home. Maybe in August? You've only been out there a month. Give it some time."

She closed her eyes tight and tears rolled down her cheeks. The memory of the spring afternoon hit her chest. She hadn't told anyone, but that hadn't been their first fight. It was just a public one. It was good when it was good. To Rilla, it made sense the bad would be that bad. Everything had a price. "It wasn't like you think. I hit him first."

"Oh, Rilla. Don't talk about it. Put it behind you."

She didn't want her mom to say that. She didn't want to hear it was behind her, because it wasn't. It was why she was here. Why she was alone. It was why she sat raw and open and bleeding. "I just..."

"Roosevelt caught a squirrel the other day and brought it in the—" Mom began.

Rilla hung up and dropped the phone to the floor, rolling over and burying her face into the couch with her throat tight from strangled cries.

So, this was what it was to be alone.

She breathed into the cushions, trying to calm down. It'd been good with Curtis—it really had. And the whole fight had started because he'd wanted more from her. He cared for her.

She sat up and reached for her phone, pulse skyrocketing as she opened her Instagram DMs and sent one to Curtis. *Hope everyone had fun at prom*, she wrote, sending it before she could stop herself.

The reply came almost immediately. *I didn't go. Miss you.*

She froze, heart stuck in overdrive, pumping a mixture of terror and longing. She started to type a reply when something thumped on the porch. Rilla dropped the phone, wiping her eyes in case it was the Staffords back already.

It came again—a dull thumping and . . . snuffling? What was that? The wind? The Staffords?

She pushed off the couch and went to the door, cracking it open.

Under the dim porch light, a squarish black blob moved under the play water table, thumping it up and down.

Rilla peered closer. What was that? Someone's dog? It sniffed like it had a cold. Then suddenly she realized.

A bear.

She closed the door, locked it, and stared at the wall. Shit!

The thumping continued. Now with added scratching sounds. Could a bear break in?

She looked at her phone and closed out of Instagram, Curtis forgotten. Hurriedly, she dialed Thea, ears straining for sounds of the bear.

It was quiet. Then. A loud, wet sniff came at her feet, just under the door.

Rilla squealed and jumped away. *Shit, shit.*

"Hello?" Thea answered.

"There's a bear!" Rilla screeched. "What do I do?"

"What? Where are you?"

"The Staffords." A long scratching sound came from the door. Rilla back against the far wall. "It's at the door. Ah . . ."

"Calm down. I'll have someone come over and take care of it."

"What do I do?"

"Just stay in the house. It's probably scared by your squealing anyhow. It's fine."

Rilla buried her face in the couch cushions and moaned.

"Stop being so dramatic. I'm surprised this is the first bear you've seen here. They're the same as they are at home. Less wild though, which makes them more dangerous."

"Oh." Rilla sat up, panic eased. Black bears were common at home. It wasn't odd to see one loping across the road when driving in the morning.

"Yeah," Thea said. "You're fine."

The thumping continued on the far side of the porch.

"Rangers will be out shortly. Call back if you need me."

"Bye," Rilla said.

She hung up and looked at the phone. Instagram was in the background—her conversation with Curtis unfinished.

A flood of shame washed over her. She'd started it . . . again. After promising everyone she wouldn't. After promising herself. Maybe it was for the best she was here. No matter where she went, she couldn't seem to get beyond herself.

twenty

A DOOR SLAMMED DOWNSTAIRS, BOLTING HER AWAKE.

Shit. Rilla pushed back the covers strangling her, in panic. Curtis would be mad if she was late. Tumbling out of the cot, Rilla hit the floor with a thud. The pain cleared the sleep from her mind.

Oh right. California. Yosemite. She closed her eyes against her racing heart. She'd forgotten.

She slumped against the cot as it all came flooding back. The trip out here, the night she'd been busted, Walker, Petra, climbing . . . and now, no more climbing. But Mom said she could go home, all she had to do was make it to August.

If there was one thing she was good at, it was not being good at anything. Rilla groaned and crawled back into bed. The sheets rubbed against her skin, still raw from the climbing the day before. The light was weak—barely above dark—and drummed in her ears as if the waterfall had moved and now pounded on the roof.

Rain!

She'd forgotten about the impending rain. Comforting and drowning everything out. It was almost like she was home. She burrowed deeper under the covers, pretending she was home. She missed her dog, her bed, and her room. She missed not failing at things she wanted. Closing her eyes, she pictured Walker asleep, and herself tucked in his arm on his bare chest, her skin on his.

Another door slammed.

Someone yelled. Muffled and loud.

Heavy steps.

Rilla's eyes flew open to the rafters. Ugh.

Pitching back the covers, she pulled on her sweatshirt and went downstairs.

Thea looked up from tying her boots. A flicker of surprise crossed her face—almost like she'd forgotten about Rilla, in her attic. "We're evacuating the park," she said briskly.

Rilla froze. "Oh my god. What? Why?"

"Flooding."

The floodwaters in Rainelle rushed back to her. Depraved. The Monroes. Going to school and watching the river from the window of her biology classroom. "What?" she asked dumbly. "Do I need to get my stuff?"

"We're not leaving. The water won't get this high. But we need to evacuate the tourists. All the snow is finally melting." Thea donned her Stetson and turned for the door. "Get dressed, and you can ride with me today. Get a rain jacket from the closet." She opened the door to a drumming rain and slammed it shut.

Rilla looked around the now empty, silent house. She couldn't imagine evacuating a park like this. It wasn't like Thea could just roll into a tent campground and herd twenty people into their cars. This was thousands. People in houses, canvas tents, campgrounds, RVs, and everything in between. It was completely evacuating the town they came from, twice over.

Rilla pulled on a pair of leggings and back to the hall closet downstairs to hunt for a rain jacket. She pulled the chain and a bare bulb flicked on. Her jaw dropped. *The closet was stuffed with outdoor gear.* It looked like a shitty, dirty version of the mountain store. Jackets, down, skis, ski poles, tents, tarps . . .

Maybe there was climbing gear. She dug in, looking for any useful piece of gear she could add to her tiny pile upstairs. But within a few minutes, she was disappointed. There didn't seem to be anything she could use. The memory of sitting at the top of Doggie Diversions, rope-less, crossed her mind and she paused. She'd forgotten. She couldn't go back after embarrassing herself so thoroughly. Petra was right, she *was* a gumby. Grabbing a blue jacket, she pulled the light and shut the closet door firmly behind her.

Thea opened the door, fifteen minutes later on the dot, and leaned inside. The rain poured off her jacket in thin streams. "You ready?"

"Yep," Rilla said, zipping up her backpack she'd been stuffing snacks into.

"Did you bring some schoolwork?"

Rilla stopped.

Thea gave an exasperated sigh and snapped her fingers. "Come on. You're going to be in the truck all day. Use your time wisely."

Rilla turned and huffed back to the attic. Retrieving some math and *The Scarlett Letter*, she stuffed them on top of her snacks and pulled her hood over her head, heading into the rain to Thea's waiting truck.

"Why does the park have to evacuate if it's not going to go that high?" she asked, shutting the rain out.

"There's only one road out of the Valley, basically. If it gets flooded, we have a bigger problem than tourists getting wet."

Rilla put her backpack on the thick rubber floor mats and knocked her hood down. The heat was blasting, despite the fact that it was the warmest morning since she arrived. The clock on the dash said it was only 8 A.M. She deflated. It felt so much later. "Does this happen often?"

"Not during the summer season, but it's been colder this year."

"Ha. Global warming," Rilla said dryly.

Thea put the truck in drive with a jolt. "You know, global warming doesn't mean everywhere gets super warm right? I just assumed they had better science at Alleghany these days." Thea gave a condescending chuckle that made Rilla want to slap her. "It means climate change. Like, more extreme temperatures, more extreme weather events . . . hurricanes, tornadoes, bigger floods." She turned out onto the slick pavement of the road. "Colder springs where the snow pack in the high Sierras doesn't melt until a large spring storm from Mexico pushes up and wallops the Valley with a deluge of water."

Rilla frowned. "Our science is good. They just don't teach about global warming. Not everyone agrees."

"Scientists agree."

"All of them?" Rilla snapped. She didn't even care, but she hated that Thea made her feel like a country dumbass who had failed out of a *bad* education.

"Yep," Thea said, putting her blinker on and waiting for the heavy line of traffic to make a space for her big park ranger SUV.

"Okay, fine. Global warming."

"Global climate change," Thea corrected.

Rilla clenched her jaw and looked out the window. Leaving West Virginia had turned Thea into an asshole. "Up in 'airs'," as Granny would have said.

Clouds clung to the cliffs, obscuring the tops from view while smaller, thin wisps floated along the bottom. A low rumble of thunder rolled through the Valley, echoing back in on itself and up into the truck where Rilla sat.

Thea drove the wrong way on a one-way street and then eased across a walking path to pull up to Rilla's old friend—the firehouse-jail. "You're not on parking duty today?" Rilla asked as Thea parked and turned off the truck.

"I'll probably have to direct traffic. But right now, I have roll call. You can get coffee and some breakfast. Just don't touch anything, or get in anyone's way. Or talk, really. Try not to talk."

Rilla rolled her eyes, pulled up her hood, and followed Thea through the rain to the side door of the firehouse.

Inside, it was a very different Yosemite than she was used to seeing—no tourists, no workers like in HUFF. These were the lifers. The corporate fast track to an Ent—the sentient trees in *The Lord of the Rings*.

Thirty or more rangers and volunteers milled around the ambulance parked inside. Their jackets glistened and boots left wet footprints on the concrete. Scraggly beards on old and young, and hair chopped short or braided off the faces of the women. The feel of weather worn, but alive and green. They talked in clumps. Looked at a phone with their heads together. A few sat on the floor, eyes closed and heads resting on the concrete walls. This was what goth Thea had become. A motherfucking baby Ent.

Rilla made a beeline for the big thermos of coffee and the tray of bagels set up on a table in the back. She grabbed a bagel and scooped out a glob of cream cheese.

"Who let the Valley rat in?" Walker said.

"Huh?" she asked stupidly, realizing a half second too late that he meant her.

His hood was up, but under the dripping edge, his eyes teased and he needed to shave. *Had he heard about the rope dropping incident?*

"You gonna just hog all the cream cheese?" he asked, voice thick with sleep.

Her stomach flipped, pulse climbing—god, his voice in the morning was quite possibly one of the sexiest things—but she made a face, and smothered the cream cheese over the blueberry bagel as if all her hormones hadn't flicked on high alert. "Back off the cream cheese."

"Oh yeah?" He reached across her for a bagel. "Excuse me," he said, purposely shoving his arm into her face.

"Git, you big lug," she said, shoving her elbow into his side, still clutching the plastic knife.

He stepped into the hit, sending her stumbling toward the coffee. "Oh, pardon me." His boot came down on her sneaker just enough to pinch. "My bad."

"Ugh, you toad," Rilla said, wholly delighted, as she pushed back against his solid weight and tried to yank her foot out from under his.

"Children," Thea snapped behind them.

Guiltily, they straightened.

"He started it," Rilla muttered.

"Did not," Walker said.

"Oh, my god," Thea said with a glare for them both. She refilled her mug of coffee and turned her back. "I claim neither of you."

"Good going, West Virginia," Walker said.

She growled and felt very pleased.

Walker grinned and demolished half his bagel in one bite.

"So, what do you have to do for this?" Rilla asked.

"Nothing very interesting . . . I mean, I was like—" his voice deepened, "rescuing babies and kittens all night."

"All night?" She put her hand to her chest and prepared to swoon.

"In the wind and rain, uphill both ways." He stuffed the rest of the bagel into his mouth, talking over it. "Nah, I was at a trailhead most of the night, telling people the park was closing. Mostly, it'll just be a long, wet day with annoyed tourists."

A woman about Thea's age walked up to the bagels, with a confused side-eye to Rilla.

Thinking she was blocking the woman's way to the table, Rilla slid out of the way.

"You rested up, Walker?" the woman said, with a soft accent that made Rilla's heart jump. The South. *Home.* Now she understood why people talked about the South with nostalgia.

"Absolutely. Adrienne, this is Martinez's sister, Rilla," Walker said. "Rilla, this is my team leader, Adrienne."

Understanding crossed Adrienne's face. "Oh, hey, Rilla."

"Rilla is a new climber," Walker said.

Adrienne nodded politely.

"And, Adrienne holds the speed record on Age of Gemini," Walker said.

"Now you're just buttering me up," Adrienne said.

"Oh, wow," Rilla said, hating herself for ever wanting to be a climber. *Goddamn, what a stupid fucking idea.* "That's awesome."

"I'm hoping you give me something interesting today," Walker said.

Adrienne rolled her eyes. "We'll see what we get. Be prepared for misery."

Walker pumped his fist. "The NPS Way."

"Boy, you don't even know." Adrienne sipped her coffee. "After this, we'll have our own debrief. I think we have a group still left on El Cap. Sawyer talked to them on the phone this morning and they're descending. I'll have you go out and check on them this afternoon."

A ranger in a more official-looking rain jacket at the front of the firehouse cleared his throat.

Everyone sort of turned.

"All right, guys," he said, lowering his radio and raising his voice. "Listen up." He glanced at a little notebook in his hand and scanned the room before beginning his weather report and instructions for road closures and evacuation processes.

Rilla quietly filled up a cup of coffee while he talked, mixing in cream and sugar.

When they finished, Walker waved goodbye and followed Adrienne to a clump of volunteers.

Rilla caught up with Thea and followed her back into the rain, careful not to spill her coffee as she climbed inside the truck.

After starting the truck, Thea gripped the steering wheel, pulled herself up, and yanked down the edge of her vest from where it pushed out under her chin.

Rilla narrowed her eyes. "Are you wearing a bulletproof vest?"

Thea ignored her and twisted in her seat to back up.

Rilla leaned into the center console. "Why are you wearing a vest? Do you have a gun?"

"OMG shut up," Thea snapped.

"You're a cop." Rilla pointed, eyes narrowed. Knowing it was annoying her sister. Knowing it was fun. "You're not a ranger. You liar. Did you tell mom?" Mom would hate that Thea was a cop. A park ranger—okay. It was law enforcement for trees, basically. But a cop? No. There was a strictly enforced anti-cop component to being a Skidmore.

"Baby girl, if you don't hush up . . . I swear . . ." Thea wrenched the wheel of the SUV, toward traffic on the main road. The windshield wipers flicked in rhythm.

"Mom is going to be so mad. Wait until I tell her." It was hilarious how annoyed Thea was getting.

"I am a ranger."

"A cop."

"A *law enforcement ranger*," Thea said.

"How could you betray mom so deeply?" Rilla teased.

Thea snorted. "Let us count the ways." She turned off the wet pavement and onto what Rilla would have thought was a bike path. Tourists scattered in front of them, looking up into the SUV with wet and miserable expressions. The pines grew close to the road and dripped more rain.

"It's so hard being an upstanding citizen. Oh, the burden. The woe. You perfect child," Rilla said.

Thea put on the brakes and turned off the truck. "Get out. You're coming with me." Thea pulled her official ranger jacket hood up and got out, the sharp patter of rain hitting the nylon before she closed the door and eyed Rilla through the glass like hurry up.

Rilla pulled up her hood and rolled out of the truck, boots sinking into the soggy needles and mud. "What are you doing? Am I going to get paid for this?" She asked, catching up with Thea.

"You are out your damn mind. I should make you sit in the truck and do your work, but I'm not sure you'd be there when I got back."

Rilla rolled her eyes and trudged after her sister. Just over the trees the edge of Half Dome loomed down on them, the patches of snow still visible at the top. All that snow on the mountains. All the snow she'd seen from her climb. It was melting and rushing downward into the Merced, into the slit of Valley before it passed on into wider places.

"We need to check on everyone and get them out of here as soon as possible," Thea said from under her hood, not breaking her stride as she walked up to the closest RV. "The river isn't supposed to hit the high mark until midnight, but by then it'll be over the roads."

Most of the campground was empty, and the ones that were left looked closed down or as if they were packing up. Rilla followed along in the rain as Thea went to each RV, one by one, reminding them of the evacuation order and asking how quickly they could get moving.

One guy was waiting until the crowds died down because he didn't want to sit in traffic. His arms were folded and his eyes narrowed, immediately hostile to Thea's calm reminder and encouragement. Eventually she gave a firm, decisive, "you need to leave immediately and not wait for traffic." A moment passed where the rain pattered and the wind rushed off the mountains above them and the man glowered in silence.

Where it shimmered right on the edge of turning into something different. The hair on the back of Rilla's neck stood up and she held her breath.

"All right, I'm leaving," he said.

Rilla exhaled.

Thea didn't thank him. Just headed on to the next RV, looking calm and unbothered.

"How do you do that?" Rilla asked, expecting Thea to ask what she was even talking about.

But Thea's eyes flickered to the horizon, high into the rain-pregnant sky and she said very seriously. "It's not fun to have your vacation interrupted. But people forget, these are still wild places. We are all visitors here. They think we're here to serve them, when it's really that we are here to serve the park. You can't be afraid of getting hurt. It keeps you from doing the most important things."

Rilla looked back.

The man, true to his word, was already in his RV with it running. Still with the same glower.

"Does Mom know about you and Lauren?"

Thea looked down, lips tight.

"Really?" Rilla was surprised. "Why not? I mean, we had two dads." Everyone who learned that fact seemed to find it exotic—which wasn't ever a good thing, but Rilla figured at least Thea should be used to it. "Mom would totally get it."

"I don't really want to talk about it."

"But why? I don't get you. You obviously talk to Mom, but you don't *tell* her anything? Not this. Not what your job is." And yet, Thea told everyone in the Valley her business.

"Mom doesn't want to hear anything," Thea snapped. "She just wants to hear everything is good. Trust me, I've tried telling Mom shit. If you and Mom have something different, that's fantastic. I'm happy to hear that."

Rilla clenched her jaw. "I tell her stuff."

"Great."

"You can't just write her off like that. You should try," Rilla said. Somehow it mattered, deeply mattered, that Thea didn't tell Mom stuff about her life. "You have to try," she repeated.

"Oh my god, Rilla!" Thea stopped and lifted her arm. "Go wait in the truck."

"No," Rilla shot back, swallowing just in time to keep the *you can't make me* from bursting out.

Thea glared under the dripping brim of her hat. "You are the worst."

"Yeah, that's right." Rilla crossed her arms, but to clutch her ribs to keep from cracking apart in the fear that she'd finally pushed Thea too far.

Thea stalked off to the next RV hunkered against the rain and an old lady in a clear poncho and plastic cap over her white hair stepped out.

The tears she'd thought she'd run dry the night before pricked in her eyes. God, if she could just stop fucking everything up. Turning her back, she rubbed her eyes and stared glumly up into the dripping pine boughs, listening to Thea repeat the same things over and over.

At the back edge of the massive campground, they crossed paths with Lauren.

"Got 'em?" Thea asked, pulling her radio from her hip and surveying the few trailers still pulling out.

"I think we're good back here," Lauren said. "Ready to hit up Half Dome Village again? Did they make a decision on employees?"

"I'm waiting to hear," Thea said.

"Can I go back to the truck?" Rilla asked. "My feet are wet."

"No," Thea snapped.

Lauren snorted. Her gaze flicked to Rilla. "She's got you out of the attic today, huh?"

Water dripped off Rilla's hood and plunked on her nose. "Yep." *Did Lauren know her girlfriend was a complete snot?*

"I'll take you back to the truck. You can do your work now," Thea said, walking off.

"Oh. Ugh . . ." Rilla followed the back of Thea's ponytail, stringy from the rain dripping off the brim of her hat.

"If you put this energy into doing it instead of complaining, you'd be done by now," Thea said.

"Is there a handbook of trite parenting phrases you get with guardianship papers?" Rilla asked. "You don't even know what it is I'm supposed to be doing. You only ask when you run out of things to say."

Thea just barked a laugh and whipped open the truck door. "You're fighting the wrong person, baby girl."

Rilla made a face and slammed her door. August. She just had to make it until August.

Thea glared out the front and rolled down the window for Lauren, who'd stopped by the truck.

"You all right?" Lauren asked softly.

Thea sighed and leaned against the side. "I'm fine."

"She won't tell our mom she's dating a girl," Rilla said, taking satisfaction in getting to tell on Thea.

Lauren looked at Rilla and didn't even flinch or make an expression.

Rilla bit her lip and looked at Thea.

Thea shook her head. "We'll talk later," she said to Lauren.

Lauren nodded. They kissed and Thea started the truck.

Rilla crossed her arms and slid into the corner, as far from Thea as she could get.

"You're a little bitch, you know that?" Thea said. It stung.

"Ohhh . . . that feels awfully Thea from West Virginia," Rilla said. "Be careful. You might wake up and Mom will know you fuck girls."

"*Shut up!*" Thea screamed.

Rilla snapped her jaw shut.

"Do you think I want my life to be like this? Do you think I hate Mom? That I never want to go home again? That I didn't love being there? That I haven't actually told Mom about three times, all of which she completely ignored like some fucked-up denial thing?"

Rilla couldn't answer.

"I'm doing it, Rilla. Day after day, I'm dealing with what I have. And all you're doing is refusing to even acknowledge there's a problem. It's okay to say someone's actions hurt you."

Rilla didn't know what to say. Or think. "Mom isn't like that," she whispered, even though it sounded exactly like Mom. "And I know . . . I'm not. No one hurts me." Shit, why did she feel like crying. Everything was hot and confusing and terrible.

Thea shook her head. "Why do I try?" she muttered.

They sat in silence, in the traffic, with everyone else—moving at a snail's pace. Rilla stared out the window, focusing on her breathing until the threat of tears receded.

Thea pulled into to the end of a parking lot and blocked the exit. "Let me know if you see anyone coming to their cars. I have to inform them of the evacuation," she said, putting the truck in park and turning down the heat.

From the front seat, Rilla could just barely see the foaming edge of the Merced as it churned over boulders along its path. It looked swollen but not flooded. But she knew rivers. Rainelle had flooded only two years ago from snowmelt and storms. Thea didn't know—she hadn't been there or called when it happened. Rilla didn't know what was going on between Mom and Thea—but it couldn't be what Thea said. It just couldn't. Rilla wasn't ready to face a problem she couldn't try and fix.

"Is this all you're doing now?" Rilla said. "Napping?"

"Yep," Thea said from under closed eyes. "Try doing some schoolwork."

Rilla sighed and looked at her bag. The deadline for all this work wasn't until August. There was no reason for Thea to be on her except it made her feel good to grind her axe about something. She pulled out *The Scarlett Letter* and slouched in her seat, curling the book's binding back on itself. The rain pattered on the windows. The fan blasted heat. She blinked at the end of the page, and couldn't remember a word of what she'd read.

"Can I go back to the house?" Rilla asked.

Thea was silent.

"Thea." Rilla droned. Come on. "Theaaaaaaa."

"What," Thea said without moving.

"Can I go back to the house?"

"No."

Rilla gritted her teeth. "Why?"

"You need to sit still and focus. You need to be making significant progress on your schoolwork," Thea continued.

Rilla deflated. "What's significant progress?"

"I need to see you working. Disciplined. With a stack of finished bigger than your stack of unfinished."

Rilla narrowed her eyes and flapped her book in Thea's face. "I'm halfway done with this book. Does that count?"

Thea didn't flinch. "No."

"I can do that at the house."

"But you don't. You know I found your mess the other day?"

"What mess?"

Thea counted them off on her fingers. "The pencils, the broken pencil sharpener, the drawer you dumped out, the garbage can you left without a bag, and you didn't latch the bear box for the garbage you did take out. Thankfully, I followed your little mouse trail of undone crumbs and latched it before something got into it."

Rilla frowned and looked out the window. She didn't want to argue with the only person left who cared about her future or wanted her to do something. And she could do the work—she *had to*. But hopelessness clawed at her throat, choking her.

She opened the door and got out.

"I said no. Where are you going?"

Rilla slammed the truck door and started off in the rain, without waiting for Thea to argue.

The park felt strange without people—foreboding, with its empty meadows and empty paths and the long string of bumper-to-bumper cars still leaving the park. Her feet were soaked, making her cold, and she headed across the Valley toward one of the stone bridges sure to still be above water.

The rain pattered on her hood and dripped down her arms. The clouds still hung heavy and foggy around the cliffs and she wondered if any climbers were still stuck up there in the storms. Shivering, she wrapped her arms around herself.

On the stone bridge, the river rushed muddy and thick with brush and bramble. Rilla leaned on her elbows and gazed over the edge, mesmerized by the lulling rush of water, current of rain, and dull roar of wind high in the mountains.

She pulled her phone out and hit the messages in Instagram, staring at the message from Curtis. She wanted to reply, but she shouldn't have even sent the first message. It wasn't lost on her that she didn't miss him until she felt alone. Her chest squeezed and she stuffed the phone back in her jacket and closed her eyes. She'd only ever gone out with him because no one like him ever liked a Skidmore. He was hot, he was a running back on the football team, he was well-liked. He made her more than herself. How selfish could she be?

Behind her eyes, she focused on the picture hanging in the mountain store—the woman with her gaze fixed higher and bigger and bolder. But it kept getting replaced with the view of her feet, bracing the wall, and the rope disappearing between them. It felt like she was destined to fuck everything up. Her home. Her sister. Climbing.

Keeping her eyes closed, she straightened off the bridge and walked, splashing through the puddles by feel. The first few steps were easy. The next, harder. The farther she went, the more she knew she might not be going somewhere she wanted. That at any second she'd bump ... her eyes flew open and she was still on the path. Empty and forlorn in the rain. The road was empty, beside her. The river roaring and the falls pouring.

She walked through the meadow, past the emptied Camp 4 and the empty SAR camp under dripping tarps. Sometimes she closed her eyes and tried to see how far she could go. Mostly she walked with her eyes open. This place that was never seen so empty, and she got to see it.

El Capitan rose over the trees. Its head in the clouds, its prow emerging from the silver and diving into the pines. She didn't know the way, but there must be one. Somewhere. And when a soggy pine-needle-covered trail led away from the asphalt, toward the monolith, she ducked into the trees.

The path wound and rose through the incline of scrubby oaks and soaked leaves that looked like rose petals wet underfoot. When she came out of the trees, she stood at the bottom of the white granite monster and looked up. The thrum of the mountain beat in her heart. The top obscured in the heavens. It felt, for one strange moment, as if she was standing on ... beside ... something alive and warm and singing to her. Like it could lift her limbs and she would float to the top, having finally reached something beyond herself.

The rain dripped in her eyes and rolled under her hood and dripped on her hair and she grew cold. But still she looked. Tracing the endless lines of its art. Its blank page littered with secret paths.

The rocks rolled to her left and she jerked away from the wall.

Walker stood under the trees. A look of understanding and knowing so thoroughly on his face it made her pulse beat toward him in a way she had never felt.

"It gets under your skin, doesn't it?" he asked.

She ducked her head and clambered over the rocks to stand under the awning of black oaks beside him. "I've just never seen anything that big."

"That's what all the girls say," he said.

"Ugh . . ." She wrinkled her nose and slapped his arm. "Gross."

He leaned on a tree trunk and looked down at her over his shoulder, a devilish grin twisted on his mouth. "You walked straight into it. I couldn't resist."

"I just . . ." She bit her lip and looked into the gaze that was teasing her. Adeena and Petra were real climbers with lives that had never crossed hers until now. Caroline was otherworldly, even if she was Walker's sister. Walker was from southern Ohio. He wasn't Caroline and admitted it readily. He knew of a Rilla back home, she was sure. All she wanted was for someone who knew her to say she could do it. Walker felt as close as she could get.

"You want to climb it," he said, as if it was the most obvious thing.

She nodded, expression pleading for him not to laugh.

"You're not going to get there top-roping the bunny crag with Dee and Petra."

"I know," she said. "But I can't ask for anything more."

He looked confused. "Why not?"

Because she was already getting more than she deserved. Because who would want to waste time on a person who wasn't very good? On a person who ruined everything. Who was terrible to her only sister. A person who sucked at everything. Especially at climbing. She sighed and put her hands in her pockets. "How did you get here anyway?"

He dragged his hand through his hair and gave a half growl, half yawn like an overgrown mangy cat. Finally, he answered, "I started volunteering for my local fire department when I was fourteen. And climbing with Caroline in Kentucky. I came out here with her."

Rilla held up her hand. "Wait."

He stopped.

"Why'd you guys leave Ohio?"

He folded his lips and looked up at the cliff. For a long moment, he didn't speak. "I don't really talk about it," he finally said. "My mom died the year before. There were six of us and my dad just had too much going on. Caroline left, and I went with her, to get out of his hair. She's in a different universe than I am as a climber, but we were always really close and . . ." He sniffed.

"Do you still talk to him? Your dad?"

"Oh yeah. And my younger siblings. It was all good. Just . . . time. I wasn't as focused as I am now. We had a lot of bills and like, seventeen-year-old me ate a lot. I still eat a lot."

"I'm sorry about your mom."

He nodded, cheeks sunken like he was biting them. "Anyway, my first summer out here, I met your sister and she was the ranger working with the SAR team and got me kind of interested in that path. After that, we moved to Colorado and I finished the number of climbs I needed to get my AMG mountain guide certification while Caroline was training there, did some swift water classes and certifications that would help, and applied for a position on the SAR team."

He didn't look at her through the whole thing.

"Well." She sat up straighter and crossed her arms. "I also am very accomplished." She paused for dramatic effect. "I once did cocaine and it made me go to sleep. So, you see, I'm really special too." It was a one-time thing. And stayed that way.

He couldn't seem to settle on an expression. "That *is* special," he said.

"I'm a winner." She meant for it come out peppy, like a cheerleader on that cocaine that put her to sleep, but it ended up a little more desperate and high-pitched. She wanted to crawl under a rock and die.

Mercifully, he moved on. "Petra mentioned you were really great on Snake Dike. That you're talented."

She had? Was Petra just saying that? "I don't know?" She shrugged, uncomfortable under the compliment. He didn't know she'd climbed in front of Caroline and *dropped the rope*.

Walker nodded. "Yeah, that's why it's so impressive. You don't know." His radio chattered. "Thea's looking for you," he said, touching the bulge of the radio on his hip under his jacket. "She said to go home and wait for her."

She nodded. "I fucked that up too."

"Sisters are hard," he said.

She chuckled, warmed to have a companion in sister misery. "Yeah."

"You can do this," he said, nodding toward the cliff. "I mean, not right this second. But you're here; and if you want to work and find your people, you can. By the end of the summer even, you could climb The Nose if you wanted."

Rilla laughed. "You're joking."

"I'm totally serious," Walker said.

She looked down. "It feels like all I can really do is fuck up. Did you hear I dropped the rope yesterday?"

He laughed. "Yeah. I heard."

"Don't laugh! Your sister had to rescue me."

"Listen. Is that what's getting you down?" He straightened off the tree. "I mean, fucking up is an integral part of climbing."

She frowned and side-eyed him. "Stop bullshitting me."

"It is!" he insisted. "If you aren't falling, you aren't climbing hard enough. If you aren't making mistakes, you aren't progressing. If you aren't getting in over your head, you aren't exploring. You try and not fuck up in a way that will kill yourself or someone else, but everything else . . ." He smiled. "Climbing makes failure a friend, not a foe."

Never had she wanted to kiss a boy more in her life. But beyond that she wanted other things more than she'd ever wanted them. She wanted to climb, to say she was sorry, to not have failure mean such big things in her life. She didn't want to be afraid of messing up—even if she didn't have much more to lose. Abruptly she tightened her fists and turned down the path.

"Wait. Where are you going?" he said with surprise.

Rilla shouted over her shoulder. "Tell her I went home to do my homework."

Walker's reply echoed off the cliff. "Copy that."

She was going to climb El Capitan.

She was going to stay in Yosemite. She was going to outrun that ranger every time, and she was going to push herself until she was scraped, and she was going to get back up when she fell, and she was going to keep her eyes open to look for where the thin path swung away from the wide asphalt, and in doing all those things—in pursuing this thing that was so much bigger than herself . . .

She was going to transform.

twenty one

FOR TWO DAYS, THE VALLEY WAS QUIET EXCEPT FOR THE RAIN DRUM-
ming the roof as Rilla worked. Her eighteenth birthday came, and just
when she was ready to throw all her books out the window and post
something passive-aggressive about being forgotten on Instagram,
Lauren came home with two chocolate cupcakes and a piece of dry spaghetti stuck in the middle of one and lit on fire as a makeshift candle.

"Don't tell Thea, I forgot to get her one," Lauren said, licking icing off
the top after Rilla had blown out the spaghetti.

"Thea probably forgot anyway," Rilla said.

Lauren snorted. "Sure, and how do you think I knew it was your
birthday?"

Oh yeah. Rilla made a face.

"Well, how does eighteen feel?"

"Like seventeen," Rilla said over a mouthful of cupcake.

Thea came home later with more cupcakes, and a new fleece
Patagonia jacket.

Rilla clutched the jacket, her smile real.

She finished all of her trigonometry before the rain stopped, the
waters receded, and tourists flowed back into the Valley.

Morning dawned—bright and simmering heat in the thick shafts
of golden sunshine slotted through the pines. The river ran high, but
within a week a fire had lit in the high Sierras and the wind shifted,
bringing the smell of smoke with it. Rilla would have imagined Thea

surely had something to do with forest fires in the park, but Thea just layered on more sunscreen and listened with a morose look on her face to the fire reports and the radio chatter.

"You hate your job, don't you?" Rilla asked one morning. They hadn't talked about the conversation during the flood. But resumed tentatively, as if it had never happened.

"I hate parking cars," Thea said, without lifting her eyes from the massive swift-water rescue handbook she was reading. "But I'm not going to be parking cars forever." She swallowed another bite of cereal. "How's school?"

"Uh. Great. I finished all of my trig."

"Great job! Keep at it," Thea said. "Mom called. I told her you'd call today."

Rilla nodded, still torn between being angry at Thea for criticizing Mom and angry at Mom for being that way in the first place. "Yeah, okay."

"All right," Thea put her bowl in the sink and reached for her Stetson. "Pray I don't get run over by an angry tourist," Thea said, and then was gone, leaving Rilla sitting at the table in an empty house.

She hadn't seen anyone since the day she dropped the rope, on purpose mostly. Even though she knew she wanted to go back to climbing, going back out to show her face and *ask to lead* was a . . . hurdle. She looked at her phone and wondered if Mom would even be up. Probably not.

Taking the computer, she opened up a blank document, determining to knock out a paper on the book she'd only half finished reading. The clock ticked loudly. The quiet in between the ticks seemed to carry a noise. After ten minutes on the couch, her body was sore from sitting still. She should just bite the bullet, go back out, and ask. No one was going to be in Camp 4 today, especially not this late. She could go and try and find a stranger to climb with—people often signed up for partners on the ranger board—but any partner would be able to tell right away she was a fake. She couldn't lead! Rilla groaned and leaned forward with the computer. She started writing and barely even knew what she was saying, she just kept her fingers moving. After filling a page, she figured it was time for a break and clicked over to movies, propping up Thea's *Wilderness First Aid* on her knees to page through.

Ten episodes of *Vampire Diaries* later . . .

Shit.

Rilla looked up, realizing the light had turned amber and her whole day was gone. She closed the computer and unfolded herself off the couch just as Lauren came in the door.

"Hey girl, busy day?"

Rilla smoothed her hair and tried not to look guilty. "Yep. You?"

"A squirrel got into the Half Dome Village store." Lauren sighed and sank in the recliner, unlacing her boots. "I swear, if I get the plague . . ."

"The plague?" Rilla said, stashing the computer under the couch and trying to think what she could do to make it look like she did something.

"Yeah, don't touch rodents. They'll give you the bubonic plague."

"Are you serious? The actual plague. Who touches rodents?"

"You'd be surprised how many people try and pet those mangy bionic rodents." She pulled off her socks and sighed. "What have you been doing all day? More *Vampire Diaries*?"

Rilla blinked.

"It shows what you've been watching."

"Oh."

Lauren laughed. "Oh indeed."

"I did get all of my trigonometry done," Rilla defended herself.

Lauran waved her hand. "That's a fight for Thea. I do not care about a few episodes of *Vampire Diaries*."

Rilla's shoulders sagged in relief.

"We need to talk about what happened during the evacuation."

Shit. Rilla studied her hands.

"I guess you've talked with her about it, right?"

Rilla stayed quiet.

"Yeah," Lauren said like she'd just proved a point. "I know your situation is complicated. I'm not pretending I understand the dynamics that are unfolding there. I know for Thea, it's been difficult to figure out boundaries and how to move forward, and I imagine you will need to learn the same things. But here's the thing." She pulled her legs off the chair and leaned on her knees. "You cannot, under any circumstance, tell a gay person she must come out. Even to your sister. Even to her mother. You crossed a line."

Rilla's face felt like it was burning up. "It . . ." She swallowed. "It wasn't about coming out. It was about her and my mom."

"It was about coming out. I don't care who is involved. It was about exposing something intensely vulnerable to a mother who has never been safe for Thea. A mother Thea has always had to take care of. It's not even remotely your business. Only Thea gets to decide that."

"But our parents are . . ."

"It doesn't matter, Rilla," Lauren said. "What matters is you need to respect Thea and her decisions about how to handle her family. Thea deserves an apology from you."

Rilla kept her head ducked. "I mean, she knows . . ."

"Not unless you tell her. She loves you and is here to help you. She was the one who suggested bringing you out here. When she heard what happened with that boy, she spent hours on the phone with your mom, convincing her that you needed to leave West Virginia."

That ache started up again in the back of Rilla's throat.

Lauren looked at her, waiting.

Rilla exhaled and closed her eyes. "I didn't know," she croaked. "I thought my mom asked her to take me"

"Nope." Lauren shook her head.

The silence was deafening.

Rilla felt sick to her stomach. All this time she'd thought Mom had wanted her to go, and Thea had just been the closest person. She hadn't realized Thea had been convincing Mom . . . wearing her down, getting her to see how serious it was. That definitely made more sense. Ugh. Rilla put her face in her hands.

"Need in the bathroom? I'm getting a shower," Lauren said, standing up.

"I'm good." Rilla bolted for the door. "I'm going to get some sunshine." Closing the door behind her, she sat on the porch and put her chin in her hands. How could she fix this mess?

With a sigh, she slid off the edge of the porch and started walking for Yosemite Village. As she left the meadow and joined the asphalt path, someone whistled behind her.

She turned as Walker pedaled up behind her in shorts and a fluorescent T-shirt with SAR printed in bold, black letters on the back. "Climbing today, Rilla?" He stopped and leaned the bike between his legs.

She tried not to grin like a goober, awkward conversation with Lauren forgotten. "Not today. You on call?"

"Just got back from carrying a hiker down from Half Dome," he groaned. "I'm going to eat before something else happens. You going that way?"

"Yep."

"Well, hop on then." He straightened the bike and Rilla gleefully stood on the back, hands on his shoulders. She was pathetic, but it was okay, she'd accepted that about herself.

"I know you'll probably say no, but . . ." He pedaled toward dinner. "Want to lead tomorrow?"

The California sun hung in a cloudless blue sky, but she was sure, at that moment, the clouds parted somewhere and shone brighter. "Yes!" She completely forgot to flirt or tease him in her desperation to have someone teach her to lead a route without having to ask Petra or Adeena.

They rolled through an intersection and Rilla spotted Thea, standing to the side, holding a long line of cars at a stop. Thea looked tired and sweaty. She waved as Rilla rolled past.

Shame crawled up Rilla's spine.

twenty two

THE SMELL OF THE SWOLLEN RIVER AND WOOD SMOKE LED RILLA
under the cedars as she walked into Camp 4 the next morning. *She was going climbing with Walker.*

Her hair was braided, and she wore her mom's cut-off "Southern X-Posure" T-shirt and a pair of Thea's fancy outdoor pants she'd stolen. Gage had wrapped a cord around her sunglasses so they would hang on her neck if she knocked them off while climbing, and her old West Virginia Mountaineers hat rested snugly on her head. In her backpack she carried her booty from turning in all her homework to Thea and spending all her money—a harness, shoes that seemed to fit, a helmet, Grigri, and a chalk bag. It made her feel equally legit and fake. But she gripped the gear and tried to look like she belonged.

She was determined.

Hoisting the harness on her shoulder, she blocked out the image of everyone laughing at her behind her back, and walked into the sacred realm of white tents of the SAR site.

Four people—not including Walker—sat at a picnic table under one of the tarp porches, sharing what looked like a cozy breakfast. Two girls and two men. Tanned and strong and worn out in the way Walker often seemed—not in the physical sense, but where his clothes and his patience didn't suffer fools. The girl on the end closest to Rilla, with her coltish limbs and a smattering of freckles, noticed her first and they all paused and looked quizzically at her, confirming her suspicion that entering this part of the camp was like entering into someone's house unannounced. She'd just waltzed into their kitchen, during breakfast. She swallowed quickly and her face burned. "Walker?" she choked out, thinking the less she said, the better she'd be.

"What?" the girl asked, tilting her head further.

Rilla swallowed. "Is Walker around? I'm Thea's sister."

The girl blinked and suddenly her face changed, warm and welcoming and smiling. "You're Thea's sister? Hey! Welcome to Yosemite."

Rilla smiled, relieved as she came closer to the table. "Thank you."

"I've seen you around. I didn't know you were Thea's sister."

Rilla nodded. "Yeah, we're half sisters."

The girl nodded like she was thinking *clearly,* but was trying to be polite.

Walker came from the direction of the road, back from a run and already sweating despite the cool morning air. He ran a hand through his hair and his eyes only met Rilla's for a second.

Adrienne nodded hello.

Rilla waved hello and fought the urge to cringe. She didn't belong here.

"West Virginia," Walker said. "Have a seat."

There was an empty chair beside him and Rilla sank into it, happy to be smaller, folded up and safe.

It was a different crowd, but the same circle in the dirt. A strange mixture of ranger, climber, and summer employee—they sat around a fire covered with a grate and a cast iron skillet and moved slowly as the sun crept through the trees.

"We almost ate your food," a man said, picking up a plate. He wore a blue T-shirt and canvas pants, and his long white hair floated out from the bottom of his ball cap. He seemed much older than Walker—in that age where men's ages become indecipherable beyond the modifier *older.* He was attractive, or could be, if one squinted and tilted their head and imagined him cleaned up a bit and the wild man beard trimmed and put into regular clothes instead of whatever sweatpants and white socks with sandals thing he was wearing.

"*Mark* almost ate your food," Walker said. "Want some coffee?"

Rilla accepted the plate burdened with little sausages, softly charred peppers, and onions—and a browned waffle—with a nervous smile.

"Who's this?" a guy said, coming up. "One of Walker's rope bunnies got invited to breakfast?"

Adrienne laughed and pressed her fingers to her mouth to keep from spilling out her food.

Rilla's face burned.

"Nah, it's Caroline's gumby," someone said.

Rilla smiled politely, as if she was in on the joke and knew why they were talking about Caroline. She took a bite of her waffle. It was delicious and crunchy and tasted faintly of golden wheat and fire, and she forgot to wonder if they knew what a rope bunny *actually* was.

Walker handed her a blue speckled mug of steaming coffee and sank back into his chair. "Caroline should be here any minute. I won't make you climb with me again," he said with a wry smile. "She's a million times better of a climber than you or I will ever be, even if we are reincarnated into better climbers forty more times."

Rilla kept chewing, but her stomach twisted and her mouth immediately dried. She was going climbing with Caroline? The sleek, *professional*, amazing Caroline.

She stared at her plate, too panicked to eat.

"Speaking of Caroline, did she hear Celine Moreau is coming in July?" the white-haired guy said, leaning over his chair for the coffee. "Did you get some of this?" He offered the carafe to Rilla.

She nodded and lifted the mug still in her hand.

"Why July?" Adrienne said with a frown. "It's maybe the worst time. So hot. So crowded."

He shrugged. "I just heard it from a buddy."

Walker leaned over. "Celine is a famous French climber."

"As famous as a climber gets, anyway," Adrienne said.

"She was on the cover of *National Geographic* last year," Walker explained.

Rilla nodded and took a sip of the coffee to hide her awkwardness. It was bitter and hot and softly nutty, and perfectly balanced the bite of the peppers and the sweet brown sugar and sage sausage.

Caroline appeared over the edge of chairs. "Hey, guys!" she said with a wave.

Rilla looked into her cup. Her stomach flipped nervously.

"We didn't save you any food," old guy announced.

"I ate at the house. Sorry I'm late, it took a while for the car to leave." She yawned and smoothed her hair. "I still need to pack up. My stuff is here." Her gaze flicked to Rilla. "You ready? Did they feed you?"

Rilla stood hastily, still holding her plate and cup. "I'm ready. Thank you. The food was amazing."

"Here girl," old guy said with a chuckle, taking the things out of Rilla's hand. "I got you. Calm down."

Caroline readjusted her sunglasses. "Okay, let's get going. Before it gets too hot."

Rilla followed Caroline around the side of Walker's tent where she opened a Rubbermaid container of gear and started pawing through it and handing things to Rilla to hold.

Rilla had her few things she'd been able to buy, but Caroline supplied the bulk of the gear. When she'd been climbing with Petra, Petra supplied it.

Her chest warmed and with her belly full of food and the camp alive and humming, she couldn't remember a time she'd ever been this sober and this nervous. It was worse than the slow slog to the base of Half Dome. Then, she had nothing to lose. Not really. Now she had some semblance of a community. And what if she killed Caroline? Or injured her? Dropped her? Took her hand off the brake to scratch her nose? What if she dropped the rope *again*? It wasn't hot yet, but Rilla started sweating anyway.

Caroline turned the pile of messy gear into a meticulous, Instagram-worthy, orderly spread on the picnic table by Walker's tent. The cams and nuts were arranged by size and color. The carabiners arranged by length of webbing sling. More odd bits of carabiners and strange pieces that looked like they did the same thing as a cam or a nut, but weren't either, were laid out beside a few long stretches of looped webbing Caroline had called daisy chains.

Alongside that, Rilla's stuff was added in, her helmet and chalk bag sitting beside Caroline's. The few pieces she'd borrowed from Petra combined with the few pieces she'd been able to buy.

Caroline added water and two apples, a bag of jerky, two little cups of canned fruit, three mashed date bars, leg-long ladders made of nylon, belay devices, rope, and a few other things Rilla didn't recognize.

"Do you know how to aid?" Caroline asked.

"Um." Rilla flushed, leaning on the edge of the table. She knew aiding is what you did to get through blank, unclimbable faces on long climbs, but Petra and Adeena had never climbed anything with her that they couldn't free-climb—with gear placed along the way.

"There's some 5.10 climbing on this route. I don't know where you're at or what you're good at, so if you can't free-climb it, I'll show you how to aid." Caroline handed Rilla a slightly crumpled printer paper of inked lines and x's with the name written in block letters at the top.

Rilla stared. She couldn't make sense of the drawing as being a climb; but that's what it was—a map of sorts. A wandering line of x's and several notations of grades ranging from "3rd class" to "5.8 C2 or 5.10 C1, which meant with or without aid" and arrows pointing meaningfully to other lines. She didn't know what to make of it, but she looked at it carefully all the same.

Caroline filled a little bag of trail mix from a giant Ziploc and added it to the pile before making a second.

"So, this here indicates a roof." Caroline pointed to a bit of straight line. "These x's indicate bolts. The double x's means there's two bolts at the anchor of the pitch. And this is an arête."

"A what?"

"It's a corner that comes out to a point." She put her hands together in a triangle, pointed at Rilla. "You'll see when you're climbing."

Rilla went back to studying the map, trying to impress it into her mind, and not replay Caroline dancing up Doggie Diversions in her head. Her stomach churned. Ever since that first day at the Grove, she hadn't even dared to dream of climbing with Caroline. And she didn't want to—not now. Not when Rilla knew how bad she was. If she messed up today, she could hurt Caroline. Or worse, lose the tiny bit of trust Caroline seemed to have in her.

twenty three

THE LATE MORNING LIGHT FILLED EVEN THE SHADE WITH CLARITY AND
brightness. Rilla stood not far from where Thea wandered somewhere,
writing parking tickets and giving directions to an endless line of cars
and visitors. But facing the wall, she was alone. In the emptiness. In the
silence. A speck on the sea of granite towering above. It was she and her—
"On belay," Caroline yelled—partner, the one she desperately wanted to
impress. She was only following Caroline on this first pitch, but after
The Great Rope Incident of Last Week, Rilla didn't feel confident about anything. She eased out a breath and wiped the sweat off her hands before
dipping her fingers into her chalk bag off her waist. More chalk. More
chalk solved everything. "Climbing," she yelled.

"Climb on," came the reply.

The ledges to reach the bolt before the pendulum were an easy
scramble. At the bolt, she carefully unclipped the carabiner from the
rope, then from the bolt, and replaced the gear on her sling.

"Got the draw?" Caroline yelled.

"Got it." Rilla's gut clenched as she looked out over the Valley. Where
Caroline had to run back and forth to work her way across, Rilla would
just have to swing over. She didn't realize what that meant until this
moment—looking sideways across the sloughed granite—but as the follower, she would be swinging over to the next piece. The one she couldn't
see. The one *Caroline* had placed.

She clenched her fists and took slow, deep breaths. Caroline was obviously a fantastic and conscientious climber. But depending solely on anyone other than herself felt uncomfortable. Depending solely on a person she was intimidated by and wanted to like her, somehow even worse. Maybe Walker was right—the more she cared, the safer it should be, the more she shied away from it. Oh god. What did that say about her on a personal level?

"You all right?" Caroline called.

"I'm good." Rilla's brain said *give a thumbs-up*, but her hands gripped the rock rebelliously. *Just having an emotional meltdown.*

"Take your time," came the reply.

It took another minute to work up her nerve, but she couldn't get down and she couldn't go on without facing it. Just do it.

Jump.

2.   3.

Jump.

She still couldn't do it. Slowly, she inched to the edge, blinked at the open space below, and walked off.

Her stomach leapt into her throat. The whole world soared as the wind hit her face. It felt for a moment or two like she was flying. Soaring through the Valley in clear light and transcendent space.

The granite block rushed toward her. Oh shit. She threw her hands and feet out, instinctively trying to lessen the impact. "*Arfff,*" she huffed out, whole body slapping the block. Her hands scrambled to hold. Rilla looked for her feet and let her hands go blind, shoving her toes into anything that seemed like it would hold her. Her body was still swinging. Still wanting to go back the other direction. For a second she started to tear away. Without thinking, she grabbed on to the gear Caroline placed. And stopped.

Rilla exhaled. Her elbows scraped the granite. Her stomach muscles clenched tight to keep her feet on the wall. She took a second to catch her breath and stood.

Feeling the pressure of wanting desperately for Caroline not to get tired of her, Rilla pushed upward. The rope slid through the gear above her, clinking gently against the stone. Up. Shift. Push. Just as she fell into a rhythm, her hands skittered across blank granite. The arête was smooth and had no cracks. *Argh.* She re-adjusted her grip and tried not to panic.

Out of the corner of her eye, a bit of the brown rock moved.

At first, she blinked in confusion, thinking she was seeing things.

It moved again, becoming three-dimensional as it lifted off the granite.

A spider.

What the fuck? With her heart in her throat, Rilla forced herself up on the tiny little divots she wouldn't have trusted two seconds ago. Desperate to get away from the ambling spider, she practically ran up the wall, screaming through her teeth.

"Are you okay?" Caroline asked.

"Spider!" Rilla squealed, shivering. It was below her now. Somehow. But she was dripping sweat.

The climb from there to Caroline was the hardest she'd ever worked to move on the rock. It wasn't even remotely pretty. Nothing like the way Caroline moved. But all she had to do was try. Just try. *Failure was a friend.*

Another deep breath, and she set to work the piece of pro—a cam—out of the crack as she cleaned the route behind Caroline.

"Is it stuck in there?" Caroline called.

"Yeah," Rilla said.

"Try wiggling it back up."

That loosened it enough so that Rilla was able to work it out and clip it next to the first piece she cleaned.

Don't drop it. Don't drop it. Putting all her mind on the piece in her hand and not on the hundred feet of empty air below, she clipped the piece to her sling and breathed. One more hurdle down.

"Okay?" Caroline yelled.

"All good," Rilla replied. Caroline was probably sitting up there bored stiff and wishing she'd done anything else.

Rilla got back to climbing—and it continued to suck. She pulled on one of the bolts, which hurt and was not at all the hold her desperate, sweating hands wanted. She slipped off multiple times. Made wretched noises. Wanted to cry. Cursed. Scraped her wrists and elbows. Twisted her legs into weird positions. But, in the end, she crawled even with Caroline on a gravel-strewn ledge. Sweating and shaky-limbed, her arms and legs throbbed.

"Did you say a spider?" Caroline asked.

"Yes," Rilla gasped. "I almost died."

"I am so impressed you didn't immediately jump off. That would have been it for me."

Rilla kept trying to catch her breath, knocking back her helmet and wilting against the wall. It cooled her back and the wind gusted against her face.

"I can see why Petra and Adeena kept climbing with you. Try not to hang on bolts or gear though, okay?"

"Those bolts are not actually helpful," Rilla said.

"Yeah and if you pull on gear, you just get it stuck or worse, pull it out."

Rilla blanched. She hadn't even thought of that. If she'd been leading, that would be a big fall.

"Plus, it's not clean climbing." Caroline shrugged. "It's bad form to get in the habit of that."

"Oh. I didn't . . ." Rilla blushed. "I didn't realize."

"You're a beginner. You didn't know. Petra had the responsibility of telling you, and maybe she did and it just got lost in other information. But if you want to keep doing it, you should know clean climbing is the rule." She smiled and looked up. "The next pitch is a good lead for you. It's easy and ledgy."

Caroline explained the pitch in detail, using the route map to show Rilla how to read both the route and the map. But when she reached for the gear on her sling to hand over to Rilla, she froze.

"Wait. Where's the . . ." Caroline paused and yanked the bag toward her, combing through the top. "Did you put that big nut in?"

Rilla's heart stopped. She remembered Caroline handing it to her. She remembered having to hold it while the smaller pieces went on first. She remembered . . .

"Fuck," Rilla breathed. *Oh no.* Tears stung her eyes.

Caroline glanced at her. "What?"

"I put it on the . . ." Rilla licked her lips. "On the picnic table. I forgot to . . ." *Oh god.* "Pack it."

Caroline groaned and leaned back.

Lauren echoed in Rilla's head. *You need to learn to apologize.*

But it was just a mistake. It wasn't . . .

It was totally her fault. Rilla squeezed her eyes shut and winced, forcing the words out. "I'm so sorry."

Caroline just laughed. "Ah, don't worry about it. We can make it work. Look."

Rilla opened one eye.

Caroline was pulling two smaller nuts out and held them up. "You'd be surprised how often this happens—something happens—and you need to figure out how to use the gear you have, instead of the gear you need." She laid the nuts on top of each other, their flat sides flush. "Just stack them to fit into the space. You'll need to be careful it's in there. But this will work."

"I'm really sorry," Rilla repeated. It was easier now that she'd said it once.

The harness cut into her legs and her back. Her arms below her elbows felt useless. Sweat rolled between her breasts. But she clipped the first bolt and scrambled up to the ledge she'd be following, a long string of rope behind her.

This part wasn't climbing—not technically. It was mostly walking up a rocky ledge to a pair of bolts that waited at the end. But with each step, Rilla felt the edge. Like the ground below, she heaved as she moved, and at any second she could be shrugged off the cliff. Her legs felt heavy. Each step got smaller and smaller until she found herself stopping.

Deep breath.

She was okay. She was doing it.

Her fingers shook. She checked her knot, and kept on. In a few minutes, Rilla clipped the bolted anchors with an intense surge of relief. With the relief came the accomplishment, and the pride and the glory and the wonder of doing it, and it was wildly fun again.

Caroline explained how to place gear along the next pitch she led, and Rilla listened with serious attention. All she wanted in life was to make it out of this climb without embarrassing herself any further. It went about as disgustingly and terrifyingly as the rest of the climb, but it *went.*

The afternoon sun shifted from white-hot into intense umber. Rilla was drenched, her sports bra chafing on the edges. The gallon jugs they'd brought were nearly emptying, but the bonus was it made the haul bag easier to haul after each pitch.

The last pitch was her turn to lead. Heralding the top . . . an obvious, tall, hunter-green pine tree.

Caroline patted her on the back. "Have fun!"

Rilla nodded, helmet bobbing on her sweating head as she looked up and began to climb.

It might have been fun for Caroline, but it all felt *awkward* to Rilla. She kept trying to have one foot on each wall and shuffle up the corner. But gravity kept yanking on her body. The stemming—her legs splayed like a little kid inching up a doorway—was easy one second and flat-out impossible the next.

Annoyed, she jammed her feet into the crack and tried to wiggle her way up. She regretted this day. She regretted ever finding it fun. What the hell was ever fun about this?

She sniffed and inched upward. Nothing felt right.

"Can you place a piece?" Caroline asked from below.

Shit. She'd forgotten. She had to place a piece *or she was going to die.* Never mind the pieces she'd placed farther down that would hopefully hold. Never mind that Caroline was below, on belay. *Die. She was going to die.*

The fear combined with the effort required to keep herself on the wall worked out into her fingers, and the cam clanked wildly against the rock. She fumbled—

Zzzzzzzip.

Oomph. Her next piece caught with a teeth-jarring and gear-shuddering jerk. She blinked and—

Zzzzzzzip.

Thwack.

She smacked against the wall, terrified and eyes wide, still clutching the piece she'd been trying to place. *Shit. Shit. Shiiiit.* Scrambling, she jumped onto the wall, clutching at anything she could touch. *What happened?*

"You okay?" Caroline called. She wasn't far below now.

Rilla looked between her legs. "No," she wailed.

"Does anything hurt?"

Rilla quickly took stock. Her heart pounded out of her chest. Her eyes watered. Fingers shook. Her breath came fast and shallow.

"I'm okay," she squeaked, wishing she believed it. She was not okay.

"Congratulations." Caroline sounded more chipper than Rilla had ever heard. "You lost a piece and didn't panic!"

Rilla stared down in mild horror. This wasn't something to celebrate. "I'm *gonna* panic, bitch," she yelled.

Caroline's eyes widened and she blinked.

Shit.

Caroline busted out laughing.

"Stop laughing," Rilla screeched. "Help me."

"Okay, okay. Look. You're at peace now. Check it."

Rilla whimpered, forcing herself to reach out and tug on the cam. It seemed solid, but so had the others.

"Can you slide in a nut to back it up?" Caroline asked.

Rilla felt sick, seeing herself reach for the gear on her sling and falling off.

"Just throw anything in," Caroline said. "It'll help you feel better."

Rilla gritted her teeth and forced herself to reach for a nut, slide it into the crack, wiggle it down, clip in the draw, and drop in the rope. Only after she did it did she realize she'd automatically done something she'd basically just learned. "Got it," she said, feeling a slight thread of relief.

"You were climbing hard," Caroline said from below. "You didn't even anticipate that you were falling. You blew a piece and kept your cool. You are the motherfucking shit right now, Rilla."

Rilla closed her eyes and shook her head. "I want to get down."

"When you place a piece, pull *out* when you're checking it. Not just down. Finish this pitch and then we're done." Caroline's tone was that of a much older girl. Thea the way Rilla kept wanting her to be. Someone in complete control. "Take a minute to regroup."

Rilla's stomach twisted and tightened, but she lifted her chin and focused above—not on the fact that she hung in a couple straps of nylon and tiny bits of raccoon fodder stuffed into thin cracks six hundred feet off the ground. She had to get control of herself. She couldn't lose it. There was no escaping this—this is where giving up meant she would lose all the work she'd put in, not only on the wall today, but in all the days she'd shown up to climb.

Drawing a deep breath in, she held it in her lungs for a half second longer and then eased it out in a long, controlled breath, imagining all that knotted her body easing out with it. "Help me," she called.

"Shake out your hands," Caroline replied immediately.

Rilla took one hand off and shook out the arm, then the other. She took another extra-long breath and swung back around to look at the wall.

"Try putting your hands into the crack on the side and pull that way," Caroline continued.

Rilla followed her instructions, angling herself out of the corner. "Like this?"

Caroline nodded. "And your feet up on the opposite wall."

Rilla put her foot up. "Oh." She almost laughed. It still felt awkward and horrible, but the forces twisting and pulling at her eased. Making her body into a right angle that in some way mirrored the right angle of the dihedral, she got back into the position and looked up.

"Shuffle your hands up. Don't try to go hand over hand like you were. Stem if you can, though. So much easier. And don't use your muscle here, hang on your bones."

Rilla frowned. *What?*

"Straighten your arms."

Rilla had thought they were straight, but she obeyed and locked out her elbows. "Oh!" She laughed. Now the bones of her arms did the work of holding her into the crack, not all her muscles, like when her elbow was bent and her arm was flexed. It was still hard—but not impossible.

She could do this.

Twenty minutes of shuffling later, she pulled over the ledge, past the tree, and clipped the anchors.

Caroline followed, and they hauled up the bag and spread out on a wide ledge under the shady boughs of an eighty-foot ponderosa pine, four hundred feet off the ground.

Rilla leaned against the wall, still clipped into the anchor and her eyes lifted with relief to the granite above her she did *not* have to climb.

"Have a treat." Caroline handed her an apple.

"Thanks." Rilla bit into it, tasting both the sweetness of the apple and the salt and grit on her lips. It was terrible. And intoxicating. "Goddamn, I'm going to do this again, aren't I?"

Caroline laughed. "Why wouldn't you? You were great."

"It was horrible."

"But wonderful," Caroline said with a dreamy grin.

Rilla closed her eyes and groaned. It was true.

"Want to know something?" Caroline said, wiping at the sweat on her face and leaving a smudge of dirt.

"Absolutely," Rilla said, perhaps a bit too hastily.

"My first big wall climb was up here, on a route just over there." Caroline gestured down the wall. "And I was so nervous and it was so hot that like ten pitches into it I got diarrhea."

Rilla did a double take. "That uh . . . is not what I expected you to say."

Caroline laughed. "I can't ever walk past here without thinking about it. I was in such a rush and so sick, it was all I could do to get my pants down. I just had to pray there was no poor soul walking below."

"Oh my god."

"I know!" Caroline shook her head and gave a little shiver. "I shit into the air!" She laughed. "I was so embarrassed at the time. Now it's just kind of funny and horrifying." The ocean of streaked granite and blue sky reflected in her sunglasses. "Did you climb in West Virginia?"

Rilla chewed her apple and stared out at the massive view. "No. I didn't know anyone that climbed at home. Plus, like, I'm a Skidmore."

"What does that mean?"

She probably shouldn't explain. If she'd been on the ground, she would have remembered this truth was not what she wanted anyone in California, least of all Caroline, to know. But up here, things felt different. She unscrewed her Nalgene and took a drink, looking up at the shadowed parts of the white granite cliff. "You know that family back home in Ohio that like . . . lives by the railroad tracks and has trash in their yard and rides a four-wheeler to the store because they have DUIs—you can get another DUI that way, sidenote—and they're always in trouble and their kids are always in trouble, and all the other parents are like yeah, I don't want you hanging out with that kid and if you play in their yard you are never allowed inside the house?"

Caroline squinted with one eye open. "Mm-hm?"

"That's a Skidmore." Rilla dropped her water bottle and pulled her T-shirt straight down. "This is actually my mom's T-shirt from the strip club dollar Thursdays."

Caroline squinted at the shirt. "Southern X-Posure?" She looked confused. "Oh, I get it!" She laughed. "I hope she taught you some moves. Always good to have a career to fall back on for extra cash. Stripping seems like an international sort of skill."

Rilla snorted.

Caroline unfolded her legs. "Well, so what?"

"I'm not supposed to be here," Rilla said, hearing her mom again at the bus stop. Girls like her didn't get chances like these.

"None of us are." Caroline laughed and leaned back. "I know it doesn't feel like it, but where you come from is part of what makes you, *you*. When I first left Ohio and started traveling for climbing, it was amazing, but also overwhelming. When you wake up every day wondering how you got there, even if it's in a good way, it's exhausting. But, the thing is . . ." Caroline paused a moment, staring out at the Valley. "I don't know. At first it felt like I didn't belong, like everyone would figure it out and send me home. But then I realized, all those things that made me afraid I didn't belong were all the reasons I was there in the first place. Everyone has a different path." She glanced at Rilla. "I'd go in your house," she said confidently. "I'd probably live next door."

Rilla smiled and tucked the apple core into her small trash bag. She wanted to hug Walker for giving her something so valuable as this climb with Caroline. The ease and elegance of Caroline's style seemed less a threat and more just part of Caroline.

Rilla's smile was real, her position on the wall was earned, and it didn't matter if she was special, or mediocre, or boring, or a Skidmore, because right now it felt like she had climbed above all that.

"Here, let's take a picture," Caroline said, fishing a camera out of her bag. "Your first lead multi-pitch!"

Rilla leaned in and smiled wide.

Caroline shaded her eyes and looked. "Cute."

"Can you take one of me with the view? I don't have any pictures . . . I want . . ." She gulped and forced herself to keep going, since she'd started. "Just to prove to everyone I'm not out getting wasted all the time. Which is definitely what they think I'm doing."

Caroline waved her hand. "Say no more. Want one of you climbing too? I can rig it up and . . ."

"No. No." Rilla flushed. "I just. I'm just being petty."

"It's not petty. It sucks when people assume the worst." Caroline stood, pulling out some slack in her rope to have freedom of movement on the ledge. "Here, stand back off the anchors and we'll get the background."

Rilla leaned back, weighting the anchors and smiling. She gave a big thumbs-up, but then it felt dumb, so she put her hands down on the rope. It was awkward—to have Caroline Jennings taking pictures of her. She looked down, trying not to seem embarrassed. The ground was far away, but she barely noticed. "Okay, thanks," she said, pulling back onto the ledge.

"I'll text them to you tonight. They look good. The light is nice."

"It's crazy that a tree can grow this far off the ground," Rilla said, tipping her head into the simmering blue afternoon and the wavering shade patterns across her face, still feeling awkward about the photos and rushing to move on. Even though Caroline seemed fine, she couldn't help but hear Petra's derision about Caroline's photos in her head. All she wanted was to shove it *once* in everyone's face back home.

"Back in the fifties some naturalists tried to get up here to see what kind of tree it was. They put in a bunch of bolts and gave up," Caroline said, over bites of her apple. "A group of climbers made it up here, and reported back that it was a Ponderosa. They looked farther up and said it was 'a real opportunity for future rock engineers',* but no one climbed above this point for the next twenty-six years."

Rilla twisted and looked up the wall. It was surprising to see how vast it looked still—especially after spending all day climbing to this point. It hardly looked like they'd made any progress at all. "Engineers? That's a weird way to describe it." Watching Caroline felt like art.

"The majority of climbers that made this Valley what it is, were white-boy engineering majors from Stanford coming down here on summers and weekends. I mean, the guy who said that was a German major, but same diff." Caroline brushed some dirt off her pants and stuffed the apple core back into her plastic bag. "So yeah, engineers. Because clearly the future of climbing was full of white-boy Stanford engineers." She caught Rilla's eye. "Definitely not a skinny girl from southern Ohio."

---

*   Allen Steck, *Camp 4*, Steve Roper, 133.

Caroline offered her a fruit cup, warmed from the sun and liquid sweet. She savored the soft peaches, leaning against the wall. In the silence and the wind, a tree frog began its song in the boughs above them.

Rilla looked up, eyes wide.

If this tree and frog could be places no one thought they belonged, maybe she could too.

twenty four

THEY WALKED BACK INTO CAMP 4 AT SUNSET. DIRTY. COVERED IN A THIN film of dried sweat and dust. Rilla's fingertips were rubbed raw. Her palms blistered and cut from the last pitch of shuffling her way up on lead. All she wanted was to take off all her clothes and go bury herself in the Merced.

Of course, when she walked into the campsite, Walker was leaning back on the picnic table with his radio sitting by his arm. He looked up, gaze flickering over the length of her in one quick glance before he swallowed and looked away.

A tremor of excitement fluttered in her stomach, and her exhaustion was forgotten.

Caroline took her pack and handed her another gallon of fresh water.

"Just in time for dinner. I'm almost done," the old man said from where he worked over a camp stove on the end of the table and a pan set over the fire.

"They've returned," Adrienne said, pushing out of the screen door of one of the canvas tents. "We were starting to get worried, but then we remembered you were with a newbie."

"That newbie," Caroline loudly declared, dropping her hands onto Rilla's shoulders and pushing her forward for the crowd. "Took a zipper fall on the last pitch and got right back on it. Like a champ."

It wasn't something anyone would brag about, but she recognized the praise Caroline was giving her was for having the tenacity to go on and not tap out. It was praise meant for a newbie, but she couldn't help but give a salty, dusty, cracked grin, and try very hard not to look at Walker, though she was dying to know what his expression was.

"Oh. Yeah. Right on." The old man smiled. "Did you have fun or have you sworn off it forever?" He looked at Caroline. "That's the true test. If she'll do it ever again."

"Let's go right now," Rilla said, her voice cracking halfway through. "Whatcha got?"

Everyone laughed. But differently than anyone had laughed at her before. And she hadn't even known there was a difference until right that second. *This* was the way she wanted to prompt their laughter—not because she said things that made people uncomfortable.

"I gotta get a ride back up to the Grove," Caroline said, sinking into a chair with her water. "Any good calls today?"

Hoping it wasn't too obvious, Rilla gingerly sat on the other end of the picnic table beside Walker.

Walker said, "Someone fell into the Merced."

Caroline grimaced. "Did they come out?"

Old guy nodded. "Took over an hour."

"Your sister came over," Walker said to Rilla.

"She was doing the rescue?"

"We put her on the line, since she's trained for it." Walker nodded. "We needed extra people, with the current so strong."

"She's okay, right?"

"Oh yeah," he said, as if there was never any question. "I bet she's pretty pumped. The person might even make it."

Rilla smiled, happy to hear something went right for Thea.

No one even asked if Rilla wanted a plate. One was just handed to her, overfilled with fried potatoes, softened and charred onions and cloves of garlic, eggplant, and corn, a piece of battered, fried fish, and a soft roll that looked familiar to the ones Jonah stole from the dining hall.

"That hiker we brought off Half Dome the other day gave us the fish as a thank-you," old guy said as Caroline lifted her phone high and took a picture.

Rilla hadn't thought she even had an appetite until she inhaled the char-grilled smell. The others chattered away and the campground swirled around them, Rilla leaned on her elbow, forcing her aching muscles to move from her fork to her plate to her mouth.

"Tired?" Walker asked quietly, leaning back on his elbows.

"Sore," she said. "I don't think I even have energy to shower."

He chuckled, gaze dropping in a distracting way. "What did you guys do?"

"El Cap Tree," she said over a mouthful.

"You weren't overplaying this," Caroline said to him as she ate.

"I told you," Walker's voice lightly sang. "You didn't want to believe me."

Rilla wasn't sure what they meant, but it seemed to be good, and she'd never felt more at home, despite being an outsider. The food went down easily, warming her belly. Her limbs stiffened and filled with sleepy lead.

They stayed there—in camp chairs propped up in a world carefully constructed of light. Shifting gold into fuchsia pinks, and deepening nearly fluorescent purple alpenglow, the sunset wove into the rocks and the water. The sky was sugar. The sheer cliffs rising up on all sides were veined granite polished into mirrors. Light gushed, frothing in iridescent foam on the Merced.

Every time she glanced at Walker, his blue eyes reflected the ephemeral joy she felt, sitting on that picnic table bench. Everyone sat around, laughing and talking. Rilla's eyes burned and she eventually pushed off the table and said her thanks.

"I'll walk you back," Walker said.

Even in her exhaustion, Rilla felt the surge of adrenaline as his long body fell into rhythm beside hers and the people they left behind hollered suggestively.

He rolled his eyes and flicked them off.

She laughed.

"Martinez would kill me if her little sister died on the walk back," he hollered over his shoulder.

Rilla groaned, tripping over the rocks in the dark. "It is possible I might die. I am so sore and tired."

"That happens." He reached over and grasped the back of her neck, giving it a squeeze like he was massaging her muscles, before awkwardly dropping his hand and pulling away.

Her eyes widened in the dark and tried to find something innocuous to say. "Busy day for you?"

"Not really. I wasn't involved in the river thing." He laughed. "I mean. I rescued bear cubs from the river, one in each hand."

"With no shirt, right? And an axe or some shit, like a deodorant commercial."

"Oh, we're past deodorant commercial. More like body spray level." He tossed his head like he was whipping back his hair in an imaginary wind.

She laughed, then cried. "Don't make me laugh, my stomach muscles hurt. Everything hurts."

"Poor baby," Walker murmured mockingly, knocking the edge of his shoulder into hers.

"Ow." She slapped at his stomach.

He grabbed her wrist and for a blissful second, they were entangled before he shook her off, laughing. "How did it go though, really?"

"Other than climbing with the most intimidating climber possible, you mean?"

"Caroline is nice."

"Yeah, because she's your sister."

"If I was answering about my sister, I would *not* say that." He snorted, still holding her wrist. "She was impressed. You did good. Does it feel good?"

Every beat of her heart pumped blood into that sliver of skin under his warm, roughened fingers. "It feels so good," she said.

They walked under the spreading, lichen covered black oaks, the darkness sweet and warm and the wind tinged with a faint hint of smoke. His skin glowed in the dark and she closed her eyes, walking beside him with her wrist still held between his fingers, a little awkwardly like he was almost holding her hand but hadn't committed to it.

Her head pulsed with the feeling of this moment.

It was everything.

In sight of the house, he let go. "See ya round, West Virginia."

She didn't respond—all the feeling was stuck in her throat. Turning, she wistfully watched the sway of his shoulders as he walked back into the dark. The wind blew and she shivered, longing rippling into something else. It was terrifying to want something she'd never wanted before—something that would expose her and risk herself in a way she'd avoided. Curtis had never been a risk, not like this. She narrowed her eyes into the dark. She wanted him, even if she had to work for it. Turning, she headed inside.

Thea was asleep on the couch when she went inside—belly down, fingers on the floor. And drooling. Rilla paused by the couch. Hopefully, Thea hadn't been waiting for her.

Rilla showered off the dirt and grime. When she closed her eyes, all she saw was dihedrals and arêtes and her body making angles to work her way against gravity. She defied gravity. Broke the rules. And had come back alive.

After her shower, she came out to Thea sitting upright, with a stack of paperwork in her lap.

"Thought I heard you come in," Thea said. "You look like you got sun."

Rilla looked at her pink shoulders and shrugged. "Want tea?"

"No . . ." Her gaze flickered over Rilla. "I mean . . . sure. What were you up to all day?"

"Playing outside," Rilla answered, pulling a mug out of the cupboard. "I heard about your river thing."

Thea made a noise.

"Are you . . ." Rilla frowned and watched the microwave numbers descend. Somehow it seemed silly to ask her sister if she felt okay. Thea was always okay. But suddenly Rilla wondered if that's just how she saw Thea because that's how she wanted to see her. She swallowed. "Are you okay? I heard they're going to live."

"Yeah. We seemed to get to him in time. I'm just glad it wasn't you," Thea said, standing and stretching her arms wide. "I didn't anticipate how I'd assume every rescue call was for you."

Rilla snorted. "I'm not *that* much of a disaster." She wasn't. She'd climbed with Caroline Jennings and everyone had lived.

"You're not a disaster, baby girl." Thea pulled her forward and kissed her forehead in a way that made Rilla feel young, in a good way. "You've been doing so well. I'm proud of you. I'm so glad you're here."

The microwave dinged.

"But just because you're not a disaster doesn't mean disaster can't happen to you. You can do everything right, and still not come back alive," Thea said. "That's just the risk we take to live our lives sometimes."

Rilla pulled out the hot water and added a teabag. She handed Thea the mug and took a deep breath. If she could do it on the wall, she could do it here. "I am sorry."

Thea's forehead creased. "For what?"

Rilla swallowed. It was a little easier than it'd been the first time, but not much. "I am sorry I made you feel like you had to tell Mom something you weren't comfortable sharing. That wasn't right of me. I didn't realize I was making it about that. But I can see now, it was easier to make it about you and your feelings than to admit how angry I felt when you left."

"Anger isn't an emotion, it's a reaction," Thea said.

Rilla made a face. "Ugh. *What do you want from me?*"

Thea smiled softly. "Yeah, I know. It's hard for me too. To talk about my feelings."

If she wasn't angry when Thea left, what had she been? She chewed her lip. "Abandoned? I felt abandoned. Everyone started leaving. Granny died. Daddy . . . Marco," she corrected. "Left. Then you did. I can't fault Granny for dying. But you and Daddy—did you just leave because he did?"

"No!" Thea sat down, looking stunned. "No, that wasn't it at all. I was angry at Daddy for leaving. I didn't even talk to him except for a few years ago. I left because I had to. I didn't mean to abandon you, but . . ." She rubbed her face and sighed. "It's hard to explain."

Rilla looked at her hands. "I can listen."

It was silent. Thea exhaled. "Mom depended on me . . . to the point where I was paying the bills, I was running the house, and Mom and Tom—they got angry if I did anything else. I woke up one morning and realized this wasn't how I wanted to live. I was eighteen and if I didn't leave then, I was afraid I never would."

"I didn't realize . . ." But Rilla could see it, now when she looked back.

Thea shook her head, dangerously close to tears. "I couldn't stay, Rilla. I'm sorry."

"I wouldn't want you to have stayed. I just didn't know that until now."

Thea smiled. "I'm glad you're here."

Rilla nodded. "Me too." It was worth the fear and the agony. Her phone buzzed and she pulled it out. Caroline had texted—three pictures.

The first was their selfie, smiling wide and messy hair in their helmets. An up-the-nose shot for Rilla, lovely.

The others were Rilla on the edge...the massive Valley framed behind her. She smiled. She barely recognized herself. Saving them to her phone, she flicked over to Instagram and got halfway through uploading a shot of her looking down, when she canceled it.

The only reason she'd wanted that picture was to prove something. But who was she trying to prove something to? Everyone at home had only wanted a spectacle. When she stopped being a spectacle, they stopped caring.

She looked at the photo again. *That is me,* she told herself over and over. Staring at the girl's thick, hardened arms. Her curious look hundreds of feet below. Her strong legs and messy braid. *That is me.* No one in West Virginia needed to believe this. No one needed to see it. It was all she'd hoped she could be, and all they'd never believed. She was the one who needed to see it. She was the one who needed to believe it.

Going back to Instagram, she uploaded the one of her and Caroline, #ValleyGirls. Upstairs, she combed through the slopped over pile of homework, pulled out her algebra, and folded her legs under the bare lightbulb. Pencil in one hand and chin tucked into the other, she began.

And didn't stop.

All night. Under the wind gusting through the open window, whispering all the things she could want, because a tree and a frog grew four hundred feet above the Valley floor.

twenty five

THE NOSE BECAME A SECRET. SHE KEPT IT TIGHT INSIDE HER CHEST, A
note she'd hidden inside her ribcage, that only she could read. A desire
so laughably out of her ability, she couldn't afford to let it escape, even as
she alternated between working for more gear and climbing with anyone
who would have her as a partner. She unfolded it and read it in her soul
while scrubbing the floor of the public bathrooms in Half Dome Village
for twenty dollars from Bethany and Amarie. She checked to make sure
it was still there when newcomers, Olivia and her partner Avery, showed
her the short, painfully big moves on the Camp 4 boulders. She picked
it out of the dirt and tucked it back away after she landed on her ass on
their bouldering mat over and over.

Olivia caught her staring at the white lightning bolt smeared onto
the granite boulder in chalk.

"It's famous," Olivia said. "Midnight Lightning. It took Ron Kauk and
John Bachar two months to do it the first time. Anyone who gets it goes
back over the lightning bolt with their chalk. To share in it."

Rilla tried the problem and could barely get on. Avery tried and got
halfway before landing on their ass. Olivia didn't get any farther.

But after they moved on, Rilla often found herself looking at the
lightning bolt as she walked back through the Camp, and reaching for
that secret note tucked into her ribs. To share in an experience bigger
than herself, a history she became a part of—it was what she'd wanted
even before climbing came into her life.

"Do you aid climb?" she asked Petra, too intimidated to ask her to teach her outright.

"Ugh. Aiding is a slog," Petra said. "Let's just find something you can actually climb."

Rilla shrugged and kept packing.

•

"Why don't you just fucking ask her?" Jonah asked as they jogged side by side one morning through the Valley.

Rilla growled. "I don't want to have to ask her. I want her to know, like, duh, Rilla is amazing. Rilla needs to aid to do anything bigger."

"Does she even know how?" Jonah said, slowing as they came to the open spring near the start of the Valley circle.

"Yeah, she knows how." Rilla came to a stop, sides heaving. She was a better runner than when she started, but Jonah had this unfair ability to run and never seem winded. "She climbs with Adeena all the time. Big routes."

"And they don't invite you?"

"They're partners. I don't know. I get it . . . if you have a good rapport with someone, and they climb at the same level, you don't really want someone new to come in and change the dynamics." She bent and filled her Nalgene with water from the spring. A cool breeze stirred the wisps of hair at her neck and brought a wet, earthy smell that made her feel of home. "You know, I never realized how much the humidity unlocks the smell of things."

"Does it smell differently on the East Coast?"

Rilla blinked. "Yes! Totally! Haven't you ever been?"

"I've never been farther east than Kansas."

"Oh. No, it's so humid and disgusting. It's like the air is a heavy, hot wet blanket. In West Virginia, I mean. I haven't actually been to the coast."

Jonah shuddered.

"But it carries all the smell and soul. The flowers and the earth and the trees. You can smell the breath of everything. You can get drunk on the smell of honeysuckle."

"You make West Virginia sound nice."

She rolled her eyes. "It *is* nice." Tipping the water bottle, she drank the sweet, clear spring water.

"If West Virginia is full of people like you, I don't know why it gets a bad rap."

She snorted. "It's full of people like me. But also, people much nicer than me. But it's terrifying when outsiders have ideas about you already. What can you do different to change a story they already think they know?"

Jonah didn't say anything, but his eyes narrowed thoughtfully and he pursed his lips as he refilled his bottle. "I still think you should ask Petra. Or, if not her, maybe Adeena would do it."

"Adeena is Petra's partner. I would feel really weird asking her. I haven't seen Caroline in a while, and maybe she hates me. Petra obviously doesn't think I need to aid. Walker doesn't find me attractive. Everyone hates me. *Wah.*"

"All right. Whoa, girl. No one hates you." He rolled his eyes.

Rilla stuck out her tongue.

"Just ask. The worst that could happen is someone says no. You'll live." He shifted away.

"You heading on?" she asked.

He nodded. "Thanks for running with me."

"Fine. *Bye.*"

"See ya." He jogged off, heading farther into the woods for more miles.

Rilla closed her eyes against the breeze that tasted like home, and then turned back for the heart of the Valley.

She stalked the Camp 4 parking lot for the next few days, until she found Adeena alone one evening.

"Do you know how to aid?" Rilla asked.

Adeena nodded over a drink of water. She lowered the bottle. "I was wondering if you were ever going to learn."

"I asked Petra, but..."

"Petra doesn't like it."

Rilla forced herself to say the words. "Would you be willing to teach me?"

"Absolutely," Adeena said, screwing the lid on as the car pulled in, Petra driving. "Pick out the climb you want to do and meet me here tomorrow afternoon." She waved goodbye.

Rilla waved back, in the direction of the car. After all her agonizing, it had been so easy.

Gage leaned across the seat. "Your turn for dinner duties. I signed you up with me. We're making bibimbap. Tomorrow."

"Sounds good!" Whatever that was. The unspoken rule was that when it was your turn to cook, you tried to make something only you could make. Rilla assumed if she ever had to come up with a dinner they'd want her to make fried chicken and collard greens, and good luck because she could barely cook rice and beans.

Stuffing her hands into her shorts, she walked over to HUFF, trying not to replay the conversation with Adeena, and thereby find a way to talk herself out of trying. She wouldn't be here if she hadn't tried. And kept trying.

It wasn't safe, but it was better than not trying at all.

twenty six

EARLY AFTERNOON WHEN THE DUSTY SHADOWS LENGTHENED THROUGH the pines, Rilla met Adeena at Camp 4 and they collected their gear, checking the route map to make sure they'd packed what they needed. It made Rilla proud and nervous that Adeena trusted her to take the lead on the trip. Adeena handed Rilla the aid ladders, and Rilla carefully dropped them into the pack.

In the amber light, they hiked the short hike along the east face of El Capitan.

"Petra won't be like . . . mad at about this, right?"

Rilla asked, even though it seemed weird that an older girl like Petra would do that.

"No," Adeena retorted. "Why? Do you think so?"

"I don't know. That's why I was asking."

Adeena frowned, then shrugged. "We're good."

"I still can't believe you two didn't know each other before you showed up for the summer."

"I knew enough people around the Valley. I knew if it didn't work out, I wouldn't be stranded."

"Still." Rilla picked her way around a loose boulder. "Do you live close to your family here in the States?"

"My aunt and uncle are like fifteen minutes from where I live now. And I'd visited before."

There was a trace of defensiveness in Adeena's tone, and Rilla clamped her mouth shut, worried she'd said something wrong or assumed something she had no right to assume.

"Petra makes you feel like she's in control of things," Adeena continued. "I actually didn't think for a second there'd be a problem, because she's always seemed so genuine and confident. But, I mean, it's also the community. Climbers help each other out."

"Petra does make you feel in control." But sometimes Rilla wondered how much of it was simply a need for Petra to control a situation.

Adeena didn't say anything else. She tipped her chin to the wall, scanning for the start of their climb, and Rilla followed her lead.

When they scrambled up the slab to the start, Adeena pulled out the aiders and unraveled them from the cordelette they'd been packed with.

"There's a rhythm to aiding," she said, the sun bathing her in amber and highlighting in her dark hair. "Efficient aiding makes all the difference in how long something takes and how tired you get. But it's not the same as climbing. The better you get at the rhythm, the faster you can move through those sections."

Adeena pulled out some gear and spent the next fifteen minutes explaining how Rilla would use the aiders. "Always make sure it's clipped to the daisy chains, okay?" she finished.

Rilla stared dumbly, trying to cram Adeena's instruction in her head.

She dusted her hands with chalk. "I'm going to free-climb. Or attempt to. This tiny face crack stuff is my weakness."

Rilla stood with the aiders in her hands. "I don't even know . . ."

"All right, let's go!" Adeena said, clapping her hands together and looking at the wall as if she was psyching herself up.

Rilla guessed she'd just figure it out. She clipped the aiders to her harness and her helmet to her head and shrugged.

In the same way chimneys had felt awkward and arêtes had felt unclimbable, the first run up the aiders felt frustratingly slow and terrible. Nothing in her body seemed to know where to go. Nothing seemed natural. She cursed and sweated and her neck and shoulders and legs ached by the end of the first pitch.

It was supposed to be faster—but Rilla swore she could have climbed it in half as much time. But this new thing was different than all the others. Now she could remember how that chimney felt and how the arête seemed impossible. She remembered failing and flailing. And she remembered working until somehow the rock relented and everything became easier. Her body had muscle memory of failing. Her mind didn't panic, because it had been there before. This was normal. This was how she learned. She gritted her teeth and pushed back her helmet and looked upward to the boundless sky and kept on, knowing in her heart the terrible awkward feeling of failure could be sweated out and left behind.

She tried to find a rhythm. Repeating it over in her head like a song to keep time to—left step, right step, left step until you're as high as you can. Click your heels. *No place but home.* Smear toe.

Reach.

Clip to the new piece.

Unclip your last ladder.

Then clip your rope.

Place a piece. Check to make sure it's solid.

Start again.

Left step, right step, left step. High. Click. Smear. Clip this. Unclip ladder. Clip there. Clip that. And again.

Left step. Right step . . .

Pulling over a roof, Rilla's stomach suddenly bottomed out. Fear rippled up her spine.

Out of the corner of her eye, she spotted the Valley floor—how far away it was. How much space echoed, ready to forget her existence. Every muscle tightened. A good hold was just above, out of reach, but easy to get to if she jumped. But if she jumped—all she saw was her hand outstretched. *Zzzzip, zzip, thump* as her gear pulled and she fell three hundred feet to smack the ground. She should have triple-checked all her gear placement. Clutching the aiders, she shifted, awkward and aching, and terrified to move.

"You okay?" Adeena shouted.

"I'm fine . . ." Rilla looked down. Her feet swung over a dusty green carpet of pines far below.

"You sure?"

Rilla swallowed.

"Trust yourself," Adeena yelled.

Rilla readjusted her grip.

"Trust your gear," Adeena yelled.

Rilla flicked her eyes to the gear she'd just put in the wall to hang the higher aider on.

Trust herself, her gear . . . her partner. She had to. If she didn't, she'd just be stuck. She squeezed her eyes shut and forced herself to move.

"No wonder Petra doesn't like this," she huffed to Adeena, pulling to the anchors. "That *was* a slog."

Adeena laughed and crisscrossed her legs. "Yeah. A slog, indeed. I like big mountains because just when I'm sick of one thing, it seems to change, at least a little. I get bored easily."

"I hear ya." Rilla brushed dirt off her knee, thinking of her piles of homework half-started and never finished. "I'm sorry . . . earlier. For offending you."

"For what? I wasn't offended."

"I mean." Rilla swallowed. "About your family. Assuming I knew your feelings."

"Oh." Adeena shrugged. "You're fine."

"Do you still want to climb big mountains, or do you like this more?"

Adeena looked out. The Valley reflected in the sheen of her eyes. "Oh yeah. I thought about doing a big mountain this summer, but I didn't know how training would work with this first year of school. But, I've always wanted to come here. My brother had been here before when visiting family, and he made it seem magical. I needed some time from that kind of climbing. It felt like a good time to come."

"Is your brother back in Pakistan? He's a guide, right?"

Adeena didn't respond right away. She redid her ponytail with her eyes fixed to the Valley. "He passed away last year, on K2. Inna lillahi wa inna ilayhi raji'un."

Rilla startled straighter. "Oh no, I didn't—I . . ." she stammered.

"It's okay. You didn't know. Rilla, I don't expect you to know everything about my life. It's fine to ask."

Rilla glanced at Adeena—uncertain whether to believe it was fine, or if she was trying make her feel less stupid. "I've never heard you speak . . ." Shit, what did people from Pakistan speak? Pakistani? No, that was what they were called. Right? Sweat pricked the back of her neck. She had to show Adeena she wasn't racist. "Your native language." Nailed it.

Adeena side-eyed her. "Arabic is not my native language."

"Uh . . ." *Shit.*

"I can speak it. But my native language is Shina. I was quoting the Quran. *We are Allah's, and to him we shall return.*"

Rilla's face burned. She swallowed and looked at her chalk-dusted fingernails. The Quran. "Oh, that's why you went off to pray. You're Muslim?"

"Yep. And just so you know, it's pronounced *moos-lihm*. Not *muh-slem*."

Suddenly Lauren jumped into her head. *You need to apologize.* Rilla frowned. No. It was an honest mistake. Not wrong. Just . . . *ugh.* She bit her lips. "I am so sorry. I just haven't ever met someone from the Middle East."

Adeena snorted. "Aaaand, I'm not from the Middle East. Pakistanis are South Asian."

"Oh my god!" Rilla shouted, pounding her fists on her knees. "Why am I so awkward? I'm gonna shut up now."

Adeena laughed. "You have *got* to give yourself a break. I'm sure there's plenty I don't know about West Virginia."

"I'm not a good representative of West Virginia," Rilla said. "I'm basically the stereotype everyone there hates anyway. Everyone else probably knows Pakistanis are South Asian." She was careful to pronounce *Pakistani* like Adeena did.

"I'm not sure *I* should visit any time soon." Adeena said with a chuckle. "But I do hear the New River Gorge is nice."

"It's not like everyone thinks," Rilla said. "I know what y'all think. It's not some totally backwoods, shitty, racist state. Some people are assholes, but that's everywhere, right? People are nice, we're just ... not ... I don't know. It's beautiful. And has the nicest people. I miss it so much." She looked down. "I hate feeling like this." This awkward urge to defend the place she'd come from, against things that might be true for some, but were not true for all. "Do you miss Pakistan?"

"Always. It's my home. But I have complicated feelings about it." Adeena smiled with understanding. "I didn't mean to make you feel shitty about where you're from."

Rilla ducked her head. "It's okay. Sorry for being a tool."

"You weren't!" Adeena said. "Now, if you'd been shitty after I corrected you, then you would have been a tool."

Rilla smiled. "Glad I wasn't shitty."

"Me too."

Rilla unscrewed the cap on her water as the wind gusted. "You're a good teacher with the aiders. I appreciate it. A good teacher makes all the difference."

"It's only what I want to do for the rest of my life," Adeena said. "So I'd better be good at it."

"Not climbing for the rest of your life? Teaching? Is that what you're going to school for?"

"I'm in school for an MBA. What I really want to do is run a non-profit to teach girls to climb. Girls at home . . . girls everywhere . . . need something like climbing in their lives, I think." She stretched her arms in front of her. "Climbing taught me I own this body. I own my mind. It gave me a safe place to grieve and grow and want something beyond the life I had. I am lucky to have this opportunity—this gift. This is a privilege not afforded to most people."

"Yeah . . ." Rilla bit her fingernail absently, terrified to take those feelings and apply them to herself. "I can't believe I'm here."

Adeena smiled. "Same." She glanced at her phone. "Err . . . Petra just texted. She's wondering where we are."

"Are you going to tell her we're climbing?"

"I'm going to ignore the text. We can just meet her at Camp 4."

They ate their apples and chucked the cores, watching them sail through the deepening afternoon shadows into the abyss. No sound accompanied their disappearance.

The sky shifted to the dark purple and hot pink of alpenglow, and they lowered out and began the short hike along the base of El Cap, back to Camp 4.

"Dee!" Ajeet's shout echoed as they picked their way through the scree.

Adeena and Rilla both looked up, into a group of climbers in the Alcove, taking turns on a swing that someone had hung from bolts on a climb arching over the slanted ledge.

"Hey," Adeena called back, and they crawled up the slab, looking out over the Valley and the sloped green-carpeted walls and gray gullys facing them.

A line of dusty climbers waiting their turn waved and introductions were made.

"You going to swing?" Ajeet asked Rilla. Ajeet was the climber who had prayed over her first meal at the Grove.

"I . . ." She watched as a climber clipped the hanging carabiners to their harness and leapt off the ledge—because of the overhang of the arch, the rope swung out into the wide open, before swooping back under the ledge. It took three others to pull the swinger back in to unclip.

"Sure," she replied.

When it was her turn, Adeena clipped her into the swing. And with the lock of the carabiner's gate, her heart jumped in her neck. What if this time, it broke? This tiny piece of string she was going to bounce on. She had to trust that the rope would hold for her, just the same as it held for everyone else. Clutching the rope, she jumped.

As the wind rushed to greet her, she laughed with joy.

•

Back at the Grove, she washed her hands and presented herself as assistant to Gage. "At your service," she said, hands outstretched. It was dark and everyone seemed to be coming in and cleaning up, looking hungrily toward the kitchen.

He chuckled. "I need you to wash the spinach." He nodded to some grocery bags stuffed with fresh picked spinach sitting by the sink.

"Where did you get this?" She hadn't seen a garden around.

"A farmer outside the park."

"I guess it could grow . . ." She shrugged. "Since it's cool at night."

"Did you live on a farm at home in West Virginia?"

"No." She pulled out a handful of spinach and tossed it into a colander, turning on the water. "I lived in a duplex. But my granny had a big garden before she died. I used to help her weed."

"My grandma gardened too. Flowers. She had incredible roses."

"Oh, roses are so beautiful. They grew on the side of our house and I always loved it when they bloomed."

Rilla emptied the other bag of spinach and started washing the leaves of the dry dirt. "What are we making?"

"Gochujang bibimbap. It's hot rice and beef with vegetables basically."

"Cool." She shook the colander and glanced over her shoulder at him. "You're in school?"

"Structural engineering." He nodded.

"How did you get into climbing?"

"I went to a friend's birthday party in fifth grade that was at a local climbing gym, and I just got hooked. I loved it. I had a lot of energy as a kid . . ." He cleared his throat. ". . . and my parents were pretty relieved when I found an outlet."

Rilla laughed. "A lot of energy is usually code for trouble. Were you a troublemaker, Gage?" She glanced over her shoulder, teasing.

He suppressed a smile as he cut cucumbers. "Of course not. I was a well-behaved, adorable child. I absolutely did not torment my parents by climbing out of my bedroom window when I was six."

She could just imagine a rambunctious little boy version of Gage with his button-up and a terrible grin. "All I did was practice the piano and read quietly," he finished.

She snorted.

"I'm kidding, I was a terror."

"No!" she said in mock surprise.

Something wet hit the back of her head. She squealed as a cucumber chunk hit the floor. "Ah. Spinach is not a good weapon." She plucked a leaf from the bowl. "On guard."

He shook his head. "You're supposed to be cleaning. Not playing."

"I wasn't the one who launched cucumbers."

She handed over the colander piled high with washed spinach and followed his instructions for laying out the food.

And when they sat down to eat, Rilla dug into her bowl of hot rice, julienned cucumbers, zucchini, sprouts, spinach, mushrooms, and radishes in colorful piles, with steaming tenderized beef to the side, and a hot chili paste for the top. "This is my new favorite food," Rilla said.

Something about it felt like home—maybe just the same things, cucumbers from Granny's garden, spicy radishes eaten raw, and tenderized beef served over cheap rice. Who knew that food could make her feel the potential for home existed in places she'd never even seen?

twenty seven

"HOW'S IT GOING?" MOM ASKED CHEERILY, A RUSTLING SOUND MIXING with her words.

Rilla frowned at the phone and put it back to her ear. "Mom, what're you doin'?" She gulped to hear the accent she'd swear she didn't have. "What are you doing?" she asked again, carefully.

"Your daddy broke his leg. I'm wrapping it with packing tape."

Rilla made a face at the bushes. "What?"

"He's got it all propped up in a brace Mr. Banner gave him, but I'm trying to secure it so he can use the shower." *Shhhhh . . .*

Rilla pulled the phone away.

"Why don't you go to the doctor?" She asked, putting it back to her ear.

"We had Granny Hutchins out, and you know, he's doing okay right now. Got some pain meds. She was able to set it. Good lord, that woman's strong. She told him to pack it with some stinging nettle and that's been working. If it get's real bad or something, we'll go. But we're still paying off my incident last year."

"Oh yeah," Rilla said. Mom had needed her stomach pumped when she accidentally mixed the wrong medications. She'd even been embarassed about that. "How'd he hurt his leg?"

"Flipped his four-wheeler." *Shhhhhh . . .* "Move it this way, Tom."

Rilla chewed her fingernail. "Can I ask you something?"

"Sure," Mom said.

"Why didn't you tell me it was Thea's idea for me to come out here?"

Shhhhh . . . "*Rilla Anne,*" her mom said in an exasperated tone. "I was the one who decided to send you. Thea just offered."

Rilla took her fingers out of her mouth and stared at them. "Oh." She sighed. "You know everything with me and Curtis was mutual, right?"

"Mutual is for divorces, not for brawls."

"But I hit him too."

Mom sighed.

Rilla swallowed, her throat tight. She closed her eyes and suddenly she could see it all the way everyone else had been telling her. The way it had started. The way Curtis had backed her into a corner, yelling at her about sleeping with other guys. She'd slapped him—yes. But she'd been terrified about what he could do with his body that close and she'd struck out to put distance.

"I don't know why you're complaining," Mom said. "You got the chance to live with Thea. You'll come home in August having seen more of the world than most people around here have." *Shhhhh . . .* "That should do it."

A dull ache tore at Rilla's chest. "Yeah, August." She didn't want to go back now. Now that she had climbing, and all her friends and everything that maybe could be with Walker. She had finally made a home for herself. But she didn't say anything. Mom wouldn't ever hold her to it, if she decided not to return, and that was one of the nice things about Mom. "Sorry. I love you, Mom."

"Love you, Rilla. Tell Thea I said to call me."

She hung up and stared out at the shifting afternoon light and the cloudless blue sky. It wasn't like that, she found herself repeating in her head about Curtis. But she laid her head on her arms and closed her eyes. *Yes it was. It was exactly like that.* And it had been wrong. She didn't completely believe it yet, but she was starting to.

And she cried, hurting all over again.

•

"I want to maybe do an overnight climb," Rilla said, twiddling her pencil as she sat on the bear boxes, notebook on her knee, supposedly scribbling an outline for an English paper. The fire flickered under the cedar boughs and the hum of Camp 4 reverberated around them. It was the end of a long, hot climbing day, and they waited for stragglers at Olivia's campsite in Camp 4. Rilla should have gone home, but couldn't bring herself to leave when everyone was still there. She'd hoped, by announcing that, someone would invite her along on a trip they'd already planned—but no one jumped at the bait.

"All right," was all Petra said, lazily from the chair where she looked half-asleep. She looked up as Walker stepped into the circle. "Look at the man whore himself."

"Love you too, honey." He made a kissy face to her. "What's up?" He said it to the group, but his gaze flickered to Rilla.

She straightened, grip tightening on her pencil.

Petra kicked at his leg. "I heard a rumor Celine Moreau is coming."

He shrugged. "That's the rumor," he said.

"I need updates. You can send it via carrier Rilla."

He snorted. "Is she your bird carrying messages down here, then?"

"Well, it's the best I got. What you been climbing?"

"Nothing special." Walker sighed and sank into a chair. "I'm stuck." He poked at the fire, gaze flickering over to Olivia. "We haven't met? Have we?"

Olivia's eye widened. "No. But I think I've met your sister. She beat me at a youth worlds in Germany when I was sixteen. I didn't realize she had a brother." Olivia visibly blushed, even in the light of the fire.

Rilla snapped her chin to study Walker, grateful for her dark corner to hide the flush of jealousy. The skin of her wrist burned. "He's everyone's vacation fuck boy," Rilla said before she thought all the way through the sentence.

He didn't look at her, but his mouth visibly tightened. "Yep," he said lazily.

That terrible sense of just having made a mistake sank in her stomach. What had she just said? Despite what Thea and Petra had said about him, she'd never really seen any evidence of him being like that. Appalled, she buried her nose back into the outline and tried to ignore everyone as they kept talking.

"Caroline!" Petra said as Caroline slumped in and dropped her pack in the dirt.

"Move," she ordered her brother.

Rilla kept her nose in her notebook.

"Ugh." He moaned, but rolled out of the chair and sat on the box next to Rilla.

She swallowed. "I'm sorry," she whispered.

He didn't reply. But his arm touched hers. Warm and reassuring in the dark.

"How is freeing The Nose going?" Petra asked Caroline, almost teasingly.

Caroline huffed into the chair and didn't answer.

Rilla's stomach clenched. She couldn't tell if Caroline regretted taking her climbing, or was just focused on her own climbing, or just exhausted and hadn't noticed Rilla was there.

Probably just tired.

Or all of it.

"Hey, that climb you did the other day. I heard there was a loose block on the fifth pitch," Petra said.

Caroline leaned over and poked around at the snacks Hico had brought. "Are these Oreos?"

"They're Hico's."

"Huh?" He was on his knees at the edge of a spread-out tarp, busy packing for the next day's climb, paying no attention.

Caroline held them up. "Mind?"

"Help yourself."

Caroline sat down and opened the package, finally turning to Petra. "The block is loose right below the fifth set of bolts. Even touching it seemed like a bad idea. I stayed far away. It's definitely coming off soon."

"*Soon* meaning, anytime between now and a hundred years from now," Petra said.

"Speaking of which," Hico said. "Did anyone get updated beta for the huge chunk of Half Dome that came off?"

"I have an update. I'll copy the page for you," Walker said.

"Everything changes. Even Yosemite," Petra said with a sigh.

Rilla looked up at the ridge—blue and shadowy in the moonlight above the warm glow of camp. At home, the mountains changed in theory, but not really in practice. The flood had changed things, but not really the mountains. Here, the ridges changed at a rate you could see. Young gods versus the old. Rilla balanced her pencil on her finger—the old gods had seen fit to kick her out, but it felt as if the new ones had yet to see her.

Deep down, she wanted to be seen. To be accepted. The pencil tipped and she caught it, coming back to the conversation.

"There used to be this really cool sign in the front of the hotel, with an etching of Half Dome on it. I guess they got rid of it when they changed the name," Caroline was saying. "I wish I would have just taken it."

"It's still there," Rilla said. She'd seen it while weeding for Aiden. "It's just in the garden. Yard decoration sort of thing."

"Caroline, you should take it," Petra said. "She knows where it is."

"There's also an abandoned tennis court back there," Rilla said.

"Really?" Caroline bit another Oreo. "I feel like I need to see that."

"And there's a school in the Valley," Walker said. "I found that out when Rilla arrived."

Rilla nodded. "Yeah, there's a school. It's teeny." She slapped her notebook. "Hence, this slog."

"Why don't you just take your GED?" Caroline asked. "That's what Walker did when we left Ohio."

"It's not hard," Walker said.

"What?" She could have avoided all this mess with one test? Rilla tilted her head. "I didn't even know that was an option."

"You have to be eighteen. There's a study book. Ask Thea."

"I turned eighteen last week." Rilla slapped the notebook closed. "I'm *done* with this shit."

"Wait." Walker held up his hand. "Your birthday passed?"

"Rilla!" Petra wailed. "Why didn't you tell us?"

Rilla shrugged. "Well, it was when the park was evacuated."

"Oh," Petra said. "We'll have to celebrate."

"Happy birthday!" Caroline said.

Everyone echoed.

Rilla ducked her head, embarrassed. "Thanks, guys."

"Okay. Take me to see this tennis court," Petra said. "On our way to take Caroline to get her plaque."

"I can't steal the sign," Caroline said.

"They obviously don't care about it," Petra said. "Come on."

Caroline groaned. "Fine. I want that stupid plaque. Let's do it."

Petra pumped her hands and glanced to Adeena. "You coming, Dee?"

"Yeah, that's a hard *no*."

"Do I have to do a dance for you? Are you just jealous?"

There was a pause and Adeena looked up with her eyes narrowed. "I'm not about to risk my visa over your pranks."

Everyone froze. It wasn't necessarily that Rilla had forgotten what was going on outside of the park—it was that she hadn't ever *applied* it to Adeena. Suddenly, it called into question how she thought about the rest of the world . . . it made everything more personal when it applied to her own community.

"Sorry, Dee," Caroline said quietly. "We won't go without you."

Adeena waved her hand. "Don't do that. Go steal it for me." She clenched her fist. "Show the man who's boss."

Petra laughed. "Come on, Caroline. Rilla will lead us."

"You coming?" Rilla asked Walker, fingers crossed.

His gaze met hers and then dropped. "Nah, I gotta sleep. I'm on call again tomorrow, and it's supposed to be really hot. I want to get some good sleep."

Fine. Be that way. She wanted to snap and flounce off, but she just shrugged and tried to make it look like she didn't give two hoots that he was still sitting by the fire with wide-eyed Olivia.

Rilla fell into step beside Caroline and Petra as they left the camp behind and headed down the dark path still randomly populated with tourists. Caroline and Petra were always polite together, but she'd never seen them *hang out*. It was a new, strange dynamic.

"Olivia was super into your brother," Petra said.

"Do I look like I give a shit?" Caroline asked.

Petra rolled her eyes and gave Rilla a look like, *OMG*.

Rilla's stomach tightened.

"I don't want to talk about my brother's dating life," Caroline said.

"Ugh, yeah. I hear you," Petra said smoothly, even though she'd brought it up. "Did you hear that rumor that Celine is coming to the park?"

"Not a rumor," Caroline said. "She's coming at the end of July."

"Rilla, do you know who Celine is?" Petra asked.

"Um. Vaguely," Rilla answered, dodging dazed and sunburnt hikers through Yosemite Village and trying not to feel dumb she didn't really know. "A famous climber, right?"

"Hopefully she's not so celebrity she can't climb with us," Petra said. "I'm friends with one of her climbing partners, and I've heard she's nice, but we'll see."

"She's nice," Caroline said.

"Oh, you've met her?"

Caroline was quiet, but she must have nodded, because Petra moved on. "Rilla wants to do a big wall," she said.

"Oh yeah?" Caroline's tone picked up excitedly.

"We should all do one together. You're the queen of big wall logistics," Petra said.

"Mmm . . ." Caroline said. "Yeah, maybe."

Petra and Caroline were going to climb together? She'd never seen that. But more importantly, they would climb with her. Rilla nearly skipped with glee, off the asphalt, onto one of the grass beaten meadow paths that the employees used to shortcut the Valley.

"Why are you so loud?" Caroline said to Petra. "Quit trampling through the undergrowth. We're stealing something, not waltzing in and announcing our presence."

"I am being quite stealthy," Petra shot back

Caroline laughed.

Rilla slowed, trying to be quieter, just in case.

Petra shoved her elbow into Caroline's side, and Caroline jumped. "Quit trampling through the undergrowth, Caroline," Petra said.

Caroline covered her mouth to smother her laughter.

Rilla crept through the gardens with Caroline and Petra in tow. Her mind ran circles around Walker, her schoolwork, and how to convince Thea she should take the exam for a GED, only half aware of what she was doing.

The oaks shivered and the moon reflected off the walls above them. A thrill rushed into her fingertips—she was going to climb those. That was all that mattered to her. As long as she could keep climbing—keep being a climber—she'd be happy.

She showed them the tennis courts, cracked and broken and shrouded in vines. It was the only thing in the Valley that hinted at eerie. "The plaque is somewhere over here" she whispered.

Creeper covered the ground. No paths through—it was a barrier island of drought-resistant grass to keep the plebeians and the proletariat in their part of the Valley.

"Did you see it?" Petra whispered. "What does it look like?"

"Why are we whispering?" Caroline asked. "Is someone going to catch us?"

"We're technically trespassing," Rilla said quietly. If Ranger Miller suddenly appeared, she was screwed. *Thea* was screwed. She should have thought of that back at the fire.

"I'm not interested in seeing how technical," Petra said.

Rilla kicked around in the grass, head bent. Her toe stubbed on something hard. "I think I found it." She bent and felt in the dark. "Nope, just a rock."

"I got it," Petra said.

"Really?"

"Yeah . . ."

They were interrupted by a flashlight and an all too familiar voice. "Put your hands in the air."

Shit. Inwardly, Rilla groaned. *Why, oh why?* Ranger Dick Face was back.

"What do we do?" Caroline asked frantically.

"I'm running," Rilla whispered.

"Are we all running?" Petra asked, grinning in the dark.

"On the count of three."

"One."

"Different directions," Rilla said, just in case—she wasn't sure she trusted either of them to know to scatter.

"Two."

"Three," Rilla whispered.

They tore off through the brush and trees.

Ranger Dick Face hollered after them.

In the chaos, Rilla ran as fast as she could through the brush, heading straight for home. The memory of running from Vernal Falls flashed behind her eyes, but home was a short distance away and no sirens followed. The flashlight dropped off quickly and she slowed to a walk as she reached the edge of Yosemite Village. Ranger Dick Face was nowhere in sight. She touched her pockets, looking for her phone to check the time to know whether to expect an angry Thea. But her phone wasn't in her pockets. Shit. She must have lost it . . .

Rilla frowned. Where had she left her homework? On the bear box? *Oh my god.* She did not lose her homework.

Rilla trudged up the steps with a sigh, opening the door. "I'm back, but I'm just getting—"

"Hey!" Thea interrupted. "Did you forget something?"

twenty eight

WALKER PATTED HER PHONE AND NOTEBOOK, NEATLY SITTING ON THE
table beside him.

"Oh." Rilla gave a nervous laugh. "Hey. Thanks for bringing those back."

"I swear Rilla, you are the most scatterbrained person I know," Thea said.
Rilla frowned.

"How'd it go?" Walker asked, a grin on the corner of his mouth.

Rilla glared him.

"How did what go?" Thea asked.

"Nothing," Rilla said quickly. "I was showing Petra the tennis courts."
Rilla opened the cupboard and got out a mug, steadying her still-shaking
hands.

"Okay." Thea looked at Walker as if he was supposed to explain; but he
just shrugged.

"Want some tea?" Rilla asked Thea.

"I gotta head to bed," Thea said.

Rilla held the tea box up for Walker. "Peppermint?"

He leaned forward on the counter, his long ropey arms tensing under
the thin T-shirt. "Ah . . ." He nodded. "Sure. Why not? I'll take some."

A rush of warmth ran up her spine, and she had to turn quickly to hide
the smile on her face by getting a mug out the cupboard and setting the
kettle on the stove.

"So, in that situation you'd want to use a clove hitch, right?" Walker
asked Thea.

Thea looked up. "Oh, yeah." She stretched. "Sorry, I was distracted. All right, I have to sleep. You're in for the night, right Rilla?"

Rilla nodded, busying herself with the mugs and teabags. "Want honey?" she asked.

"Nah. I'll just drink this and be heading back. Night, Thea. Thanks for talking."

"Anytime," Thea said. "Thanks for bringing Rilla's stuff back."

They were left in silence.

Walker's gaze flicked to hers. Judging by his tensed mouth and furrowed brow, he was holding something back.

"What?"

His mouth twitched. "Nothing."

She raised her eyebrow.

With a wide-open palm he rubbed his mouth, eyes somehow exasperated when they flickered to her.

Her heart raced. "Oh come on, what?"

The kettle began to whistle and she turned off the stove and poured the water.

He straightened up sober and his expression in control, accepting the mug. "So I'm just everyone's vacation fuck boy?"

She cringed. "That was not okay. I don't even . . . I was . . . Everyone just..."

"Everyone what?"

She shrugged. "You have a reputation. I've been warned."

He nodded, lips pursed. After a minute of awkward silence, he said, "What are their warnings?"

Rilla swallowed. If she told him, her feelings would be obvious. Explicit. She turned away and put the tea back. "Just that you move through girls quickly."

He didn't respond. Didn't look at her. She slid over his mug and waited.

"Climbing any better after Caroline?" he asked, changing the subject.

"I think so? I still suck, but like in a better way?"

He smiled. "That's all you can ask for."

"Hopefully I won't be there forever."

"You don't think the best climbers feel that way?"

"Do you feel like you suck?" she asked.

"All the time. On and off the wall."

She rolled her eyes. "You're supposed to tell me about your feats of nerve and daring."

He blew softly on his tea, sending ripples over the liquid. "Sometimes it's nice not to have to lead with that."

She smirked. "If I had that to lead with, I would."

His eyes popped up in amusement. "What about you with that whole . . ." He shimmied his shoulders.

"Wait, what is that? That's not me. I *am* offended."

Now it was his turn to roll his eyes. "Right, who's that guy you run with?" He drummed his fingers on the counter.

"Jonah is actually just a friend," Rilla said primly.

"Sure." Walker nodded. "Sure. Do you have a boyfriend back home?"

Something flashed hot and panicky across her chest. Rilla sipped her tea. It burned the tip of her tongue. "No. I've actually only had one boyfriend. A few other casual things . . ." Just at that moment, the memory of being backed against the truck and slapping Curtis across the face shimmered alive in her head. Her palm stung. Her heart raced. She swallowed and looked down, trying to regain control. She was fine. It was fine.

"Really?" Walker asked with surprise.

"What's that mean?" She realized too late it sounded intense and defensive.

"No. It's fine. I just . . . I don't know. I expected—" He stopped abruptly and clamped his mouth shut. After a long drink of his tea he said, "Nothing. It means nothing."

She narrowed her eyes.

"Was it serious?" he asked.

For Curtis, not for her. She'd been using him. She'd never thought about it like that, but she could see it now. *It still wasn't okay. It wasn't okay.* She told herself, but for the moment it was hard to believe what happened to her hadn't been something she deserved—the price she'd had to pay.

"You don't have to talk about it if you don't want."

Rilla looked up. "Oh. Sorry. No, it was complicated. Not serious, but complicated."

His forehead creased and those blue eyes locked tight with hers. "Yeah?"

She tried not to squirm.

"Complicated but not serious. Hmm . . ." He put his chin in his hand. "That's pretty vague."

She spun the mug, not looking at him. "I never got close to anyone. I didn't want to. Then I might get stuck somewhere. People are dangerous. Ya know?"

"Yeah. Totally."

She glanced up. "How about you? A girlfriend back home?"

He snorted. "No. No. The rumors are true," he said with a touch of bitterness. "I'm not known for having serious relationships." He studied his tea. "It's like climbing with a stranger. The idea of a relationship, I've done it, but . . ." He shuddered.

"Right? How are you supposed to even know? They could, like, tell you just to hang on, while they pick their nose. And you're screwed. You're up there, trying not to die. While your partner just has a thumb up his ass." Or wants more than you can give and is angry with you.

Walker laughed. "People are the worst."

"They really are," she said, trying not to replay the worst of her memories.

He took a large swallow of his tea and straightened off the counter. "Maybe it doesn't have to be a risk. Just like . . ."

"Like climbing with you?" She said it as a joke. And then suddenly flushed, realizing what she'd said.

"I'm much better . . . than . . ." But he seemed flustered too.

She looked at his hands, curled around the mug.

"This valley is so small," he said after a moment. "It's just like Ohio in a weird way. It's hard to keep anything quiet. Turns out you can never escape certain things."

"Except it's the most international small town I never imagined." Too late it occurred to her that he might have meant something else, something she hadn't addressed—she couldn't tell.

"Well, thanks for the tea." He slid the mug over.

Rilla took it, stomach nose-diving in disappointment—clutching after something she'd missed. Some opportunity.

He straightened and stretched his arms, rolling his wide shoulders. Delaying?

She swallowed. "I'll walk you back."

His eyes flickered to hers.

"Caroline would be so pissed if you got hurt on the way back," she said, rolling her eyes.

He chuckled.

Her heart raced even faster. This was it. This was it. Somehow, this was totally it.

It was silent, and only a little awkward, as Rilla slipped on her sandals and looked up to find Walker watching her.

He had brought his bike, which made it more ridiculous that she was "walking" him home; but she hopped up on the back sprockets, and he kicked off, and the night opened up as they sped out of the meadow.

Her hands were on his shoulders, her chin above his head. *Trust yourself. Trust your gear. Trust . . . your partner.*

She ran her fingers up the side of his hair and back, tugging at the long, dirty strands. His chin tilted up toward her, his head hitting her chest. He couldn't see where he was going, but they knew the paths so well he didn't need to. His throat was bared in the moon, his lips slightly apart. Eyes closed. The wind kissed their faces.

Slowly, she lowered her lips to his, nipping gently at his lower lip.

The bike dipped to the left and they yanked apart. He pulled forward to right it, the spell broken.

Her heart beat against her ribs as he leaned away from her and pedaled slowly to the edge of Camp 4.

She got off the bike, aching and bursting at the seams to keep on in that moment. He leaned over the front of the bike and watched her. "Tired, West Virginia?" he asked.

Her pulse throbbed in her head. "Not right now," she whispered.

He opened his mouth to say something, but a shrill beeping interrupted.

They stared at each other, confused.

And realized at the same time. His pager.

"Oh, *fuck*," he said, digging it out of his pocket like it was a bomb about to explode.

Her shoulders sank.

He looked up. Grabbed her chin, and pulled her up to his mouth. "Later, West Virginia," he breathed onto her lips. And was gone.

Later. She turned for home, fingers crossed it was a promise.

twenty nine

BETWEEN CLIMBING WITH CAROLINE, HAVING ADEENA TEACH HER TO aid, and all the ways in which Rilla's world was unfolding out from this narrow thing it had once been—something invisible unlocked in her brain. Suddenly, The Nose route seemed possible. And as soon as it became possible, Rilla realized how much work she had ahead of her. Like she had to be at this point to see both its possibility and its challenge.

The route consisted of thirty-one pitches. It would take her roughly four days. That meant she'd climb straight through four days. It meant she'd sleep on the wall, live on the wall, and haul all the food and water she'd need throughout those four days. It meant peeing on the wall. Shitting on the wall. *Somehow.* It meant having the mental fortitude to be in a harness and not touch solid ground for four days.

All day long, she found herself thinking of the route, imagining how she'd feel to have it completed. To reach the summit and look down the thousands of feet and have accomplished it. It felt like, if she could somehow do that—do all the work, do all the climbing, and stand at the top—she'd be the person she'd wanted to be all along. In her attic at night, she fantasized about what she'd pack, what she'd wear, how she'd smile. She pictured herself as Caroline—beautiful while she ate out of a can in a portaledge. Under the light of the bare bulb, her homework forgotten, she studied a route map she'd found on the Internet.

When Jonah asked if she wanted to work someone's shift at the hotel, she agreed immediately—never mind she had no idea what that job entailed. If she wanted to climb The Nose, she'd need as much of her own gear as she could get. Her backpack was full of Petra's gear, but she wouldn't be able to always use that.

"Meet Allie at the laundry at five thirty A.M.," Jonah said. "I'll tell her you agreed."

Rilla took the coffee he slipped over the counter and went back into the intense July sunshine.

The Nose.

She was going to do it.

One by one, she asked everyone what they thought went into something big and bold and out-of-this-world like climbing The Nose.

"Being responsible," Thea said, eyes narrowed. She dropped her chin. "Also, how's your schoolwork going?"

"Learn to aid climb efficiently," Adeena said.

"Controlling your mental state," Walker answered, before getting called out on the radio.

"Learn how to pee in your harness without peeing on yourself," said Petra.

"Discipline," answered Caroline, after finishing climbing and Rilla had showered and climbed into the backseat on the way to the Grove for Petra's turn to cook. "You have to commit to one thing for a long time."

She asked Gage during dinner at the Grove, partially to distract herself when Walker walked in. Petra had made sushi. "Believing you can do it," said Gage, dipping his tiger roll into a bowl of soy sauce. He pointed his fingers at her as he talked over the food in his mouth. "Even if you have all the physical skills, to be able to believe you can put together something that big is a huge component. If you don't believe it, who will?"

Rilla picked up a roll and studied it. Petra had said there was avocado, fried shrimp, and cucumber in the rice wrapped in seaweed. She'd never eaten sushi before, but she followed Gage's example and dipped the roll into the bowl before popping it in her mouth.

"Oh shit," she muttered over the bite. "That's delicious."

Gage grinned. "Yeah, I was dubious, but this is pretty good."

"I heard that," Petra said, putting another plate onto the table.

Gage reached over Adeena to grab one. "I'm just saying. The amount of people who say they can make sushi, versus the amount of people who can actually do it, is a big difference."

"I took a class with a Michelin star sushi chef," Petra said.

Rilla had no idea how tires and sushi connected, but she caught Walker watching her from farther down the table, and forgot to ask.

He looked showered—for once—and his sandy blond hair from all the days in the sun. He wore a clean, white T-shirt, and his blue eyes were shocking in his tanned face. He lingered for a minute, a little smile on the edge of his mouth. She scrunched her face, uncomfortable with the intensity but wanting so badly to be that uncomfortable always.

Someone said something, and Walker looked away.

Rilla stared at her plate until her pulse resumed a semi-normal speed, and Gage passed her a platter with spicy tuna rolls.

"Rilla, you doing anything tomorrow? Want to do a route on El Cap with us?" Tam—a visiting climber—asked.

Rilla sat up straighter, the *yes* immediately on her tongue. Then she sank. "I agreed to work. I'm sorry. But I would have loved to."

Tam moved on, but Rilla glowed with the feeling of being invited—being part of them. Maybe she could bail on the shift she'd picked up.

The house was full, the windows open to the cool mountain breezes, and the beer and sake were poured liberally. Rilla eyed the platters of fish Petra kept bringing, unable and unwilling to calculate how much this had cost, or how far Petra had to drive to get to a town where she could buy it all. For the first time, she realized everyone but her pitched money in for these meals. After this, she decided, she'd pull her own weight.

She ate until she was bursting, and drank until she was warmed and glowing and could practically feel Walker at the other end of the table. Their eyes kept connecting in between the laughter and the stories; and when his eyes grazed over her, she felt it as a pulse of electricity in her whole body.

Long after dinner had ended they sat there, drinking slowly and sipping tea Petra had put out. Rilla's thighs were sweaty and stuck to the chair, and her cheeks ached from smiling.

Walker stood and patted his chest. "I'm stuffed. That calls for a smoke."

It was like her whole body had been waiting. She jumped up. "I'll . . . uh . . . come with you." She tried to be cool, but Adeena laughed outright, and Gage even covered his mouth with his hand.

"Shut up," she muttered. "Can I bum a smoke?" she asked Walker. And then she blinked, because she had been bumming smokes all summer—which didn't really amount to quitting, but it was something like once or twice a week, which was basically quitting. And hey, look at her. *She'd quit!*

"I was going to ask you," Walker said. He winked. "I can lend you one."

She pushed out her chair.

Adeena smacked her on the ass on the way out, and she yelped.

Walker glanced back at her with a confused face. "You all right?"

She swallowed her laughter. "I'm good."

"She's spectacular," Adeena said.

"Y'all are juvenile," Caroline said.

"What are they talking about?" Walker said, holding the door for her. "I missed it."

"I have no idea," Rilla said with a roll of her eyes.

And then they were outside.

She took a deep breath of the cool breeze, the moonlight bathing the wide-open meadow, and the mountains.

Walker started down the road, lighting the smoke and then handing it over for her to share.

"Thanks," she said, suddenly shy.

His white shirt glowed in the moonlight, blue on his skin. "Man, that was good."

She exhaled and nodded. "Oh my god, yes. That was the first time I've had sushi. I didn't expect it to be that good."

"Petra's a good one. She's got some . . . *quirks*, but she's never stingy about sharing an experience. Did you see the bathtub in that house yet?"

"The copper one?" Rilla asked. It was the only bathtub she could imagine him meaning.

"Did you try it yet?"

"Is the experience worth its weight in scrap?"

Walker laughed so hard he choked.

She took the smoke from his fingers as he bent over gasping. "I mean, it wasn't that funny," she said, pounding his back.

"It's funny," he gasped, grabbing her wrist and using her to stand up. "Because that was exactly what I thought when I first saw it." He grabbed the smoke back, still leaning on her.

"Are you drunk?" She laughed, not sure whether to push him up.

"I am not." He ground the butt carefully into the gravel and picked it up. "But you're going to go sit in that ridiculous copper tub."

She snorted. "I am not."

"You are. When in life are you ever going to get to sit on that much scrap? This is luxury. We have to take it when we can."

She laughed. "No! It'd be so weird. We just had dinner."

He shook his head, bent his shoulder, wrapped one thick arm around her thighs and hoisted her over his shoulder.

Rilla yelped and swatted at his back. "Walker Jennings, put me down." *Never.*

"Not until you sit in that tub," he declared, marching back down the road for the house.

"I don't want to be a weirdo."

"Too late, buttercup." He hitched her higher, his hands gripping firm on her thighs in a way Rilla was completely and utterly there for.

He hauled her up the steps and threw open the door, stomping right through everyone, to Rilla's total embarrassment and utter delight.

"Uh . . ." Hico said.

"We'll be upstairs," Walker said.

The silence must have made him realize what he said.

"Not like that," he said. "She hasn't used that bathroom yet."

More silence.

"The tub!" he roared. "The door will be open, people!"

Hico busted out laughing and Caroline groaned at the same time.

"I mean, I'm not opposed to a closed door," Rilla said into his T-shirt.

He lightly slapped the back of her thighs. "Stop."

A flush of power ran through her body and she pushed her head up off his back so she wouldn't pass out.

He put her down in the bathroom and she wobbled unsteadily as the blood rushed back into her head.

"Hey guys . . . what's uh. What's going on?" Petra asked, stopping as she walked past.

"Rilla hasn't used the tub yet," Walker said as he leaned over the edge and turned on the faucets.

"Oh, Tam hasn't either." She leaned out the door and hollered over the railing.

Rilla wanted to shake Petra.

"Come on," Walker ordered. "Take off your clothes."

Rilla laughed, her cheeks pink. She folded her arms over her stomach. "I'm not doing this."

"I'm not saying get naked. Just leave your underwear on." He swiped at her knee with a grin.

She shook her head, stomach trembling.

Everyone traipsed upstairs. Rilla didn't unbutton her pants until everyone else did too. She was used to being around everyone in her swimsuit or climbing in a sports bra and pants, and her cotton underwear and sports bra weren't anything skimpier. But still, Hico handed her a cold beer as they all crammed into the oversized tub, with Tam and Walker sitting on the edge behind her.

"Y'all are weird," Rilla said happily, her arms up on Walker's legs. "If this tub disappears one day, it's because I sold it for scrap."

Hico leaned back and looked at the floor. "Is it not bolted down? That'd be super easy."

"Let me tell you something," Petra said, lifting her bottle out of the steaming water to gesture. "If you're going to steal anything from people as rich as my grandparents, don't go for the tubs. Go for the watches or electronics. My grandpa has a broken watch around here you could pawn for more money than this tub. And then you don't have to carry it out."

Hico laughed. "I guess if someone has a copper tub, you shouldn't stop there."

"A watch though?" Rilla asked. "Really?"

"I got a watch for climbing Everest," Adeena said. "From the Pakistani government."

Rilla nearly choked on her drink. "You've climbed Everest?"

"When I was fifteen," Adeena said, her eyes tracking away. She took a drink.

"Oh my god." Rilla blinked. "That's incredible."

Adeena shrugged. "It was . . . memorable."

"Really?" Caroline said. "They gave you . . . a watch? Not money or a scholarship?"

"An engraved Rolex," Adeena said with a nod.

"Did you keep it?"

She laughed. "It basically funded my entire education."

"Will you ever climb it again?" Tam asked.

Adeena exhaled, looking at the ceiling. "I'd like to. For my brother. He was with me the first time."

There was a moment of silence. Walker's legs tightened on her sides.

"Do you really want to do The Nose?" Petra asked Rilla. "We all know you've been asking everyone about it. Time to woman up and tell us if you're serious."

Rilla gulped her beer down and looked at everyone—terror freezing her tongue. She wanted to say *yes*. But what if everyone was laughing behind her back?

"We'll do it with you. Me and Adeena." Petra rolled her eyes. "Caroline doesn't want in. She's doing it on her own."

"Oh, right." Rilla said. She's forgotten—from that day when she dropped the rope, Caroline was climbing it free.

Adeena nodded. "I'm in. It's The Nose." She shrugged, as if that said everything.

"Yes," Rilla said.

"Yes, what? Come on. Yell it," Petra said. "Yes, what?"

"Yes, I want to climb The Nose," Rilla said.

Hico put his hand to his ear. "I didn't hear you."

"*Yes, I want to climb The Nose!*" Rilla roared from her gut, shaking the foundations of the redwoods with her desire.

Everyone laughed and lifted their bottles. "To The Nose."

thirty

PETRA GAVE RILLA AND WALKER A RIDE BACK TO THE VALLEY, SPENDING
the whole time talking with Walker in the front seat about some trip they'd done together. They laughed and reminisced and Rilla found herself slinking farther into the dark backseat like a forgotten child. Finally, Petra dropped them off in the Camp 4 parking lot.

Rilla waved goodbye as Petra pulled off.

Walker pulled out a smoke. "Want to go look at El Cap?" he asked.

Her pulse jumped. "Sure. I'm not dressed for it though." Her arms were chilly in the cool night air and she was still wearing shorts and sandals. At least her underwear was dry, thanks to the dryer at the Grove.

"You can borrow a sweatshirt. I just did laundry."

"Oh, what, I won't get the pheromones of greatness?"

He laughed. "I don't need no pheromones."

They turned off the path for his tent and he put his finger to his mouth.

Rilla took the smoke, waiting as Walker disappeared up the slope into his tent.

It was late—the entire camp was asleep, and fires were put out or burned down to embers. But she wasn't a bit tired. Adrenaline hummed; and when she closed her eyes she saw his long, lean body stretching out in the sunshine.

He was back in only a minute and handed her a worn hoodie. She slipped it over her head and it came down over the thighs and off her hands, warm and soft and smelling like clean laundry soap and dusty canvas.

"I brought you a headlamp, if you need it," he said, tucking something into her front pocket. "How's training?"

"Training for what?" She asked.

"The Nose. I mean, tonight wasn't the moment you realized you wanted to climb it, right?"

She laughed and slipped her hands into the pocket of his hoodie. "I didn't realize it was obvious."

He laughed. "Rilla, if you looked at a man with half as much lust in your eyes as you looked at that granite, you'd put him to his knees."

She frowned. "That makes me sound—"

"No," he interrupted. "I mean you want it. You can tell."

"Well, that's awkward." She laughed. But if he could tell what she wanted, how come he couldn't tell she wanted him? She followed him off the asphalt and into the darkened trees. They lost the moon in the wood, and she blindly reached for him and found his back.

"Can you see all right?" he asked.

"Not really."

"You can turn on the headlamp if you need to."

"If I just follow you, I'll be fine." She stumbled over a root and crashed into him. "I think."

He reached behind and took her by the hand, this time letting his warm fingers twine with hers.

"I never realized how big your hands are," she said. "How do you get these paws into those little cracks?"

He laughed. "Only in climbing is *wow, big hands,* not a good thing."

"I'm just saying... those tiny crimps." She ran her thumb across the top of his fingertips, smiling at the way his pulse fluttered in his wrist. "And your drawings. They're so intricate." She hadn't seen them since the time she'd accidentally picked up his journal, but she wondered about it. She wondered what he drew and what he wrote. But it felt too personal to ask.

"Some things are harder. But then I can reach things you can't. Your awkward off-width is my perfect hand jam. Your perfect hand jam is my finger crack. Everything is equal on the wall. And it's not like my hands are freakish and can't hold a pencil."

"It's not equal," she said. "But I get what you mean."

He squeezed her hand and pulled her on a bend in the path. "Mountains do not care who you are, they will kill you all the same. That's what I meant."

"At home the mountains always felt personal," she said. "Here it feels like they don't even notice you. They feel young and brazen and new. Not old and full of secrets and shadows. It's beautiful. Like, beyond beautiful. Every day feels like a dream drenched in sunshine. I love being here. But sometimes I miss that old feeling of . . . brutality, or something. Where everything is terrible and great all at once. It feels strange to live without it. I didn't even know I would miss something like that. I wonder sometimes if I *am* that, and that's what I like about climbing."

"Stop," he groaned. "Ugh. Why you gotta be like this?" He pulled her under his arm, tight to his chest.

It was too easy to roll into his hug, to slip around in his arms and push up on her toes with her face tilted toward him in a patch of moonlight pouring through the silver leafed oaks.

They still held hands, twisted behind her back. He pushed her fist into the small of her back, driving her closer.

The breeze rustled the leaves above them.

She felt his breath pull and ease. His chest expanded and relaxed. The rhythm. A cadence. His gaze flickered over her face and came back to her eyes, his long body hard and alive against hers. She closed her eyes and her lips parted in a smile.

"There it is," he whispered. "Open your eyes."

But she couldn't. She tightened her mouth, trying to bite down on the smile.

"Open," he whispered, softly kissing between her eyes. A flush of heat drove down to the base of her spine.

She laughed. "No." But she parted her eyes just enough to reach for his neck in the moonlight and pull his mouth to hers.

He kissed her slowly.

She pushed back with urgency.

He pulled away, his laugh tinged with a growl and he cinched her fist tighter into her back, against him. This time he kissed her with that intensity that she'd seen rippling under his skin since the bus stop in Merced. An intensity that made her stagger, even as he held her pinned.

It felt like a thing she expected to know, suddenly bigger and wider and taller, the world expanding inside her own chest.

It was almost too much. She needed to breathe. She pulled away.

He held her there as she caught her breath. His thumb circled lazily on her neck.

"You okay?" he whispered. "Am I okay?"

The oaks rustled a papery sound.

"Yeah," she breathed. "More."

The sky turned pink and found them still kissing in the shadows of the black oaks.

thirty one

FORGET CLIMBING EL CAPITAN, SURVIVING A DAY IN THE SERVICE industry was what was going to do her in. Especially since she'd been up all night, making out with Walker. Rilla's stomach rolled with excitement at the fresh memory of his hands on her.

"Do your hair," Allie said, her messy top-knot bobbing.

They stood in the warm laundry room—the machines all quiet. The sun had not yet risen. Rilla buttoned the skirt of the uniform and rolled her eyes. "Yeah, yeah. I know how tips work."

She stood on her tiptoes to use her reflection in the small, dark window to do her best old-people makeup—a nice pink lipstick, mascara, and blush. Her concealer didn't work anymore because of her tan, and her hair had gotten so long she had to ask Allie for scissors to cut off six inches of straggly ends, but finally she turned from the window, slipped on the borrowed flat dress shoes, and waited for Allie to approve.

Allie shrugged. "It'll do. I'm going back to bed." She handed over her badge. "Don't get me fired."

Rilla threw on a sweatshirt and headed across the Valley, her bare legs pricking with the chill. She'd never been inside the big hotel, and her heart beat a little faster as she crossed through the meadows and headed up the paved and landscaped drive.

In the lightening purple dark, the sleep-hazed faces of Braeden and Christian stood by the entrance's stone columns—still fixing their uniforms. She'd hung out with them often around HUFF, but had never seen them at work.

"What you doing here so early and so dressed?" Braeden asked as Rilla came up.

"Taking over for Allie today." She smoothed her skirt.

"Ugh. Allie is smart. Can you get us coffee?"

"I have to clock in first," Rilla said. "Where's the coffee?"

"Go to the kitchen and ask Darien to make it," Christian said. "Please." She nodded and headed inside.

"You're the best," Braeden called as the door swung shut behind her.

Inside was a whole new Yosemite. Freshly polished wood floors stretched under her feet, and the weak light of new dawn filtered in the southwestern patterned stained glass windows that stretched from floor to ceiling. Leather couches were arranged around solid tables in the lobby. Giant copper pots held succulents and ferns. Above it all, the coffered ceiling was trimmed in southwestern painted designs and from the beams, lights made to look like candles on circular wooden chandeliers hung, giving the whole room a warm, cozy glow.

It was the nicest building she'd ever been in, except for a field trip to a museum once.

Rilla tried not to look out of place, practically tiptoeing down the quiet corridor to find the employee room and the kitchen.

At the end of a hall, past the bathrooms, she found it—using Allie's card to open the locked door. Inside, she breathed with relief. The hotel lost its veneer, going back to linoleum and dingy painted drywall. An old-fashioned punch clock sat on the wall, with a hanging file of cards. Rilla found Allie's and punched it in.

The timestamp read 5:59 A.M. Just in time.

She relaxed and stuck the card back in. A notice on the bulletin board beside it caught her eye and she looked closer.

Shit.

REWARD: $1,000 FOR INFORMATION LEADING TO THE ARREST AND RECOVERY OF STOLEN HISTORIC AWAHNEE HOTEL PLAQUE.

Pictured was the plaque she stole with Caroline and Petra.

Her stomach dropped. *Ranger Dick Face.* At least he couldn't possibly know it was her. Right? She rushed away from the bulletin board, feeling like her guilt was written all over her. Unless someone talked to a ranger, they probably wouldn't find out. It was fine. She'd just make sure to tell Caroline and Petra.

It was a good thing Adeena hadn't come with them after all.

Back in the hotel, she found her way to the kitchen through the massive dining room, already bustling for breakfast and the few early risers sitting at tables. After delivering coffee, and getting one for herself, she found Allie's supervisor—Tammy—and began.

Tammy was also a temporary employee and liked Rilla, so she'd been fine with her switching out with Allie. With minimal instructions she sent Rilla wheeling a room service cart and taking the stairs to deliver whatever the guests kept calling down to the desk for. In between calls, she restocked housekeeping carts, watered plants, swept the lobby, and dusted off the tops of doors.

Allie would keep her day's wages, but Rilla kept the tips.

She shoved fives and ones into her pockets and ran back down the stairs for the next call, trying not to think about the stupid stolen plaque.

After Allie's shift ended, the sun was low in the sky. Rilla changed in the employee locker room, took the uniform back to Allie, and immediately went to the outdoor store and pushed over all her tips and collected wages from the last week, in exchange for a shiny cam.

It was fuchsia and silver, and glinted in the evening sun, glimmering without a scratch. She couldn't wait to get it dirty.

Running back to the house, she burst in to find Thea sitting at the table, filling out paperwork.

"What's that?" Thea asked, staring at the shiny cam.

Rilla looked down. "Um." Rilla hadn't talked to Thea about climbing, and even now she was afraid if Thea found out how much time she'd been spending on the rock, she'd be forbidden from it. The last thing Rilla wanted to do was start *that* fight. Casually, she moved the cam behind her back and changed the subject. "I want to take a GED test."

"You want to drop out of high school?" Thea said.

"Not drop out. Just . . . finish differently."

Thea frowned, looking between Rilla and where the cam had been. "Where did you get the cam?"

"I bought it."

"With what money?"

Rilla bit her lips. "I've been working."

"You have a job?"

"No. I . . . I do odd jobs for other people," Rilla said.

Thea's eyes narrowed. "Like what?"

"Like, today I worked at the hotel."

"In that?" Thea took in her ratty shorts and tank top.

"Uh. No." Rilla looked down, her cheeks warming. "I had to return the uniform."

Thea sighed and rubbed her temples. "Rilla . . ."

Rilla didn't move.

"You can't *do* that." Thea put her head in her hands and groaned.

"Why not?"

"You're not trained. You're a liability. It's illegal."

"It is not illegal," Rilla said. "You're a cop, not a lawyer."

"I'm not a cop," Thea yelled.

Rilla rolled her eyes.

"You want to take the GED, huh?" Thea said. "Let me ask you this. How's your schoolwork?"

Rilla gulped. "It's fine. But why do it, if I can just take a test?"

"It's not just taking a test," Thea said. "You can't use this as a Get Out of Jail Free card just because you're behind on your schoolwork. You need to spend less playing and more of the work you're actually supposed to be doing."

"Pretty sure it is just a test," Rilla said.

"And you still haven't answered about the cam," Thea said. "I don't want to hear you've been spending all the time I'm at work playing instead of doing your work, and now that's why you think you can take a test and make it all go away."

Rilla stilled, her face burning. "I'm . . . I'm . . ."

"I'm what? And who taught you to use that? That's for experienced climbers. You're going to hurt yourself."

"I am experienced," Rilla shot back.

Thea rolled her eyes. "A month of playing hooky to climb does not make an experienced climber."

She was right. She was . . . Rilla gulped and looked down at her hand. What was she doing? Thea was right.

"You are not allowed to climb. Not until you are caught up and enrolled in school. You can't afford to risk your future for a little fun. And you aren't responsible enough to be climbing with stuff like that."

Any argument got choked in Rilla's throat. No climbing? She stared at the cam, tears burning her eyes.

Thea straightened. "I'm done." Grabbing her hat, she stormed down the hall and slammed her bedroom door.

Done?

Rilla glared at the door. *Done* done? "Of *course* you are," she yelled, before stomping outside. She kicked the dirt all the way through the meadow. Hating the gear and all it represented—not her hard work anymore, but the things she'd never be able to climb beyond. Thea was unfair—but she was right. A month of climbing wasn't anything. She'd give it all over just to have her sister not think she was a useless annoyance. To have her *not* be done. And what was she going to do about climbing now? The Nose?

The Nose!

If Thea found out about The Nose she'd send her back to West Virginia for sure.

The grass was dry and dead at the edges of Camp 4, and on her first walk through the camp, no one was there. She sat at the picnic table at Tam's empty campsite, waiting for someone to show up. The afternoon light shifted through the trees and Rilla put her head in her arms and sank into the heaviness in her chest.

Someday she was going to go so far away no one would know who she was or where she came from, and she could start over with no memory of her mistakes.

Rilla kept expecting someone to show up. But no one did. She glanced at the SAR site, but no one was there either. It was sunset now, the tourists had all lit fires and climbers and hikers she didn't know were beginning to come back to camp. She pushed off the table to go find Jonah, still carrying the cam with her.

On her way across the Valley, she caught sight of the old man at the SAR site who'd fed her the morning she'd climbed with Caroline—hustling somewhere in his fluorescent T-shirt. She wanted to ask where everyone had gone, but his face was set in a grim line, and he seemed not to notice anyone or anything except the place he was trying to be. Her chest tightened and she picked up her pace. Something felt wrong. She felt wrong. Her stomach churned, hating that she'd made Thea mad, hating that Thea was right, and hating Thea for being unfair. The temptation to message Curtis hit her in the gut, and then she only hated herself for having to fight so hard against it. Rilla couldn't go back—not when she kept screwing things up like this.

Rilla found Jonah in the cafeteria. "Do you know what's going on?" she asked.

He looked confused. "I haven't heard anything," he said with a shrug. "You okay?"

She nodded.

"Run later?"

"Yeah, sure." Thanking him, she left the building and wandered back outside. The crowds seemed on edge too—people talked with each other in urgent, curious tones. She wanted to stop and ask everyone what was going on, but didn't know how to intrude. Maybe it was all in her head.

There were no sirens, but she followed a passing ambulance anyway, out of the woods and into the meadow below El Cap. The massive cliff stood in shadows. Only the tip-top of Half Dome held light now. And a dark haze seemed to creep out of the trees.

She edged to Lauren. "What's going on?" Rilla asked. Even Ranger Miller was there, looking like he was actually doing work as he talked with other rangers and then spoke into the radio.

"They're doing a rescue."

Rilla looked up. The dusty orange-and-cream granite was darkening and if she squinted, she could spot tiny stars of light beginning to dot the cliff—they were each climbing teams, she knew that. But which one . . .

"Where is it?" Rilla asked.

Lauren pointed. "See under that big shadow."

Rilla put both hands on her forehead, straining, trying to see. There was nothing but dusky granite.

Her pulse raced in her neck. Who was on the wall? And who had been sent to get them?

"Everyone's gone for this? What happened? Do you know who?"

"I don't know. We have a broken arm from a dropped haul bag. Half of us are here. Half are split between some hikers missing in Tenaya Canyon. And a turned ankle on Four-Mile Trail."

"Shit," Rilla breathed.

"When it rains, it pours." Lauren's radio bleeped. She turned away and answered. "Thea's coming over," she said. "Hang around. We might need bodies for Tenaya Canyon."

Rilla startled, but Lauren didn't seem to notice. Hang around? As in, to be useful? She wasn't useful. To anyone. But suddenly, she wanted to be. Her pulse pounded in her neck and she nodded to Lauren, a sense of purpose flooding her body and rooting her to the meadow.

Rilla moved in the grass, pushing through the dry stalks until she came to a man with binoculars. "Can I borrow those for a second?" It was nearly impossible to spot climbers on the wall without binoculars.

The man pulled the glasses away and blinked, but he handed them over and pointed at the wall. "Right there, below the big flake."

Rilla's hands shook as she put the binoculars to her eyes and blinked. The wall came into focus. Empty. She moved it, slowly, scanning, straining her eyes in the fading light. With every second she couldn't find them, it felt as if the possibility it was someone she knew increased.

"Here." The man moved the glasses.

A thin trail of rope came into focus. At the bottom, two figures in shadow.

She couldn't tell who it was.

Overhead, a chopper thumped. She pulled down the binoculars and handed them back to the man, tipping her chin to watch the chopper fly overhead. Its belly was white and the grass shuttered around her.

"Rilla," Thea called.

Rilla turned and headed back through the grass to her sister, standing in a sloppily tucked shirt and a ball cap. Lauren was beside her.

"What were you doing today? Any climbing? Hiking?" Lauren asked.

Rilla gritted her teeth. "No," she seethed.

"She can come with me," Lauren said to Thea.

Thea blanched.

Go where?

"She needs to go home and do her homework," Thea said.

"I'll watch out for her," Lauren said. "It'll be good."

Thea softened. "Well, okay."

What? Thea just gave in like that? Rilla had never seen that happen. Ugh.

"Rilla," Thea said. "You can go with Lauren, Walker, and Kamika. They need a body. Listen. You do what they say, okay? If you don't, you'll put everyone's lives in danger."

Rilla glanced between Lauren and Thea. "Okay?" She'd heard of climbers who were around Yosemite being used as volunteers in SAR events when they needed extra help, but she'd never thought she'd be included in that.

"Go get some boots on, and pack a daypack for yourself," Lauren said. "Pack a rain jacket, food, water, headlamp, extra batteries, and a basic first aid. Go as fast as you can and meet me at the trailhead for Mirror Lake. We're just going hike up to the start of the canyon, but it'll be dark and tough terrain."

"Okay!" Rilla turned and ran off across the Valley.

Within twenty minutes, she'd changed, packed her bag, and started running through the early twilight to meet Lauren.

"There you are," Lauren called as Rilla huffed to a stop. Walker stood behind her, and a young ranger whom Rilla only knew as Kamika. "Okay. We're looking for a hiker, male, age twenty-five. Medium height. Name is Mike. He was wearing . . ." Lauren peered at her notebook in the last bit of light. "Ugh. Red shirt. He left Olmstead Point yesterday." Lauren flipped over her notebook. "He was last seen leaving the Olmstead Point trail to head into the canyon. Rangers have entered from there, but so far haven't found anything. We're basically doing a containment search. We're going to be hiking up to the entrance to the canyon—only a few miles past Mirror Lake, but a talus field they might have gotten stuck in. After that, we're going to hold tight at the canyon output and wait for the rangers from Olmstead Point to join us." She flipped her notebook closed and pulled her headlamp onto her forehead. She glanced at the group. "Ready? We're in teams."

Rilla's heart thumped in her throat, like the first time she'd started across the Valley for Half Dome. And the first time she'd gone with Caroline on lead. She tightened down the straps of her backpack and slid her headlamp on her head.

"Walker, you've got Rilla," Lauren said. "And I'll be with Kamika."

Rilla swallowed and looked to Walker, but his face was serious, watching Lauren. "We going off the trail at all?"

"No. Just sweep the left and we'll do the right side. We'll take turns calling. When we get to the talus field, we'll spread out a little more."

"What do I do?" Rilla asked quietly.

"Just walk in front of me," Walker said. "Make sure you look into the woods to your left and on the trail in front of us for the hikers. Go slow. That's it."

"Okay." She nodded.

He turned and looked to Lauren. "We good?"

She put her thumbs up. "Let's do this."

They started into the woods, on the wide path leading to Mirror Lake. Tourists were still out and walking, and Rilla scanned every person on the path and the stands of trees and looming boulders for anyone who might have wandered into the woods.

Lauren called out their names occasionally, especially when big clumps of people came by. But by the time they hit Mirror Lake and Half Dome rose straight above them, there were only a few tired-looking stragglers, and none of them were the hiker they were looking for.

"All right, we're going off-trail," Lauren said, veering off into the brush in the twilight. She radioed a similar update.

Rilla followed Lauren's pace—slowing down when she found herself a few steps ahead, picking up when she fell behind. At first, it felt as if she'd surely miss the hiker—it'd be just her luck. But she fell into a rhythm and soon there was nothing but the dim trail. Walker's body moved behind her. Lauren and Kamika to her right. They moved as one unit, as a team, as the trail ended and they began picking their way through the rocks and brush—slowing even more to carefully sweep the rocks and call out.

"Listen," Lauren ordered them as they broke out of the woods. A river bed opened wide before them. It was almost dark—that deep purple haze of evening and all the light gone from Half Dome.

Perched on a boulder in the dry riverbed, Rilla stopped with the others and tilted her head to the wind. Straining to hear its cries.

Nothing came.

"At least the sky is clear," Walker said.

"One less thing to worry about," Lauren agreed.

They crawled around a boulder bigger than Thea's house, breathing hard, but quietly sending their headlamps around them.

"Canyons have their own strange forces," Lauren said. "I never like a call into Tenaya. To me, it means I'm going after a body."

Rilla tried not to shiver in the dark as they worked their way to the far edge of the Valley and the walls of granite began to close in on them. The night became darker. The stars were only a strip above them. A faint trickle of water caught on the wind, and by the time Rilla was certain they had to be halfway through the canyon, they stopped at the edge of a dark pool. "Well, we've reached the start," Lauren said.

Rilla tilted her head and the small burst of light of her headlamp swept up a wall of granite with a dark, narrow gash in the middle. From the darkness, a strange sound came—water, but water as Rilla had never heard before. It echoed, like the sound was pulled liquid and dark.

"He has to come out somewhere along here," Lauren said. "If he's coming out."

It wasn't wide—just a rocky sweep between the big walls of granite on either side and the rocks rose higher in front of them. A thin waterfall poured over and pooled in the middle.

Rilla sat and clicked off her light, relieved after her long night and long day to be sitting. Her gaze flickered to Walker, in the dark. He'd spent most of the night with her, knowing he'd have to do something like this.

"Are we still supposed to be looking?" she asked him quietly.

He turned off his light. Lauren had a large flashlight sweeping across the narrow valley as she talked on the radio, but the darkness seemed to suck it in, not illuminate anything.

"We're at a choke point," Walker said. "It's narrow enough here if anyone comes through, we'll see."

Lauren nodded. "Most people only think of something like a grid search—which is actually the most ineffective way of searching. In all the places between here and Olmstead Point, the only way they can come through this point is by coming right here." She swept her light across the waterfall and the rocky hillside between the granite cliffs. "So, we send a group of searchers on the other side. Experienced canyoneers. They sweep the inner canyon and we make sure no one leaves."

"It feels weird," Rilla said. "The canyon is there."

"Some people say it's cursed," Lauren said. "The army killed the son of Chief Tenaya to *incentivize* the Ahwahnechee from the Valley. And the story is, he cursed the canyon. But I think the earth just hangs on to the memory of injustice and revisits it on people. No one can escape the past, not even the land." She flicked on her headlamp. "All right, you guys stay here. Call if you see anything."

Lauren and Kamika disappeared across the tight gorge, but their lights bobbed along. If she strained, she could just make out their shadows.

"Can I ask you a question?" she said to Walker. Hating herself even more that when someone else's life was on the line, she was still thinking about her fight with Thea.

"Shoot."

"Am I . . . Am I . . ." She swallowed, trying to find the courage to ask. "I know I'm out of my league. I know I'm new. But am I still . . . a gumby?"

He laughed. "No. You've been new, but you've never been that. You've always been smart and careful. Even when you had bad habits from Petra, you fixed it right away, Caroline said. You are trusted."

"Am I inexperienced?"

This time he didn't answer right away. "Yes and no. But I think we all have to nurture a feeling of inexperience. It can keep us safe and cautious. But without letting it make us overly afraid. I think. And yeah, you haven't had as much experience as some. But more than others. Most people would not have progressed as fast as you have."

She nodded. It didn't really help like she thought it would.

In the quiet, the day and her fight with Thea come roaring back to her. She couldn't give up climbing. Climbing had given her everything else. It had brought her here, helping, useful. It had left her beside Walker, as something like an equal. It had even pushed her to do the homework she'd gotten done—not enough, but something.

She'd have to disobey Thea and continue to climb. She'd have to keep it a secret. But she didn't see any other way. Losing climbing felt like losing the only thing about herself she liked, the only thing that had value.

Rilla pulled her knees to her chest and stared into the dark, waiting and hoping that the lost hiker would emerge out of the night.

thirty two

THEY SAT THERE ALL NIGHT. RILLA FELL ASLEEP. CURLED UP WITH HER
backpack on the cold rock, dreaming strange, lucid dreams. She woke
to the rich smell of coffee on the dry wind. Opening her eyes, she looked
into the clear shade and the sun touching the cliffs high above her.

"Youth," Lauren said bitterly. "You can sleep anywhere."

Rilla frowned. "You mean me?"

Lauren laughed.

"Coffee?" Walker asked.

Rilla pushed up, pawing at her hair to try and tame it into something
passably cute. She nodded and took the blue speckled mug of coffee he
pulled off the burner and handed to her. "Did they make it out?" Rilla asked.

"The rangers are in the inner canyon. The SAR team had to wait for
light. We should be here until the afternoon," Lauren answered. "On our
way back, if they haven't been found, we'll do another sweep. But, I imagine we'll find something today."

Rilla sipped the hot, bitter liquid, closing her eyes as the steam hit
her face. The air was dry and face felt puffy. "Did they say who was on El
Cap yesterday?" she asked.

"Some climbers," Lauren said. "They're all right."

Walker glanced at her. "It was Tam and Avery."

Rilla froze. "But they're okay?"

"We don't know how it happened, but somehow their haul bag came
unclipped and it hit Tam on the way down. Broke her arm pretty bad."

"There's such a thing as a not-bad arm break?"

Walker screwed up his face. "The bone came through the skin, I heard."

"Oh." Rilla looked at the coffee. She'd sat at Tam's campsite yesterday, all while Tam had sat up on El Cap with her bone coming through the skin. "She's going to be okay?"

Walker patted her ankle. "She's going to be fine. It happens. You try and do everything you can to minimize the chance of it happening, but it still can happen."

But Rilla sipped her coffee, certain it would not happen to her because from this point on she'd be *so* careful. More careful than she'd ever been. And it wouldn't happen to Walker because he was so experienced. And it wouldn't happen to Caroline because she was just as experienced as Walker, but better. And it wouldn't happen to Petra, because Petra didn't do anything she couldn't handle. And it wouldn't happen to Adeena because Adeena had climbed Everest. And . . .

Lauren's radio bleeped, a loud squawking sound that shattered the stillness. She picked it up.

Located in the inner canyon. The only thing that followed was a number that began with ten.

Lauren lowered the radio and exhaled.

"They found him. He's dead," Walker explained.

Rilla's stomach dropped and they all looked away in silence.

It wouldn't happen to her. She clenched her fists tight. She would be so careful. She wouldn't go into places she didn't know. She would be safe. She would think twice and do once.

It wouldn't happen to her.

thirty three

RILLA KNEW SOMETHING WAS DIFFERENT WHEN SHE WALKED INTO
Camp 4 later that week, and all the climbers seemed to be trying to figure out which way to look over their coffee, and all the non-climbers were rubbernecking and confused.

She found Adeena, Petra, Hico, Gage, Caroline, and Knox sitting in a line on the bear boxes at a newcomer, Abby's, campsite, trying very obviously to look casual. Abby and her partner, Langston, sat in their chairs, eating cereal out of mugs, also trying to look cool.

"Um. Hey y'all." For a second, she heard the West Virginia in her voice and was surprised. Is that how she always sounded?

"Morning," Abby said at the same time as Langston lifted his spoon, and Adeena and Petra said hey, Caroline said *hey girl*, and Hico, Gage, and Knox nodded, *sup*. All at once and hardly at all.

Rilla put her hands up. "What the hell?"

"Celine arrived," Caroline said, tilting her head across the camp. "With a Nat Geo crew."

"And Andy Thomas."

"Who?" Rilla asked, tapping Gage on the shoulder and waiting for everyone to slide down the bear boxes, creating space at the end for her to plant herself down.

"How do you *not* know who Andy Thomas is?" Petra asked.

Rilla frowned at her, trying not to blush.

"Andy Thomas is that guy who's famous for free soloing. He's an amazing climber," Caroline said. "Almost as good as Celine."

"Want some cereal?" Adeena shook a box of Frosted Mini-Wheats in her direction.

Rilla shrugged and extended her hand for the box. "Sure."

"What are we looking at?" Rilla asked Gage, grabbing a handful of cereal.

"All the way at the end. They're in two campsites all on their own."

Rilla shifted straighter, peering over the tops of the other campers waking up, pulling out breakfast from their bear boxes, and lighting the morning fire.

Through the people, the trees, the brush of wind on the glimmering morning dust, the far end of the camp came into focus.

It was mostly men—maybe ten to two. Similar looking to the climbers she saw all the time, except less . . . grungy, and with better equipment.

"Which one is Celine?" she asked Gage.

"The brunette in the blue jacket."

Rilla looked her over carefully. Celine had all of Caroline's ease and grace, but in a shorter, rawer body like Adeena's. Her hair was thick and long, tied back in a low ponytail. Her face looked like the manifestation of the articles always popping up online about how to be more like a French woman—not quite beautiful, but interesting.

"And Andy is the one in the green."

Andy looked . . . dopey. Muscled and hard and weather worn. But dopey. Like life had intended for him to be inside playing video games, but he got wires crossed somewhere and ended up a world-famous climber. He had his hands tucked into his pockets and leaned over the shoulder of Celine, looking at something Rilla couldn't see.

"So, is this what we're doing today?" she asked over her mouthful of cereal.

"Caroline, go over there and talk to her," Adeena said.

"They're eating breakfast," Caroline replied. "I've met her, but we're not like best friends."

"Yeah, but you're the most famous of us," Gage said.

"Being in *Climbing Magazine* like *one time* does not make you famous," Caroline said. "She's probably never heard of me."

Petra hopped off the box. "All right, I'll do it." Stretching her long legs in a purposeful stride, she headed toward the group.

"May we all have the balls of rich white girls," Hico said.

Adeena snorted.

They all watched quietly as Petra paused at the edges of the campsite and waited until Celine lifted her head. Whatever she said must have worked.

Rilla leaned forward, fingers curled tight. It seemed ridiculous, but what if Celine would climb with them? What if Rilla could join them?

Petra looked over and waved, while Celine stood out of her chair.

"Does she mean we go there?" Caroline asked, nervously tugging at her shirt.

"All of us?" Adeena said.

"OMG. OMG," Bea said, smoothing her hair. "We're going to meet Celine Moreau."

Rilla stood and dropped to the back of the group, trying not to be noticed, even as she hoped a beam of sunlight would burst out of the clouds and shine on her like a Chosen One.

Petra's true gifts were never more appreciated by everyone, Rilla included, as they were just then, as Petra took an awkward, gangly group of half-washed climbers and introduced them to the National Geographic team and climbers. Rilla hung at the back, watching in awe as Petra somehow pulled Adeena to the front and talked about her experience on Everest, current education, and future aspirations toward teaching young girls in Pakistan to climb, without making it sound forced or weird. When Adeena was safely in conversation about Gilgit's street food and the last rainy season—one of the photographers had just returned—Petra grabbed Rilla's elbow and yanked her to Celine. "From West Virginia," is all Petra said about her. Though Rilla guessed that's all there was to say.

Celine's eyes lit. "Oh, the New is so beautiful. I loved climbing there."

Rilla fumbled with a reply, shaking hands with her and Andy, while trying not to let on she was new to climbing.

Then, somehow, they all got to stand there, as if they were equals, and Celine was just a newcomer to the Grove as they talked about updated route information, what had been happening in climbing recently, which routes were closed for peregrine falcon nests, and what Celine was planning on climbing.

"I'm going to do some free-climbs on Half Dome," Celine said. "Maybe a solo attempt if I feel good. But, we're really here to . . ." She glanced at Andy, a half smile on her face. "We're getting married at the end of the trip."

"This is where I grew up climbing," Andy said with a smile. "We had a small ceremony in France already. But with so much of my family here, we decided it would be perfect to do a bigger wedding here."

"Of course, any of you are welcome to attend the ceremony," Celine said. "And we'll probably be needing some haulers for the climb. We're sorting all that out now with the team."

Rilla nodded excitedly with the rest of them, and they all hung on just a little too long before Petra said goodbye and they went back to Abby's campsite with wild and awkward grins plastered on their faces, at the hope they'd be chosen.

•

By the end of the day, someone had come over and requested climbers by name—Hico, Gage, and Caroline.

"Caroline?" Petra said. "That's it?"

"Hico, and Gage, and Caroline," Rilla repeated.

"*What the fuck?*"

"Oh . . ." Adeena said, blinking at the ground.

Rilla's chest pinched in disappointment, but she hadn't really expected to be asked. It was clear she wasn't the leader. All in all, if it had been her making the decision, the only change she'd make was to sub Adeena for one of the boys.

But Petra was furious, and there was nowhere for her fury to go. "When you're putting together teams," she ranted to Adeena. "Don't think that one woman at the top, in front, is what counts for feminism when the whole fucking team is men." Petra looked over her shoulder at Half Dome. "Ugh . . ." And she stormed off.

Rilla and Adeena stood still, looking at each other.

"I mean, I didn't think anyone would get chosen," Rilla said. "If you ask anyone, it's clear I'm the least experienced."

"Caroline is the best climber," Adeena said to Rilla.

"But you're a better climber than Hico and Gage." Petra wasn't, Rilla was realizing. It was strange though—everyone seemed to know Petra wasn't, but still found her an important part of the group.

"It's not really climbing so much as hauling," Adeena said. "I know they probably looked at me and thought I couldn't wrangle the pig fast enough to keep up. The boys and Caroline make perfect sense."

"But you can haul!" Rilla said. "I've seen you!"

"I know. But maybe not fast enough?" Adeena shrugged. "I don't know if I'd think the same thing if I were them. Probably."

"What use is it to complain about it anyway?" Rilla said, kicking at a rock with her toe. "Nothing you can do to change it."

Adeena laughed. "Oh baby Rilla," she said smoothing Rilla's hair like a mom.

Rilla squirmed uncomfortably.

"I will never forget about it. I'm always going to wonder," Adeena said. "But I agree, there's nothing to do about it *right now*. But someday, Petra will be right, I'll get to decide the team and I'll remember this moment and give a girl like me a chance."

Petra had run into Caroline at the edge of the campground and they could see Petra talking, arms moving dramatically.

"Can I ask something?" Rilla asked, hesitant.

"Yeah?" Adeena asked, watching them.

Rilla patted her pockets absently, forgetting she didn't have smokes on her. "I don't really get them. How did they meet?"

"Who? Oh, Petra and Caroline?"

"Yeah."

Petra was still talking. Caroline crossed her arms.

"Same place I met Petra," Adeena said. "Petra was a volunteer for the competition. Me and Caroline were talking when she introduced herself and started talking about Yosemite."

Rilla's stomach turned.

Adeena looked uncomfortable. "I think they hung out a few times and climbed together. But like . . ." She shrugged. "Honestly, I was just excited to come to Yosemite, and Petra doesn't bother me. I'm the middle child of six—I know how to go with the flow. But I get that other people can't deal with her personality."

Rilla understood. Petra was competitive even in places where it wasn't okay to be competitive. She didn't do things she wasn't good at, and she exaggerated how good she was. But at the same time, Petra was the one who'd brought her in and took her climbing. If it weren't for Petra, Rilla wouldn't be there now. And if it weren't for Caroline, Rilla would have never been able to grow as a climber. It was a terrible, icky feeling in the pit of her stomach with no visible resolution.

Adeena looked like she felt the same way. "I want some ice cream. Let's get ice cream."

"Sounds like a plan," Rilla said, and they rushed away from Petra and Caroline.

•

The temperatures rose and the tempers stayed short—especially between Petra and Caroline, now that Caroline was hauling for Celine. Adeena and Rilla just tried to stay out of it and listen sympathetically to Petra's rants—knowing they all wished they could be on the wall, hauling in the ridiculous heat and sweating like a pig for Celine and Nat Geo photographers. Despite the heat, the crowds grew even thicker, flocking to the dried-up waterfalls and the slow-running Merced.

"It's just . . . I don't understand how Petra doesn't understand that they didn't mean anything personal by only asking Caroline," Rilla complained to Walker after Petra had finished complaining to *her* and had gone back to the Grove. They were stretched out, opposite each other in Walker's hammock outside his tent. He had his notebook open, sketching, or *doodling*, as he called it. It'd been a quiet day in a busy week and the first time they'd really gotten to hang out since Celine had arrived. They were both dirty and tired.

Walker's pencil moved across the paper. "I know, but Celine knows Caroline. Caroline has a reputation in the community. And Hico's a famous boulderer. Gage is Hico's partner. Petra and Adeena aren't known."

"Adeena climbed Everest when she was younger than me!"

Walker shrugged. "That's . . . I mean. Women just aren't as well-known for their accomplishments. I would have asked Adeena. She can haul ass. But I know her, and Celine doesn't. I would feel pissed if I were Petra too. I'd take it personally too."

Rilla frowned. "It just . . . it's like a splinter I can't get out. Festering and shit." She plucked at the strings on her shorts.

His knee nudged hers.

"It just seemed like if I climbed as well as everyone else," Rilla said, "I could have been picked. But Adeena and Petra both climb as well as Hico and Gage. But they weren't picked." Petra didn't climb as well . . . but it felt disloyal to think it, and it still left Adeena on the ground. "Adeena has the most climbing experience of everyone."

"Except Caroline," Walker said.

"Okay, but still. Adeena should be up there."

"This is the first you're hearing of sexism?" Walker asked with a chuckle.

"Is that what this is?"

He shrugged. "I don't know. It could be bias. Or not."

She frowned, not feeling any better for the conversation. "Can I see what you're drawing?"

"No," he said immediately.

"Please? Is it me? Let me see." She tried to sit up and look.

"It's not you." He clutched the notebook to his chest. "Go away."

She made a face. "Please?"

"It's an infographic."

"A what?"

He rolled his eyes. "You know, like an illustration demonstrating how to do something?"

"What are you demonstrating?" She gave him an exaggerated wink. "Ooh . . ."

"Don't tell anyone I showed you." He handed her the notebook.

Settling the leather binding in her lap, she carefully opened the cream pages. A smile split her face. "Walker! It's so good. And so interest-ing!" The panels showed setting up a high-line for high-angle rescues. "I guess if you aren't drawing me, this is acceptable. Why don't you want people to see?"

"I just don't like people knowing."

"Well." She fought the urge to turn all the pages, and handed the book back. "You're very good."

He shrugged and tossed the book to the picnic table. Sliding his hand up her leg, he gripped the back of her calf. "Ugh, it's hot."

They were surrounded by people, in the afternoon light, in a Valley bursting at the seams with tourists. Walker tipped his mouth up, eyes sparkling. "Want to go for a swim?"

She grinned and swung her legs over the side of the hammock. "Let's go."

They crossed the road and ducked into the woods, tramping through the pine needles to come out onto the sandy bank of the Merced. The river glimmered cool and clear in the afternoon sunshine, and the air smelled like dry, warm pine. Despite the busyness of the Valley, they found the river mostly quiet and only a few visitors with small children farther up where it was shallow.

"I needed a shower anyway," Walker said, pulling off his T-shirt and hat, and dropping them on a fallen tree along the water's edge. They were shaded from the brutal afternoon sun, but the river was bright from the sun coming through the pines and reflecting off the granite rising above them on all sides.

"That's disgusting," Rilla said, adding her T-shirt to the log. "Rivers don't count as a shower. Only pools."

"I like your tan lines," Walker said with a chuckle, gaze flickering across her neck and shoulders.

She stuck her tongue out. "You're mean." Between running and climbing and spending most of her days outside, no matter how much sunscreen she put on, she had a deep tan and a crisscross of sport bra tan lines.

"No, I'm serious," he said. "They're hot."

She rolled her eyes and waded in. The water was crisp and cold, soothing her aching feet.

"Ah," Walker breathed, walking straight into the current. The muscles in his back and sides rippled under his tanned skin and the water licked up his torso.

Rilla stood ankle deep, motionless, and her mouth was suddenly dry.

He put his hands together above his head and made a shallow dive into the darkest part of the pool, disappearing under the water.

This was a dream. This couldn't possibly be real. Rilla blinked rapidly and sucked in a deep breath of the dry hot air. *Holy shit.* This was her life.

Walker resurfaced downstream, shaking the water from his face before he looked back at her. "Come on," he called. "It feels good."

Rilla's heart pounded in her neck and chest, but she walked into the water, trying very hard not to trudge into the current, but glide like some effortless water nymph. By the time it reached her hips, the pull was so strong, she surrendered—sinking under its calm surface and kicking her legs out like a frog to swim across the current and reach him in the middle of the deep pool, where the river slowly bent.

"Hey girl," he said, smile wide as she floated to him. His blue eyes were lit with the light bouncing off the granite walls—so beautiful they took her breath away. Rilla would never ever forget this moment, she was sure.

"Where are you going?" he asked, reaching his hand out.

She blushed—she'd been so distracted, she'd forgotten to keep swimming against the current. She kicked off the rocky bottom and swam back toward him.

He grinned, pulling her arm under his.

Rilla wrapped her arm around his back and without even thinking, pulled her legs around his stomach.

"This really is the best way to drown," he said, bobbing under the combined weight—long arms moving under the water to keep them afloat.

"Ah, I'm sorry!" Rilla blushed harder, loosening her legs to let him go.

"No, I want to die." He half laughed, half groaned, as he stopped treading water and gripped her hips, pulling her legs back. His head dipped under and they were picking up speed in the current.

He was kidding about drowning, but it wouldn't be long until it wasn't a joke. Rilla pushed away from his chest, legs slipping out from his grip, ducking under the water to swim away.

"I'm cold now," Walker called when she resurfaced downstream. "Come back."

"I'll race you back upstream," she said, leaning back in the current. Her toes lifted out of the water and she stared past them to the Sentinel, standing like a massive throne in the afternoon light. If there was a heaven, she imagined it was this—hot air, cold mountain water, over-looking granite, and a boy swimming her direction.

"What do I get if I win?"

She shrugged, too embarrassed to suggest anything she'd like him to win.

"Do I get to see *all* your tan lines?" he asked.

She laughed—partially from embarrassment and partially from the thrill of joy that ran up her spine.

"We'll see," she said, twisting in the water to ready to swim. "On your mark. Get set."

She started swimming.

"Hey!" He hollered.

She couldn't help but laugh—which made it hard to swim. She'd had a good head start and managed to stay ahead, kicking and trying not to laugh.

He grabbed her ankle, but she kicked away, laughing and getting a mouthful of river water as a consequence.

"Come here, cheater," he growled, grabbing her arm with one hand and shoving her head straight down with the other.

Water filled her mouth and she choked, kicking away. A hot panic tightened on her ribs and she suddenly could think of nothing but Curtis's fingers digging into her shoulder as he held her down and hit her in the face.

When she resurfaced, coughing and pushing her hair away from her face, Walker was on the bank, laughing. He stopped as soon as he saw her. "Are you okay?"

She coughed, and found she could stand on the bottom. Her hands trembled and her heart raced. She was okay. She was okay. But for the first time, she realized she wasn't okay. Not really. Was this always going to happen?

Walker rushed back into the river, patting her on the back. "I'm sorry. You all right?"

She nodded, gulping back her tears. She couldn't cry in front of him.

"You sure? What happened?"

Rilla shook her head, unable to talk for the fear that had wedged itself into her throat.

"Come on," he said, pulling her tight against him and leading her to the bank.

"I'm okay," she managed on dry land.

"I'm really sorry," he said, lightly touching her waist.

"It's fine. It wasn't you. Don't worry about it," she said, swinging her hair over her shoulder to gather it from where the lengths were plastered down her back. He still touched her waist, thumb rubbing against her skin.

"Did you just choke on the water?"

She bit her lip and shrugged, watching the river.

"Rilla," he said softly.

She closed her eyes against the threat of tears. "Oh my god, I'm so embarrassed," she chuckled, even as the tears dropped to her cheeks.

"Oh baby, come here." He pulled her in against his chest, arms wrapped over her shoulders, squeezing her tight. His skin was cool from the water and she buried her face into him, letting the tears just run their course as he stroked her hair. Fuck that it was embarrassing. Walker made her feel like it was okay . . . that she was safe. And somehow that made her cry a little harder.

"What it is?" he asked. "Are you sure I didn't hurt you?"

"No. I . . ." She pulled away and wiped her eyes. "It's nothing. I mean, it's not nothing. Back at home, before I came out here." She took a deep breath and sniffed. "That complicated boyfriend? We . . . fought." Somehow, it felt so shameful to say it out loud. She shrugged. "It's catching up with me, I guess."

"Fought? Like, he hit you? Is that why you came out here?"

She nodded, biting her tongue to keep from explaining it wasn't like that.

He ran his fingers through his wet hair and sat on the log where they'd laid their shirts. He patted the space beside him. "I'm sorry that happened to you."

Rilla sat down, stretching her legs out on the sandy dirt. "Thanks."

He leaned into her.

She rested against his shoulder and sighed. The sun shifted into the deep gold California haze—with the tinge of campfire and food on the dusty breeze.

And suddenly, she was okay. More than okay. Rilla kissed his shoulder and sighed happily. "Thanks."

His fingers tightened on her side, sinking into her skin. They were still smudged from his drawing.

"Why don't you want anyone to see your art?" she asked.

His chest tightened under her. "They're private. And it's not art."

"But they are so good. They are. You don't want to share them ever?"

He sighed. "I don't know. I like doing it for me. Maybe, someday . . ." He shrugged. "Maybe someday, it will be something that let's me stay outside and working for myself. That's really what I hope it will do. Make just enough money, my way, to be able to work on things I love. Maybe travel some more."

"More?" she asked in surprise, thinking of Caroline's Instagram. "Don't you guys go all over the world?"

He shook his head. "No. No. I don't go. Caroline does. We share an apartment in Denver in the winter, but she's not there very often. I work as a guide there."

"Oh. I had no idea." Of course, that made sense, she just hadn't thought of it. "So you guide in the winter and work here in the summer? Do you want to keep doing that?"

"I love this job. It's been such an amazing summer . . ." His smile was wide and genuine—a smile for himself. "This is my dream."

She smiled. "Mine too."

"Hey," he said.

She tipped her chin up to look at him.

He smiled. "I like you."

"*Like me* like me?" she teased.

He pursed his lips and nodded. "Pretty much."

She was still smiling when he kissed her.

thirty four

RILLA KEPT CLIMBING, BORROWING PETRA'S STATIC ROPE AND SETTING
it up, early in the morning by herself, on top-rope with two mini traxions—a kind of pulley system—to self-belay. She soon got used to the fear of being alone, and the only drawback was she had to stop every once in a while and pull the slack as she went. She kept to easy climbs where she could work on movement—trying to mimic the grace and power Caroline had without anyone watching. Remembering Tam and the hikers, she often found herself checking and rechecking the locking mechanisms, her rope, the anchors, and any fixed gear she passed.

Most of the gear she depended on was still Petra's, and every time she looked at her few pieces mingling in, she thought of Johnny Cash's "One Piece at a Time" and cringed a little. She was saving for a rope, but then she'd still need most of the gear she used. One mini traxion was over a hundred dollars, and the setup required two. She spent a week self-belaying before Petra needed her rope back, and Rilla had to stop.

In order to climb The Nose, Rilla needed to climb every day. She needed the experience of touching a lot of rock, figuring out a lot of problems, and doing it enough that when she got on The Nose, nothing but the view and the sequence would be new. Unwilling to wait around when she could have been climbing, Rilla forced herself to go to the bulletin board outside the ranger shack. Scanning the scraps of paper looking for a climbing partner, she crossed her arms and dug her fingers into her skin. The papers all had names and campsites. Some of them had ratings of what they typically climbed. Rilla looked for someone who could climb around a 5.10. It was where she felt most comfortable.

While she looked, a thin boy with an undercut and long braid came to the board and pinned up a paper.

She glanced him over. "You need a partner?" she asked quickly, before he left. At least this way she wouldn't have to do the awkward walk into someone else's campsite.

"Yeah. Do you know someone?" he asked.

She supposed it wasn't obvious. "Me. Are you looking to climb now? I'm ready. I don't have a rope though." Wait. She needed to ask other things. "How long have you been climbing?"

He shrugged, looking her over.

Rilla felt the sudden urge to pull down her shorts. They were cut-offs, not technical fabric or spandex everyone else climbed in.

"A few years," he said. "You're a climber?"

She nodded. "I live here."

"That's awesome," he said. "How long have you been climbing?"

"This summer, but I've gotten a lot of time in."

He smiled. "You know, I think I'm looking for someone with a little more experience. Thanks though." And with that, he walked off.

Rilla's cheeks flushed and the heat prickled over her scalp. She wasn't as experienced as Adeena or Caroline, but she was a good partner. She knew what she was doing. Was it that she didn't look like a climber, even now? *Would he have said that if she'd been a boy?* Stomach churning, she trudged out toward the parking lot. She couldn't muster up the courage to ask anyone else and be rejected. Looked like she wasn't climbing today.

At the far edge of the parking lot, Rilla heard someone call her name. Turning back, she looked around.

"Hey! Wait up!" Caroline shouted, waving her hand. She had a huge pack on her back and carried another one.

Rilla ran back. "Need help?"

"Sure!" Caroline handed off the bag in her arms. "But don't drop it. There's like a million dollars worth of lenses in there."

"Shit." Rilla looked down. "I don't know if you should trust me."

Caroline chuckled.

"How's it going?" Rilla asked.

"Hot and gross and annoying." Caroline groaned. "I kept thinking because we'd be higher up, it'd be cooler. I didn't count on having to go up and down a million times. I think I've lost like ten pounds just from the sweating."

"How has it been? Climbing with Celine?"

"I'm not really climbing." She shrugged. "Ascending and hauling. But it's really cool to watch the photographers and Celine and how they work together while she's climbing. She's been working on the route on a rope this week. I think she'll finish up and go for it at the end of the week. If she feels good." Caroline readjusted the straps. "I don't know. It's cool. Petra still pissed?"

"Madder than a rooster who lost all his hens."

Caroline snorted and shook her head. "I feel bad. But . . ."

But no one would have asked Petra anyway, was the thing Rilla felt they both would say but didn't. Rilla looked down. "Is there sexism in climbing?"

Something she said must have been funny, because Caroline started laughing so hard she had to stop walking. She bent and braced herself on her knees, still laughing.

Rilla raised an eyebrow. "It wasn't a joke."

"I know," Caroline asked. "You just . . . oh." She stood and wiped her eyes. "*Yes* is the answer."

Rilla readjusted the lens bag and looked around at the tourists staring.

"Do you know what happens when I pose for a climbing photo and I'm wearing a sports bra and tight shorts? Or, god forbid, a bathing suit?"

Rilla was silent, falling back in step beside her as they entered Half Dome Village.

"A thousand people leave comments about whether the aesthetic of my body pleases them—a body that is a tool to take me where I want to go. A hundred people email me their opinion that I am setting women back a hundred years by trading sex appeal for attention. Ten people actually write think-pieces that are published online or in print about the same thing, but adding in how the values of climbing are being lost in today's generation. How no matter their opinion on what I did, I am a symptom of the sickness that is plaguing this culture. When Hico does it—nothing." She sighed. "Everything a woman in the public eye does is a disaster. Adeena was in *Rock and Ice* in a hijab, and the amount of shit she got for that . . ." Caroline rolled her eyes. "It was in the millions. Because Huffington Post picked it up. She was wearing it because she was around her family that day, and Adeena is one of the most respectful people I know. But god forbid a woman make her own decisions about how she conducts herself, or bridges her cultures, or deals with her faith. What a thousand men have done, one woman can't do without being a symptom or a symbol."

Rilla's shoulders sagged, feeling put in her place. "Oh."

Caroline snorted. "Yeah."

"Well. That's . . . yeah. Gross." Rilla didn't know what words would make sense after that. But then, suddenly, it came to her. "I'm sorry that happens to you. If it means anything, that's the thing I admire most about you. That you are just yourself and also a climber. It makes me feel like, in some way, I can be Rilla and a great climber."

Caroline smiled. "Thank you. I appreciate hearing that."

"Have you been to Pakistan with Adeena?"

Caroline shook her head. "I'd love to climb there with her someday. That's how she met Hico—that *Rock and Ice* shoot. They asked her to bring him. That sort of bugged me—that Adeena, a hugely talented climber—wasn't enough of a draw on her own, but it was good for Adeena's career overall. I think Adeena feels that way too."

"I don't know why I thought this was all this paradise where none of this went on. I feel very naïve all of a sudden," Rilla said.

"Because on the rock, it's not real. It all falls away when you climb. On the ground, it's different." Caroline stopped and reached for the bag. "If I didn't love climbing so much, I'd never be able to deal with the bullshit on the ground. Thanks for carrying the lenses."

"Have fun," Rilla said.

Caroline laughed, heading into the woods. "Pray I don't die from heat exhaustion."

Rilla turned back, taking her time through Half Dome Village to see if anyone needed a break from their work for a few dollars. She fished a condom out of a toilet, removed a troop of baby mice from a cabin, and bought Thea a cold Gatorade before heading out into the heat to find her.

She looked so miserable, in the only patch of sunlight coming through the trees, waving cars through the intersection with Yosemite Village, that Rilla felt guilty. It wasn't her fault, but it somehow made her remember all the ways she'd let her sister down. She was climbing, even though Thea had forbidden it. The WANTED posters for the stolen plaque had made it onto the doors of the store and cafeteria in Half Dome Village, and her homework wasn't even remotely finished, while Rilla held hope Thea would realize the GED test was the simplest solution.

Thea spotted Rilla and stepped out of the intersection, letting another ranger take her place.

"Will you just look into me taking the GED?"

Thea rolled her eyes. "You can't use it—"

"I'll keep working. Just please consider it."

Thea shrugged. "Fine. I'll look into it."

"I brought you this," Rilla said, handing over the sweating bottle.

"Aw . . ." Thea unscrewed the top. "Thanks."

A thousand prickles of guilt stabbed her chest, but Rilla just nodded. "You're welcome."

•

The next morning, after Thea had left for work and Rilla was working across the bottom of the Camp 4 walls, partnerless, Celine emerged out of the brush.

Rilla jumped away from the wall, brushing off her hands guiltily. If she had hated climbing in front of Caroline, she definitely didn't want to be caught by Celine.

Celine only said, "Good morning," politely.

"Morning."

Celine shaded her eyes against the early morning glare of light bouncing off the granite and looked upward.

Rill stood awkwardly. Not wanting to climb, not knowing what else to do.

"You're the one from West Virginia, right?" Celine said after a few minutes.

"Yes ma'am."

"Caroline said you only started climbing this summer."

Blushing, Rilla nodded. When would she stop being new?

"How exciting. What a wonderful place to begin a journey," Celine said. She tucked back a strand of her hair and looked up. "I'm just looking at this route here. Have you climbed it? Henley Quits?"

Rilla glanced upward. "Uh, yeah." She had. She had led it, even. Blood rushed to her fingertips and she bit down on a smile. "It's fun."

"Mind belaying me on it?" Celine asked.

Rilla's eyes widened and she looked down at her gear. *Really?* "Sure." *Be cool, Skidmore.*

And even though she stood on the ground, carefully minding her rope as Celine quickly moved up the ever shrinking crack, Rilla felt like yelling to anyone who might hear, "*I'm belaying Celine Moreau!*"

It was only after, when Rilla lowered her, that she understood why Celine was Celine.

Methodically. Quietly. With a strange sense of balance and poise, she unclipped her harness and turned again to the wall.

Rilla stepped back, confused.

Celine turned to the wall and raised her hands. And while Rilla watched with an unhinged jaw, Celine proceeded back up the climb. The rope limp beside her, the only sounds were the birds and the gusts of wind in the trees.

"Wow," Rilla breathed when she returned to the ground. "I don't think I could ever," she started before snapping her jaw shut.

Celine smiled. "You shouldn't. Unless you know you can."

"How do you manage that risk?" Rilla asked, still in awe.

"For me, it's not a risk like it is for most people. I know what I'm capable of. I know my limits because I've pushed every one of them on the rope. To go off the rope, it's because I know I can physically, and the mental challenge is all that's left."

"But you could die!" Rilla said.

"Of course I could. And so could you. We shouldn't fear what might happen. We should fear what we want and might not do because of fear."

Rilla laughed. Then, without thinking, she leaned on the rope and blurted out, "Why didn't y'all ask Adeena to haul?"

Celine blinked twice and her forehead creased. "Adeena is the Pakistani climber, yes?"

Rilla nodded, her words catching up with her. She looked down, embarrassed. "Yes. She's from Pakistan. She climbed Everest when she was fifteen. I've learned so much from her. She's one of the best climbers and teachers in the Valley."

Celine smiled. "I only met her that one morning. She sounds wonderful. I'm so glad to see you girls all supporting one another."

Rilla frowned, wanting to ask if she'd known Gage except that he was Hico's partner. The quietness of it was what bothered her most—the shadow that seemed like it would never be caught and dealt with. Even now, what could she say? Get to know some girls? Celine probably knew plenty. Walker was right. And so was Petra. So was Celine. And Adeena. It seemed just when Rilla was over one mountain, there was a whole range of challenges ahead to navigate. Complicated and uncharted.

"Thanks for belaying me," Celine said.

Rilla looked her in the eyes and nodded.

"Want to take a turn?" Celine wiggled the rope.

Rilla looked to the wall and to Celine. This was life, she realized. From now on there would be no final resolution that led her into truth. It would be a series of this—shadows she had not seen and gods who were less bright, less high. Finish one pitch and another remained ahead.

"Yes," Rilla said, stepping forward to tie-in.

In some magic of early morning light, when she climbed the route, she felt her breathing and her body sync into a place she didn't know existed—where everything worked and sang together beautifully, and the world existed in that moment just for her and the glory she felt.

thirty five

AFTER THE PHOTOGRAPHY CREW LEFT AND THE CIRCUS SUBSIDED,
Celine and Andy's wedding became the thing everyone talked about at
the Grove and in Camp 4. They'd been given things to do at the event—
treated like family as an honor to the community of climbers who
became family everywhere.

Two days before the ceremony, Rilla told Thea she was going on a
camping trip, and just didn't tell her it was camping on a wall. The climbing was easy. Rilla wasn't there to learn the climbing. She was there to
learn the logistics in preparation for The Nose.

Adeena and Petra taught her to pee into the air, or into a container to
pour out away from the belay, and shit into a container, while in a harness. Rilla learned how to set up a portaledge and sleep in her sleeping
bag on the small nylon cot hanging off the side of the wall, while still in
a harness.

No one was on her period, but Adeena showed her the easiest way
to change a tampon or menstrual cup—which some climbers used,
apparently—midair. It was a task much simpler than she'd expected.

It was not glamorous or cool, but if Rilla wanted to climb The Nose—if
she wanted to climb like them—she'd have to learn to live on the rock.
They made it easy though. The two girls somehow made Rilla laugh as
she hung ass out in the air, trying to relax enough to pee. And when she
learned where to lash the waste container in the anchors or pack it in the
pig, so she wouldn't drop it, and it wouldn't touch anything else.

They spent the night, not far off the ground, talking as they stared into the Milky Way and watched the tiny dots of lights moving on the valley floor below.

In the end, it all was less gross and less fuss than she'd imagined. But she returned to Thea's house eager for a shower, and trying hard not to pester her sister about the prospect of getting her GED.

The afternoon of the wedding, Rilla felt like she spent at least an hour scrubbing dirt out of her nails and feet and slathering her sun- and wind-dried hair with conditioner. The hot water ran out, but she clenched her chattering teeth and cursed the goose bumps on her legs as she finished shaving. Her stomach trembled with anticipation and excitement and she tried not to let herself dream up a thousand different ways Walker could fall to his knees and worship her, but she couldn't help a few. She hadn't seen him in a few days, between climbing and his work, and she missed him. Missed him like she hadn't even known was possible.

Grateful for the warmth of her attic bedroom, she toweled off, smeared lotion into her suntanned limbs, and spent a long time sitting on the floor half-naked, brushing out the snarls of her hair.

Outside, the afternoon sunbeams lengthened. The air sizzled. The chill from the shower faded and she was starting to sweat again as she blow-dried her hair and carefully smoothed it out with a brush.

She had brought three dresses from West Virginia. One was white, so she put it back right away, hearing her grandmother in her head about never wearing white to a wedding. One was an Easter dress an aunt had given her when she was fifteen. It was pink with darker flowers. Perfect wedding attire. She picked it up and began putting it on, but as soon as she pulled it over her head she broke out in more sweat, and her stomach cramped. She paused, stuck in the polyester lining, the dark pink flowers wrinkling like a bad metaphor. It wouldn't go any farther. She was fitter, tighter, and leaner than when she'd arrived. But also bigger. Well-fed and healthy and bigger. She only wore stretchy pants or the new things Thea had bought her to replace what she'd outgrown.

She took a deep breath and clawed the dress back up over her head. What was she going to do? This was the dress for the wedding. The last dress was a blue sundress. Cute for putting over a swimsuit. Cute for a long day with her legs up on the dashboard of a jeep. Not for a wedding.

Hands on her hips, she took a deep breath and glanced out her window. The sun was deep and golden, and she was definitely late. She tried to make the pink flowered prison work, forcing it somehow over her hips and trying not to sweat as she put her makeup on and smoothed oil on her hair. Finally, she was ready.

And ready to die.

With a groan, she peeled herself out of the dress again and wiggled out of her bra like she was escaping a spider. She grabbed the blue sundress and pulled it over her head, pausing only to add big, dangly earrings and a bracelet to dress it up before scurrying downstairs. The right thing be damned.

Even with rushing, she got to the road just in time to see Walker, waiting with white ribbons hanging out of his pocket, looking worried. He wore a pair of light pants. A white dress shirt. His hair was combed, and his shirtsleeves rolled up. The ribbon trailed along beside him. He caught sight of her, and his chest lifted for a brief enough moment that it made everything worth it. She had to duck her head; her smile was so big.

"You're late."

"I know! I'm sorry."

"They're almost here." He pulled the ribbon out of his pocket and shoved one end in her direction.

"What are we doing?"

"Stay there. We're stretching it across the path. They're walking from Camp 4 to the chapel, and we'll join when they come on through. It's a local custom where Celine grew up."

She grasped her end and tried to slow her heartbeat, watching his big body as he moved to the other side of the path. The ribbon fluttered between them.

He smiled. A slow, liquid smile. "Hey," he said, his voice deep and sexy.

She couldn't help but grin. "Hey."

"You look nice."

"It's a bathing suit cover-up."

"Oh. Well." He blinked. "You still look nice."

She nodded. "Thanks. So do you."

"Oh, this?" He looked down. "It's a bathing suit cover up."

She laughed and tossed the ribbon between them. "What is this anyway?"

"They walk together to the chapel. We're um, supposed to stand here until they come get us and cut through the ribbon."

Rilla squinted and frowned. "Are we . . . are we an *obstacle* to love?"

"Not us!"

"Right?"

"We're the most pro-love people out of everyone," he said.

Rilla did a fist-bump into the air. "Pro-love. I love it."

"We can't be an obstacle."

"Never."

But they didn't look at each other anymore. And they gripped tighter to the ribbon between them—not an obstacle, but true love's ability to cut through obstacles.

Rilla held tight to the flat ribbon, melting a little in her damp hand. She closed her eyes, feeling Walker's heartbeat in the line. Louder than the people and the cars passing on the road. Louder than the rushing Merced and the wind through the trees. Louder than her mind. At least for a moment.

She wished she could have a picture of this. Whatever it was. In a way that would capture her body underneath the dress and the wind on her skin and the feeling of Walker's broad and muscled body facing hers, in the same wind and the same layer of clothes. Maybe it was all the talk of love. Maybe it would fade. But right this second, it felt like the closest she'd ever been to saying she was in love with someone.

She opened her eyes, both startled and unsurprised to find Walker watching her. Her face. Her eyes. His gaze locked with hers and they stood there, watching each other. Their heartbeats thrumming in the white ribbon stretched under the watching granite.

Walker took a step, ribbon sagging, his lips tight and eyes full of something that made Rilla terrified and excited and . . .

And then Celine and Andy rounded the path.

They both straightened, and pulled the ribbon tight.

Rilla swallowed and tried to look calm, turning her attention to the bride and bridegroom.

Andy looked a little like Rilla felt. *Trussed up.*

Even though his suit—cream, with a white shirt and smoky purple tie—looked like it fit impeccably, it immediately betrayed his athletic-not-aesthetic body. His long hair looked trimmed and smoothed back; but it was still long, shaggy hair on a man who probably needed a good sit-down with a barber.

But Celine? Celine looked like the goddess she was. She walked with her arm in Andy's, holding a cluster of white and purple flowers in her other hand. Her dress was long sleeved and close fitting. A frothy chiffon and lace paneled skirt swirled from her knees as she walked. It was the perfect balance between the idea of a classic French woman and a rock climber who traveled the world and peed out of her harness.

Behind them, a crowd had gathered, walking and talking and playing sweet, lulling melodies on guitars and mandolins and ukuleles. Celine and Andy led them on.

They paused before the outstretched ribbon, and Celine smiled at them before Andy sliced through it.

Rilla felt the cut. And found she missed the connection.

Walker caught her eye, and they waited as the procession passed before falling in at the back. Caroline wasn't there yet and neither was Petra. Amid the lilting guitar and the happy chatter, Rilla felt a sudden dive in her chest of loneliness and longing for something she didn't know how to put words around. She didn't think it was just Walker, but something bigger ... beyond ...

The back of his knuckles grazed her hip as they walked, and her breath caught.

They crossed the meadows, collecting Adeena and Hico, Gage and Petra, Caroline and newcomer Leland on the way to the chapel, in the evergreens under the watch of the Valley cliffs. Adeena wore a long fuchsia dress with ornate gold trim and gold jewelry, and Caroline was in a simple black silk dress. They were like Celine, in that they wore their dresses as well as they wore their climbing clothes. Petra looked totally different from them, but right in her own way—with a floral dress that touched the ground and flowed easily in the breeze as they walked.

They all were definitely in dresses and not swimsuit coverups from Walmart, but each girl complemented Rilla as if they didn't notice, and Rilla tried her best to stop comparing.

The service was short. Rilla listened in a stupor of late golden sun through the glass into the tiny chapel, enjoying the feel of Walker breathing beside her, and the dry dust smell of the inside.

Afterward, they all proceeded across the Valley to the hotel's gardens. It was so very Celine, and you knew that without knowing Celine.

A great bower stood heavy with snapdragons, asters and freesia and greens, dripping forward into a curve over an empty spot on the lawn. Someone had even climbed up into the great live oak to drape long trails of twisting greenery and flowers and lights.

They ate sweetly seared scallops and lobster in cups while they laughed awkwardly and fumbled with their hands and limbs in unfamiliar dress clothes. Rilla hadn't ever tasted either dish, and copied others dipping the lobster in butter. They sat all together at a table on the edge of the crowd. Hico knocked over a glass, and Petra talked at length about her time in Paris. Walker slid his hand onto Rilla's thigh and squeezed gently. Rilla leaned on the table and smiled. They were served duck with crisp skin and fatty meat that pulled off the bone, potatoes, and soft bread. Champagne drunk, they grew more at ease and laughed at each other, all copying Caroline and Petra, who seemed to be the only two who knew how to eat duck off a bone with a fork and knife.

The dancing began, and Rilla leapt up, with Walker's hand tightly held in hers. They joined Celine and Andy. Rilla laughed as she realized that as much as she often thought of climbers as dancers, on two legs and flat ground they weren't that great.

They danced and drank and shoved the lightly sweet almond cake into their mouths, washing it down with champagne. All around them, the night was cool and pleasing on their arms.

And then it was time to go.

Celine hugged the four of them. "I already told Caroline, but you're welcome to visit my home in France. Come climb with Caroline. She's coming for spring. I'd love to climb more with you."

"Oh my god, totally," Petra said from across the circle of people.

"I'd love to . . ." Rilla said. *But I have no idea how I'll manage.* France. It was a weird country in a geography book—a joke even, at home, because it didn't exist except in stories—and suddenly it was real, a place that existed and was so close she could taste it on the air around them.

"Adeena?" Celine asked, touching Adeena's arm. "I would love for you to make it."

"Thank you so much for asking," Adeena said. "I'll definitely consider it."

They hugged and moved aside for Celine and Andy's family, waving goodbye.

Walker draped his arm over Rilla's shoulder, and she tipped her head, studying his profile in the dim light. He was gorgeous, and he was hers. Rilla wrapped her arms around his waist and leaned into his hard body. "Let's go look at the stars on El Cap," she said.

He smiled, biting his bottom lip briefly as he looked over her face and pulled her so tight she could barely breathe.

They left the crowd on the paths they walked every day. The moon was high over the Valley, making the shadows dance in the wind.

"I heard Celine invite you to France. That's gotta feel great," he said, his fingers rubbing the curve of her shoulder.

"To think, I started this summer not even knowing how to tie a figure eight."

"I'm so blown away by you. I feel like the biggest ass for writing you off that day. You completely amaze me and everyone else, every time you start climbing and we realize somehow, you've gotten better than you were yesterday. I've never seen someone do that."

Rilla laughed and pulled away, dancing ahead on the path. "You should feel like an ass."

He watched her. Then with a quiet roar, ran after her. She squealed and ran. Head back, arms pumping. He couldn't catch her. Or he chose not to.

She slowed and circled back.

"You're beautiful," he said.

"I know," she said, laughing. Even though she didn't really know, she felt it right then, and that was all that mattered.

Hand in hand they crossed the road, turned off the path, and threaded through the tall grass.

In the middle of the meadow, they dropped to the ground and looked up.

El Capitan stood over them, tall and foreboding in the dark.

"Come closer," Walker said widening his legs and dragging her tight to his chest. She tipped her chin, leaning against his shoulder.

The lights on El Cap—tiny white lights—looked like stars fallen from heaven to decorate the granite. And above them, the haze of the Milky Way stretched wide and clear.

His fingers softly stroked the skin of her calves, running up and down the lines pushed into her body by running and hiking and climbing. The night air was sweet and his fingers stirred a deep ache in her stomach. She pretended to watch the flickering pinpricks of headlamps on the massive shadow of granite under the moonlight, but all she saw was the haze of stars and the sweep of Walker's fingers up her legs, to her knees . . . to her thighs.

Her breath came fast, feeling the stillness in his body—the focus and attention. When she looked up at him, in the dark, his chin was tucked, watching the rise and fall of her chest in the sundress. The heart beating just under her skin.

They were in the meadow, but in the dead of night, the Valley had fallen silent. Tourists were tucked in their tents. In a room of rustling grass and the cool mountain wind, Rilla reached up and slid the straps of her dress off her shoulders.

His fingers stilled.

A shiver ran up her spine as the wind touched her skin, bringing the ache to the surface. She reached up and touched his lips; and in response, his fingers crushed the flesh of her thighs with desperation.

This was more than she could have ever dreamed for herself, back home. And here, she'd not only dreamed it into reality, she'd brought it to be so. *Somehow.* This gorgeous boy. The stars so clear and bright. With France ahead, and The Nose just within her grasp. Her body felt strong and capable. She slid a hand up her body, relishing in the hitch in Walker's breath. She did it again. Teasing him with a body she possessed. A body that was hers.

He kissed her neck, hands moving from her thighs upward, dress clutched and caught in his grip. The cotton bunched around her waist, and his hands stilled at her hips.

She slid her feet closer to where she sat, letting her knees open wide in invitation.

When he didn't immediately move his hands, she pressed back against him and slid her fingers between her legs.

Walker gave a low moan as he watched. His breath a rush of warmth on her skin, mixing with the cool breeze. The grass tickled her thighs. She owned this night. This body. This moment.

Tilting her chin up, she closed her eyes and sank into the ecstasy of both the moment and the journey. Her fingers moved under the edge of her underwear, trembling a little from the cold and desire and the idea that Walker was watching. Confidently, she touched herself—urged on by the hardness pressing in her lower back and the way Walker nearly whimpered before softly sinking his teeth in her shoulder.

"Can I?" His breath caught. "Touch you?"

The urge to deny him leapt in her throat; but she wasn't ready to play that game. Maybe someday—but she was too hungry for the newness of his touch right now. Instead, she smiled dreamily and pulled his hand downward. His fingers were warm, and she shuddered at the way the hard grooves of his callused fingertips stroked her wet and exposed skin.

She moved her hands away, allowing him to take over. Desperate to touch him, she shifted over and reached behind her back.

He moved for her, pausing for a moment so she could unzip his pants and find his skin in a way that made him bite his lips tight to keep from crying out.

She smiled as he pulsed under her touch.

His fingers moved slowly at first. Teasing. Exploring. Responding when she reached down and gently adjusted his fingers. Pulling the strings of her need deep down along her spine until she was engulfed in her desire, panting and gasping and pushing her hips up in little shakes in an effort to get more. She tightened her grip on him, her arm awkward, feeling messy and raw, but not willing to lose hold of him and his pleasure at the same time as she chased hers. She arched her back, falling to pieces as he brought her to the edge and pushed her over. The stars exploded and showered her in effervescent sparks behind her eyes.

"Fuck. Keep going, please," he whispered in her ear.

She leaned to the side, twisting between his legs to kiss his mouth as her hand moved. His hand closed over hers and, together, their shared breath roaring in her ears, she brought him with her.

His head fell back and the moonlight touched his lips.

thirty six

RILLA WOKE UP ON THE COUCH. WALKER WAS ON THE FLOOR. THEY were still dressed.

She sat up and frowned, vaguely remembering him walking her home. By that time they'd been so tired they'd just fallen asleep. The memory of what had happened the night before hit her brain, and she grinned like a loon.

"Uh-oh," Lauren said. "Jennings. Who let you sleep here?" She sat in the recliner and laced her boots.

He didn't respond.

"We just got too tired . . ." Rilla said, certain her body had her night written all over itself.

Lauren eyed them both and shook her head. "I'd get breakfast and avoid your sister if I were you. She and your mom got in a fight last night."

Rilla made a face. "Oh. Thanks!"

"No problem." Lauren grabbed her Stetson and backpack. "Time to go save people from stupidity."

Rilla shook Walker's shoulder. "Hey. I'm hungry. Take me to breakfast."

He grunted.

She licked his ear.

He bolted up. "What?"

Laughing, she stepped over him. "Be quiet. I'm going to put actual clothes on. You're taking me to breakfast."

"Oh, sweet Jesus," he gasped, clutching his ear as she left. "Don't do that again."

A sense of power—way too evil for whatever the hell time it was—flooded her veins, and she had to muffle a giggle in the hall. Quietly, she climbed up to her attic and pulled on a T-shirt and sweats over a pair of shorts.

Thankfully, Thea hadn't made an appearance by the time she got outside.

Walker sat on the steps, his dress shirt unbuttoned. He leaned on the railing, asleep.

"Breakfast. Now." She smacked him lightly on the top of the head.

"I need clothes," he said. "And I prefer the first way you woke me up."

They walked over to his tent and Rilla tried to look like she'd not . . . in the . . .

"How's it going?" Adrienne asked, pouring granola over her yogurt. "Is Walker up this early? I thought with a day off, he'd be asleep still."

"I'm hungry," Rilla said.

Adrienne shoved a spoon in her mouth. "I'm late for a meeting," she said over the food. "See ya."

Walker biked them across the Valley in the early morning light, to the cafeteria, where they filled their plates and coffee cups and sprawled out on one of the gleaming tables.

"Want to go climbing today?" Walker asked. "With me?"

She smiled, dumping hot sauce on her hash browns. "I *guess* you've earned it."

"I mean. I can keep working toward it," he said hastily, a twinkle in his eye.

She laughed and mixed her food with a fork. Before she said anything else, someone ruffled her hair. "Look what the Valley churned up," Hico said joyfully, sitting beside Rilla and grabbing the hot sauce off her tray. "You two disappeared last night." He eyed them both. "Some emergency I missed?"

Rilla snorted and didn't look up.

"You know. There's always something in Yosemite," Walker said.

"Mm-hm." Hico twisted in his chair. "Dude, over here."

Gage slid his tray in beside Walker. "The girls are here too. I saw them come in."

Sure enough, in a few minutes, a sleepy-looking Adeena, Caroline, and Petra appeared at the table.

"The Valley girls themselves," Hico said. "Good morning sunshines."

"Like, why are you, like, so awake?" Petra said in a fake accent.

Adeena busted out laughing. "I have never heard you talk like that. When I was little, I thought that's how all girls in America talked."

Petra salted her eggs and pushed her tray out so she could lean on her hand while eating. "So, what were you two up to last night?" She pointed her fork between Rilla and Walker.

Rilla glanced at Walker.

Walker shrugged. "Nothing." He leaned over and stole a sausage from her plate.

Petra pretended to stab him with her fork, and looked to Rilla. "You two together now?" she asked.

Rilla waited, breath tight in her chest.

"We're eating breakfast together," Walker said. "If that's what you mean."

Petra smiled a small smile at Walker's evasiveness—like a satisfactory little curl she couldn't control.

Rilla hid in her coffee cup. She was starting to hate Petra's competetiveness. Petra didn't even like Walker. Everything in her stomach turned sour, and she pushed away her plate, trying to look like she didn't care.

"Please stop asking my brother questions about his love life while I'm eating breakfast," Caroline said, not looking at any of them. "You're ruining my food."

"We were talking on the way down and decided it's a great Middle Earth day," Caroline announced, pushing back her hair. "It's supposed to be a hundred today, so it's either that, or I'm going to Tuolumne."

"What's Middle Earth?" Rilla asked.

"It's the inner falls of Yosemite Falls—you can't see it until you're inside," Gage said. "It's so beautiful. It's literally like you've been dropped in New Zealand or a Tolkien book or something."

"You coming?" Petra asked Walker.

He nodded. "Sure."

Rilla didn't know how she felt, but she knew she felt something. She stood with the others, taking her tray back and trying to shake off the awkwardness that had crept up and ruined her breakfast. There was nothing wrong. Nothing at all.

•

Caroline free-soloed up Sunnyside Bench—something Rilla hadn't even thought Caroline would do. Once Petra saw Caroline did it, she followed suit, leaving the taste of unease in Rilla's mouth as she watched her disappear up the cliff. Petra could do it, Rilla was fairly certain. But she trusted Caroline to make a better decision on risk than Petra did.

The rest of them simul-climbed up Sunnyside Bench—a new experience for Rilla. It made the easy route go quickly, as they were all attached on the same rope. Gage went first and placed the protection. Walker went last and cleaned it. Everyone else climbed along in between. In that way, they ran up the cliff quickly, laughing and joking as if they were all out for a walk under the brilliant sun.

At the top, Caroline and Petra sat under a tree in the shade, waiting and looking more relaxed together than Rilla had ever seen. The slabs wore down into a faint trail and she fell in step behind the others as they all headed single-file along a great granite terrace, toward Yosemite Falls.

It'd been hot and not rainy, and the falls had become a steady, thin trickle, plummeting well over a thousand feet from the upper edge. The gray and tan-streaked cliffs ran each direction as far as the eye could see. They had spent two hours climbing out of the Valley and had barely made it off the floor. She kept looking up at the falls, at the glisten of the splash of water on granite, squinting under the intensity of the sunshine.

"It never gets old," Petra said, raising her arms up as the trail wound down to a wide opening at the bottom of the falls. Thick green manzanita bushes flattened and puffed in the wind in between the smooth granite boulders and slab. The trickle of a thousand-foot waterfall turned into a glassy creek slipping around the boulders and falling over the rounded edge of the shelf. Beyond the shelf, the water dove into a narrow fissure—a slot canyon—that kept falling toward the Valley floor.

"We're going down there?" Rilla asked, equally scared and excited. It was a clear, beautiful day and she was with a team; but she would never forget that hiker in Tenaya.

"Down there is Middle Earth," Caroline said.

At the top of the shelf, chains were bolted to the rock—shiny and well-kept—clearly waiting for their ropes. They pulled the ropes, put on their harnesses, and began dropping down into the canyon on rappel, one by one. When it was Rilla's turn, she started off and then paused to drink in the full sight of the still stunning waterfall. She'd listened to this fall every night. She'd seen it when she didn't know what she was looking at. And now she stood right beneath it.

Walker stepped in front of her, grinning. "Yo, Rilla." He snapped his fingers. "Focus."

"I was admiring the view," she said.

"See ya in a bit." He waved.

Over the edge, the main falls slipped out of view and she followed the short, bulging wall to the bottom, joining the others in a shrunken pool walled in on all sides by the rock. The far side of the walls were water-polished and Rilla shuddered to think of standing here in the spring, when the falls were rushing at peak, and this pool would be covered in fathoms of tumultuous water, thrashing at itself to get over the next edge. Warm fingers gently touched her spine, and the shiver looped around itself and spun into a warm, aching hook that dropped to her toes as Walker gripped her shoulders.

"You cold?" he asked.

She smiled and spoke over her shoulder as they trudged through the pool, their packs floating alongside them. "No. I was thinking about the water being high." And how fast and powerful it would be churning through this arm-width channel.

"Oh. Yeah. That is a scary thought. Wait for me, I need to get the rope." He turned and pulled long stretches of the rope down over the drop, and coiled it back up to carry over his muscled shoulder through the waist-high water.

Out of the first pool, they walked along the thin stream of water still flowing, deep in the heart of the falls, past the stacked shelves of white granite, being careful not to slip on the granite, to another set of anchors before a drop. It was like being on an amusement park ride. Rilla waited in line, laughing and talking and enjoying the scenery until it was her turn. Walker followed last of all and pulled the ropes.

Over the next edge, she followed a sheer, long drop to a pool of blue-green water.

A narrow stream of sunshine funneled through a long granite hallway, lighting it as if it were sun pouring into the open doors of a great granite cathedral, refracting off the pool of emerald-blue water at the bottom of the long cathedral walls.

In the shaded corner of the wall, the water rushed as a stream of white froth, and lower, it washed over her, cooling her sun-warmed skin with tiny droplets of icy mountain mist.

At the bottom, she pulled herself off the rope and stepped into the rush of the water, standing on the rocks and letting it gush over her head just to feel part of the whole thing that surrounded her.

Shivering, she slid back into the pool and swam down the narrow cathedral pathway, bobbing toward its wide-open doors and an unmitigated sliver of stunning green and empty space of the Valley. Like she was tucked into some secret, lush paradise. The water was clear and green and perfect. The sun was bright and warm. The breeze, clean. Flipping onto her back, she treaded water and watched as Walker lowered himself and slid into the water.

He pulled the rope, kicking and swimming backward. The water rushed in great sparkling droplets as his arms moved. She'd never wanted to touch someone so badly as she did right then. But she knew it would not be enough and she didn't know what the answer was for that. It'd always been enough before. She hadn't known it wouldn't until he hadn't said anything at breakfast. It felt like she'd betrayed herself.

They all arranged themselves, spread out on the rocks at the end of the pool, lying back in the sun and passing around the beer and the bag of chips and Adeena's bag of apples she'd hauled up. They were a sweet treat. The light traveled across the granite and Walker's arm was beside hers on the rocks, and it felt like the only thing in the entire world that mattered was his bare muscled arm brushing hers. She didn't even feel guilty; the longing was so great and all-consuming. She could live with this. They were alone and above the crowds, and she needed nothing more from life than a handful of chips, a cold beer, and this afternoon in Yosemite Valley.

They moved farther down, loose-legged and dopey, as if they were all high, but still able to scramble over the massive, river-smoothed granite boulders to the top of the rounded boulder looking out over a twenty-foot drop into another pool.

Caroline tossed the rope first, and then jumped into the deep, clear water. The edge of this pool pushed up against the view of the open Valley and the haze of blue-emerald trees like a massive, natural infinity pool.

She jumped feet first into the blue pool, and felt the water rush past as Walker jumped beside her.

Above the surface, he grinned at her, gaze flickering ahead before he pulled her close and kissed her.

Rilla melted against his wet skin, against his hot mouth. It was wonderful, but when she pulled away a sick guilty feeling flooded her stomach—like when she'd message Curtis and she *knew* she shouldn't. But this was Walker—and he wasn't that at all. She looked at him, pulling the rope down with long stretches of his arms and it felt like everything they'd done together that summer was all in one feeling. *She loved him.* And he didn't love her. He didn't want anyone to know they were hooking up.

It felt like the rawness of her feelings was alive on her face, and she dipped under the surface to try and wash them off.

When she resurfaced, she was in control—but still with the echoes of it all in her chest. She loved him, and he didn't love her.

He flipped his backpack over and held it toward her. "Hang on, I'll tow you."

She grabbed on to it and kicked easily as he swam them both for the rocks at the edge of the pool. *She loved him.*

What was she going to do? How could she make him love her?

They sat in the sun with easy smiles, drying off before beginning the next rappel over the next set of falls. Anywhere in the world these falls wouldn't be little, and they'd be stunning all on their own; but here they were just another beautiful thing in a string of beautiful things. Water shot out in a graceful arc, crashing down the granite. Rilla hung back, waiting for Walker on a boulder above everyone else. She lay back and closed her eyes.

"Is Rilla planning to come?" Caroline asked.

Rilla's ears perked up, suddenly awake and straining to listen over the sound of rushing water.

"No," Petra said.

"I doubt it," Adeena said. "She still doesn't have a full rack."

"I think she's still messed up with school too."

"Usually climbing helps people figure shit out. Rilla's just . . ." Petra trailed off and Rilla couldn't hear if she said anything next.

"She's young still," Caroline said.

"Her home life is a disaster," Petra said. "Like with jail and drugs and super white trash. Her mom was in a long-term relationship with two men, and one of them left. So, it was like a dad leaving. Except it wasn't her dad, it was Thea's. Walker told me."

Rilla's face burned. *Walker told her?*

"Oh, I didn't realize," Adeena said. "Like a polygamist?"

"That's marriage," Petra said. "She wasn't married to either. It's more like polyamory. Where you're in love with more than one person at a time," Petra explained.

"Climbing probably is the first time she's done anything, like, in the larger world," Hico said. "It takes a lot of guts to do that."

"Yeah, going to France would be a huge thing. Too much, too soon," Petra said.

"She's got time," Caroline said.

"She could do it," Adeena said.

"Even if she could, it requires money," Petra said. "And *that* she doesn't have. She's still using my gear. I should probably get that back before she thinks I gave it to her."

"Yeah, her stories about West Virginia are . . . confusing."

"Like, *lying about it* confusing," Petra said. "Do we really think her mom was a stripper? It's all a bit much. I think she likes the attention."

"I don't know . . . she's young," Caroline said. "I don't think she's lying, but . . . "

Rilla had never known as much agony as she felt right at that moment, where all her worst fears had materialized as real from the mouths of people she most idealized. It was standing in a dry canyon and a sudden torrent of water unleashed and drowned her. One second she was fine. The next, there was no escape. It was over.

Tears sprung, bitter and hot. And she turned back and jumped into the water until it closed over her head and she imagined the steam rushing over the top of the water as it cooled the misery and heat of being alive and turned her into iron. She imagined she was the mountains, fresh and new and cooling into granite.

She rose to the surface just long enough to breathe and feel the sun against her eyelids before returning to the cold glacier water.

She heard Walker's voice calling before she understood his words. She felt his body move the water around her. His fingers on her waist. She kicked away and up.

"Rilla," he said as they surfaced.

Her name sounded odd in his mouth. Like she had the sudden urge to scratch it out and forbid him from ever saying it again.

"We're going," he said

"I'm coming," she said, and kicked for the rocks at the edge of the pool.

She finished the rappels in silence, at the back.

No one seemed to notice.

thirty seven

THE ONLY REVENGE WAS TO PROVE THEM ALL WRONG. OR AT LEAST, that they, like home, had underestimated her. Yes, she might be what they thought. But she was more. And could be capable of more. Celine had seen that. Celine had climbed with her! She could go to damn France if Petra could.

Petra was right about one thing though: Money was an issue.

"You can always find money," Jonah said, after rolling a blunt and listening to her vent as they sat on the granite couch, overlooking the Valley.

Rilla finished holding a tight breath of smoke before blowing it out and handing it back to Jonah. "Life doesn't let me find jack shit."

He rolled his eyes. "You sound hangry. Did you eat?"

"I ate," she muttered, elbows on her knees. "I'm not going to care about this. I'm going to get revenge for this."

"That sounds an awful lot like caring."

She turned to him, eyes narrowed. "Well, *you're* being super helpful."

Jonah shrugged. "Don't shoot the messenger."

She exhaled and looked out over the Valley. Everywhere she could see, she had memories of climbing with those people. Memories that felt ruined and tainted by what she'd overheard. "My mom said I could come home."

"To West Virginia? I thought you didn't want to go back?"

Rilla shrugged. "I miss it. Sometimes.

Jonah was quiet for a moment. He sniffed and looked away. "It's shitty to hear the things we are afraid everyone is saying. And shitty that they didn't think you were being honest. But I mean, have you talked to them about it?"

Rilla clenched her jaw. "I just thought. I thought this would be different."

"People are shitty. Friends can be shitty. I don't think it means they aren't your friends. That's certainly a better option than running home to West Virginia, don't you think?"

Rilla was about to say something snotty in reply when the sound of a rock tumbling caught her attention.

They both froze and looked at each other.

What was that? Rilla furrowed her brow.

Jonah grimaced, looking worried.

It wasn't that people didn't know about the couch—most everyone in HUFF used it. It was that people announced themselves. One rock tumbling could be a squirrel. A coyote. A deer? A bear . . .

She crept over to the edge and peeked over the rock to look down the trail.

A tan Stetson stood at the bottom, waiting.

Or a Ranger Miller.

Shit. Shit. Shit. If he caught her up here smoking weed, he'd definitely be able to drag her back to Thea's like AHA.

"COPS," she mouthed to Jonah.

He looked confused and didn't move.

She grabbed the stuff and chucked it as far into the trees as she could.

"Hey—" Jonah started to protest but she slapped a hand over his mouth and shushed him. Was that it? She patted his pockets just to be sure, pulling out an empty bag. Quickly, she put a rock inside and threw that too.

He made a squeak as it sailed to the ground.

"So, yeah," she said, letting go and trying to sound casual as she sat back down beside him. Her hands trembled. "People are the worst," she said.

He glared at her. "Yeah. They really are."

"Good afternoon," Ranger Miller interrupted, suddenly appearing over the top of the trail.

Thank god he'd bumbled the sneak up. Rilla tried not to look guilty as she turned over her shoulder and looked up at him. "Afternoon."

"I smell some paraphernalia. Have you been smoking weed?"

"Nope."

"It rises out of the Valley," Jonah said.

She wanted to elbow him, but it'd be too obvious.

"Rilla, I think you should come with me anyway. I don't feel comfortable leaving you up here alone with an older boy. Your sister would be upset."

"What?" Rilla asked. "You can't do that."

"I'm doing it. Let's go."

Normally, she would have fought him. Dug her heels in. What did she care about getting in trouble? But with Thea's future on the line, she didn't want to risk it. "Fine," she snapped.

"Rilla!" Jonah said.

"Be quiet now, son," Ranger Dick Face said, like he was a parody of himself and learned his policing from watching *The Dukes of Hazzard*.

Jonah stood and crossed his arms, glaring at Dick Face.

"I'm going. It's fine. I don't want to get Thea in trouble," Rilla said.

He nodded, still glaring.

"Let's go, Di—" She swallowed. "Ranger Miller."

"I'm keeping an eye on you. Don't even think about running."

"Oh my god, you can't be serious," Rilla said, starting down the steep, rocky path. Could this get any more ridiculous? Sighing, she followed

Ranger Miller back to Half Dome Village, to his truck, where he told her to wait and called Thea.

She rolled her eyes and leaned against the truck. Now Thea would certainly be mad. Talk about making a mountain out of a molehill.

"I wasn't smoking," she shouted so Thea could hear her.

Ranger Dick Face glared at her and turned his back.

She should bolt. Old Rilla would have bolted. But she folded her arms tight over herself and stayed put. Some things were more important. Thea was more important. She tightened her grip on her ribs and closed her eyes, repeating it over and over.

"All right, she's coming by for you."

"You're just trying to make something out of nothing."

He shrugged. "I don't think it was nothing. I think you were up there smoking weed with your friend."

He was right. But it was unfair. She ducked her head and glared at the ground. "You're a . . ."

"What?" he snapped. "Go ahead. Give me a reason."

She practically bit her tongue off trying to keep it still in her head.

Thea showed up ten minutes later, ignoring her while assuring Miller she appreciated it.

"He's an asshole. I wasn't doing anything," Rilla said, after he'd pulled off.

Thea shook her head. "It doesn't matter."

Rilla bit her lips tight.

"I have a final interview for the position next week. He's just trying to get anything he can."

"He must be feeling desperate," Rilla said hopefully.

"Or just petty," Thea said. "Just try to avoid him. Please." Thea sighed. "I needed to tell you anyway, your meeting with the principal is Tuesday at nine A.M.," Thea said.

"Wait. What?" Rilla froze. A red wash of panic came over her. "Why?"

"To see if you can be reinstated or if you have to repeat eleventh grade. Whatever you haven't done, do it now."

She had done nothing. Basically nothing. "I thought you were considering the GED?"

"What are you talking about?"

"I talked to you . . . like, a few weeks ago. About taking the GED—instead of school. I want to go to France. I want to get a real job and go to France to climb. Celine invited us."

Thea didn't speak. She just stared.

"I talked to—"

"Are you out of your mind?" Thea roared, full accent in her voice like Rilla hadn't heard all summer.

"As a matter of fact, I'm not," Rilla snapped. "But you seem not to have one this whole summer—at least when it comes to my existence."

"France? Celine?" Thea yelled.

Rilla rolled her eyes. "Oh, great." Thea was going to do the inexperienced climber thing again.

"What planet are you living on?" Thea said. "You aren't going to France. You don't even have a passport. And you weren't supposed to be climbing—and what . . ." She sputtered and stopped. "What's this about Celine. *Celine Moreau*?"

Rilla crossed her arms. "I climbed with her. She invited me to France along with Caroline. I'm a climber. A good one."

Thea rubbed her face and groaned. "What? You have got to be lying."

Why did everyone suddenly think she was lying? Rilla swallowed down a sick feeling. "I'm not. Ask Walker. Ask Caroline. Ask any—"

"I don't know how to do this," Thea interrupted. "I don't know how to be a parent."

"I don't need a parent. I already have two." There were no vacancies, despite the situation.

"An *actual* parent is what you need. For once in your life."

The same horrible, shit-brown feeling crept over Rilla's shoulders and tightened up her neck. Thea should be the one person, at least, who knew that her life wasn't a ridiculous stereotype she needed to be saved from, even if it sounded that way. "You can sell that load of shit to everyone else about Mom, but you can't sell it to me. I know the truth," Rilla snapped.

"The truth?" Thea swung around to face her, black hair nearly blue in the shade and uncharacteristically wild around her face. "Mom's chaotic, in and out of jail, unstable, addicted to a variety of substances including men, and does not see a problem with her lifestyle." Her tone was serious. Intense. "She refuses to even acknowledge her own history. Or how much danger you were in."

Rilla pulled back.

"*Your* dad's got the IQ and reasoning skills of a golden retriever and we both know he just does whatever Mom does," Thea continued. "Mine is the *non*-functioning addict. And as much as I understand you wanting to defend them, trust me when I say there's nothing to defend."

How could Thea say that? Had she forgotten how Thea's dad, Marco, read stories and her dad, Tom, taught them to ride dirt bikes. How Lee encouraged them to live wild and unfettered, and to not give any mind to what others might say. How all three showed them how to live and love even planted in a place that kept trying to pluck or poison you out like some rampant weed? "You don't know shit," she seethed, too furious to even argue. "You can't even see you're just like her."

Thea froze, her face white. "You know mom had a baby before us. I mean, she was pregnant—when Grandma kicked her out. Do you know what happened?"

Rilla froze.

"Her boyfriend beat the shit out of her and caused her to miscarry."

Rilla's stomach plummeted.

Thea leaned forward, wide-eyed. "Yep. And you know what? She went back to him."

She didn't want to hear this. Rilla closed her eyes, hating the sudden eruption of heat in her chest. "But she sent me here," she whispered.

"I convinced her. Yes, she sent you. And it's my job to do what she can't do. You are not going to France. You will graduate high school, so help me god."

Rilla's face twisted, fighting the coming tears. "She left. She did the right things, in the end. She did the best she could."

"In the end, sometimes it doesn't matter," Thea said. And she headed back to her post, leaving Rilla all alone again.

She could go home now. Mom had said, in August. Mom had said she could take the GED. All it would take was one phone call. Rilla could use the last bit of her money for the ticket. By that night, she could be on her way. It would solve everyone's problems—Thea's, Petra's, Walker's, everyone's. Even hers.

Rilla lifted her chin to the view of El Capitan staring over the trees and her heart wrenched. She couldn't leave. Not without trying The Nose. It was the thing she'd been working toward. The thing that mattered more to her than anything else. Somehow, she'd have to find a way to even the score and make them all wrong.

It came to her while setting aside Petra's gear to return it. It went, money—copper tub—everyone said it was dumb to steal a copper tub because—*watch!*

Rilla would pawn that broken watch of Petra's. Didn't have the money. Couldn't make it. Rilla pulled Petra's gear into her bag, and slid down the ladder. She'd show her. Her heart raced and bolstered her courage.

•

Rilla waited with her bag between her knees on the boulder by Petra's car until they arrived in the parking lot.

"Hey. I looked for you this morning."

"I had some work," Rilla answered, trying to seem at ease. As if nothing had changed. She picked up the bag. "Anyway, I wanted to get this to you, before I forgot."

Petra took the bag and looked inside. "Are you going to have enough gear for The Nose?"

"Oh yeah. I'm good." She'd been working nearly every day, and with some luck, duct tape, fishing line, and absolutely *nothing* going wrong, she thought she could manage.

Petra frowned. "You sure? You can totally keep these longer. It's no big deal. I know you're working. It takes time to build up a rack."

"No." Rilla swallowed. "I'm all good. I'll be ready."

"Two more weeks," Adeena crowed. "I'm nervous already."

"Two more weeks." Rilla nodded. A pit in her stomach started. "And after that, France."

Petra's brow pinched, but she smiled and looked over. "Yeah. France."

Rilla watched her go, her hand in her sweatshirt pocket to grip the gold watch she'd taken from the Grove. A stab of guilt cut through her stomach, but she swallowed it away.

Yeah, in France.

thirty eight

THE VALLEY WAS SILENT AND COOL, AND RILLA TIPTOED HER WAY OUT
of the house, keys clutched tight in her fist. A quiver of unease drifted through her stomach, but she'd been over it all night. It would be simple and quick. It was Thea's interview day—immediately following work—so she'd be gone longer than normal. Thea wouldn't even notice her truck was missing. In the end, Rilla would have the money she needed for France. There was no reason to back out now. All she had to do was drive to the closest bigger town and pawn it.

The drive to Merced went smoothly. The sun slipped up the canyon walls and she emptied out of the mountains in the desert just as the last bit of sunrise melted away into day. She was making great time, arm out the window, and all her unease melted away.

By the time she slowed, looking at the GPS and shifting the truck along the roads, the heat of the day descended and the back of her shirt and her thighs were drenched in sweat. It was hotter out here in the open desert than the last few days in the Valley.

Finally, she pulled up along the street, where the GPS announced her destination. It was a row of flat stucco houses with small aluminum windows on a wide, cracked concrete street. She was halfway done. With a breath of relief she hadn't realized she'd been holding, Rilla switched off the engine and slid out of the hot truck. The pawn shop was a gray stucco building with a chipped red door and bars on the windows. A full sycamore stood in the lot next door, dancing patterns on the sidewalk. Rilla took a few deep breaths and walked in.

The man wore a ratty Harley T-shirt and cargo shorts and even though she knew she should be afraid, nervous, there was something so familiar in him that she almost cried and hugged him as if he was a long-lost cousin. All summer she'd been working so hard to be something better, bigger, bolder, and feeling so alone when no one around her looked recognizable. Knowing she was the bottom regardless of whether she examined it by class, economy, and culture. And in a pawn shop in Merced, California, she felt all that slip away and she only had to be Rilla Skidmore.

It wasn't a great feeling. But it was home.

"I need to pawn this," she said, dropping the watch she'd stolen from the Grove onto the glass.

The guy rubbed his face and nodded.

In less than five minutes, she was back in the truck, and heading out of Merced. The fields flashing past her window, endless, eternal, and washed out in the bright sun.

About a half hour in, a faint, sweetly burning smell started, and she scanned the fields and horizon looking for the smoke.

She noticed the engine light too late. And the speedometer falling, even though she was pressing the gas harder. *Shit.* She yanked the truck over to the side of the road, the dust kicking up and mixing with the smoke now pouring out of the seams of the truck hood.

Shit. Shit. Shit. She jerked the handbrake up and jumped out of the truck. She had her phone, but who could she call? She wrapped her hand in her shirt and tried to open the hood, but it burned when she touched it. A vision of herself on a criminal clip flashed in her head. She looked around, shading her eyes against the heat and the sun. She'd figure something out. There were nothing but orchards as far as the eye could see. Dark mountains shimmered faintly on the horizon, partially hidden by haze. A dust devil whirled, soft and delicate and eerily silent in the dry dirt field, spotted with sparse almond saplings, across the road.

A heaviness hit her chest. What had she done? She was out in this wasteland of farms, alone, panicking while the truck poured smoke, knowing she was a hairsbreadth away from the same thing she'd always been.

She exhaled and put her hands on her hips. Okay, what next? Maybe she could walk somewhere. Pulling out her phone, she opened the maps and zoomed out. And out. And . . .

Was this even working? No signal. She looked both ways on the empty road and the sweat rolled into her eyes. Shit. She had to do something.

The hood had cooled enough to open carefully, her hand wrapped into her T-shirt. She wasn't sure what she was looking for; but if the engine was smoking, she figured she should take a look.

With the engine open, she could only peer blankly inside.

And feel thirsty and hot. Sweaty. *Shit.*

The road was still empty. How could it be empty?

She glanced down the long row of trees.

Across the road, the dust devil kept spinning.

A car approached, and she rushed out to the road, waving her hands. But the car zoomed right on by.

This was fast becoming a problem. She was melting. A hot wind puffed in her face and she wished it were cooler. The haze on the horizon seemed darker. Brewing. She squinted.

And suddenly, she heard the chug of a tractor.

Rilla whipped her head around, scanning the clementine trees. A cloud of dust rose above the trees a few rows over. Turning, she ran down the road, looking down the rows until she spotted a tractor, pulling it's trailer down a row of trees. Shouting, she ran down the row, sandals sinking in the surprisingly soft dirt.

The tractor kept moving. Shooting heavy streams of water onto the bases of the trees, soaking the desert. She caught up with it and the worker pulled back in surprise, cutting the engine.

He was dark skinned and dark haired, and he waited with a bandana covering his mouth, eyes crinkled in concern.

She'd only taken two years of high school Spanish. All she could remember was hello.

"Hola?" she asked.

The man yanked down his bandana. "¿Hola?"

"Uh. Soy llama . . . *shit.*"

"I speak English. Are you okay?" he asked.

Relief flooded over her. "I broke down. I think my truck overheated."

"You're on the road?"

She nodded. "Can I . . ." But she wasn't even sure what to ask.

The man came back and looked over the truck. He filled the radiator with water, and she was able to restart. By that time, the dust devil was long gone; but the horizon had thickened, and the haze had given way to a sharp anvil of clouds, soaring into the blue sky.

Only an hour and a half to go, and she'd be back at Thea's. Hopefully before Thea got home and realized the truck was gone. Only an hour and a half. She eased onto the road and gripped the steering wheel.

The road led right into the clouds. She lifted her eyes to the edge as she passed under it—from intense blue to swirling dark. But she was in the mountains now, the hills rising steeply on both sides into the canyon as she dropped down to ride the road along the bubbling Merced.

An hour. Maybe. She kept her eye to the narrowing sky above the mountains and kept the pedal toward the floor as much as she dared. After another stop to fill the coolant, she climbed back into the truck as it began to rain.

She was almost there.

Almost.

She entered the start of the Valley. The road dimmed. The rain drummed in her ears. The river beside her rose and roared and foamed.

Why had she done this stupid drive? It felt as if the shoulders of the gods twisted and turned, trying to swat her off like she was an invisible gnat that tickled their shoulder blades.

The windshield wipers flicked angrily back and forth. The river rose. She leaned forward in the seat, eyes glued to the road, speed down to under twenty miles an hour but it felt fast. The water seemed all around her. The edge of the river rippled up along the edge of her sight. Reaching.

Her pulse thumped in her throat. Hands sweaty on the steering wheel. Almost there. Almost there.

Water rushed down the wallows of the hills. Across the river, the hill rushed with it. Rilla yelped, pressing the pedal to the floor as a chunk of thick mud crested into the river and sprang upward to her side of the river. Too fast. She was too fast. The water was too fast. The road was too fast. She slammed on the brakes and the back end skidded behind her, fishtailing in a hydroplane. The river seemed to reach for her. The mountain was pressing against her, pushing her off the road.

The truck stopped, half off the road, facing the river.

Fingers shaking, she unbuckled and got out. The rain drummed on her head. Her heart pounded; she was sick to her stomach. She couldn't do this. What had she done? This was punishment for revenge. She put her hands on her knees and bent, water dripping in a long stream off her nose and over her lips. She was almost there. She just needed to keep going and everything would be fine. Get back in the truck. She stared at it for another few minutes, willing herself to get back in and keep going. If she kept going, she'd make it.

If she kept going...

Rilla straightened and got back into the truck.

•

The rain had lightened to a drizzle by the time she pulled into the meadow in the Valley. She wanted nothing more than to rub her ticket to France in Petra's face, but the rain had sobered her up and left her empty. Thea wasn't home. No one was.

In the silent house, safe and sound, it felt like a hollow victory. Particularly given what she'd had to do to get there.

She got in the shower, hoping to wash off the guilt. The sight of the hill rushing into the river and the water spinning around her in the truck flashed as the shower hit her back. The drive was over. She had done it, and she had fifteen hundred dollars to her name. She pulled back her hair and took a deep breath.

No one was home yet, and after getting out and dressed, she grabbed Thea's *Wilderness First Aid* and sat on the porch with a box of cookies.

She'd only been out there ten minutes when Walker came up the steps. "Hey, girl,"

She froze. She'd been avoiding him since Middle Earth as best she could, but somehow it had only been making it harder.

He smiled, bending down to kiss her.

She twisted away, pretending she hadn't seen.

He frowned and pulled away. "What's up?"

She shrugged and studied the page—the words going to nothing. *Shit. Why today?*

He sat on the floor and folded his legs. "Are you okay?"

"Nope," she said, turning the page. The next page didn't make sense either. But she'd been stupid—stupid to allow herself to trust another person and . . . why had she thought she could have feelings about him? Confide in him? Love him? He should have been nothing but a friends-with-benefits.

She'd gotten attached to everyone. And they all sucked.

She flipped another page, fingers trembling.

Walker took the book out of her hands. His tone was serious and made her think of the day in the river and how happy she'd been to be cared for. "Hey, what's up?"

She crossed her arms over her chest. "Nothing. I made a mistake is all. I'm just . . . I'm." Her face burned. Her eyes watered.

"Did I do something?"

"Nope. You didn't do anything." She wasn't trying to be vague, she just didn't want to admit how she felt.

"Rilla. Talk to me."

"I misunderstood you is all. I misunderstood everyone." She sniffed and threw her arm over her face. "I just thought. I thought we were . . ."

"Oh."

If she'd harbored any hopes she'd misunderstood, they were dashed to utter destruction in his quiet, sad *oh*.

"It's fine. It was all new and exciting to be here. I got confused."

"I really like you," he said. "I think you're awesome."

She tightened her arm over her eyes. "You don't have to—"

"I thought we were just going to have fun. Climb and hang out. I'm going back to Colorado in the fall. And you . . . I mean." He bit his lip and didn't say anything, blue eyes tight with worry. "Who knows where you'll be?"

She swallowed and swiped at her eyes. "Yeah. That was fine with me," she lied. "I just didn't think you'd deny that to everyone."

"I don't like people to know my business. Petra—"

"You told Petra my business," she snapped. "And I wasn't saying you had to tell them your business, but like . . . I didn't expect it to be a secret."

"I'm not trying to keep it a secret."

"You made me feel like shit. You told your friends things I'd told you in confidence. I don't want to do anything with someone who makes me feel like shit afterward."

"Rilla . . ." He sighed. "You're overreacting."

She pushed up, eyes narrowed. "Oh, okay."

His jaw tightened.

"Get the fuck off my porch, Walker."

"Rilla . . ."

She looked him dead in the eyes., going for broke with nothing to lose. "The worst part of this shit? You made me think you wouldn't leave me hanging on a wall, with your thumb up your ass. It was too easy. Too good. You fuck head." She swiped at her tears. "Dummy me fell in love with you. I should have known the first time I climbed with you that you weren't any good."

Twin spots of red jumped into his cheeks and his eyes flashed. Without a word, he turned and strode off into the meadow.

An incredible sadness filled her chest as she watched him go.

•

The next morning she had to go to the principal's office with her pile of undone work and the sloppy pages of things she'd completed.

"I want to drop out and take the GED," she said as the principal made a face and peered at a soda-stained page of math work.

The woman put down the paper and looked at her over the edge of her glasses. "You realize it's not the same as a high school diploma."

Rilla shrugged. "It lets you do the same thing." *Get out of school.*

She shook her head. "A GED is for someone who cannot go back to high school and finish. It's never going to be a high school diploma, and it will always tell an academic institution that you were unable to complete school and instead had to take this option. Now, that can be just fine for some people, when it's their only option. But that isn't your only option. So, why are you intent on limiting yourself?"

"I'm . . ." Rilla started to argue and then snapped her mouth shut.

The principal sighed. "This work is more than halfway done. We have another two weeks until school starts. I might be able to make this work. It'll mean extra work for you, even as we start. It probably means you won't graduate until next summer. But I don't think you should take the GED. I think you can finish."

Rilla looked at her hands. "I'm going back to West Virginia and taking the GED." As soon as she finished The Nose.

"CLIMB ON."

From the depths of the struggle comes one relief: to run out of options. The going gets easier when the only thing left is to just get going.

—Josie McKee, YOSAR veteran, wilderness medicine and rescue instructor, alpine and big wall speed climber. McKee climbed The Nose solo in 23.5 hours, seven Yosemite big walls in seven days, and holds five Yosemite big wall speed records.

thirty nine

RILLA STOOD AT THE BOTTOM IN THE DARK, HER BORROWED JACKET zipped to her ears as a light breeze touched her face, and the black oaks quivered behind her. The ground that El Capitan rose from felt alive, with a beating heart deep down in its granite belly that thundered through her feet and pulsed in her ears. The stars were still out. The moon was waning and blue.

It felt like she'd come full circle. She lifted her hands and began.

They climbed, the first two hundred feet un-roped. Familiar from the many treks to haul the gear they'd need and stash it farther up the climb. The wind picked up and the sky lightened to purple. It was easy scrambling, but the higher Rilla went, the more aware she became of the trees, and the sky, and the start of the biggest thing she'd ever done.

They began up some crumbly rock, into a wide corner crack. The climbing wasn't hard, and feeling well, they climbed easily in a quiet rhythm. At the top, they set up the anchors on the bolts.

Rilla led the next pitch, into a left corner, using a little tri-cam to slip into the crack, double back a piece of webbing, and clip herself it. The movement felt easy and fluid, and it filled her with confidence—almost as if she just watched herself do something she'd never expected. She swung over to another crack, moving up to the bolts.

As the sun rose bright and clear, they reached Sickle Ledge, where they had stashed their haul bags—the *pig*, Adeena grunted, lifting hers. The wind whipped against their skin, and the sun was so bright off the white granite she squinted even behind her sunglasses. After hauling everything to the ledge and making sure anchors were secure and untangled, they sat three across, legs sprawled on the thigh-wide ledge, and dug through the bag for food. Rilla chewed on a few pieces of jerky and a nutrition bar. After some water and waiting to let another group get off the ledge as they hauled things for their climb the next day, they stood and began to push on toward their first night bivy.

On the next pitch, a burst of wind caught the rope at the end, yanking it toward the flake.

"*Nooooooo!*" Adeena yelled.

"I got it." Rilla yanked harder. The rope pulled up just before catching.

"Crisis averted," Petra called.

The climbing was easy. The sunshine was hot and the wind cool. They pushed on at a pace that made Rilla feel like there would be no way they'd spend four days on this rock—*half of it was already done?* Rilla kept tipping her head and trying to match it to the route map, but she felt sure they were way ahead.

"The Nose," she scoffed. "The Nose is going down."

The Nose was going down. Until it was time to haul the pig—the huge bags lashed to the rope that carried all their food, gear, and water—up to them at the top of the pitch.

Goddamn it, why had she thought they would go fast? Sweat drenched her shirt and the sun broiled her shoulders, and her lips and mouth became so dry from the wind she kept sucking down water, which made her have to stop and pee, and then wind caught her pee and splashed it on her hand and . . .

"*Goddamn it*," Rilla snapped when the pig got caught again as she hauled it up. Hauling required her to pull and walk a length of rope down the wall, and then, holding the tension, slide the ascender back up. It was a constant fight. Her fingers were continually in danger of getting smashed into the gear on the up, and her thighs and stomach straining to pull down. Impossible when the bag got stuck. She leaned down and wiggled the line.

"It's your lead," Petra called.

And just like always, it switched back to being glorious.

Rilla led. Then Adeena. Then back to Petra for the pendulum over to the start of the Stovelegs. Rilla's neck ached as she watched Petra lower out. "Why is it called Stovelegs?" she asked Adeena, eyeing the long, straight crack of pitch seven, eight, and nine-ish.

Adeena adjusted her sunglasses. "Before this was first climbed, a climber—working on the route with Warren Harding—went to a scrap yard to find something he could use for protection in the cracks. This was the fifties, so there wasn't much. He found some legs from, like, a woodstove, and shaped them into a piton that would fit this crack and be easy to carry. It's been the Stoveleg crack ever since."

"Lower me," Petra yelled.

Rilla shifted the hard candy in her mouth, trying to rewet it. The afternoon light waned. Hopefully Petra would be quick on lead. She tipped her chin again, shoulders screaming from the hauling and the sun.

Petra's long legs furiously pumped against the rock, the gear clinking and her silhouette against the sky. She swung, hopped over the rise, and reached.

"Got it," she called.

Rilla exhaled and peeled a clementine she'd meant to save for farther up. "I'm just going to eat all the food now, so I don't have to haul it," she said to Adeena.

Adeena laughed while she kept feeding out rope for Petra in the Stovelegs.

When it was Rilla's turn to climb, she ended up aiding. On the ground, fresh, she could have climbed it. But after a long day of climbing and hauling, she was so exhausted that the aiders were hard enough to manage.

In the evening, they reached Dolt Tower, a natural ledge wide enough to sleep on. By the time they hauled up all their gear and got everything sorted into a mess of anchor webbing, gear, and haul bags, the light was nearly gone.

They pulled their sleeping bags out and collapsed onto the ledge, exhausted.

"It always seems so easy," Adeena said. "And then I start and, *ugh*. I forgot."

"I am so sore," Petra moaned. "But so far, so free." She pumped her fists to the sky.

Rilla opened one eye and looked to Adeena, who seemed to be thinking the same thing. *There was no way Petra could climb the whole route free, but . . .*

"I'm hungry," Adeena said, sitting up. "I'm going to pray and then make some oatmeal."

After a meal of oatmeal with fruit, brown sugar, nuts, and more water, they brushed their teeth, spitting toothpaste into oblivion, and curled up in their sleeping bags.

The light faded and the wind whipped the dark and the stars came out. Even though Rilla had seen the stars before, seeing them here, from the edge of a sleeping bag with her harness digging into her legs and sides, Adeena's knees in her back, and Petra's elbows in her boobs made the stars seem magical and new. She closed her eyes, a smile on her face, and remembered the first day of climbing—with Walker, and how it was horrible and how nothing had changed, except that she was *here* now. But then she heard Walker and his "oh." And she heard the way they'd talked about her and her past. No matter how long she looked at the stars, she heard it in her head. The wind sharpened until it stung tears from under her closed eyes.

In the morning, she was feeling better. Sore, a little swollen and weird, but better. "What pitch number are we on anyway?" Rilla asked, grateful for Adeena's mountaineer coffee pour-over skills as the rich, sweet scent of coffee tinged the dry wind.

"Lucky thirteen," Petra said, sitting cross-legged and looking over the edge.

The sky was blue and boundless, streaked with the pink gold of sunrise. Rilla rubbed more sunscreen on her burnt face and used the remaining lotion on her hands to smooth back the flyways as she finger-combed through her knotted hair and re-braided it. She ate a packet of tuna and an avocado with salt and hot sauce packets she'd stolen from the dining hall. It wasn't the most satisfying—she could have used a huge plate of French toast with bacon, grits, and gravy, and a glass of whole milk alongside her coffee. But the tuna made her feel strong and ready to climb again, and the avocado made her feel something like full. She packed her sleeping bag and the three of them organized their gear, took down the portaledge, and studied the route map one more time—looking over the ten pitches they were slotted to do before bivying at a spot named after Camp 4.

Petra was tying in to lead, when there was a sudden crack, like thunder and lightning at once. All three of them jumped. Rilla looked automatically to the sky, but Adeena and Petra yanked her tight to the wall as something roared past.

Rilla blinked and watched, her mouth open. *A person.* It was a person in a red suit and he fell. Her heart stopped beating. A red plume billowed out behind him, pulling him up below as he gently finished soaring to the ground.

"Damn BASE jumpers," Adeena said. "I about peed myself."

Petra laughed weakly. "I totally thought something had come off. Ack! I'm awake!"

Rilla's heart resumed beating—faster to make up for lost time. "Oh, my god," she said, still staring at the person floating to the trees.

They watched until the jumper landed in El Cap Meadow, and then they turned back to the wall and began the rhythm, branching off pitch fourteen to wait for Petra on the Jardine Traverse—the route variation you took when you were trying to free-climb.

On the ground it'd seemed harmless, but now Rilla knew there was no way Petra could free-climb The Nose, and waiting for her to struggle through left Rilla annoyed in a new way. She'd spotted Petra pulling on gear, but couldn't say anything while Petra was climbing. Her neck ached from twisting to look up.

"I don't know what she's doing," Adeena said at one point. "But it's not free." It was the closest they came to talking about it.

Climb.

Ascend.

Haul.

Curse the haul bag for getting stuck.

Curse everything.

Get the haul bag up.

Begin again.

The sun rose high and bright. Halfway through the morning, Rilla pulled on a thin, long-sleeved shirt because she couldn't imagine how any more sunscreen was going to help against the sunshine trying to burn her off the face of the earth.

Rilla took it upon herself to make salami and cheese crackers for everyone for a mid-morning snack, which they ate before hauling. It was a good idea she took credit for when they spent the next few hours in a long slog, belaying Petra's attempt to free-climb.

In between, they snacked on apples and thick globs of peanut butter, slowly working their way up a leaning ramp of sun-soaked granite toward the Texas Flake.

The shadows slipped over them as they each wiggled up into the chimney.

With her back to the flake and her feet pushing on the wall, Rilla tried not to think of coming off the wall. There was no protection here. The more she tried, the harder it was to not think about it. Her feet slipped and her arms hurt from trying to keep from pushing so hard on the flake.

It was her fear right now, she could feel it. She was tired and sore, yes. But it was fear locking everything tight. She winced and forced her body to move, putting the fear into its place and not allowing it to weigh on her body.

With a relieved sigh, she pulled out of the chimney to the top of the flake and sat astride, one leg on each side of the flake—one in sun and one in shadow. She put her arms up into the wind and tipped her head, sweaty helmet shifting back. *Done.*

The Boot Flake was next—and it was Rilla's turn to lead. She found a good rhythm in ascending the aiders, clipping the bolts and fixed gear until she reached the bottom of the boot-shaped flake and needed to dig at her side for a cam.

She was higher than she'd ever been climbing, but the higher she went, the more the ground lost its sense of reality. It faded into gray and blue and greens of otherworldliness. All that existed—all that was real and permanent—was the granite beneath her raw fingers. The rub of the harness on her legs and waist. The dryness of her mouth. Her body moved like a machine—doing exactly what her mind told it to do. Focused. Strong. She'd never felt like this in her entire life. She was in control—and more out of control than she'd ever been. A body held in perfect tension. Maybe this was what life was—a constant state of seeking perfect tensions.

They didn't talk much as they kept climbing. Everyone was starting to feel the effects of two full days of climbing. But the summit felt manageable. Within their grasp.

Petra had grabbed gear, but still insisted on climbing free—Rilla and Adeena didn't argue, but it was starting to annoy Rilla more and more. Especially as the afternoon waned.

Adeena did the run for the King Swing—the famous, huge pendulum—was a different experience than it was for Petra and her long legs. Her swings took time to build, but had a power Petra's hadn't had.

When it was Rilla's turn, she swept through the last of the sun lighting the shadows of the Valley and reached for the rock. The force pulled abruptly, and she felt this surge of superhuman strength course through her arms and connect her mind to her feet to find a foothold. Petra and Adeena grabbed hold of her shirt and secured her beside them.

The sun was beginning to set—twisting that familiar deep amber—but with three more pitches until they reached their camp spot, they were either climbing well into the night or bivying below the ledge.

"Maybe both," Adeena said with a sigh.

"What is that on the horizon?" Adeena asked when they were working over the anchors, switching belay for the next pitch.

Rilla peered into the twilight near the last bit of sun. It was bright and seared her vision. It was hard to tell. "Clouds?" she asked.

"It's probably just the sunset doing weird things. Or whatever…clouds."

"Fuck," Adeena said, swiping hair out of her face.

They all kept their eyes to the horizon, even when they put headlamps on and kept climbing in the dark, and couldn't see what might be coming.

The wind picked up.

"It might rain," Petra yelled.

In the light of her headlamp, Adeena's eyes rolled.

Rilla wasn't having it. She glared up at Petra. "*No shit!*" she yelled back over the wind.

"We'll be fine," Adeena said. "Let's just get to the bivy before it starts."

The dark was all around them then—biting with cold teeth on the back of Rilla's neck as she kept blindly following Adeena, who had taken over on lead.

The first lightning flicker sent her pulse screaming—the granite lit wildly as if there were ghouls and goblins in each shadow. The face turned menacing. But in the fear, she suddenly felt, for the first time, as if the rock was hers. As if she belonged here—more than the other two. She was ugly, and terrible, and full of shadows where she kept finding terrible things. It always felt as if the bright sunshine of the mountains would kick her off; but here, in this night storm on El Cap, her fingers tingled and her body hummed, and she finally felt secure.

"*Fuck! Your hair!*" Petra pointed.

Rilla tipped her head up to see her hair on end, dancing above her helmet. "*Fuck fuck fuck!*" she screeched. She was about to be hit by lightning. She could feel it—the hum of the clouds gathering energy and seeking her body.

"Curl in a ball," Adeena yelled. "Grab your ears."

Rilla let go, immediately falling on the long stretch of cordelette of the anchors, and bumping against the wall as she hugged her knees to her chest and tucked her ears down. Thank god she'd been anchored. Thank god, because she'd just let go without thinking, and hadn't double-checked anything. Cringing, she waited to be struck.

The lightning flashed. Thunder echoed.

Her heart beat ferociously.

"Come on. We have to get to the ledge," Petra yelled.

Rilla only heard "ledge," but she didn't need Petra's encouragement to know they were in deep shit and needed to get up to shelter.

She kept her head down and climbed until she reached the anchors and helped haul the pig.

"Be careful of the next pitch," Petra said. "There are loose blocks."

"Perfect," Rilla moaned.

Lightning and thunder drowned out Petra's reply. In the flash of light, Rilla realized Petra was scared. And Adeena was calm. Adeena was the leader. Maybe she had been all along, despite Petra's bluster.

Rilla met Adeena's gaze. "What do we do?"

"We can't climb in the lightning," Adeena said in a lull of the wind. "We need to spread out and hunker down until it passes."

"Let's just keep going," Petra urged. "We're almost there."

Petra was delusional. Rilla yanked the route map out of her pocket and kept a firm grip on it in the wind. "The rap bolts are to the left," she told Adeena, showing her the paper under the light of her headlamp. "I can head out over there. You and Petra anchor to the bolts here."

"Guys . . ." Petra protested. Lightning flashed on her face, turning it white and blanched.

"We're listening to Adeena," Rilla snapped. "She has the most experience." On the ground, what Adeena had lacked in technical ability was, up here, less important—now Rilla could see how Adeena's experience with the situation and the stress made her a calm and able leader. It was heartening to realize not everyone showed their potential. That maybe there were things, hidden on the ground, that gave Rilla value. That she didn't have to be Caroline. She could just be herself.

Thunder drowned out Petra's protest. And Adeena handed her a rain jacket.

Rilla headed out across the granite, headlamp yanked down to her neck. With the lightning, she couldn't see anything anyhow. Adeena belayed off the anchors, but if she fell, it would be a swing back *underneath* Adeena, hitting them with the rope. The light flashed and she spotted the glint of silver bolt hangers. It went pitch black; but Rilla kept her eyes trained ahead. She exhaled, bringing her belly in closer to the rock. They could make it. The storm would pass soon.

The lightning flashed again and she reached out to clip the bolts, fumbling in the blind dark. Quickly, she turned her headlamp on, and clipped another set of bolts and long draws to the anchors, getting herself secure.

The wind gusted and roared. The dark seemed a thing to consume her. "Off belay," she yelled into the wind now that she was anchored to the wall.

She couldn't hear anything back.

Rising up on the balls of her feet off the rock, she crouched like Adeena had instructed, ducking her head to her knees and covering her ears with her hands. Lightning-safe position—ready to be fucked by a bolt. She closed her eyes and tried to mentally be okay with sudden death.

The rain started. Pelting her back like ice in the driving wind. Lightning and thunder came at once, shaking her to her teeth. Her calves cramped. Her back tightened in the cold rain. Now she prayed *for* sudden death instead of this slow one where she froze. The rain came harder. And the thunder melted away into the mountains.

She straightened. "Guys?" she yelled into the dark.

No sound.

For the first time, panic seized her heart. She'd always had a partner in this. And even though she knew Petra and Adeena were across the wall just a little ways, she didn't *know*. She couldn't convince herself to believe it. The rain lashed her face. Rilla clutched the jacket tighter and bent her head, hanging in her harness.

She must have fallen asleep, because the next thing she knew she was gasping for air under a waterfall. Automatically, she straightened her legs, pushing off the wall. Was she dreaming? She looked around and it was still dark. Still night. The waterfall gushed over her shins, pouring icy water into her shoes and already wet pants.

"Rilla," she heard someone yell.

Instantly, she realized the storm had lifted. The wind had died down and the rain had stopped.

"I'm okay," she forced through her chattering teeth. "I'm in a waterfall."

"Can you make it back over?" Adeena yelled. "We can bivy and find something dry."

Rilla looked down at her waist. Her legs were cold and shaky, numb. But they were likely to only get worse, especially if the water didn't let up soon. "I'm coming."

It took her three times longer than normal to haul herself up into the rush of water to unclip from the anchors. Torrents spurted over her jacket and into her clothes, dripping ice through her whole body and any layer that might have still been dry.

Shaking uncontrollably now, she clipped the biners to her side and began inching along the still dark wall. After a few steps, she realized it wasn't pitch-black anymore, but faintly dark gray.

The morning shadows of Adeena and Petra waited against the wall, quiet as she made her way to them. The going back was a lot harder than leaving. A lot harder. She shuffled slowly, hands open on the wet wall. What had she done? What had she done to be here? She sniffed and the misery she'd felt when looking at them turned into misery at looking at herself. She'd stolen Petra's watch. When all Petra had done was help her. Invited her in. Took her climbing. She kept getting pissed at the rules Petra broke on this climb, because she was pissed at herself.

Rilla reached Adeena, waiting as Adeena clipped her into the anchors. "Thanks," she said.

"You need to get dry. Petra's getting you clothes."

"Are y'all dry?" she muttered through the shivering.

"Mostly. We'll bivy and rest up. Get something warm."

"Take your shirt off," Petra said. "I got a sweatshirt."

Rilla worked out of her jacket, handing it to Adeena, and then peeled off the soaking layer of thin technical shirt she'd been wearing and the soaking wet bra underneath. "It'll dry as soon as the sun comes up," Adeena said, taking her sports bra and handing her a sweatshirt. Rilla yanked it over her head, worried somehow it would slip out of her hands and disappear into the wind.

They wrestled with the portaledge as the sky lightened and the wind whipped the cliffs dry. By the time Rilla had her wet pants off and hanging off the edge to dry, she was in her underwear in her sleeping bag, watching the sunrise.

No one talked. They didn't even eat.

They all just fell asleep.

forty

"SLEEPING BEAUTY," SOMEONE YELLED.

Rilla peeled her eyes open to the bright sky. Fuck. She was soaked in sweat. Moaning, she pushed back her sleeping bag and sat up.

"Hey-o, one is awake."

"Didn't even have to kiss her."

"Just from the power of your manhood that close, it woke her anyway."

Rilla made a face and turned. A group of four climbers were hauling off the bolts that had been under a waterfall. The one looking at her, not hauling, wore a T-shirt on his head under his helmet. "Did y'all get caught in that storm last night?"

She rubbed her face and leaned against the wall, pushing her feet out over the edge of the portaledge. "Yeah. It was brutal."

"I bet. Everyone okay?"

She looked to the other sleeping bags. "Yeah. We're good. What time is it?"

He glanced at the watch on his wrist. He looked military maybe, now that she thought of it. "A little after one."

She nodded. "Do you have a smoke?"

He laughed. "I think I can spare one for you. Hang on."

Leaving his friends to finish the hauling, he dug it out of the top of his pack and picked his way easily on a long leash from the anchors.

Rilla made room beside her, stuffing the sleeping bag into her pack hanging beside her.

He crawled to sit beside her and lit the smoke for her.

She took a deep breath. "Oh my god. You are a lifesaver." She crossed her bare legs and took another deep pull on the smoke.

"We were lucky. We found a bit of a dry spot . . . almost shit my pants with the lightning though," he said, lighting his own cigarette.

"Tell me about it. My hair stood on end."

"And you didn't get hit?" he asked.

She exhaled a long rush of smoke and shook her head.

"Lucky girl. You're all good."

His shoulder touched hers and her skin thrummed alive. She wondered what Walker was doing. And a sudden sadness over the way that happened rushed over her. She shook her head and kept smoking. Walker was up here somewhere. Hopefully they'd survived the night.

"Well, you're about halfway there. Going to keep going or are y'all heading down?" the man asked.

She startled and looked at him, confused. "Why would we go down now?"

He laughed and put the smoke to his mouth. "Damn straight. Good luck!" He scooted off the portaledge with smoke trailing from the cigarette still held in his mouth.

Stretching on the harness she leaned across Petra and Adeena, forgetting she was in her underwear until the breeze hit her ass. "Yo, Adeena," she yelled. "Wake up."

"Do you want lunch?" The man behind her asked. "We have extra MREs. I'll cook for you."

She glanced over her shoulder, holding her cigarette away from the nylon. "Uh . . . sure? Yeah." *Why not?*

He nodded and gave her a thumbs-up, still heading for his buddies.

She finished waking Adeena and Petra—and putting on pants. And by the time they were packed and ready to climb, he handed them each a packet of beef stew.

"What're your names?" his friend asked as the three hungry girls poured the stew straight into their mouths.

"I'm Rilla," she answered for everyone. "This is Adeena and Petra."

"Oh, Petra. Nice." He nodded. "Petra is beautiful."

"The place," one of his friends helped.

"Well, and the girl." He gestured across.

"My parents visited during their honeymoon, hence . . . " she waved her hand. Petra looked . . . busted. Her eyes were sunk deep in exhaustion and her hair was knotted on top of her head. Sunburn touched her cheeks. They all looked terrible, and Rilla laughed to realize she literally couldn't care less. Smiling, she drained the rest of the stew.

"Thanks for this. It was actually really great." Rilla stuffed the empty packet into their trash bag and looked up. "Did y'all mind if we jump on ahead of you?"

"No problem."

It was a good thing they went first. With four men waiting for their turn behind, Rilla found she was motivated to move faster than her aching body would have wanted. They hauled ass up the pitch, moving gingerly over the loose blocks and to the left, where they were able to collapse on a ledge and drink water, and eat another meal.

"See ya at the summit!" The man waved as they pushed through to the next pitch.

Rilla bit into her salted avocado and waved back. The same wind that had lashed angrily at her now gently caressed her face, cooling her as the sun warmed her bones. She wondered again about Walker.

•

It was late afternoon when they reached Camp 4, putting them a whole day behind. It was full of people, including the men from earlier.

Rilla turned back to Adeena and suggested making up time and keep going into the night. "If we can get past the Great Roof tonight, we'll be in okay shape," she said. "I just want to get . . . off this wall."

Adeena agreed.

Tentatively, they turned to Petra.

"Absolutely not," Petra said.

There was a moment of tension-filled silence.

"Okay, help me. What makes you want to bivy here? How are you feeling?" Adeena said, which was a lot nicer than the way Rilla would have done it.

"I'm free-climbing. I can't rush the Great Roof."

Adeena and Rilla looked at each other. They'd both assumed Petra would have given up by now. She wasn't going to do it. She had, in reality, already failed by grabbing on to gear, and the hardest climbing was still ahead. To climb it now seemed beyond delusional.

"Petra. Honestly. You think you can free it? You've only done a third of the leads and . . ." Rilla trailed off.

"What the hell is your problem?" Petra said.

"I don't want to bivy here," Rilla said. "We have time. I want to get higher."

"We're okay on food."

Rilla gritted her teeth. "You're fucking delusional. You aren't that good of a climber. We're gonna run out of water."

Petra's cheeks got redder.

"Rilla," Adeena said softly. "It's fine. We can figure something out."

Petra glared at her.

Rilla rolled her eyes. "Let's bivy under the roof. You can climb it first thing in the morning. At dawn."

SARAH NICOLE LEMON

"That's *another* night on a portaledge."

Rilla shrugged. "The ledge doesn't have room anyway."

They all looked longingly at the packed gravel ledge. Solid ground.

"All right," Petra said. "You're hauling though."

The wind died in pitch twenty-two. And the heat crept in. Sweat gathered under Rilla's helmet as she slowly worked her way up on lead, to the base of the Great Roof.

The hauling felt like a personal punishment, and Rilla got more pissed off the harder it became. Petra was finishing eating by the time she was done and Rilla had nothing to look at but the satisfaction on Petra's face. She kept trying to swallow back her anger and pettiness. Her guilt. But it flavored everything. She choked down a piece of sausage and cheese and some water and ignored Petra, staring across the Valley as the stars lit the sky.

•

What day was it? It was her first thought when she woke before dawn.

It was day four. They were supposed to be done today, but they had only reached halfway. And Petra wanted to free-climb. Rilla rolled upright and shouted, "Petra, get climbing or I'm leading."

Petra slept on.

All her anger flooded back. But it was hard to remember the start or end of her reasons. It was like a fire licking out of control. She peed into her container, emptied it away from the belay, and clipped it back onto the gear. "Let's go, Petra. Adeena can belay. I'll pack."

Adeena sat up groggily. "I need so much coffee. I hate this climb," she moaned. "I want a shower and a real bed."

Same, Rilla thought.

•

Two hours later, they were still waiting for Petra. Not for her to climb, but for her to realize what everyone else already knew—she wasn't that good.

She was capable. Knowledgeable. Competent. But not great. She wasn't Caroline. She wasn't Adeena. She had not free-climbed The Nose.

Rilla crossed her arms and looked out over the Valley in her sunglasses. Waiting and furious. She hated that Petra couldn't see herself realistically...hated more what that annoyance might say about herself.

Finally, Petra gave up and came down for the aiders. She was dirty, and scrapes covered her knees and elbows and thighs and even her cheek, *somehow*. She'd wrestled with herself and had to face the truth.

Rilla's stomach turned. "Well, thanks to you, we'll be lucky if we get to the summit by midnight."

"*What is your problem?*" Petra shouted.

"I'm fine. I'm not the one up there trying to free-climb The Nose," Rilla scoffed.

"I cannot believe you, of all people, are here shitting on people's dreams."

"*Oh my god, what the fuck crawled up your ass and hatched?*" Rilla yelled.

"Guys," Adeena said.

"Shut up," they both yelled.

Rilla immediately regretted it.

"You're the one who never climbed before this summer. Now look at you. You're on the fucking Nose. Why the fuck are you being a bitch about me just trying this." Petra started crying. "And failing."

"Hey. You're fine. It's been a hard couple of days," Adeena said, rubbing Petra's shoulder. "Rilla's probably just exhausted."

"Yeah. I'm exhausted," Rilla said flatly. "I'm also white trash and no way am I going to France, right Petra?"

Petra and Adeena looked confused.

"I overheard y'all talking," she said.

There was a moment of silence.

"Did we say . . ." Adeena frowned. "Something that wasn't true?"

Rilla flushed, her cheeks feeling crispy from the blush and sunburn and windburn. "Oh, I'm *going* to France."

"Is *that* what you're all upset about? Grow up," Adeena said, in as a close a thing as Rilla had ever heard her snap.

"You can't say that shit about me."

"Oh, the shit that's true?" Petra said.

"It's not true. I'm not only that. You made me sound like I'd . . ." *steal from her.* Which Rilla had. To prove what? She closed her eyes and tried not to cry.

"No one is saying you're only that. No one is saying you're this forever. It's just right now this is what you are. You get pissed at Petra for trying to climb something way out of her range, and you're too scared to even try the shit you *can* do." Adeena exhaled and crossed her arms. "You're not the first or the last. Even if you don't go to France, you'll go someday. Get the fuck over yourself, Rilla. You're not that special."

Rilla and Petra stared.

"I'm ready to climb," Adeena said. "I don't want to be doing this anymore."

"I stole your watch. And pawned it," Rilla said to Petra. Immediately, a tension she hadn't known she had dissolved. Replaced by misery, when Adeena and Petra stared at her.

"Are you serious?" Petra asked. "You . . . *stole* . . ."

Rilla blinked. "You have no idea how much shit is attached to me. Hearing y'all say those things was my worst nightmare come true. I came three thousand miles hoping to never hear someone talk about me that way again. I spent all summer doing everything . . ." She had to take a breath. "*Everything.* To make everyone see me differently."

"No one saw you the way you see yourself," Petra said. "Why would you take that?"

"I couldn't take the tub."

Petra didn't laugh. "Fuck, Rilla. How am I supposed to trust you now?"

Rilla bit her cheek. "I just wanted to prove to you I could make it to France. That I was worthwhile."

"People come and go all the time. People can't do stuff because of money all the time. If we all had money, we'd be ... fuck, I don't know ..." Petra looked around. "I'd be at a spa right now."

Rilla rolled her eyes. "You'd be in Yosemite. The place every climber wants to be."

"No, right now, I'd literally be getting a chartered helicopter and going to a spa to get the fuck away from you." Petra snapped her fingers. "Adeena's right. You need to grow up. Even if I said the shittiest things about you—even though I made you feel like that. You should have talked to me. Asked for help about France. *Anything.*" Petra bit her lips tight and looked away. "You know what your problem is? Your problem is you want to do it all yourself, or it doesn't count. That's not the way it works, climbing or life. You hold all of us at an arm's length. You aren't honest—"

"Oh, that's right. I'm telling lies about my life. I couldn't possibly have experienced everything I said, right? Because *you* didn't experience it."

Petra glared at her.

Rilla gritted her jaw. "Let's just get this climb over with." They were too far from the summit to think about anything else.

"Great. Yeah. So excited," Petra said sarcastically.

"I'll lead," Rilla snapped. Mostly because it was the only way to escape the two of them for a moment.

The afternoon heat hit the wall as she focused on the rhythm of the aiders. *Step. Clip.* Her brain fell quiet. The wind roared in her ears. She wanted to escape. To leave. But she was stuck on this thread, dangling between the place she'd left and the place she wanted to be. *Step. Clip.*

Rilla wrestled herself and the aiders around the edge and pulled the anchor off the Great Roof. It was one of the most recognizable and famous parts of the climb, and already she couldn't remember anything but how she felt.

Dejected, she carefully set her anchors and gave Adeena a thumbs-up. Belaying was also rhythmic—*pull, take, lock, feed out.* Adeena's long hair blew like a raven's wings in the wind and the swallows and baby falcons twittered around them. The line connecting her and Adeena became shorter with each movement. The lines running to the gear and Petra, laying against the rock.

She'd pursued it. She'd gotten it. But all she'd wanted from the beginning was a thing she didn't have—a sense of community, a place to belong, and love that couldn't just give up. In climbing, it felt as if, for a moment, there was someone she trusted, someone who trusted her. It didn't feel that way; it *was* that way. Except for now, again. She was in the same place she'd begun. And would be again, she saw that now.

"Over halfway," Adeena said

Rilla nodded. "I'll haul. You can belay."

"You sure?" Adeena asked.

She wanted the punishment of the hauling. The agony. "I'm sure," she said.

While Adeena belayed, Rilla pulled herself up and down the thread, hauling the bags up, pushing herself until everything cried for relief, and then she was crying. In her harness. She put her head to the rock and sobbed. She'd come this far and was still alone. She was connected, *literally*, but cut off. Walker had done the same. Thea . . . *everyone.*

Her tears stained the granite until she had no more water left for tears and wiped her wind-burned cheeks and finished hauling.

No one said anything as they began to the next pitch. And for the next two and a half pitches there was nothing but the sound of the wind, the occasional shouts of other climbers, and the talking of sparrows and falcons nesting on the wall.

They paused only to take a few photos at the Glowering Spot—the Valley so far below it was unreal. Rilla could barely believe anything but this wall existed, and all she wanted was to be done with it.

Lunch was her last avocado and summer sausage, sitting in the middle of what smelled like a giant urinal on the Camp 6 ledge. Not that they particularly smelled better.

"Why do boys have to ruin everything?" Adeena grumbled, finishing peeing into her container. "If you can pee on a rock, you can pee on plastic. And then the one seat here wouldn't be disgusting."

The men from the other day were below, catching up. Rilla shoved her food in faster, not wanting to be overtaken. "Ready?" she asked through her last mouthful.

They were only a few pitches from the end, but the granite that towered above them seemed as if would truly never end. The rest of her life would be lived here, trying to get somewhere she'd never find. Rilla worked the aiders, relaxing in the exhaustion—the relief of having her brain rest, even if it came at the price of her trashed body.

The next section involved tensioning off a piece into a corner, where each piece she placed seemed small and not great, and she was so tired she didn't even care when the memory of the *zzzip* tried to taunt her. Finally, she reached the anchors and the pitch was done.

She hauled again while Petra belayed.

This time, it felt easier.

They had just managed to delicately move around the *death block*, as Adeena called the house-sized boulder ready to peel off and kill, when the yelling started.

Rilla looked down, straining in her harness to see what the commotion was. "Do you hear that?"

Petra looked with her. Adeena scanned above them. "Check your gear. Maybe they see something wrong." Everyone automatically touched their knots and harnesses, fingers traveling to the anchors.

"I think they're calling for help," Petra said. "One of us should rap down."

They looked to Adeena.

"All right." She flipped her Grigri closed. "Double-check me."

Rilla and Petra silently studied the setup. Knots. Rope. Everything closed. Knot at the end of the rope.

"Check me," Petra said, offering her belay setup to Rilla and Adeena.

Again they checked.

They were tired. Worn down. The simplest mistake would be easy to make and could be completely catastrophic.

Adeena headed down, leaving Petra and Rilla to look over the edge, trying to figure out what was going on.

The afternoon sun burned her face and Rilla reached into her bag to smear more sunscreen on. "Want some?" she asked Petra.

"That's okay."

"I don't blame you. Feels kind of useless right now," Rilla said.

The radio crackled and Adeena's voice came through. "Come down."

Rilla and Petra looked at each other. Did she mean for them to go down there?

"It's another group across from them. Leader fell. He's unconscious. They called—" The radio cut out.

Rilla looked at Petra. For a split second it was totally still—the intensity of everything overwhelming. Then they sprang into action. Petra started setting up the rappels. Rilla dug through the pig for the bottom—finding their phone. The emergency number for Yosemite was taped on the back.

Rilla stuffed the phone into her pocket and checked Petra's rappel.

Even after they both checked, they stood there, unable to start the descent. The fear felt like a viscous thing, a wall keeping them from moving.

"We're good," Rilla said.

"Check again," Petra said.

"Knot," Rilla said, pointing and going through it out loud. Petra nodded and took a deep breath. She did the same for Rilla.

"One. Two. Three."

Simultaneously, they lowered, leaving their gear fixed to the rock.

Below, the group and Adeena were starting their way across. "It's the boys," Adeena shouted, eyes wild. "I see Hico's socks. Rilla, I think it's Walker."

Rilla had never felt such a panic and terror and hatred of climbing as she did just then. That he was only a few feet away, but she was stuck, on this rock, in her harness. That they couldn't call 911 and immediately get him to a hospital. She swallowed and forced her fear into a ball. Putting it aside so she could move, she handed the phone to Petra. "You call. Let's go."

Rigging a line and managing to traverse across the face, they found the boys. Walker lay on a portaledge, in his harness, and limp. He looked asleep. Except for the blood. His helmet was cracked.

"Fuck, Rilla. I'm so sorry. Caroline is going to kill me," Hico said.

"He's alive?" Rilla asked Hico.

He nodded, lips tight. "His breathing is shallow, but he's breathing. He fell but it was from rock fall. Just a little . . ." Hico made a ball with his hands. "Knocked him right out."

They could hear Petra talking behind them.

Everyone stared at the portaledge soberly.

Blood covered his face—from his mouth and nose, Rilla thought. And his arm was folded onto his chest looking wrong and unnaturally white.

The feel of his fingers against her skin flashed into her mind and she swallowed a sob.

"They're going to send the chopper for a short haul," Adeena said.

Everyone took a breath.

Rilla clipped into the runner and tensioned herself out, careful not to jostle the portaledge. She reached for his neck, amid the blood and gore. Under her fingers, he was cold and his pulse beat shallowly. All the pages of Thea's *Wilderness First Aid* ran through her head—the ones she'd read when avoiding her homework. She peeled off her shirt and used it to apply pressure over the gash on his arm. She went back to his pulse, staring with dry eyes at the watch on his bent arm to time it. Trying not to think of the hikers. Trying to think, like Tam, maybe it was just a broken arm. How had this happened to *Walker*?

"He needs to be covered," she said. "I think he's in shock. His body temperature is falling."

Hico jumped into action, pulling a sleeping bag from their pig. She took it and spread it over his shoulders.

They were all quiet, staring out at the view of the Valley, scanning the hazy afternoon sky for signs of the chopper. What if there were crosswinds? What if this happened again, while they took him to the hospital? *What if . . . what if . . .*

Rilla closed her eyes and tried to shut off her thoughts. She checked his pulse again and it seemed weaker. *What if they didn't make it in time?* There was nothing she could do for him.

Walker's eyelids flickered.

"He's awake," she said.

Everyone straightened.

He met her eyes and tried to say something, but nothing came out. His eyes had a lost and dazed look—and even though he was awake, she was afraid it wasn't any better.

"Shhhh . . ." she said. "You're okay. The helicopter is on its way." She touched his blood-spattered jaw and gently patted his skin, careful not to accidentally move him. If he moved a lot or got panicked, he could hurt himself more. "Stay calm, they're almost here. I need you . . ." Her voice broke and she swallowed it. "I need you to be a dick to me some more."

The afternoon light deepened, and the wind died. Rilla was never so happy to be sweating as she was just then—the rescue team should have no problem getting there.

Finally, almost forty-five minutes later, they heard the thrum of the chopper and Adeena pointed it out as it rose from the meadow.

Rilla held her breath, watching the copter as it came closer and closer, feeling Walker's pulse faintly beat under her fingertips. It wasn't like she could keep him alive by counting the beats of his heart, but it felt like maybe she could anyway. It felt like it would hurt to stop.

She started humming. Trying to keep calm.

"Get a figure eight on a bite," said the guy from the other party on The Nose who'd followed them down. His group sprung into action, getting an anchored rope ready.

They all lifted their chins as the chopper flew above them and the two people dangling from the long line beneath the belly gently swung lower.

It was Adrienne and the old man. Her face was set and hard, but worry was in her eyes.

Rilla wanted to cry. She moved away, traversing back to Adeena and Petra as Adrienne took over. It was all a blur as she deftly wrapped Walker in a red bag that kept him prone and secure, clipped him to their line, and motioned to the people in the helicopter.

The wind of the blades beat against her helmet, but Rilla watched in a stupor as Walker was gently lifted away, Adrienne holding him still. Adrienne met her eyes and then . . . they were gone.

Heading to the Valley, to help.

It wasn't until the chopper landed that anyone stirred. They had to finish climbing still. Soberly, they all worked back to the route. The men from that morning were now right behind them. Everyone moved carefully. Slowly. Double- and triple-checking, though they all knew accidents happened regardless. The rocks fell at random.

Their bivy that night was silent and dark. Rilla laid under the stars trying to keep a grip on her sanity. She couldn't afford to lose it—not with climbing still ahead.

"Caroline says he's okay. A concussion, broken ribs, and a broken wrist. That's it," Petra said, looking at her phone.

Rilla eased a sigh of relief. *Thank you, god,* she breathed to the stars.

•

After a slow start the next morning, they fell into a steady rhythm in the long stretches of aiding. Finally, deep into the night, they staggered up the final scramble, past a tall pine and dropped the bags and themselves to the rock.

The stars glimmered in the dark.

"We did it," Petra said.

Adeena fist-bumped the sky.

Rilla stared miserably at the edge of the Valley. She'd done it, and she was still the same. She'd done it, and nothing had changed. She'd done it, and Walker had left the Valley and was in the hospital. Hot tears pricked her eyes, and before she could stop it, she was crying.

"You're okay. You're okay," Adeena said softly, rubbing her back.

"Deep breaths," Petra said, motioning her through.

"I'm sorry," Rilla gasped, the second she had enough air. "I am so sorry. What I did was so wrong. I'll give you the money. You can get it back."

"It's okay. You're okay," Petra said.

"I'm not okay."

"You are okay."

"I'm *not* okay."

"You *are* okay."

Rilla shook her head as a fresh round of sobs wracked her. She lay down on the granite and curled up into a ball. It hurt so deeply. She missed her home. She missed feeling as if she had a place where she belonged, even if it wasn't the place she wanted to be. She missed believing someone loved her. She missed the connection of the rope to Adeena and Petra—to Walker. To her sister. She wept for the boy who'd shared her cigarette at a bus stop, challenged her to open her heart, and had fallen when she thought he would be the last to fall.

"Here," Adeena said, pulling out her sleeping bag and draping it over her.

"I'm not going to tell anyone about the watch," Petra said. "I know you're sorry. I forgive you. And I'm sorry I said those things about you. That wasn't okay."

"Y'all were right." Rilla sniffed. "I've been trying so hard. But it felt too risky to ask for help. I didn't want to have to do that. You made me so mad. But it was anger . . . it was hurt. I regretted it the moment I'd done it, but I just couldn't admit it."

"I'm sorry we made you feel like shit," Petra said. "You're right, we were unfair."

"I'm sorry too," Adeena said. "We all know how crummy it can feel to hear that from your friends."

"I violated your trust," Rilla said. "I was such a bitch to you."

"It's okay." Petra looked down at her hands. "I have some things to work on, I'm realizing."

"I'm going to pay you back. I'm going to get the watch back," Rilla said.

"I know." Petra nodded. "And you're *going* to France."

"I have summit chocolate!" Adeena said.

Rilla sat up, clutching the sleeping bag around her dirty shoulders.

"Ah! We've revived her with chocolate," Petra said, digging in her pack. "And I've got the alcohol." She pulled out three little bottles of vodka and passed them around. "I didn't feel like warm beer, sorry."

Adeena unscrewed hers and tipped it back. "Summit vodka is excused. I love you," she declared to Petra.

Rilla took a piece of chocolate and the little bottle. "I love you both too." It was not as hard to say as she'd thought. It was like placing a piece and hoping it wouldn't fall, but knowing if it did, she wouldn't have done anything different anyway. She was climbing. There was risk. But there was also reward.

She toasted and drank the vodka, welcoming the warmth of the swallow in her exhausted body. Nibbling on the chocolate, she looked out over the dark blue shadows of the Sierras under the moon.

"Think about it," Petra said softly. "Just three months ago, we sat on top of Snake Dike. Do you remember that? You're here now. You've climbed The Nose. We've climbed The Nose."

"We climbed The Nose," Rilla repeated. It didn't feel real. It didn't feel connected to the moment three months ago when she hadn't even known what The Nose was. "I climbed The Nose."

"Wait . . ." Adeena turned, digging through her pack. "We need a picture." She set a timer and ran out to place the phone on the rock, before coming back.

They put their heads together and the flash went off, blinding them all to the shadows.

"Am I any different?" Rilla asked quietly as they blinked. "From Snake Dike?"

"Yes," both girls said simultaneously.

"Really?" she asked.

"You're a leader," Adeena said. "You're more confident. Not just in climbing, but everywhere. You proved yourself a team player, over and over. Not everyone can be part of a team," Adeena said.

"You hooked up with Walker—which is more than any of us managed," Petra said with a chuckle. "You saved his life, maybe, by keeping him stable. You're less afraid. Kinder. Not nearly as closed off as when I met you. I remember it was so hard to talk to you because you didn't answer," Petra said.

"You are less ignorant," Adeena said with a nudge. "And you apologized to me right away the last time, which you didn't do when I met you."

"Oh my god." Rilla lowered her chin and pinched her nose. "Dee..."

"Calm down. It's fine."

"You owned up to the watch. I probably would have never known," Petra said.

Rilla exhaled. "I'm so—"

"The point is you took responsibility for it. You knew you'd fucked up. You knew what you'd done. And you are making it right." Petra looked down. "You've made me a better climber. A better person."

"Me too. And you spent all summer working for the gear. Working for this climb. Working for this moment," Adeena said.

Rilla took a deep breath and stared at the stars. The same stars as at home—in West Virginia. "We did it," she said. "We climbed The Nose."

"The Nose," they toasted.

forty one

IF YOSEMITE IN SUMMER WAS A GOLDEN DREAM, FALL WAS THAT DREAM
sharpened and deepened. The air was cool and the path from Happy Isles
thin of crowds. Rilla walked, her old West Virginia boots back on her feet,
and her hands stuffed into the pockets of the fleece Thea had gotten her
for her birthday.

"Rilla, wait up."

She half turned, smiling at Walker rushing to catch up with her. He
had the thin puffer jacket pulled over his sweatshirt, reminding her of
the day last spring at the bus stop.

The evergreens stretched their boughs overhead, the sky cloudy
above them.

"I've been looking all over for you," he said, falling into step beside her.

"You leaving?"

He nodded. "I'm leaving."

Rilla nodded. Adeena and Gage had long ago left to go back to school.
Petra had left after that, going back to her parents' home in Long Beach.
Hico had pulled up roots and gone to Joshua Tree two weeks earlier. The
house in the meadow had emptied, and Rilla got to move downstairs
with Thea and Lauren. Walker and Caroline were the only ones left; now
Walker was heading back to Colorado and Caroline would be there only
a little longer. Thea, and Rilla, were staying.

"It was a good summer, in the end. No one died," she said.

He laughed. "No one died."

"Though you certainly tried." After recovering from his fall during The Nose, Walker came back and even finished the season with YOSAR—though Rilla was fairly sure Adrienne didn't send him on anything. He'd turned into a good climbing partner, but Rilla knew it was because *she* was a good partner, and not him.

He inhaled a sharp breath and stopped, looking around at the trees, the cliffs, the sky. "You're going to see this place in winter. In snow. It'll be really special."

"I'm excited to see it."

He seemed like he had something else to say—his mouth tightening and relaxing as the seconds of quiet passed.

"Well . . ." Her throat ached, watching him. She'd loved him. Loved him still, if she was honest. It hurt, but it wasn't a bad hurt.

He pulled something out of his jacket. "I wanted to . . ." He swallowed. "Thank you." He handed her a folded piece of cream paper, his fingers smudged.

His notebook paper, she recognized with a thrill. Carefully, as if she was unfolding her own heart, she opened the paper.

In the gray light under the evergreens, she blinked.

It was a girl. A girl with dirt on her face and a helmet snapped under her chin. She was crouched low, her harness on, her rope tied. Intensity in her eyes and the abyss behind her. The wind whipped her hair across her strong shoulders.

It was her.

"I remember you up there. I kept meaning to draw you, when we were . . ." He chewed his lip. "I just never did. After the fall, I couldn't get this out of my head."

Tears pricked her eyes. "It's beautiful. I've never . . ." She had to steady herself to keep going. "I've never seen myself like this."

He smiled. "You've never truly seen yourself, then."

That undid the tears. She folded the paper and put it in her pocket, head bent. "Thank you," she said through a scratchy voice and dripping cheeks.

He took a step toward her, hesitant at first, then all at once. His long arms coming around her shoulders as she went to him, and he pulled her close. "I'm sorry for the shitty things I said. How I made you feel. You were right. You were right about everything. My climbing. Everything."

She buried her face in his chest and wished deeply for this moment to last forever.

He dipped his head, mouth to her temple. "I screwed up something special I didn't even know I had. Maybe, if there's a next time, we'll get it right."

She chuckled and rolled her eyes, turning her head to lay her cheek against the soft flannel of his shirt.

His gaze flickered to hers. His heartbeat picked up under her ear. The shattered golden leaves of summer whirled in the mountain breeze.

She tipped her chin just enough, rising on her toes to meet his kiss.

forty two

A FEW DAYS LATER, RILLA SAT HIGH UP ON WASHINGTON COLUMN WITH Caroline, eating an apple in the cold wind, and Caroline tilted her chin and said, "We should climb The Nose."

Rilla barked a laugh. "You about made me drop my apple."

"That would have been tragic," Caroline said. She kicked her legs and looked down. "Anyway, I'm going to try and climb it free. I'd love it if you were part of my team."

The wind whipped in the silence.

Rilla nibbled on an edge of her apple, trying to figure out what to say. If any one of them could climb it free, it would be Caroline. But how . . . ?

"I've been working it from the top all summer. I didn't want to tell anyone about it. Like, make it into a big thing." She shrugged and leaned back against the granite. "I think I've got it. Or at least, I'm going to try. And we leave soon . . ."

"You want me?" Rilla asked, still in shock.

Rilla nodded, and tucked her apple core into her bag. "Can I think about it?"

"Sure. I'm doing it Friday."

"Damn, you really held this close to the chest."

Caroline shrugged in her reserved sort of way. "I don't need any voices in my head except for mine. I think I can do this. I couldn't do it when I first wanted to do it, and it was such a big thing to want. I decided to save every bit of that energy in words to use for the climb. I'm going to need every bit I can get."

"I'll do it," Rilla said. "If you trust me."

Caroline smiled. "I couldn't trust a partner more."

forty three

"BACKPACKING THROUGH EUROPE?" THE MAN SAID.

"Huh?" Rilla looked over her sip of iced coffee and the bagel she was trying to balance on her carry-on. She blinked at the man in khakis and glasses and a fleece vest. He had white hair and was reading a paper.

He flicked the edge of the paper to her pack. "Are you backpacking through Europe?"

"Oh, um." She swallowed. "Climbing. Um, I'm meeting some friends to climb for the summer."

His eyes lit. "I was a climber once."

She smiled awkwardly. "Um. Cool."

He opened his mouth to say something, but was interrupted by the loudspeaker announcement for the gate boarding to Milan. "That's me," he said, when it finished.

She nodded, eyeing passersby and chewing on her bagel, trying to look at everything all at once and not seem as if this was her first time in an airport. It was LAX, so there could even be celebrities, which seemed totally surreal.

The man folded his paper and stood. "Climb hard," he said.

"Oh." Rilla's smile was involuntary and wide. "Thank you!" Rilla waved goodbye as he rolled his suitcase away.

Her phone buzzed—Thea checking in that she'd made it through security. Mom sending a picture of Roosevelt staring at a dangling French fry. *Because France.* The next text said. *Get it?*

Rilla texted a reply and leaned back in the wide airport gate seat, chewing her bagel and careful not to let her bag and elbows spill over to the woman sitting next to her.

Her bag between her feet, the setting sun flushed crimson over L.A. outside, she waited for a place she couldn't believe she was about to go to.

A place she'd never been.

Glossary of Terms

anchors—The bolts or gear setup to secure a climber and their gear to the wall at the top of a pitch.

ATC—A simple device used to control braking during belaying.

belay—The act, person who is acting, or the place the action is occurring to control the tension of the rope of the climber.

belay loop—The part of the harness where the carabiner and belay device are clipped in.

beta—Information about a climb.

Camp 4—The walk-in campground in Yosemite Park famous for its role in the Golden Age of Climbing.

cams/nuts/hexes—Types of protection. Climbers carry many sizes. Route descriptions in guidebooks will often indicate what kind of protection/gear you will need.

double back—Commonly used phrase to describe attaching the harness correctly on older harnesses.

double overhand—A backup knot to the figure eight.

El Capitan—A three-thousand-foot monolith located at the north side, west end of the Valley.

figure eight—A basic knot used to attach a climber to their rope.

firefall—A custom of dumping hot coals over the edge of Glacier Point every night for the tourists in the Valley to witness a thirty-two-hundred-foot waterfall of fire. The practice began in 1872 and ended in 1968.

gear loop—Loops on the climber's harness for easy reach of gear.

Glacier Point—An overlook above the south point of Yosemite Valley with views north and west, including Half Dome, Tenaya Canyon, and the Valley floor.

grade—The degree of difficulty on a given climb.

Grigri—An assisted braking belay device, originally manufactured by Petzl (the name is from Petzl, but is applied to any device of this type).

gumby—A new and inexperienced climber.

Half Dome—A granite dome located at the east end of the Valley, rising 4,373 feet off the Valley floor.

Half Dome Village—Used to be called Curry Village, canvas tent camping under the Glacier Point Apron, with views of Half Dome.

harness—A set of straps made to fit over the pelvis and secure a climber to a rope.

HUFF (Housing under Fire Fall)—The name of the temporary employee housing tents near Half Dome Village.

lead—The first climber who places the protection.

leg loops—The part of a harness the legs step into.

locked off—A phrase used to communicate from belayer to climber to indicate they have locked the rope off the ATC or Grigri, exerting the most amount of tension possible. Typical before a big move that might end in a fall.

Merced River—The river flowing through the Valley.

multi-pitch—A route made up of several pitches.

pig—Nickname for the big haul bags.

pitch—One section of a multi-pitch climb.

portaledge—A collapsible cot that can be set up on the wall.

protection/pro—Bits of gear placed into cracks in the wall for anchoring the climber along the climb.

quickdraw—Two carabiners with a piece of webbing between. Used for connecting climbers or gear to anchors. Climbers carry many sizes of these.

rappel/rap—To lower on a rope from top to bottom, using a belay device or Grigri to control your movement down the rope.

route—The entire climb, named and graded.

runner—Webbing and quickdraws on an anchor setup, attaching the climber to the anchors but giving room to move. Leash.

slack—A word used to communicate from climber to belayer that they need more rope fed through the belay device up to the climber.

take—A word used to communicate from climber to belayer that they need tension on the rope.

top-rope—A style of climbing where the rope is anchored to the top of the climb prior and as the climber moves up the rope passes through the fixed anchor (either set up on trees or on fixed bolts) and back down to the belayer. It is the easiest form of climbing and is what you see in climbing gyms.

the Valley—Yosemite Valley inside Yosemite National Park.

Yosemite Decimal System—The scale or grade on which climbs in North America are rated.

SELECTED FURTHER MEDIA ON YOSEMITE, CLIMBING, AND CLIMBING IN YOSEMITE

Getting to the top is nothing.
How you get to the top is everything.

—Royal Robbins, who met his wife and fellow climber,
Liz Robbins, during a summer in Yosemite

BOOKS

Blanchard, Barry. *The Calling: A Life Rocked by Mountains.* Ventura, CA: Patagonia, 2014.

Caldwell, Tommy. *The Push.* New York: Viking, 2017.

Davis, Steph. *High Infatuation: A Climber's Guide to Love and Gravity.* Seattle, WA: Mountaineers Books, 2007.

——. *Learning to Fly.* New York: Touchstone, 2015.

Denny, Glen, and Yvon Choiunard. *Yosemite in the Sixties.* Santa Barbara, CA: Patagonia/T. Adler Books, 2007.

Farabee, Charles R. "Butch." *Big Walls, Swift Water.* San Francisco: Yosemite Conservancy, 2017.

Fieldman, Dean and John Long. *Yosemite in the Fifites.* Santa Barbara, CA: Patagonia/T. Adler Books, 2015.

Harrer, Heinrich. *The White Spider.* New York: Tarcher/Puntam, 1998.

Hill, Lynn. *Climbing Free.* New York: W. W. Norton, 2003.

Honnold, Alex. *Alone on the Wall.* New York: W. W. Norton, 2015.

Johnson, Shelton. *Gloryland.* San Francisco: Sierra Club, 2009.

Jones, Chris. *Climbing in North America.* Seattle, WA: Mountaineers Books, 1997.

Krakauer, Jon. *Eiger Dreams.* Guilford, CT: Lyons/Globe Pequot Press, 2009.

Leonard, Brendan. *Sixty Meters to Anywhere.* Seattle, WA: Mountaineers Books, 2016.

Long, John, with Jeff Jackson and Dean Fieldman. *The Stonemasters.* Santa Barbara, CA: Stonemaster Press/T. Adler Books, 2009.

Muir, John. *The Yosemite.* New York: The Century Co., 1912.

Rébuffat, Gaston. *Starlight and Storm.* New York: Random House, 1999.

Robbins, Royal. *Basic Rockcraft.* Glendale, CA: La Siesta Press, 1971.

Roper, Steve. *Camp 4.* Seattle, WA: Mountaineers Books, 1994.

FILMS

Meru, by Jimmy Chin and Elizabeth Chai Vasarhelyi. Music Box Films, 2015.

Reel Rock 9: Valley Uprising, by Peter Mortimer, Nick Rosen, and Josh Lowell. Sender Films, 2014.

Note from the Author

IT'S NOT A COINCIDENCE THAT MANY CLIMBERS ARE ALSO WRITERS OR artists. There is something about climbing that strips away all the things you want to believe about yourself, leaving you with just who you are and the great beyond—something so big you will never fully understand it and are always trying to explain.

Yosemite, specifically, is an incredibly special place, with a special history of climbing. Women have always been part of Yosemite's history, though their stories are often forgotten or summed up into being girlfriends (who happen to make ascents). The climbing community is not immune to the struggles of culture at large. And like Petra says to Adeena, heralding one woman at the top for her success is not the same thing as supporting all women. Some of the best climbing in the world has been done by women.

I am a lifelong climber, including throughout my pregnancies, but I am the worst climber to ever write a book about climbing. Without climbing, though, I wouldn't be a writer. No one will ever be inspired watching me shuffle up a 5.8 top-rope, but hopefully my words will inspire girls to go out and find themselves on the rock.

Acknowledgments

THIS BOOK WAS BORN THE MOMENT I WALKED ACROSS SPORTROCK Climbing Center's gym floor for employee training, and the girl who was training me pointed to Sasha DiGiulian banging out pull-ups like a badass, and said, "There's Sasha. She's kind of a bitch."

I never found out if it was true or not, since I am a terrible climber and was hired to belay birthday parties, but I knew then and there I wanted to write a book about climbing girls.

Ten years later, it's real! So thank you, Sasha, for being unforgettable and an amazing climber. And thank you, employee I don't remember, for talking shit behind someone's back.

Thank you, Amanda, for meeting a stranger at LAX on a whim and heading to Yosemite. That trip will forever be one of the greatest experiences of my life. Zion next! Thank you, Mom Lemon, for taking care of my babies (and me) then and all the other times. Without you, almost more than anyone else, I wouldn't be able to do this.

Thank you, Jeff, Toothless Guy with Insane Arms, Old Man Who Knows Everything, Virginia Good Old Boy, Red Shirt Guy, the Guy Who Packed His Pillow in the Pig, and Joe, for letting me interrupt, ask questions and poke around your box (snort) truck. Thank you for trying to impress us by smoking your summit cigars while you were packing. Our ovaries will never recover.

Thank you, Josh, for being so willing to share, and bringing us into the circle at HUFF. And for showing us the couch!

Thank you Alix Morris and Ken Kreis, for being excited and willing to share even when I walk into your camp uninvited. I came back with whiskey, but I feel like it didn't get to you (at least, full).

Thank you so much, Josie McKee, for coming around when I interrupted your breakfast and for your invaluable feedback during revisions. You made me look like I knew what I was talking about. Your quote brought me to tears. Thank you!

The characters in this book are all versions of people that always seem to exist in climbing circles, and I'm so inspired by the young generation of girls dominating climbing and taking it to new levels.

Thank you to all my writer friends who have kept me sane and grounded throughout this whole second book experience—Ricki, Rénee, J. J., Emily, Henning, and Lee. The Coven. The Fight Me Club. You know who you are.

B! You continually have my back, encourage me, and talk me down. I am so lucky to be your client.

Thank you, Anne and everyone at Amulet, for believing in this book.

Thank you, NRG climbers and residents! I tried so hard to write a book about West Virginia climbing, but I guess I leave that for someone else!

Even now, at the end, I can think of so many other things I learned from climbing that I wasn't able to write about, so forgive me climbers!

Thank you, J, for being my partner, through the shit climbs and the great ones, through the times someone forgot gear, dropped gear, froze up, or fell off. Through the times we've tapped out, been scraped off, and the times we've had great ascents. We've been through it all, and I wouldn't do it any other way. Except the time I got stung in the ass. I would take that back.